THE
ROAD
OF THE
INNOCENTS

THE
ROAD
OF THE
INNOCENTS

A NOVEL

Bryan D. Rockwood writing as
ERNIE LABBAYE

For more information contact:
Stephen Rockwood
theroadoftheinnocents@gmail.com

978-0-9971218-0-3 (hardcover)
978-0-9971218-1-0 (paperback)
978-0-9971218-2-7 (ebook)

Library of Congress Control Number: 2015960861

Book design by Dotti Albertine

The Story Behind this Book

Bryan Rockwood spent three years writing what would become his first and only novel. The book was completed just six weeks before Bryan's death in a tragic accident. We, the Rockwood family, are publishing this work in his memory and trust you will enjoy getting to know a bit about Bryan from reading *The Road of the Innocents*. It has been said that a part of an author lives on in their writing and that is certainly true in this case. For all of us who knew Bryan, we see him and hear him in every scene.

He had a contagious zest for life. He loved being with people and could hang comfortably with those from diverse backgrounds and cultures. He loved music and was a trained pianist who also enjoyed playing the bass guitar in a rock band. He was an avid outdoorsman, skier, runner and rock climber. When it came to marathons, he was both a cheerleader and inspiration to many others who later became infected with his passion for running. And, of course, he loved to read. He would often say how much he enjoyed the feel and smell of opening a new book and sitting down with a glass of Jack Daniels. We hope readers may capture some sense of Bryan's spirit, a spirit that led many others to expand their horizons.

The Road of the Innocents is an intricate and thought-provoking book, just as Bryan was a complex and thoughtful person. You will find that he doesn't give absolute answers, but he will give you all the clues you need to draw your own conclusions. He wanted the reader to become "invested" in the story and believed ambiguity was to be expected, because we all bring different perspectives to what we experience in life. The characters are strong and well-developed and drive the story. They are neither all bad nor all good and strive to do the best they can in chaotic circumstances.

While fictional, *The Road of the Innocents* is in many ways Bryan's life's story. The locations and many of the events and characters presented in the book are drawn from Bryan's life's experiences. Just as these aspects are true to his life, we wanted this finished book to remain true to Bryan's.

In our mission to publish the work on his behalf, we have come across notations and comments in Bryan's writing papers that indicate his vision for a sequel or possible edits to this book. We made an editorial choice to leave certain aspects of the book *unimproved* because although there is room for touch-ups, we agreed to leave the manuscript essentially as we found it. In absence of having the original author to approve edits, we felt it most just to leave it slightly flawed, as we all are.

To all of Bryan's readers, old and new friends, we present with pride, *The Road of the Innocents.*

The Rockwood Family

Principal Characters
Listed in alphabetical order

Ahmed	Youngest son of successful Dubai businessman College friend of Asher Daniel
Sarah Anderson	Executive Assistant to Roy Daniel
Andreas	Founder of German security firm A regular subcontractor to CASTOR Personal friend of Roy Daniel
Asher Daniel	Husband of Kimberly Daniel Father of Tyler and Sammy Daniel Son of Roy Daniel Vice President, Product Development
Kimberly Daniel	Wife of Asher Daniel Mother of Tyler and Sammy Daniel
Roy Daniel	Father of Asher Daniel Sector Vice President—CASTOR
Eva Engelhart	Program Manager—Andreas's firm
Jabe Evans	Chief Executive Officer—CASTOR
Al Green	Executive Vice President, Business Development—CASTOR
Grantham Hayward	General Officer, United States Marine Corps
Jessica Kelly	Executive Assistant to Asher Daniel
Tamara Maybin	Executive Vice President, Public Relations—CASTOR; Former Public Relations Attache to Grantham Hayward
Sandy McRae	Former Executive Vice President—CASTOR
Bill Morton	Chief Financial Officer—CASTOR
Roger Taylor	Executive Assistant to Jabe Evans
Pete Vasilescu	Program Manager—CASTOR College friend of Roy Daniel

THE
ROAD
OF THE
INNOCENTS

one
—

On Monday, Ahmed hadn't answered his cell phone, and still—three days later—hadn't returned any of Asher Daniel's calls. Ahmed's cell phone was his constant companion. It was never silent, and he would answer regardless of the circumstance. No meeting was important enough, no dinner special enough, no woman fine enough to warrant ignoring a call or—God forbid!—silencing the ringer. A beautiful, spoiled child, Ahmed's mobile provided his screaming, whining, insisting background music, always indulged, never ignored. So for Ahmed not to have answered—much less not to have called back—something was wrong. Something was most definitely wrong.

Asher first visited Ahmed and his cell phone outside the customs hall in the Dubai airport. Ahmed stood a head above the crowd outside the sliding glass doors, Bluetooth device attached to his left ear. In his right hand, waving to catch Asher's eye, was his cell phone, swaddled in black leather and glowing coy above the fray.

"*Marhaba,* my friend! We meet again at last!" The handshake was eternal. Ahmed's obsidian eyes bored through Asher's and sifted slowly through his thoughts. His smile gleamed through his immaculately trimmed beard.

"Ahmed. So good to see you. Thanks for picking me up."

"Nonsense, my friend. It is my pleasure. I trust you had a pleasant flight?"

"As pleasant as a thirteen-hour flight can be."

"Maybe not. Many things can happen in thirteen hours," he said with a suggestive smile.

"True, true. But none of them ever happen to me."

Ahmed's laugh echoed through the hall. Dracula channeling Santa Claus. A wide-eyed little girl hugged her teddy bear. Her mother looked away from us.

"Come, you must be tired. I have a car just outside." Ahmed's free hand grasped Asher firmly on the shoulder as his cell phone beckoned them through the doors and into the damp, sodium-lit evening.

A group of men in *kanduras* and *guthras* stood and talked. Families from either Pakistan or India—somewhere east of here—pushed carts loaded head-high with TVs and computers and brightly colored shopping bags. Westerners in jeans pulled tiny suitcases, stared into cell phones, and looked around for the taxi stand. Ahmed's phone urged Asher toward a silver Mercedes. The driver got out to take Asher's suitcase. Inside, the air conditioning was on high and it smelled like a duty-free shop—expensive cologne and French cigarettes. Ahmed's driver pushed into traffic.

"We'll go first to your hotel. If you are hungry, we can get something to eat. My colleagues from Riyadh arrived earlier today and would be interested in joining us if you're not too tired."

"No, no. I slept some on the flight." A lie. But Asher was anxious to get things moving. "Let's do it. I can't wait to meet them."

The smile approved. Ahmed conferred with his phone, gently stroking its keys. The phone brightened. Ahmed returned Asher's gaze and began speaking Arabic. The smile apologized for the man's rudeness and promised to keep Asher company while Ahmed talked. Asher smiled back and gazed out at the buildings as the Mercedes made its way through the late-evening traffic.

• • •

Six months had passed since then. Today, the harbor below Asher's office window offered no answers. It was the kind of late-summer evening that New England lived for—warm and lingering, a goodbye kiss from an old flame. Well, transplanted New Englanders lived for them, anyway—they reminded them of friendlier climates back home. True New Englanders, it seemed to Asher, lived for the January nor'easter—wet snow howling sideways, foot upon foot ripping down tree limbs, power lines, and roofs, and winds pushing icy waves up piers and over roads and through homes. Mentioning the blizzard of '78 was like playing the national anthem—it brought a room together while silently but definitively separating members and guests. Battling the elements defined the true New Englander. Take away the fight, lose the character. It made Asher wonder whether a winning Red Sox club could really hold their fans the way they had before breaking the curse.

It had fascinated him to no end when he'd first moved here, around this same time of year, the mornings crisp and clear and the evenings warm and bustling with students just back from summer vacations. He and his roommates would drive out after dinner and get lost on purpose—not a hard thing to do, really—just to discover new streets and stores and bars on the way back home. They'd navigated by dead reckoning and testosterone, the only rule of the game being never, ever to ask the way. Jimmy would invariably steer them toward women, the rest of them giving him hell but still right behind him, embarrassed by the hunt but counting on the spoils. He never failed to produce, but you couldn't count on the quality. Asher still laughed at the way Jimmy would look at his friends like a young bird dog that's jumped a hen pheasant, wondering why they didn't shoot. Jimmy would jump a hen anything, and never could quite fathom how the rest of them could be so damned picky.

They'd rented a house in Somerville from the Catholic Church, something Jimmy had worked out through his brother, a Jesuit who lived in Jamaica Plain. It was an old three-story house painted that pale gray-blue only New Englanders seem to love, and it shared a parking lot with a Knights of Columbus. The screened porch leaned a little west into the parking lot and was almost completely blocked from view by the biggest climbing rose Asher had ever seen. It looked almost like kudzu—kudzu covered with big flowers the color of old claret. The afternoon Asher had driven up to the house for the first time, he'd sat there in the humid, sticky-sweet, late-summer-afternoon rose smell waiting for everyone else to arrive. He'd felt that familiar tingling in the pit of his stomach, inching its way up to the back of his neck, making him shake off the dizziness that always came before. He'd lit a cigarette and wished he had a key. There were "before," "during," and "after" people. Asher knew for certain he wasn't a "before."

He admired "during" people. The true New Englander was a "during." When the sleet cut through the downtown alleys, glazing ice across the windowpanes and piling slush in the doorway corners; when the hot, dark clouds rolled in and the summer rain slapped the windows in waves and filled the streets with mud; when the Red Sox were down 7–1 in the bottom of the eighth, two outs, nobody on; that was when the New Englander was truly alive, the gleam in his eyes betraying his look of disgust as a mask, his blasphemies as lines from a script. He didn't long for the day before, the season before, or the morning after. He loved the bite of the wind, the crack of the bat, and the growl of the thunder. He didn't expect much and he didn't gloat—at least not for long. He simply loved the way it all felt and sounded now, before "after" showed up to ruin everything with meaning and perspective.

The year they'd spent living in Somerville was about as close as he'd ever come to being a "during." They were all, he supposed, "after" people, and pretty soon—as it always did—"during" lasted long enough that it started to feel like "before," that tingling starting up again, and the only way to make it go away was to move on. But looking back, they'd rushed it. He remembered the dinners. Get five overachievers living in one house, assign them each a night of the week to cook dinner, and after a few months the dinners are lasting hours, each trying to outdo the other. Friends are invited, friends spread the word, and pretty soon it's dinner for ten every night, three or four courses and half a case of that cheap Bulgarian wine they'd found and a whole bottle of Sambuca to finish it off. Maybe a joint on the porch, just to help body and mind digest it all. Hormones still burning off fat faster than the body can pack it on, and overriding worries about what needs to get done the next day. Living in the now, at least for now. At least until that drive that got you there in the first place started to drive you away.

• • •

Asher met Julie that year. Jimmy's college girlfriend, Kate, had come up from school for a fall weekend road trip, three years younger and in awe of life after graduation. Julie was Kate's roommate, and had come along for the ride. Dinner that Friday was especially extravagant; the opportunity to appear mature and sophisticated was too much for any self-respecting twentysomething man to resist. He'd seen Julie first as he walked into the dining room, carrying the salad and mushroom fettuccini that would be their second and third courses. She'd looked up as he appeared, her jet-black hair pulled back on one side and tucked behind a tiny, perfect ear. Her eyes in the candlelight caught Asher by surprise. She looked a little lost at their huge wooden table between Kate, who had already settled into the task of reeling Jimmy back in, and a bubbly blonde who Chuck had imported from somewhere for the occasion. Asher sat down across from her and offered her more wine. Her smile was sweet and grateful.

After dinner Asher and Julie had tried the porch but it was already occupied by Jimmy and two girls from Ohio who had come to one of their parties as friends of a friend and had been inviting themselves back ever since. Jimmy said the smaller of the two could suck a watermelon through a garden hose, so maybe they weren't actually inviting themselves. Not really wanting to find out, Asher had suggested to Julie that they go elsewhere. They'd found Kate in the living room, talking without much interest with the imported blonde while Chuck, George, and Twoey (Albert Tracey Colbert, Jr. to his parents, but who'd fought his whole life against being known by any of those names) watched *The Terminator* with the sound down, making up their own lines. Julie sat on the arm of Kate's chair and the two whispered something to each other for a while. Arnold Schwarzenegger was saying something about little boys in Chuck's voice. George and Twoey laughed and rocked in their seats. The blonde looked at her red toenails. Kate looked toward the porch window, but Julie pulled her up and the two of them followed Asher upstairs to his room.

Asher's bedroom was on the third floor, beneath the slant of the roof. He opened the window, lit some candles, and put on some old R.E.M., and they smoked the last of his Thai weed. He couldn't say now what they'd talked about, but they'd laughed a lot and Kate had decided they had to name their band The New Buddhas. Then she was off. Julie looked after her as she walked down the stairs, then at Asher, then at the floor. Asher suggested she stay. Her eyes surprised him for the second time. She left and Asher lay on his bed, staring at shadows flickering in the breeze and wondering if she'd come back. When he'd decided he'd been wrong, he heard bare feet on the stairs. She'd changed into a T-shirt and old sweatpants and carried a little suitcase. He closed the bedroom door and her mouth tasted like mint. The small of her back fit in his right hand. Under the covers she turned away toward the open window, her body curved soft and warm against his. He kissed the back of her neck and she turned so he could reach a little further. Her eyes were closed, but she was smiling. The candles danced and sputtered in the damp night air.

She was still asleep in the morning when he went downstairs to make coffee. Chuck and the imported blonde were already in the kitchen, wishing each other elsewhere. Chuck gave him a quick smile and a wink. Chuck's bedroom was next door to Asher's.

Asher poured two mugs and brought them back upstairs. Julie was awake now and smiled when he walked through the door. She sat up cross-legged, feet tucked beneath her T-shirt, and took her mug in both hands. Asher watched as she blew into it, steam playing through her black hair in the cool morning sun. He sat on the floor and leaned his head back against her bare leg. She kissed his forehead. He leaned further back and kissed her mouth. Her hands were warm from the coffee mug and soft on his cheeks.

He and Kimberly were engaged the following Christmas.

• • •

Asher's computer screen offered no answers, either. And no replies from Ahmed on his BlackBerry. He looked through the glass that separated his office from Jess's desk. The fax machine? Nobody sends faxes anymore. Face it, Asher, he hasn't replied. He isn't going to reply. Something's wrong.

"Jess?" He got up and walked over to her desk. "See if I can still get on tonight's flight to Dubai. There should still be enough time to make Dulles, if there's room."

Jessica Kelly was one of the nicest people Asher knew, which did not make her one of the best assistants. She came from a big Irish family in which the men went to Boston College, became naval officers, and went into politics. You never heard much about the women. Asher knew Jess was recently married—he knew this from the day he interviewed her for the job, which was the only time they'd ever really talked—and he knew bits and pieces about her family from the newspapers. But it occurred to him, as she leaned closer to her computer screen, that he knew little more. She came to work on time, did what he asked, and left—again, on time. She wasn't one to volunteer a lot of information, and he never really asked. Odd how you can see someone more than you see your own family and still barely know them. But maybe that's for the best.

"There's room on Air France tonight at eleven." Jess's voice went for sultry, but a nagging trace of Southy landed her closer to the vicinity of frump than her not-even-thirty years deserved. "It's a little cheaper and would give you more time. If you go through Dulles, you'd really need to leave soon—like now."

Asher thought of the unreturned phone calls, and of what was at stake. "Now's fine. Book me a seat through Dulles. That way I'll get there in time for dinner tomorrow." In time to walk through the hotel bars and Lebanese restaurants and shisha joints Ahmed called home. In time—he hoped—to stop whatever was happening. Or to start whatever wasn't.

He walked back to his office and looked around. Best leave the laptop here—don't want to take any chances, and it won't find Ahmed. He pulled out a couple of pairs of boxers and two T-shirts—the kind you can wash in the sink and dry overnight—from his bottom desk drawer, next to a plastic duty-free bag full of hotel shampoo and soap. He folded them into the empty laptop compartment of his briefcase and checked—even though it had been in the same place for the past five years—for his passport. A few dirham notes left over from his last trip would cover the little stuff—credit card for everything else. He had a suit and a couple of dress shirts waiting for him at the dry cleaner in the mall next to his usual hotel. That, plus what he had on now, should cover him. Toiletries they'd have at the hotel. One last e-mail check and he shut down his computer, packed his reading glasses, and tucked his BlackBerry into his jacket pocket. Ready to go in two minutes flat. Someday he'd have to get that organized to *not* be on the road all the time.

Jess was still working on his boarding passes. The 5:00 ferry to Hingham was just pulling away from Rowes Wharf behind the courthouse. Asher had always wanted to live where he could commute by boat—ever since he'd moved here, anyway, and had learned that doing so was even a possibility. Get on the boat, buy a drink, maybe bump into a neighbor, and sail off through the islands every day after work. Had a good ring to it. The reality, of course, was that the boat had all the charm of a bus station, the drinks were expensive, you probably never saw anyone you actually wanted to see, and half the time the weather was so bad you probably fantasized about being stuck dry and warm in your car in Southeast Expressway traffic. But on an afternoon like this, with the city shadows stretching out over the water and the sea breeze cooling the people on their way to bars and restaurants, friends, lovers, children—the afternoon Technicolor turned everything into an old movie, where work ends at 5:00 and the office doesn't call and your family runs to greet you when you walk in for dinner.

"Your boarding passes are ready."

The ferry had passed the trade center now, and Asher turned his back on it. Jess stood at his door, always a little more formal than he felt good about. "I also booked you a room. I didn't know when you'd be returning, so I reserved it for a week." She hesitated, lips parted but words reluctant to come. Was she intimidated by him, or just slow? Or did she actually sense the truth? "Do you know how long you'll be staying?"

Asher looked at her and she returned his gaze, but her eyes scurried for the corner when the silence wasn't immediately broken. Maybe she does sense something. Or maybe it's just that it's after 5:00 and she's got someplace to be. The Technicolor returned and she was explaining to an irate husband he'd never met why that horrible boss had made her work late and that was why his dinner wasn't ready yet.

"I really don't know, Jess. Sorry. I'm staying till it's settled."

· · ·

He'd said that line before, of course. Six months ago after Ahmed's first call. One of those mornings that would have, in December, been beautiful—doily snowflakes floating down out of the gray dawn hush, no wind to hurry them along, blanketing the day to day, stilling the workday roar. In December, it would have been fresh and magical, a holiday pageant newly staged, a feast to be wondered through frosting office windows over cozy hot mugs of coffee and laughter. But in March, the magic was gone, too much of a good thing by half, and those same floating flakes, still just as miraculous as ever, now inspired nothing more than exasperated groans skyward, beseeching that great source of all things beautiful not to play that song again—that song no one could get enough of when it first came out—to please, please move on to another tune—something warmer, upbeat, filled with color and noise and light.

Ahmed's first call had come on that kind of morning. Asher's overcoat dripped from the hook on the back of his office door while, outside, the harbor sulked like frozen lead behind the endless sheet of slushy gauze slowly smothering the smoke-yellow dawn.

"Good morning, Asher—it is Ahmed calling, from Dubai. How are you?"

"Ahmed! Hey—great to hear from you, man! What're you up to?" Fantasies of warm, soft sand and warm, blue water and tall palms and sweet dates put a smile in Asher's voice that urged his old schoolmate on.

Ahmed, who'd lived down the hall from Asher freshman year. Roomed with that guy whose dad had been ruined the first time in the crash of '29, and whose latest stepmother bought pot from them. Ahmed, who'd explained that he'd ended up at Vanderbilt because his father believed the university was still associated with the family of the same name, and would therefore provide his youngest son with useful business connections. Ahmed, whose laugh was legendary, reverberating down the hall upon explaining his father's confusion—his father, of all people, a successful businessman, an intelligent man, by all accounts, not realizing it was only a name? Another laugh, rattling closed doors and nerves alike. Ahmed—the only Ahmed in school as far as anyone knew, sparing them all the trouble of remembering a completely unpronounceable last name (but, according to Ahmed, a highly respected one, known all around the Gulf).

"I'm doing well, Asher—very, very well. And you, too, I hope, doing well?"

Ahmed, bursting into Asher's room in the wee hours of the morning with yet another Gauloises dangling from his lips and yet another paper due in a few hours, asking for a typewriter but really looking for a typist. Ahmed, always good for a six pack of beer or a fifth of Jack—much more valuable than cash since the drinking age went up—in exchange for these last-minute secretarial services. Ahmed, returning two weeks late from Christmas vacations in Paris or from spring breaks in St. Barts. Summers working at his father's import/export firm in Dubai a duty, not a privilege. Ahmed, telling people at parties to call him "Abu Ganja"—and they'd all laugh, of course, at the word "ganja," but never really understood the joke. Ahmed, whom they'd all been quietly amazed to see graduate.

"Yeah, Ahmed—great. Excellent. You know—a little sick of winter, but hey—it's March. I live in Boston. What're you gonna do?"

The laugh back again, in all its glory. That same laugh conspicuously absent a few years after graduation over dinner one evening when they'd both happened to be in New York. Ahmed—haunted by the success of his older brothers. Money still more plentiful than motivation. Connections endless as ever, but true calling still nowhere in sight. These qualities once his greatest assets, but drifting now with every passing year closer to the other side of life's ledger, the old party-boy mask wearing thin from the inside out. His dark eyes, twin reflections of the candle waning on the table between them, betraying real fear that life was moving on and taking everyone but him along with it.

"Well, maybe I can help you get out of the cold. I got your e-mail a few weeks ago, and I think I may know just the people."

Bright, confident, optimistic. No trace of that fear remaining in the voice on the other end of the line that sloppy March morning.

"Really? That's great news, Ahmed! Tell me more. Who are they?"

"They are Saudi, Asher. Big time Saudis. They've just started a new fund—money from the royal family, I understand, as well as from some high-end business guys—and they're looking for that special edge. Okay, that's what everybody says, of course, but still, I think these guys may be different. I met them through the cousin of a guy I went to school with in England . . ."

Ahmed had explained the connections, but Asher lost track after the first three or four. He really did seem to know everyone over there. Of course, that was his only real occupation, but still, it was a big city, and no mean feat. And he sounded genuinely enthusiastic. Happy. Like his old self again.

"Anyway, I explained to them that I knew this guy from college who was in the financial information business, and they were very interested. They were especially interested in some sort of private feed—I didn't really understand all the details, Asher, you'll have to excuse me. Can you do that sort of thing?"

"That all depends, Ahmed. I'd need to ask them some questions. Do you think I could meet with them?"

"Yes, of course—they said they would love to meet with you. They're willing to come to Dubai, although you know these Saudis, Asher, they're *always* looking for an excuse to come to Dubai!" The same tone of voice that had planned frat parties for hundreds back in the day. Deep-fried alligator on the front lawn when Florida came to town. The laugh that carried farther than the smell of the frying meat, all the way down the street, around the corner and away off toward the booming stadium.

"I thought that was Bahrain. But whatever. I'd love to meet them, Ahmed. Just find out when would be a good time for them, and I'll fly over. We can discuss all the details then."

Ahmed hummed contentedly, like a horse anticipating his oats. "That's great, Asher. I think you will like them. And it will be good to see you again. It's been a long time. The last time we saw each other was that evening in New York, wasn't it? Ten years ago, at least. That's too long, Asher. You must come a few days early, if you can, so we can catch up. Perhaps you can meet my father. I've told him about this deal, you know, and he, too, would like to meet you."

Even at college, Ahmed had never introduced them to his father.

"That'd be great, Ahmed. It has been too long. So I'll stay as long as it takes—as long as it takes to get everything settled."

. . .

Jess had wondered all day when Asher would make up his mind to go. She might not be able to keep up with everything—*he* didn't think she could, anyway—but when you spend most of your working life staring through a glass wall into somebody else's working life, you can't help but pick up on a thing or two. Monday he'd called Ahmed at least ten times, something he never did. Yesterday he'd tried to do other things, but she could tell where his mind really was. Today he'd just stared—stared at his computer, stared at his BlackBerry, stared out his window, sucking on a pen. She knew he'd end up going. Only question was when.

She sat back down at her desk and looked at her clock. Five twenty. She really didn't mind staying late if there was something to do, but most of the time she was just making it up. She wished he'd give her more to do. It really seemed like he just didn't trust her. She knew she could do a lot of the things he did himself. Maybe she should suggest it. Just didn't seem right, though—her telling him what to do and what not to do. She'd seen that kind of thing happen with her father and uncles and brothers, and it wasn't them who ended up afterward with no job. There were worse things than boredom. That was another thing she'd seen with her father and uncles and brothers—excitement isn't necessarily something to go looking for. Growing up a Kelly, she'd learned younger than most that, more often than not, excitement means a scandal is just around the corner. Really, Jessica, you have nothing to complain about. Get to work on time, do what you're asked to do, go home. Stay out of the spotlight.

But the red light glowing on her phone told her that the message from those people looking into Asher's business was still there. She'd seen the number, a Virginia area code, when the phone rang around lunchtime and just sat and watched as it rang two more times then stopped. She couldn't talk to them again. She'd kept watching for what had seemed like an eternity, willing the light not to come on—but it had. The message was there. And it had remained there all afternoon, daring her to listen. Daring her to move downstage, into the spotlight. When she took this job, she assumed it was a basic, boring routine thing where she could turn off the anxieties and the memories of her past. Ever since they started calling and asking questions about Asher, she felt the familiar panic and flashbacks zapping her brain again. The only way to cope was to deny it was there, stay in the moment, count her paperclips until her heart stopped racing, and do her job. No questions asked.

Asher turned off the lights in his office and closed the door. She looked up as he paused in front of her desk. He was good-looking for his age—a little thin, maybe, but in good shape, with hair the color of maple syrup that didn't show signs of leaving anytime soon. His battleship gray eyes moved around her cubicle, taking in everything and nothing all at the same time. This happened every time he stood there. Nervous? Why? Interested? Come on, Jess, be real. She straightened up a little in her seat without really meaning to, but it didn't do anything to hide the fact that losing ten or twenty pounds wouldn't hurt. Curse of the Irishwoman, her mother used to joke, but Jess had noticed at a pretty early age that not every Irishwoman suffered from that curse. Curse of the Kelly woman was more like it.

You've let him stand there a little too long—again. Dammit, Jess, if you want him to trust you more, you've got to stop acting like a little girl. She tried to look him in the eyes—nice eyes, but awfully tired—and forced a smile. "Have a good trip, Asher. Let me know if I can do anything for you."

Thanks, Jess. Enjoy your time off. That's what he should have said, anyway—his usual joke before leaving on a trip, with a smile and a look straight in the eyes, a split second that made you believe anything was possible. But he didn't. He just nodded and kept up his distant inspection, pausing a little longer than normal, she thought, on the picture of her and her husband. Then, as if just waking up, he looked around, breathed deep, and started to walk away.

"I'll let you know, Jess. Thanks." And that was it. He was off toward the elevators, swinging his bag onto his shoulder and contemplating his footsteps.

She looked at the red light again and for a fleeting moment, the time it took for her heart to race a little faster, she wondered if she should run after him. Tell him everything. But she didn't. The slap she got from knowing too much in her Kelly home still stung too much. Nothing was worth going back into a reality of being the snitch who spilled the beans. Growing up a Kelly, as her brother knew even when she didn't, it was often better not to know.

Stay out of it, Jess. Let them find him themselves. You have one job to do. And that's to mind your own business.

• • •

Kimberly Daniel had tried over the years not to be surprised. Much to her surprise, she'd succeeded.

She noticed this fact for the first time—for the first time she could remember, anyway—as she hung up the phone. Asher hadn't told her everything—she was quite certain of that. But apparently she hadn't really expected him to, because the only unexpected thing that had just happened was that she'd realized she'd expected it all.

Kimberly looked around the kitchen at the beginnings of supper: linguine with shrimp in a lemon cream sauce. It was a recipe she'd gotten from Williams-Sonoma years ago that her daddy wouldn't have thought much of but that had remained an everyday staple, anyway. Quick to make, just as quick to call off, and keeps well for later. Just like our sex life, she thought with a smile the underlying truth couldn't erase.

Come on now, Kimberly, that's not fair. Does make a good line, but it's really not that simple. It's just a stressful time, she tried to reason, with Asher's big deal in the works and school starting up again and all the little things that just seem to multiply every year the kids get older. She put the lid back on the pot of water and set the cup full of cream and lemon zest on the top shelf of the fridge. Stack the linguini boxes and tuck them in the corner, against the backsplash. Soap and hot water on the washcloth, and scrub down the counters. Everything neat, no sign of a fuss—all set to go when the door opens and Asher walks in, whenever that might be. The fact that it wouldn't be tonight didn't make a difference. Organization was her primary defense against the unknown.

The kids would be home soon. Strange not having to pick them up—she hadn't had time yet since Tyler got his license to fill up what had, for more than ten years, been driving time. She looked around for what to do next. The liquor cabinet was tempting, but no, not a good idea. Always put a spotlight on her mood, whatever that mood might be. Right now she really wasn't sure what her mood was. Drinking didn't seem like a good way to find out, even if she'd wanted to know.

She poured herself a glass of iced tea instead and went out the kitchen door onto the deck. It overlooked their backyard, mowed down to the trees that bordered the creek. Asher had always loved mowing the lawn, but lately Tyler had taken over, kicking and screaming. Seemed a shame, taking a job away from a person who loves it and giving it to someone who hates it, just on principle. She leaned on the railing and held her glass in both hands, feeling the icy water drip down the glass and through her fingers. The evening was warm and the smell of grass mixed with the smell of somebody's grill up the road. How long had they dreamed of a house like this? A couple of bugs chirped, but nothing like back home. Her grandma used to say that the biggest difference between the north and the south was that the south smelled more, which was true, but it was the sounds on a summer evening that Kimberly missed the most. Bugs and tree frogs and bullfrogs big as dinner plates. Lightning bugs dancing like little fairies to the music. All filled up the gaps a bit. White noise to keep you from noticing the dark corners.

She could hear the Davis kids splashing in the pool across the street. Seemed silly to have a pool up here, really. In another few weeks, it'd be drained and covered for the next six months at least, waiting for the snow to thaw and the mud to dry and the rains to back off enough to let you even think about getting in. But Tyler and Sammy sure would love to have a pool. Tyler wouldn't get much use out of it, of course—he'd be off to college in just a couple of years (How could that be?). But Sammy, she'd get a kick out of it. At least she would for another year or two until she started dating and couldn't wait to get out of the house. She'd already started to show the signs. Just the other day, she'd gone off to her room and slammed the door and for the first time in her twelve years Kimberly had no idea what was wrong. Kimberly felt the tears coming. Okay, girl, enough of this. Time to do something.

Do what, though? That was the big question. Kimberly hated being alone this time of day. Best time of day there is, but not if you're by yourself. Time to fly back to the tree with the other birds and preen and scold and crow and get ready to ride out the night. Back when they'd first gotten married, it seemed as though she and Asher had never been by themselves. Work every day, bars after work, dinners with friends every weekend—one big social engagement. How'd they managed? Made her tired now just thinking about it. But it had been fun. They'd had a little one-bedroom apartment on Mass Ave, right across the street from the Christian Science building. Only after they'd moved in did they discover that most of the other residents were older, but one thing to be said for it: She'd had no lack of attention. "Hello, Peaches," one had said to her as she'd stepped into the elevator, and the name had made its way around to all the retired gentlemen in the building. At the time it had bothered her—not the attention, she'd loved the attention, but the being different—and she'd worked hard not to be. These days, though, she found herself thinking back a lot to who she'd been before, and why she'd wanted to change so much, and whether she couldn't somehow get back at least a little closer to where she'd started.

The bedroom in that apartment had faced due east so the sun came in through the blinds on sunny mornings and made little zebra stripes across the sheets and Asher's naked back. They'd spent a lot of time naked in that bedroom, as she recalled—in all the rooms, actually, though how they'd found the time she had no idea. Asher sneaking up behind her in the shower, his soapy hands slipping across her breasts and down her belly and his fingers, not so experienced then, fumbling a little between her legs. Asher over her on the living room floor, the movie credits still rolling, but their clothes already strewn from the sofa to the kitchen table. And that time her plane back from her sister's graduation had been late, she'd walked in wearing that little red sundress she'd had and he'd come home from work early and she'd had to pee so bad the whole time but a sundress doesn't offer much protection against the advances of a gentleman deprived for—what, three whole days? "Welcome home, Peaches," he'd said in his best dirty-old-Yankee voice. When was the last time he'd called her Peaches?

Where are those kids, anyway? They should've been home half an hour ago. Tyler had just had cross-country practice, so he'll be starving, ready to eat anything in his path. And Sammy—Sammy wouldn't have held him up, she'd have just been waiting, doing her homework, until he picked her up. Maybe this hadn't been such a good idea, after all—letting Tyler do the driving. Like most teenagers, he'd been all for anything that got him behind a steering wheel. He'd go to the gas station, go to the grocery store, do any of the things he'd hated all his life if it involved driving the car. Including "Driving Miss Sammy," as he called it, imitating the accent Kimberly swore she'd lost. But still, he'd barely had the license a year. It was a safe little town, but . . .

Kimberly went back into the kitchen. Her purse was on the little built-in desk next to the pantry. She put down her iced tea and looked behind her wallet for her cell phone. The little red light was blinking. Dang it, Kimberly, you have *got* to remember to keep this thing with you when the kids are out. She looked at the missed call list—sure enough, Tyler's number. She called voice mail and pushed the command to play messages before the recording told her which buttons to push. And then she stood there, waiting, watching the water from the iced tea glass make a little dark puddle on her clean granite countertop.

• • •

The flight to Dulles was, naturally, late. Perfect weather up and down the east coast, but still late. Probably a thunderstorm in Pueblo or Cheyenne or God knows where delayed flight thirty ought six to Saint Louis, which was carrying the deadheading pilot of flight 1492 to Boston, the plane destined to become flight 1776 to Dulles. The beating of a butterfly's wings.

So he'd land about the same time they started boarding for Dubai. Fantastic. As much as he traveled, Asher had never been able to shake the dread of a close connection. Never mind that he'd never actually missed a plane—not by minutes, anyway. He'd had complete schedule meltdowns when a flight was canceled and had to rebook the whole trip, but that wasn't what he hated. He hated the twenty-minute connection, sitting helplessly on a plane taxiing up to the gate knowing others were already sitting on his next flight, finding their seats and checking their seatbelts and filling up the overhead bins. He hated waiting while the Jetway driver missed the plane door for the third time. He hated watching the flight attendants as they stood and talked and laughed and generally didn't seem to give a damn. He hated, he supposed, having absolutely no control.

Asher tried not to think about the connection. He stared out the window as the clouds went from white to blue, a slow autumn light show of apple and honey and pumpkin. Sunlight winked off glassy evening ponds till it abandoned the ground altogether and the plane was left alone, the last sunlit body, pushing up and up, a wingbeat ahead of the night. Icarus couldn't be blamed. He had great intentions. Any man with any ambition at all would have done the same.

And the plan had been ambitious. He remembered when he'd first come up with the idea, running one Saturday morning through the state park near home. It was more a feeling than a thought at first, pumped through the cerebral aqueduct to warm the stems and glands of the lower brain. It was a good feeling, clever and proud, and he'd smiled as he ran faster through the rare winter sun, the ice on the pond blinding white and the squirrels out to take advantage of their brief good fortune. By the time he'd gotten back to his car, the feeling had evolved into a full-blown plan, and the car windows had fogged up as he sat in the driver's seat, still breathing hard and writing the details in the margins of an old AAA map.

All his life Asher had felt something eluded him. Not that he was unique in this. Most people, at least most people with any intelligence or passion, felt like something was missing from their lives, but couldn't put their finger on it. He'd always wanted to do something big. Really big. But not just big. He wanted to do something important that would help a lot of people in a surprising way. He knew there was ego involved in wanting to make the help something unique and memorable. But ego was useful in driving ambition. When the plan had occurred to him, a true inspiration, any concern he had about whether or not he could pull it off disappeared in the drops of sweat that trickled down his face.

The lights of New York City flickered in the dusk as the plane passed by. The guy next to him was snoring, his shirt deserting the confines of his aspirational waistband. The flight attendant wanted trash. He'd heard once that the line "When you get caught between the moon and New York City" was written by a guy while his flight was in a holding pattern over JFK. "The best that you can do is fall in love." Asher looked from fat snoring man to trash lady then back out the window. *I don't know. He must have been flying with better-looking people.*

Asher's reflection stared him down from the darkening cabin window. *What makes you so sure you can fix this? What makes you so sure there's* really anything wrong? Nothing—nothing is what makes me sure something's wrong. You outline a plan, research who might be interested, make some calls, set up some meetings—then see where it goes. That's the way business works. Push the rock uphill, and at some point you either get tired of pushing or you get to the top of the rise and the rock starts to roll on its own. Then you've got a deal. If it stops, something's wrong. Time to start pushing again. Either that or the rock's rolled off a cliff and it's time to find a new rock. But you've got to know—you've got to have information. You've got to know whether you're still chasing the same rock, or if you're even still on the same hill.

And what makes you think you can fix ... that? His conversation with Kimberly before taking off from Logan played back in his head. More dead space than words, but the dead space said more, anyway.

Nothing. Nothing makes me think I can fix that.

The approach into Dulles seemed even longer than usual. Endless circles over endless Virginia farms and suburbs and highways and shopping malls, office buildings housing the companies that actually did all the things the government supposedly did. Companies like his father's. No time to call today. He wondered how his father was doing, whether he was still down there in one of those buildings. Maybe—if he was in town. More likely than not, he was far, far away working in some other time zone. Like father, like son.

The plane finally resigned itself to the tarmac, engines roaring into reverse to make the first turn toward the terminals. Asher turned on his phone and stared at the screen, willing it to say something to keep his mind off the time. A few e-mails trickled in, then one voice mail. He looked out and saw the flagman already waving them into the gate. Messages will have to wait. He pulled his briefcase out from under the seat and got ready for a quick escape.

Asher had to run the length of the concourse to get to his gate, but at least they'd landed at the right terminal. Having to take one of those "mobile lounge" things would have doomed him. He made it to the gate with a couple of minutes to spare, showed the attendant his boarding pass, and made his way to his seat. The cabin was already full, business people mostly, preparing to bed down among strangers. He had a window seat next to a graying woman doing her best to look inconvenienced. He squeezed past her and sat down as the announcement came to turn off your cell phones and fasten your seatbelts. As he pulled out his cell phone, he saw the message indicator. He looked around and a flight attendant smiled at him, knowingly. No chance. But wait thirteen hours to find out who'd called? No chance. He pushed the CALL button, tucked his phone into his shirt pocket, and smiled back at the flight attendant. She turned away. Asher sank into his seat, took his phone back out, pressed it to his ear and waited, staring after her as she walked away, asking the couple in the exit row if they'd be willing to assist in an emergency.

two
___

"They're cavemen, for Christ's sake. We'll smoke 'em out. Shouldn't take more 'n a couple months, tops."

Outside the conference room window, the Virginia sky was melting. A blood orange sun dripped through the premature dusk.

Al Green looked nothing like his namesake. Both men were born within five years and a few hundred miles of each other, but the parents of the less famous of the two would have chosen almost any other name had they known that "Al Green" would one day be best known as the name of a black man. They'd started calling him "Alan" when he was in his midthirties in an effort to correct their mistake, but it was too late, and Al, for his part, didn't take up the cause. What people called him was of no concern to Al Green. He never even appeared to realize there was another one.

He leaned against the conference room windowsill, his back to the storm. "Why are you boys so worried about a bunch of camel jockeys? They eat with their hands. They shit on the ground. They fuck their cousins. They—"

"Hell, Al, sounds like a Green family reunion." Bill Morton leaned back in his chair, tapped his pen on the table, and smiled. He still had a thick head of hair, silver waves now, combed back from his high forehead. He wore company cufflinks.

Roy Daniel laughed. Even Jabe Evans looked up from his notebook long enough to smile.

Al Green didn't acknowledge the insult, but was obviously annoyed by the interruption. "Gentlemen, they got nothin' on us. Not one tiny little thing. We get our boys in there fast, keep 'em in ammo, get 'em plenty of air cover, and in a few weeks Haji's tellin' us everything. He'll be sellin' out his own grandma just so he can get back to kissin' the ground seven times a day and fuckin' his goats at night."

"Then why do they need *us*?" Roy Daniel glanced at Jabe Evans to make sure he was listening. The old man was bent over his notebook, as usual, but he acknowledged the question with a nod and a glance at Green.

"Same reason they always need us. There's just some things they can't do themselves."

Bill Morton nodded, still tapping his pen.

"I'm not sure I buy that, Al," said Daniel. "Not in this situation. The U.S. military has more buy-in for this operation than they've had for anything they've done since World War II. The UN, NATO—even the Russians aren't standing in our way. Everybody wants this mission to succeed. And if success means a few extracurricular activities on the side—well, as long as they're not too obvious, I don't think you'll hear a word out of anybody."

With some effort, Green pushed himself away from the windowsill and walked around behind Daniel to the coffee thermos. His belly was threatening a jailbreak beneath his button-down shirt and he was breathing a little more heavily than a walk around a conference table should warrant.

"Got nothin' to do with gettin' caught." The thermos wheezed and spit four-hour-old coffee into Al Green's cup. "These boys'd outsource knockin' up their own wives if they could figure out how to fill out the damn J&A."

Daniel and Morton laughed, but this time Jabe Evans hadn't heard.

He finished writing and looked up at Roy Daniel. At seventy-five, Evans no longer sat up as straight as he once had, but he still commanded the room's attention whenever he spoke.

"There are some things they can't do themselves. They can't do science. Not the way we can."

Green stared at his feet and stirred his coffee. Bill Morton, a bobble-head of himself, continued to nod and tap his pen, smiling as if everyone had finally understood what he'd been saying all along.

"Well, that's true." Roy Daniel nodded, too, tapping his lips with his thumb as the wind began to hiss outside the window. "But is science really what's required here? They are, after all—as Al's so delicately pointed out—living in caves."

"Science can always help, Roy," said bobblehead Bill Morton, glancing across the table at Evans.

Daniel either missed or ignored the body language. "True, true. Science can always contribute something. But I think the question here is, can it contribute something on a timescale and at a cost point that makes sense? By the time we think of what we want to propose, find the right people to propose it to, get them to issue an RFP, write a response—guys, the war's over by then."

Thunder growled in the distance and startled the streetlights on Leesburg Pike into early service. Al Green gulped his coffee and cleared his throat. "Roy's right. Now ain't the time for science. Now's the time to move in quick and get the job done."

"So what are you suggesting, exactly?" Evans asked his notebook as he wrote.

Roy Daniel opened his mouth, but Green beat him to the punch. "I'm suggestin' we talk to Colonel Jaworski and get some of our fellas in theater ASAP. He knows who we are—we helped him out back in Kosovo, helped him get the full bird. We can do it again here."

"Do we have anybody ready to go?"

"Sure we do! Nichols and Hernandez are chompin' at the bit. Hell, I wouldn't be surprised if they haven't already booked their tickets all by themselves. And Smoke—you remember Smoke, Jabe—used to work with that cocksucker Schwartz at Belvoir before he retired? Smoke's already workin' on a C4I project over at Ramstein and knows a lotta the deployin' intel boys there. I bet he could make a couple calls and get himself on the next bird out. Happy to go, too—I hear that ol' girl he married's been tryin' to get him to redo their kitchen—"

"We'd need a contract vehicle," Morton cut in as Green chuckled into his coffee cup. "Roy's right that there's no time for proposals. What have we got that we could use?"

He was looking at Daniel, but Daniel wasn't listening. He was doodling on his notepad and tapping his lips like he did when he was thinking. So Morton looked at Green, who'd apparently never noticed that the question wasn't directed at him all along.

"Well, the C4I contract Smoke's on might work. Like I said, most of the boys he's been workin' with are deployin' anyway. Or maybe that—"

"Everybody needs money." Roy Daniel was still doodling and talking to no one in particular. Evans looked up from his notebook and waited.

" —that sustainment contract Burgess's boys have got with PM-FPS. Shouldn't be too hard to slip a couple extra warm bodies in under that one."

"Everybody needs money," Daniel said again, this time more firmly. Green finally noticed that no one was listening to him, so he leaned back against the window and waited, watching his fingertips tap the metal sill as the first fat raindrops splattered against the glass.

"I think we can all agree on that point," said Bobblehead, flashing his company cufflinks and grin.

Roy Daniel finally looked around the table. "It takes money to do just about anything. It took money to get those guys into the U.S., to keep them fed and clothed and looking like respectable neighbors while they went to flight school. It's probably costing money to keep their old mothers in the manner to which they've become accustomed for the rest of their worldly days. But that's all peanuts compared to the money they're going to need. If they're seriously going to take on the best and brightest of the Western world, they're going to need a hundred times what they've been spending—a thousand times—more. Think about that. Think about them as a corporation, or a not-for-profit for a moment. Think about planning for that kind of growth. How do you do it? How would we do it?"

He had their attention, but nobody answered.

"Okay, think of it this way. Where does money come from?"

"The U.S. government." Al Green responding to a drill sergeant: loud and without a trace of doubt. Bobblehead Bill laughed appreciatively.

"Well, okay, fair enough, but I suspect Al-Qaeda's got other sources. Mom and Pop donors around the world, a couple of rogue dictators, maybe the odd arms dealer here and there—I'm just thinking aloud. That's not really my point, anyway. Where does money come from? I mean literally. Money comes from . . . the bank. Regardless of who's giving them the money, eventually all this money has to end up in some kind of institution—some kind of a bank. You can't finance this kind of operation on cash stashed under your mattress. Just like us, Al-Qaeda's got to have ways to accept money and ways to pay money out. They've got to have some sort of banking system."

Bill Morton leaned forward, put his elbows on the table, clasped his hands beneath his chin to stop his nodding, and closed his eyes as the conversation turned to his one true god. When Daniel stopped, he opened his eyes suddenly, awakened too early from a pleasant dream.

"How do you suppose they pull that off?" Morton asked, more to himself than anyone else around the table.

"That's the question, isn't it?" Roy Daniel smiled. "It must be extremely complicated. You're the CFO, Bill—you know how complicated it is for us, and we're not even trying to hide anything."

Morton raised his eyebrows, and his grin reappeared behind his clasped hands. "Not much."

"Imagine how complicated it would be if we couldn't even let on publicly that we had any assets at all. Imagine not being able to show any revenue. Imagine not being able to pay anyone directly."

"Some of that sounds pretty good. But okay, I see your point. What I don't see, though, is what this has to do with us."

"If CASTOR has a payment to make, how do we do it? If you want to move money from one account to another, how do you make that happen? If our clients want to pay us, how do they?"

"We cut checks. Or we wire money. Same as you do at home, basically—just more checks, and bigger numbers. Maybe." Bill Morton winked. "With your alimony, can't be sure."

Roy Daniel let it go. "But how does the money physically get from one account to another?"

"Well, it doesn't—not physically. One account registers a debit, the other a credit. It's all done electronically."

"Exactly. It's all electronic. It all goes through computers. Computer systems control every financial transaction of any size that happens in the world today. And computer systems—now there's something we understand."

"So you're saying we should use our technical expertise to stop Al-Qaeda's flow of funds?"

"Something like that. I actually think we might be better off just watching it—at least for a while. Figuring out who's paying them, who they're paying, who's handling their transactions, who's helping them cover it all up—we could learn a lot about who the good guys and the bad guys are and what they're trying to accomplish just by watching the money trail."

Al Green watched for the second head to sprout from Roy Daniel's neck. "Are you tryin' to say we should just sit here with our dicks in our hands and watch while Haji gets ready to fuck us all over again? I'm sorry, Roy, but I'm just an old country boy, and that just don't make no sense to me. We just got done watchin' him take down a few thousand people in a few minutes. Now it's time to show 'em sumbitches what a real war looks like. And we need to be with 'em, Roy—right there with 'em, pullin' 'em rats outta their holes by their big ol' fuckin' whiskers."

No one spoke. Jabe Evans turned the page in his notebook and his pen kept scratching across the paper. The wind was whipping sheets of water across the window of the conference room. Down below, traffic was snarled on the Pike, red lights swinging in the wind. The fluorescent lights hummed, faraway insects swarming to a flame.

Roy Daniel took up his doodling again and talked to his sketch as he drew it. "CASTOR is a science company. Science is what we know, better than anyone else, and technical know-how is what we sell. If we can use that know-how to learn how the enemy earns money, how they spend money, and who helps them along the way, then we can make a real difference. We can find bad guys we never even knew were bad guys. And sure, maybe at some point we can gum up the works, keep somebody's money from getting where it's supposed to be going and maybe stop somebody from doing something we'd all rather he not do. But in my opinion, we'd be more useful doing things like that—things we know how to do—than by signing on as soldiers for hire. NATO's got soldiers. But maybe they could use a few good scientists."

A quick knocking at the door broke an awkward silence. No one answered, but the door opened anyway, and Roger Taylor, Jabe Evans's assistant, walked in. He was fifty-something and a bit overweight, white hair military cropped above his wire-rimmed glasses. He didn't acknowledge anyone in the room, walking his runway walk straight to Jabe Evans's chair and leaning to whisper in the old man's ear. Al Green glared at Roger Taylor then turned to look out the window at the storm. Evans listened and nodded.

"Okay. I'll be right there. Is he on the line now?"

"No, sir. He's in the lobby."

Jabe Evans stared. "General Hayward is in the lobby?"

"Yes, sir. He should be up any moment now. Marcia's on her way down to get him."

Evans gathered up his notebook and followed Roger Taylor out of the room. Roy Daniel returned to his doodling, tapping his lips as he drew. Al Green smiled at his reflection in the conference room window. Bill Morton smiled, too, put his pen back in his shirt pocket, adjusted his cufflinks, and bobbled out of the room.

• • •

Some men, when they reach a certain age, buy a Lamborghini. Some jump from perfectly functional airplanes, or pay vast sums to shoot waning third-world species. A few move to the Village to write poetry. Far more start chasing girls half their age, both parties eager to convince themselves that there's more than money shoring up the relationship. Some, constitution and portfolio permitting, do it all.

Very few keep their old car, old wife, old frugal habits, and start a new company instead. Jabe Evans was one of the very few.

The only resemblance borne by Jabe Evans to his contemporaries trying to purchase the fountain of youth was that CASTOR was, for him, more hobby—an all-consuming hobby, but a hobby nonetheless—than business. He founded the company on pure patriotism: Use science to solve the United States' most pressing problems. Financial reward was secondary. "It's for the good of the company" was a phrase employees of CASTOR quickly learned never to use in Evans's presence. "It's for the good of the country," on the other hand, was a phrase that could get you promoted.

It wasn't a phrase you heard much in the early '70s, when Jabe Evans abandoned his career in the nuclear power industry to set out on his own. He recruited a few like-minded scientists, got a small blast-modeling contract from a good friend at the Atomic Energy Commission, and set up shop in an old warehouse on the Georgetown waterfront, next door to a ballet school. He loved a good physics debate with his colleagues in front of the blackboard while the ballerinas floated by across the hall. Theory meets practice. Life was beautiful.

He was not a believer in the division of labor. "You eat what you kill" was one of his favorite phrases, and he hired only people with the contacts and egos to thrive in such an environment. Every person was essentially his own company, bringing in contracts and staffing up to fulfill them as he saw fit. Those who did well saw their divisions grow and were asked to take on more. Those who did not—and there were a few—made so little money that there was no need to fire them. The only official rules of the game were that every contract had to involve the application of science to solving a problem, and had to be to the benefit of the United States. And the ultimate prize to be won was the one thing that Jabe Evans never let out of his personal control: CASTOR stock.

And so CASTOR—the Corporation for the Application of Science and Technology to Operational Realities—grew as a loose confederation of scientists ostensibly unified by these simple principles. The company employed no salesmen—the scientists themselves were expected to talk with prospective clients and drum up business. CASTOR gained a reputation as an easy company to do business with—naïve, some may have said, given scientists' general lack of interest in the financial details of the contracts they signed, so long as the science involved was going to be fun. CASTOR gained a reputation for doing consistently good work—only the fun work, some may have said, given that no one but the scientists themselves were deciding what contracts to pursue. But however you chose to describe the CASTOR formula, one fact was perfectly clear: It worked. The company grew, faster than Jabe Evans had ever expected. And as it grew, the value of its stock grew, too. Stock that Jabe Evans continued to distribute personally.

The real unifying force behind CASTOR evolved, therefore, into loyalty to Jabe Evans. In spite of the laissez-faire structure that he initially put in place, it simply wasn't in Evans's DNA not to know everyone in the company by name, to know every contract in detail, and to know every client personally. He kept detailed notes in every meeting. Nothing happened at CASTOR without at least his tacit approval. Beginning a phone call with the words "Evans wants us to . . ." guaranteed quick and unquestioning cooperation. By hiring the right people, tirelessly working his internal networks for information, and rewarding those he saw doing what he liked, Evans was able to assure himself that the company remained true to his founding principles. But a side effect of this management style—and the tremendous success of the company—was that he built a cult of personality that even Caesar or Charlemagne might have admired. Jabe Evans came to inspire fear—fear in that ancient, biblical sense, mixing love and terror in a manner unfamiliar to the average citizen of today's pop-culture democracies. He came to be known among the employees of CASTOR as the great provider—but also as judge, jury, and executioner. To please Jabe Evans was to achieve Nirvana. To incur his wrath was to perish in the fieriest rings of hell.

All of which, said his supporters, would have come as a great surprise to Jabe Evans himself, who had never wanted anything more than to use his scientific talents to serve his country. But his detractors whispered that that was exactly what he wanted you to think, and that everything—everything including his virtual deification—had been part of his plan from the beginning.

It came as a surprise to no one that the supporters tended to have a lot of CASTOR stock, while the detractors had little to none—or were often no longer with the company.

The only debate was over cause and effect.

. . .

Roy Daniel sat at the conference room table and watched as his doodling turned into a full-blown sketch. Al Green had grinned at his reflection in the window for a few minutes after Evans and Morton left the room, avoiding eye contact as he glanced in Daniel's direction. Daniel hadn't said a word. Al Green's image emerged in graphite strokes between the lines in his notebook—narrow, deep-set eyes beneath used-up bottlebrush eyebrows; meatball nose; chin like a tiny, legless ass. He stared for a moment at Green's fingers—fingers were always the hardest part—wrinkling and unwrinkling themselves behind his back as he stood facing away from the table. Green turned and tried to return the stare, but Daniel just tapped his lips with his left hand while his right hand coaxed his pencil. Al Green grunted and left the room.

Cause and effect.

Every portrait is an editorial, thought Daniel. No matter how hard you try to be objective, your opinion of the subject comes right through. He put down his pencil and tried to meet Green's lifeless stare. CASTOR: Corporation for the Advancement of Several Thousand Old Rednecks. Still, he could dig up business among the military crowd like nobody else in the company. No end to the guys Green had, at one point or another, crawled through the mud with—either literally or figuratively. Vietnam for him had been one big networking event. The Iran hostage crisis, Nicaragua, Granada, Somalia, the Gulf War—he'd hit them all, keeping his Rolodex up to date.

And now he couldn't wait to get his ticket to the next big convention. He and hundreds, maybe thousands of other Al Greens—so many, in fact, that a big convention every few years was almost inevitable. Back by popular demand.

Not fair. This one's different. We've been attacked. Thousands of Americans are dead on our own soil. We have to respond. Roy Daniel understood the argument, felt the urge himself. Hell, he'd felt it personally. Remember the day it happened? Remember your first thoughts? That morning, he'd been preparing for a 9:00 presentation to In-Q-Tel and several other potential investors in a new venture interested in using some of CASTOR's video processing technology. He'd walked into the conference room where the technicians were setting up the demo, using live satellite images of Manhattan. Nothing like Manhattan to guarantee you something to look at any day, any time. One of the technicians was on the phone when he walked in: A plane had hit one of the Twin Towers. So they trained the live satellite images on lower Manhattan, zoomed in close enough to see the smoke trailing away from the south tower. Somebody had a radio. Sarah Anderson, his secretary, had shown the investors into the room and they'd greeted one another in whispers, but all eyes remained fixed on the image, all ears tuned to the voice of the radio broadcaster, and they were there when the second plane exploded into the other tower. And that was when Roy Daniel had muttered an apology and stepped into the hallway.

Didn't Asher have an office just a block or two from the Twin Towers?

Didn't Asher seem to spend half his life visiting investment bankers in lower Manhattan, bragging about how many meetings he could cram into one day by taking the first shuttle down from Boston and planning his routes correctly?

Weren't some of those bankers in the World Trade Center?

Hadn't the radio announcer said something about a flight from Boston?

Roy had stood in the hallway, dialing Asher's numbers. Cell: voice mail. Asher's voice.

In the conference room, the planes hit the towers again.

Office: voice mail. Asher again.

Instant replay, waiting for everyone else to catch up.

Roy Daniel could feel the shaking coming but pushed it down hard. He dialed Asher's home number: voice mail again. Asher.

Are they out of town? Damn it, Roy, you should pay more attention to these things—did they tell you where they were going to be?

Of course not. He's what, thirty-five years old? Thirty-six?

Never mind. Get it together, Roy.

Sarah Anderson was coming back down the hall toward him, slowing when she saw his face. He tried to speak, but all that came was a silent "no."

Sarah stopped.

Guests. "Sarah, could you please make sure our guests are okay? I've got something I need to take care of." He hadn't waited for a response, hadn't thought that maybe Sarah had wanted to tell him something. He walked away toward his office.

Does Kimberly have a cell phone? "Sarah?" She was already gone. His fingertips were getting cold. He needed the restroom. Get it together, Roy. He dialed Asher's cell phone again: voice mail.

Roy Daniel stood in the hall and stared at his cell phone. Ring, damn it! Ring!

Get it together, Roy. What are the chances, really? Take a deep breath. One thing at a time. Just like in the old days. You're the quarterback. Focus, find your man, complete the pass.

He turned again and walked back toward the conference room. Inside, the investors were still standing or sitting on the table. A couple were staring at their BlackBerries. Sarah was coming back through the door. She tried to smile.

"They're fine, Roy. Do you need anything?" Her voice a whisper in a dream.

"I can't reach Asher." BlackBerry.

"Let me try. Why don't you stay here, I'll come and get you when I find him."

Roy nodded and turned to his BlackBerry. Asher has a BlackBerry. He typed in Asher's e-mail address, wrote "Are you okay?" in the subject line, and hit "send."

Mark Simmons, Roy's contact at In-Q-Tel, was standing next to him when he looked up.

"You okay, Roy?"

Roy Daniel nodded. "My son has an office near there." He waved his BlackBerry absently at the screen. "No answer."

Mark Simmons seemed about to speak, but only reached out and squeezed his shoulder. Both men watched the thick smoke chugging across the screen, away from the Statue of Liberty.

Time stopped.

One of the technicians had somehow tied into a CNN satellite feed—it had replaced Roy's forgotten PowerPoint on the conference room's second screen. Screaming people in work clothes and firefighters running against the tide filled the room.

None of them was Asher.

The meeting was clearly over, but no one was going anywhere. Sarah caught his eye from the doorway, shrugged an apology, and left.

The red light on Roy Daniel's BlackBerry blinked. The same planes hit the same towers over and over as newscasters with nothing to say talked on. Everyone but Roy listened.

He pushed a button and his inbox appeared. One new message. From Asher.

"I'm okay."

Roy Daniel leaned back against the conference room table and breathed. The Pentagon exploded in front of him, but he felt only gratitude.

• • •

Al Green sat down in Bill Morton's office and smiled. Golf trophies and mementos of deals long forgotten cluttered the top of the wooden cabinet beneath the window. Bill Morton turned a picture on an otherwise perfectly clean desk toward Green.

"Did you see my new picture?" A toddler wearing a pumpkin costume laughed inside the hand-painted "I Love Grandpa" frame. "My daughter's first. Already walking. Cute as she can be. And can she *talk*! Oh, Lord have mercy, some man better look out one of these days—he won't know what hit him!"

The two men studied the picture as the rain pounded the window. "So I assume you had something to do with that, right?"

Green leaned back and put his hands behind his head. "I talked to Jaworski this mornin', told him we had a meetin' this afternoon with the old man. He asked how Evans felt about the whole thing, I told him I had no idea—but that a little string-pullin' couldn't hurt nothin'. Guess he pulled."

Morton was still smiling at his pumpkin granddaughter. "Tell me again why you think this is such a good idea? Daniel does have a point—it's not really in our lane, so to speak."

"I agree with Roy on one thing—this iwar's gonna be over quicker 'n a shot dog in a barn. If we don't move quicker 'n that, we'll miss the whole damn thing. Biggest damn Thanksgivin' dinner in years, and we won't even be at the table. And we all know that if you ain't at the table, you ain't gettin' dessert. And dessert"—Al Green tipped his chair back and patted his stomach—"dessert, Bill, is what it's all about."

Morton nodded at his pumpkin. "I hear you, Al, I hear you. But you know how the old man feels about this kind of stuff. It's not what we do. It's not science. It's—you know—beneath us."

"Hell, I know that, Bill—ever'body knows how Evans feels. But the fact is, we've been doin' it for years now, here and there, and you can't tell me he don't know about it—not the way he is."

"That doesn't necessarily mean he likes it."

"Oh sure, he might say no up front if he gets a vote. But once it's goin', if it's makin' the client happy, he ain't gonna pull the plug."

Bill Morton laughed. "He does get a vote, Al. You do realize that was the whole point of the meeting we just had."

Al Green's eyes narrowed and he grinned like a pig dozing after a particularly good feed. "You really, truly believe he's gonna say no to General Hayward?"

Morton studied Green's face and his head began to bobble, slowly at first. He sat up and put his hands on his desk, adjusting one cuff so the CASTOR cufflink showed.

"And if it's making us money, and getting us more work, why should he?"

"Why the hell should he?"

Bill Morton gave a final nod and looked around his office. A couple of e-mails to read, and the message light on his phone was lit. Lightning struck out toward the airport, and out of old habit, he counted the seconds until the thunder. He looked back toward Al Green and nodded again, but Green showed no sign of leaving.

• • •

Roy Daniel looked up from his sketch when the lightning flashed. Sarah Anderson's smile ghosted in the stormy black of the window. He turned to look at the real thing in the conference room doorway.

"Hi."

"Hello."

She grinned and wafted by to put away the sugar and cream packets and unused coffee cups. She smelled like long-ago flowers and chocolate and a hint of sweat late in the day. He touched the soft skin on the back of her knee and she didn't move away. She picked up the coffee thermoses and turned to face him.

"See you later?"

Roy swiveled and saw, nose to navel, a child playing dress-up. The tilt of her head asked the question, her blue eyes gave away the answer. Her blouse was wrinkled from sitting all day, offering a preview of coming attractions between the lower two buttons.

Roy Daniel nodded.

Signature strawberries-and-cream smile, hip bump on the way out, and Sarah Anderson disappeared down the hall.

three

The days were really long by the lake since we got up so early to fish—so early that we had to turn the lights on in the kitchen. Dad and I'd eat our cereal at the counter then walk down the hill through the wet grass to the dock where the boats were. The sky was just starting to light up behind the trees to the right, but to the left I could still see the stars as clearly as I had the night before when I was chasing fireflies with a pickle jar Grandma'd washed out for me. The air was cool but humid, and I could tell it'd be hot later, and we'd go swimming.

On the dock, I'd open the door to the shed. It always smelled like motor oil, fish and mildew from the old life jackets, and nylon from the new ones. I'd pull out the fishing poles and the big plastic tackle box and check to make sure the stringer was in it and not still tied to a cleat somewhere with fish from yesterday on the other end, hiding under the dock. It was in the tackle box that day. Dad took the rods and the tackle box and put them in the fishing boat and I got in, careful not to grab the spot on the edge where the fiberglass was rubbing off that'd make your hand sting if you touched it.

It was just the two of us that morning so I got to sit in the white swivel chair in front instead of on the live box in the middle where I had to sit when Grandpa or one of my uncles came. Dad flipped the red switch and yanked on the starter cord and the engine just grumbled and rolled over the first time, sputtered and smacked the second, and then on the third pull finally woke up, coughing black smoke into the morning fog. I untied the old nylon rope from the front cleat and Dad untied us in back and then clunked the engine into reverse. It grumbled under its breath as we backed and turned away from the dock. I could smell the oil smell of the exhaust that still hung where the engine had fired.

When we were pointed out of the cove toward the main channel, the engine clunked and roared again and the front where I was sitting reared up into the air. I braced my old sneakers inside the bow and smiled facing straight ahead as the boat surged forward and pushed me back in the plastic seat. I could hear the bow hiss through the green glassy water beneath me and feel the damp wind on my face as I flew into the mist that always looked heavier ahead but was never so thick once you were in it. The air smelled like fish. I couldn't wait to have one hooked.

The other side of the lake was wild and thick with trees whose branches hung low above the water. Brush grew right up to the miniature orange cliffs where the waves cut into the clay. Sometimes deer watched us from behind the brush and the mist, but if they were there that morning I couldn't see them. The engine's pitch lowered, then it choked and spat and went silent. The bow settled back down into the water and the waves from our wake kept time against the shore for a few seconds, and then they, too, went silent.

Dad opened the tackle box and rummaged through the lures. He untangled the treble hooks of a big, black Hula Popper, hitching the eyelet in its wide mouth to the snap swivel at the end of his line. He lobbed the lure over next to an old, rotten stump near the bank. The lure bobbed there for a second or two, disappeared with a *blurp* as Dad gave the line a jerk, then popped back to the surface, its big red mouth and bug eyes gasping in the dark glassy water.

I grabbed my favorite lure—a Pico Perch. It was shaped like a little brim, dark green on top fading to silver on its belly, with little red spots and a flat, red forehead. I snapped the lure onto the end of my line and cast it, two handed, parallel to the bank. It splashed down next to a leafy branch that lay low against the water and I started to reel it back in. I could see it wiggling through the green as it swam as fast as it could back to the boat. I hauled it out of the water and cast it back toward the shore.

Dad's lure popped and splashed and the gears of my reel whirred and somewhere in the mist back near the middle of the lake another boat's motor whined from right to left, toward the rising sun. Dad and I both watched the sound go by. That's when I felt the fish tug at the other end of my line and my reel began to scream and the tip of my rod danced like a willow in a fast stream.

I sat up straight and hugged the end of my rod low and close. I reeled as fast as I could. I watched the spot where my line disappeared into the water, watched it jump back and forth and try to pull toward the leafy branch. Dad reeled his own line in and moved up to sit on the live box just behind me and reminded me to keep the tip of my rod high. The spot where my line hit the water suddenly cut away from the boat and Dad said, "Be careful, now, Ash, he's gonna jump!" and I reeled faster still to keep the line from going slack. The fish was in the air before I could remember seeing it jump, greenish silver with drops shaking away from its tail. Then it splashed back into the water and I could still feel it tugging at the end of the line and I realized I was holding my breath.

"That's a nice one, Son. Did you see how fat he was?" I smiled and nodded but kept my eyes on the line. "I think that's the biggest fish you've ever hooked." It jerked left, then right, then back to the left, and left again, but not as fast now and I hoped the fish was tired and that I'd have it in the boat soon.

The line jittered and inched nearer to the boat and then suddenly the fish jumped again. It was closer this time and I could see its dark back and the greenish stripe down its side and its fat, silver belly. Its tail flapped and sprayed water from side to side, and its head shook, rattling the lure snagged in its big mouth. "Keep her tight," Dad muttered as the fish rose into the air, and "That's it!" as it fell back into the murky lake. I felt my rod handle dig into my stomach, and my arms were starting to ache from trying to pull the fish up out of the deep water and down out of the air and back away from the snags near the stump and under the low branch. I could feel Dad leaning close behind me, could smell the coffee he'd had for breakfast and the sweatshirt he wore every morning to fish. I knew his face would be scratchy if he hugged me, because he never shaved until after we got back.

The fish fought on for another minute or two, moving left, then right, but not running the way he had been before. Then the line stood still where it went into the water. The fish pulled down hard and the tip of my rod bent toward its reflection. I tried to reel but the reel just whined and the wet line ran out, leaving drops on the eyelets of the rod as it wound back out. I hunched over the reel and fought to keep the tip of the rod from hitting the water, but the fish was strong and just kept pulling, straight under the boat. I watched my rod tip inch closer to the lake and I hunched down further and pulled back as hard as I could but the rod tip just kept going and I said, "Dad, help!" But Dad didn't help. He just grabbed the dip net and leaned in closer.

"Keep that tip up, Ash. You can do it. You can beat him."

I could envision the fish lying exhausted in the bottom of the boat, his gills opening wide and closing and one eye staring bewildered into the unfamiliar sky. I could feel Dad's scratchy hug, could smell him through the warm sweatshirt as he pressed my face into it. I could picture pulling on the stringer later in the day, watching the big fish emerge from under the dock into the greenish brown sunlit water and hearing Grandpa's slow laugh and "Well, looky there!" and Grandma's "That's a beeg feesh—I think he's as beeg as you!"

But the tip of my rod dipped into the water, and with a dull pop I felt the weight go. I reeled fast, begging it to come back, but all I saw was my Pico Perch, squirming like a guilty dog, wiggling head down through the water toward us. I heard it break the surface with a limp *splish* and felt its treble hooks rattle the wet tip of my rod.

Dad's hand squeezed my shoulder, but I didn't look back. The switch clicked and the engine sputtered as Dad pulled the starter cord. I braced my feet inside the bow and the boat surged forward. The mist was clearing now, and I could see our house on the other side of the lake. Dad steered us to the left, away from the house, away from the fish. The wind dried salty spots behind the corners of my eyes as we howled into the red-hot sunrise beyond the dam.

four

Julie walked toward him down the long hall. A hot morning sun glazed the tall windows on the left and made her wet hair glow like a summer lake at midnight. She was wrapped in a white towel tucked closed under her left arm. Her left thigh teased through with each step forward, then shied back into the warm, damp folds. Julie smiled at him and the hall stretched, taking her farther away with every step of her bare feet. The doors lining the right side of the hall opened one by one. Chuck stepped through the first into the hall and winked. Ahmed talked silently on his cell phone in the next, smiling and watching Julie glide backward through the sun. Asher's father stood in the next doorway down but said nothing, his eyes as white-hot as the windows. Asher reached out toward Julie, stretching as far as he could, but it wasn't enough. He willed his hand toward hers until even the joints in his fingers strained and popped, but she faded back into the distance.

• • •

Asher's arm lay across her lap, stretched toward the aisle. Eyes the color of tropical waves. Honeycrisp cheeks. Hair the color of warm sand.

Hadn't she had gray hair a few hours ago? Hadn't she been about twenty years older? A hundred pounds heavier? Hadn't she done everything she could to ignore him, indignant at his very existence?

"Bad dream?"

Asher closed his eyes. His pillow smelled like his doctor's office. Dishes clinked somewhere not too far away. A man's laugh burped over the hum of the engines.

When he opened his eyes again, she'd put her book down next to his arm. No indignation in her coral smile.

He could see his arm lying there, but it obeyed another master.

"Sorry. Asleep." He propped himself up through a tangle of blankets and seatbelts and headphone cords and tried to coax his wayward arm back into his own lap.

"I see."

Asher's senses booted up one by one. Tiny hummingbirds pecked at his arm. His mouth tasted like freeze-dried whiskey. His shorts were twisted around and hiked up and he realized he should keep the blanket over his lap until tensions subsided.

"Need some help?"

James Bond would have a line for this occasion. "I must be dreaming" to Pussy Galore's full-screen bust.

"Not anymore," he sang.

Mute function apparently not yet online.

Asher bumped and tugged and fluffed himself more or less upright with his one functioning arm. Something still tugged awkwardly across his crotch. "Are you any good with knots?"

"Yes, I am. Very good." A coral pout. Her "very good" betrayed a mother tongue other than English.

He looked for whatever it was still holding him down. "Well then I may need your help before I can get off."

"I think I can see your problem." She shifted in her seat and reached for his lap. Long fingers milk-soft. French nails. A simple gold ring, like a little girl's.

Asher's mind hung, cursor flashing on a blue screen.

She grabbed his seat belt and gave a yank, freeing a foot of slack from beneath his thighs.

Tropical blue waves swelled and broke. "Better?"

Asher raised his knees, opening the airways. She smelled like mangoes and airline lotion.

"Much better. Thank you."

She nodded and wriggled herself back into her seat. Asher watched her return to her book. Coral pout and tropical sparkle didn't watch him back.

• • •

"You have . . . one . . . new message. To listen to your messages, press two. To . . ."

Asher thought back to the voice mail.

"First . . . new message. Received . . . today . . . at . . . nine . . . thirty-seven . . . P.M."

A squirrel was stuck in a cardboard box on the other end of the line. It ran, hit the side, scrambled up, fell, lay briefly stunned, then started again. Deep voices through heavy scarves commented on his predicament. The goddess of airports, train stations, and voice mail systems chanted in the background. The squirrel took another run at its cardboard walls, with similar results. The scarf brothers laughed as the goddess began a new mantra. A couple of backflips in the box, and the line went dead.

"To replay your message, press one. To delete, . . ."

Press . . .

Instant replay. Was the goddess chanting in English? French? Western intonation. A doorbell introduced her second set. Europe, maybe? Don't they have those doorbell sounds before announcements in European airports? But maybe they have those everywhere. They all run together.

The engines surged a little and Asher felt cold air blowing on his head. He reached up to close the vent and saw his neighbor's hand already there. He reached instead for his glass of water and stole a look in the process. He'd been wrong. She wasn't ignoring him.

Which wasn't the point, of course. What was with the voice mail? Pocket dial most likely. But that would mean it was from someone who'd called him before. Who did he know who was traveling? Better question would be, who did he know who wasn't? Seemed like the only constant was perpetual motion, at least among his friends and relatives.

Except for Kimberly, of course. And his kids.

His stomach twisted a little. Kimberly wouldn't have called—not after their little "chat" on the way to the airport. Unless, of course, something was really wrong. His neighbor's smile called the idea ridiculous, far-fetched, conspiracy-theory stuff. But the smile winked at the idea and the idea gave the smile a sign and Asher wished he knew how much longer they had to go.

• • •

He still wished he knew. He never had known—ever since the beginning.

They'd had a great time his senior year in high school, ever since that party at her house when her parents were away for the weekend. Actually, all three of them had had fun that night—Asher, Kimberly, and a girl whose name Asher was embarrassed that he couldn't remember. Lisa maybe. They'd all been playing spin the bottle on the floor in the basement, taking turns hamming up kisses to the cheers of the other players. But after a few beers or rum and cokes or whatever it was they were drinking that night, the other players had wandered away and eventually it was just the three of them. Asher had taken turns kissing first one, then the other, long into the night. On Monday he'd apologized to the one girl and started going out with Kimberly. Why he'd chosen Kimberly over the other girl he couldn't remember at all. It was high school. Senior year. The future was so big that it lost all meaning. To make it manageable they just redefined it as the coming weekend, or the next dance, or the next time somebody's parents were leaving town.

A few days before he left for college he took her out to dinner at a French place nobody their age went to. He ordered wine and they actually brought it and they sat on the patio eating snails by candlelight, pretending they were older than they really were and that the next four years were already past. After dinner they walked around for a while then drove back up to Kimberly's house on the mountain and walked out to the bluff. The moon was out, turning her long hair white and making her eyes look tearier than maybe they really were. He told her he loved her. She looked away and told him not to say that.

When he went away to college, neither of them wrote or called. He saw her at a party when he came home that first Christmas and she told him it was okay, she liked empty mailboxes. He apologized and promised he'd write. But he got back to school and neither of them did. And they didn't cross paths again—not until that summer, more than a year later, when he sat down with his friends for lunch and she showed up to take their orders.

Actually, she never made it to the table. But he saw her, and she saw him. He sat up, smiled a little and nodded, trying not to catch his friends' attention. She stopped and smiled like you do when you're too surprised to do anything else. Then she seemed to remember her uniform that time forgot. She touched a few blonde hairs that hung lose below the little cap, looked around anxiously, then turned and disappeared. A minute or two later a middle-aged veteran of more years than Asher had chest hairs arrived and asked what they'd like to drink.

After work, Asher went back to the restaurant, but she was already gone. When he got home, he just stared at the phone, knowing that he had to make the call. Not able to stand having such a terrible task in his immediate future, he picked up the receiver and dialed her number without having any idea what he was going to say. Her mother answered. Asher had only met her a couple of times, picking Kimberly up. He hoped now that she didn't remember him.

"Oh, hi. Is, uh, Kimberly there, please, by any chance?"

"No, I'm sorry, she's not. Could I ask who's calling?" Asher could picture her unclipping an earring and shifting the receiver, tilting her hair-helmeted head to hold it against her shoulder.

"Uh, yes ma'am, this is Asher Daniel. Would you mind asking her to give me a call?"

"Of course I will, Asher." She did remember. "Are you staying with your parents?" She knew about that, too, then. Everybody did, he supposed. It wasn't really such a big town.

"Actually, no, ma'am, I'm not. I'm house-sitting for Dr. Fazio, not too far from your place. Would you like me to give you the number?"

"Oh, that's okay, Asher—we have his number. I'll be sure to let Kimberly know you called. Are you home all summer, then?"

"Yes, ma'am. I am."

"Well, that's fine. I'll give Kimberly the message. Goodbye, Asher."

"Goodbye, Mrs. Gardner."

He hung up the receiver and took a deep breath in the strange kitchen. Outside, the sky was going dark, and the summer bugs were tuning up for the evening's concert. Maybe a run would help. He changed into his shorts and running shoes, turned out the lights, and locked up the house.

He smiled as he hit the road at full gallop. Glad that's over with. Glad I'm living here. Glad I can do what I want. Don't have to be home for dinner, don't have to get up on Sunday for church. Don't have to listen to the two of them argue about whatever they've made up to argue about this time. I'm free. To do what I want. Any old time.

The Stones rolled through his head as he ran the mile or so down to the park. The night smelled like mown grass and old wood and burgers from somebody's grill. His stomach growled and he wondered what he'd have for supper. At the park he cut left and ran along the other side of the mountain, thinking maybe he'd catch a last glimpse of the sunset, but it was already down, and the leaves were too thick, anyway, to give much of a view from the street. He ran past the big old limestone church and thought about all the Civil War ghosts that as kids they'd told one another they'd seen there on Halloween nights. No ghosts tonight. I've done my duty, placed my call to the exorcist, sent those ghosts on their merry way. Burgers sound good. Wonder if Dr. Fazio left any meat in the freezer?

Asher stopped running when he came back around to the house and walked slowly up the street, hands on his hips, feeling his breath slow and his heart rate drop. Up above, past the hedges, the house was dark. No dinner waiting. He felt a twinge in his stomach that had nothing to do with hunger. But never mind. He turned into the driveway and pushed up toward the house. Maybe I'll have a beer. A beer would be good. Hope Dr. Fazio left some beer.

Kimberly was sitting on the front steps. Her uniform was gone. She wore khaki shorts and white Keds and a lime green polo shirt with the collar up. Her legs and arms were already tanned, even so early in the summer, darker than her hair, which seemed to Asher to have sucked up the last of the sunset. It was longer than before, down below her shoulders, but her eyes were the same.

"Hey, Kimberly."

"Hey." She didn't smile, but she didn't sound angry, either.

"Mama said you called. I was out for a walk, anyway. Thought I'd just stop by."

Asher watched her talking, familiar but different. He was still a little out of breath and sweaty, but he sat down next to her, anyway. Her white shoes rocked a little back and forth, and she held her hands tight between her legs.

"Sorry about earlier," Asher said. "I didn't know you were working there."

Kimberly smiled just like she had when she saw him in the restaurant. "It's okay. It was just a surprise, that's all. I'm okay now." She looked away into the trees to the side of the lawn.

"How was college?"

"Haven't been yet. Decided to take a year off first. Went to Italy. Italy was great."

Asher turned and watched her back as she talked to the trees. "Must've been. I hear it's beautiful."

Kimberly turned, looking him in the eye for the first time today. "It is. Perfect. But home's nice, too. Don't you think?"

Asher nodded, looking back down at his shoes. A cricket revved up somewhere out on the lawn. A couple walking their dogs waved from the street.

"I was going to make some hamburgers. Are you hungry?"

Kimberly smiled and nodded. "That'd be nice."

"I don't know if there's any meat, though. I just moved in last night." Asher stood up and stretched. Kimberly watched and smiled.

"First, though, I need a shower." Asher knelt down behind her to get the key he'd left under the doormat. She still used the same shampoo. "Would you like to come inside?"

Kimberly looked across the lawn and out to the street. "It's nice out here. I think I'll stay for a while."

"I was going to have a beer. Would you like a beer while you wait?"

"Do you have some beer?"

"I don't know."

Kimberly looked back over her shoulder and smiled. Asher was smiling back down at her.

"You're a terrible host."

"You're a terrible guest. Just showing up, not even a call."

"Don't talk to *me* about not calling."

"What, you don't know how to dial a phone?"

Kimberly looked back out toward the street. "I didn't want to talk if you didn't want to."

Asher followed her gaze. Another couple was walking by, talking to each other in low tones. They didn't wave, didn't even seem to notice anyone was watching. He looked back down at Kimberly. She watched the couple pass by, resting her chin on her hands. He couldn't see her face. He stepped forward so he was standing just behind her. She leaned back, just a little, against his legs. The couple walked on up the street and disappeared around the corner.

A lightning bug glowed then faded, then glowed again, closer this time. The cricket had stopped at some point, but now it started up again.

"So, I guess I'll go see if I have any beer." Asher didn't move.

Kimberly shrugged and put a little more weight onto his bare legs. "Okay. Whatever you've got. I'm not picky."

"What do you think goes on up there?"

A thunderstorm earlier in the day had cleared away some of the August humidity, and the moon seemed to have taken the night off. Kimberly couldn't remember ever having seen so many stars.

"Up where?"

"Up there. Do you think there's somebody up there on some other planet, lying around like us after a swim, staring up at the sky and wondering the same thing?"

"Yes, I do."

"Really?"

"Really."

"Why?"

"Why not? Why should we be the only ones?"

A shooting star scratched the black film of the night sky, but it healed so quickly Kimberly wondered if maybe it had just been her imagination.

"You don't think we're special?"

"No, I don't."

"How come?"

"Just don't. Seems like too big a coincidence to me."

"What do you mean? Wouldn't it be a bigger coincidence if there *were* somebody else like us?"

"There are only so many elements. Seems to me there are only so many ways they can go together. With so many stars and planets out there, it just doesn't make sense to me that they've never come together like they did here in at least a couple of other places, sometime in all the trillions of years they've been around."

Kimberly pulled the damp towel a little closer around her and squirmed over onto her side. The big, smooth rock was still warm from the late-afternoon sun—she could feel it on her arm and her leg and soaking through the towel to the bare skin underneath. Asher lay on his back on his towel, hands behind his head. If there were Somebody up there looking down at them, he wasn't leaving anything to His imagination.

"What about God?"

"What about him?

"You don't believe He created us? Made us in His image, all that?"

"Even if he did, why wouldn't he have done it in a few other places, too?"

"Why should He have?"

"I don't know. Why not? Something to do? Eternity could get a little dull, I'd think—especially without a little company here and there. Practice, maybe? Didn't like the way things worked out the first time?"

"It doesn't say anything about other people in the Bible."

"It doesn't say anything in the Bible about giraffes, either—not as far as I can remember. Don't you believe in giraffes?"

"Come on, Asher. I'm serious."

"So am I."

"Heathen."

"God squad."

The water falling into the pool surged a little, as if a wave moving downstream had just reached them. Kimberly looked at the waterfall, barely visible in the moonless dark, against the big rocks at the other end.

She'd come here in high school a few times before she knew Asher. The first time that a couple of boys had taken off their clothes and pushed shouting and swearing off those big rocks into the deep black pool, she and the other girls had shrieked and covered their mouths to disguise delight as indignation. Pretty soon all the boys were in pretending to splash one another while trying to splash the girls. The girls pretended to try to avoid getting splashed.

Patty had gotten completely soaked by a sneak attack from behind a rock. She sputtered in legitimate shock for a moment and wiped the water out of her eyes. Then she stood up straight, yelled "Fine!" to no one in particular and, staring into the darkened woods on the other side of the pool, defiantly unbuttoned her shirt and threw it at her feet. The boys hooted and splashed, but she paid no attention. Her shorts were next, wet cotton wriggled free of tanned hips and dropped unceremoniously around her ankles. The shouts from the gallery continued. She reached around behind her back and unfastened her bra. The hooting faded into murmurs and nervous giggles, and the rest of the girls huddled together and stared as she tossed away her last bits of soaked clothing.

Patty stood at attention by the edge of the pool, right where Kimberly and Asher lay now, shivering in the sticky summer heat, eyes on some distant horizon. For just a moment there was only the sound of the waterfall, exactly like it sounded now. Then, suddenly, Patty crouched and shrieked and dove into the pool, and the boys resumed their splashes and shouts. Patty, though more fully clothed than ever by the dark, churning water, was the center of attention. The other girls watched as boys hauled themselves out of the water and ran right past them without a second glance, rushing to the rocks to win Patty's attention with ever-more-elaborate leaps.

When Kimberly stepped away from the crowd and took up Patty's former post by the edge of the pool, lifting her polo shirt over her head, the boys took no notice. But all of the girls noticed and fell into line, some enthusiastic, some hesitant, but none wanting to be known as the one who went home. That got the boys' attention. They pointed and cheered and splashed as never before. Kimberly saw Patty right there with them, clapping and splashing and shouting along. Trail blazed, ribbon cut, nothing more to prove. Spectacle turned spectator, shuddering raindrop returned to the all-embracing sea. One of them now.

Only for her did the night go quiet.

Kimberly sat by the edge of the water, staring up at the stars and brushing her damp hair off to one side with her fingers.

"Do you think they look like us?"

"I doubt it."

Asher swam toward her and she smiled, aware of being watched. "Definitely not as good-looking."

"I'm not sure I really want to go, you know."

"I know how you feel. Leaving's the worst part, though. Once you're there, it's great."

"Did you feel the same way?"

"Sure, I did. Everybody does."

"How long did it take you to get over it?"

"First night was tough. You lie there in a strange bed, listening to some stranger breathing in the next bed, and you wonder what you were thinking. But then it's morning and you clean yourself up and have breakfast with that stranger from the next bed and with a bunch of other strangers who're in exactly the same situation as you, and you don't feel so lonely anymore. You all register for classes together and buy your books together and figure out where your first lecture halls are. You put up your posters and you play your music loud and your neighbors stop by and somebody knows where there's a party later on and you all make plans to meet there. You dance and have a few drinks and meet some more people and stumble back to your room and that night you discover that the person in the next bed's not a stranger anymore—he's your friend. And after a couple of days of that, you're not thinking of home anymore. You *are* home."

"Are you going to call me this time?"

"Of course I will. Will you call me?"

"Of course I will."

• • •

The reason for the rubber band war was still a mystery to Asher. He supposed the reasons behind most rubber band wars were.

One fact was clear: Chloe had started it. She may have had some provocation, but if so, it was subtle. Her reaction, on the other hand, was not. She grabbed a handful of rubber bands from the jar beside the printer, picked the heaviest one she could find, stretched it a good two feet back from her left thumb to her right ear, and let it fly. As she did so she let out a rebel yell that drew looks of concern through the glass wall from a more conventional class of employee.

Her target, like her reason, was unclear. It certainly was not James. James was dressed in tight black jeans and an old black leather jacket, sported a Lyle Lovett haircut, and since Asher's arrival earlier in the day had mostly cowered at his desk, apparently hoping no one would notice he was there. But his job seemed to involve carrying the occasional milk crate full of files to some shelves along the wall, and he'd picked Chloe's moment to fulfill this task. Her cruel attack left a sizable welt on the right side of his pale neck, and sent him burrowing back into his cubicle.

Tom, Asher's bearded, mountaineering supervisor; sporty Erika, obviously the production department's brightest star, who had apparently run all the way from home in Brookline to the office that morning; and several other bored individuals were quick to abandon their desks and come to James's defense—or, at least, to attack Chloe for reasons of their own. Their counteroffensive provided others with sufficient grounds to join forces with Chloe. And so it went. Soon the floor was littered with rubber bands. Otherwise tame office workers crouched behind walls, dragged themselves commando-style with their elbows across the carpet, and screamed as the opposing side stormed their cubicle foxholes. No one was safe. Even David, who worked out daily, planned his meals a week in advance, and saved with his partner to buy a B&B in the islands (Asher had learned all this during his interview), was forced into action, firing out of his cubicle and then cowering under his desk, fists to his perfectly groomed face, as the inevitable reprisals ensued.

Asher's desk stood in the middle of the room, exposed from all sides. He had tried to stay out of it all, not really knowing anyone and therefore not really wanting to take sides. But as the fighting continued and the pile of rubber bands on his desk rose, it became ludicrous to resist. Both the man who hired him and the man who supervised him had stocked up on ammunition and showed no signs of standing down. So Asher picked up the biggest rubber band he could find and searched the room for a suitable target.

Chloe. No one could call Chloe an innocent bystander. Asher looked around in vain, but heard her on the other side of David's cubicle, ordering some unfortunate soul to die. He could only see the very top of her head, garnished with a green and a tan rubber band. To get a better view, he climbed onto his desk and stood there, taking careful aim so as not to antagonize anyone else. But suddenly the room grew quiet, and Asher became aware of being the tallest object in the room, the only person standing above the fray, the only person without allies, the only person without a story. A target visible to all and valuable to none.

That was his first day of work with his first and only real employer: Investor's Information, Inc. Even the GM saw him taken down that day in a barrage of rubber unequalled to this day. The GM had been fond of saying that we all make our own luck. Asher chose to stand on his desk that day. The rest was really just luck.

There was no website then. The Internet itself was still an obscure world inhabited by scientists, the military, and off-duty grad students. No one had ever used the term "World Wide Web." Only the top managers had PCs, which they used mainly to compose letters and memos that they then printed, photocopied, and mailed—or, if they were really important, faxed.

So it wasn't until Asher's interview that he learned anything at all about the company he hoped to work for, answering a three-line ad in the

Boston Globe. According to the literature in the wobbly rack that greeted him outside a very slow elevator, Investor's Information, Inc.—"3I"—was "The World's Leading Provider of Company and Industry Intelligence." Behind this rather uninspired moniker lay a global network of data feeds and research experts working around the clock to bring you the most accurate, up-to-date information available from and about the people who move the world's markets.

Again—according to the literature.

David rescued him from the lone chair in the tiny, abandoned lobby and walked him around the corner into the fishbowl conference room. David was a compact, fit man in his thirties wearing a tight Gumby T-shirt, baggy pants, and unnecessary rainbow suspenders. "You don't *look* like an axe murderer." His voice was the barbed treble hook beneath a lure's brightest, laciest feathers. "I guess you won't fit in. Goodbye." He smiled through a fire-red, impossibly close-trimmed beard.

The offices were on the fifth floor of an old warehouse on the waterfront of South Boston, and aside from new teal carpeting, a handful of glassed-in offices along the front wall, and new beige cubicles throughout, they seemed to be in largely original condition. Rough brick walls surrounded the space, and worn wooden pillars supported high, plank ceilings that rained down the dust of ages when something heavy fell to the floor above.

"Do you actually *care* what 3I does, or do you just want the test?"

Asher had never expected to wonder whether showing interest during an interview was a good idea. "I *am* curious, sir. I like to know what I'm getting into."

"So do I. *Sir.*" David's blue eyes twinkled and flitted ever so quickly across Asher's twenty-two-year-old chest.

"Basically, we're creating a database of Wall Street analyst research. Investment banks—*obviously*—follow the companies and industries they invest in pretty closely. They write reports on these companies and industries for their clients. We have deals with several investment banks to get these reports sent to us in the mail. We key them into our computers, index them to make them easy to search, and then add them to our database so clients can access them online. Bored yet?"

"No, sir."

"Well, I am. So that's it—that's what we do. What *you* do—assuming you pass the test and I decide I like you—is compare what we've keyed into the computer to the original report. Base pay is six dollars an hour; quota is six pages an hour. The faster you go, the more you make. I'll get you the details after you pass the test. Assuming you still want to take it."

Asher nodded. "Sure, I do."

David attempted a disappointed look that the gleam in his eyes spoiled. "This is where the last guy who came in asked for the men's room. He never came back."

Asher laughed, to David's poorly concealed delight.

"Okay, if you'll follow me, then, I'll introduce you to Tom, who'll give you your test. We'll pass the men's room, by the way—just in case you change your mind."

"Could I ask you just one question, sir, before we go?"

"Yes? *Sir?*"

"Do you like working here?"

"No."

David sashayed out of the conference room, Asher in tow.

"I hear you went to Vandy."

"Yes, sir."

"Pledge?"

"Yes, sir. Sigma Chi."

The GM smiled and pointed Asher to a chair, then settled in behind his desk. "I dated a Vandy girl for a while. Tri Delt. Met her on spring break in Florida my junior year. Made a couple of road trips down there, went to formals with her, even visited her at her parents' house that summer. Don't know what happened, really—we had a good time. Everybody got along. Said we'd keep in touch, but—well, you know. Good times, though." Did he glance at the picture of his wife on purpose? "Another one of life's 'what if's.'"

Asher smiled and nodded and held his tongue.

"I saw you on your first day, you know. You got clobbered in that rubber band war."

Asher's laugh was half apology. "I did. Not my brightest move, I guess."

"Oh, I wouldn't say that. Showed some initiative, anyway. Set you apart. Broke the ice. Everybody knew who you were after that."

"I suppose that's true."

"Everybody likes you, Asher. David says you have a brain, which is high praise, coming from David. And I liked how you handled the meeting yesterday. You showed insight you wouldn't normally expect from someone at your level. You talked like a businessman."

"Thank you, sir. Guess I'm a pretty good actor."

"What do you think most of business is? Especially in a start-up?"

Asher shrugged. "It *was* fun, sir. I hope it was useful. Frankly, though, it didn't seem like a big deal to me. It's all sort of obvious, don't you think?"

"It was very useful, Asher. Maybe more than you think. Could save us a lot of money. As for obvious—well . . ." The GM smiled and looked Asher straight in the eyes. "*I* never thought of it. Never even occurred to me."

"I'm sorry, sir—I didn't mean—"

"No, no, don't worry. I'm not that kind of guy." The GM waved his hands in the air, shooing away a swarm of bees over his head. "I *like* people who are smarter than me. Means I don't have to work so hard. Means I have a better chance of making more money. No, I have no problem with smart people. The more, the merrier, in my opinion."

"Well, thank you, sir. I'm glad I could help."

"You did help, Asher. You did, and you can. I'd like you to do more here, if you're interested. We're getting bigger, and we have some buyers starting to poke around. We need to make sure we not only *have* our act together, we need to *look* like we have our act together. Need to show a little bench strength. I think you could help. If you're interested."

Asher smiled and looked at his feet. He had moved here *not* to be interested. Prolong the good years. Give yourself some time. Make sure you know what you want to do before you get in too deep. Here he could wear shorts in the summertime, big sweatshirts in the winter, shave when he wanted to, get to work when he wanted to. His life was, for the first time in his life, his own. No finals coming up, no papers due, no grades to make, no college to get into. No parents' pressing smiles. No snakes slowly coiling in the pit of his stomach ready to strike when he lost sight of "after." He was a "during." Just getting up in the morning, getting on the bus, getting the job done, getting home, seeing what the evening offered. Sleeping like he hadn't slept in years—every night like a night in June, the last school year past, the next one still a distant shore. Give that shore a wide, wide berth. Nothing but blue water here, no rocks or reefs to split the belly and let the waves wash everything away.

But he *was* interested, dammit. The siren's song of praise and recognition, promising acceptance and peace. A better life. You think you have it good now? Just look what's over the horizon. Just navigate through this one last reef and you'll have the whole beach to yourself. Miles and miles of soft, pink sand. Climb the cliffs and see how much better the view is. A man could really find peace here. But look at those hills a few miles inland! Look at the way the rains cool the gentle slopes on the hot, summer afternoons, how the sun arcs low in the evenings and turns the clouds pink and the hills blue and the sky silver and bronze and copper and gold. Tranquility lives there, just a little farther on. Finish your peas, then you can have dessert. Finish your homework, then you can watch TV. Finish high school, then you can go to college. Finish college, then you can go out on your own. Save for retirement. In my father's house there are many mansions. When I die, hallelujah by and by.

Asher searched the GM's office. Windows pierced the brick on two sides and looked out onto the harbor and the building next door. A glass wall looked out at the cubicles of the less fortunate. His desk was nearly empty; a PC stood in one corner and a wooden inbox in the other. Keys on a leather BMW fob lay on top of the few papers in the inbox.

The bookcase behind him held very few books. Lucite icons memorialized deals and achievements, trophies of a life of success. Family pictures stood on top. In the center, between a photo of kids in Mickey Mouse ears and another of kids bundled up in ski gear, was a black-and-white portrait of a woman Asher assumed was the GM's wife. She leaned her head on one hand and fixed Asher with a sidelong, coy invitation. Come on, Asher—what's not to want?

"So how about it, Asher? You *are* interested, aren't you?"

The GM's wife was sad but knowing, sympathetic to the young and naïve. That was me, she said, nostalgic in black and white but assured, at least, of her place on the shelf. I thought I was standing on the shore, too, waiting to choose my moment to jump into the stream. But it turns out, I wasn't on the shore after all. Turns out I'd been in the stream from the beginning. We all are. Might as well go with it. Just lie back and enjoy the ride. Seriously—what can you do about it, anyway?

"Well," said Asher, still to the picture, "I'm at least interested in hearing what you have in mind." The practical answer. Don't jump in just yet. But yes, dammit, maybe you're right. Maybe I've been in all along.

"I'm flattered you'd consider me, sir. I do like being part of the team. I've been thinking maybe I should go to business school, though." Among many, many other things, and not very seriously, but yes, over the past two years or so, he'd thought about it here and there. And it seemed like something the GM would appreciate. And he didn't want to answer the question.

"Why on Earth would you want to do that?" the GM asked through a smile designed for watching monkeys in zoos or small children in the sand.

"I don't know," Asher shrugged. "I mean, business seems pretty straight-forward, but still, there are probably a few things they'd teach you in business school that might come in handy—don't you think?"

The GM riffled through a drawer in his desk. "Asher, I went to business school. Wasted two years of my life there, and I'm still paying the bills. Let me do you a favor, save you the trouble of making the same mistake."

He pulled a piece of paper out of the drawer and began to write on it in red ink. Asher leaned forward and watched, wondering whether this was a joke. The GM sat up straight, put down his pen, and picked up the paper to admire his work. Then he handed it to Asher.

"Here you go. Here's your business degree. It's more useful than mine, because it actually contains everything you need to know about business. And it's free."

Revenue – Expense = Profit

The GM leaned back in his chair with a self-satisfied grin. "That's all there is to it. Make more than you spend. The rest is just BS."

It was a win-win.

. . .

"I heard you were home. I thought you might need to get out."

Kimberly, the guardian angel, phoning from heaven above.

"Feel like a walk?"

"How about a little hike up to the blue hole? Work up an appetite before supper?"

"I'll meet you there."

The afternoon sun was bright but low in the December sky when Asher parked his car beside Kimberly's. Kimberly was down by the stream, sitting on a picnic table and watching him. She wore faded jeans and old cowboy boots. Her hair was longer than it had been before, hanging in a thick, blonde braid down the back of her dark wool coat.

"Hey." She smiled.

"Hey, Kimberly. Thanks for calling. If I'd've had to play one more game of dominoes, I think I'd've killed somebody."

"Well, we can't have that, now can we? Especially not at Christmas."

"No. The neighbors would talk."

"How've you been?"

"Pretty good. Want to walk?"

"Sure, let's do. It's kinda cold to just sit here."

Long, boney shadows pointed across soggy oak leaves and black walnut husks. Mountain laurel and holly and hemlock groves ornamented the brown. Squirrels rummaged and stared and sprang across the path in front of them. Water like sweet tea chased and tripped down snow-cloud–colored boulders and laughed off the cold wind wheezing over the bluffs, rattling the bare treetops.

"How long are you home for?" Asher asked, watching her boots kick through the leaves. The wind smelled like the leaves and the pines and somebody's fireplace up on the bluff.

"Till just after New Year's."

"That's a pretty short vacation, isn't it? When did you get home?"

"Just a couple of days ago. Classes don't really start up again for another week after that, but—well, you know."

"I do. Did I mention the dominoes?"

Kimberly smiled. "It's not that bad. It's just that—well, you told me, four years ago, all my friends would end up being there, not here. And they are."

"All of them?"

Kimberly looked up at Asher, no smile this time. "Seems that way sometimes."

Asher put his arm around her shoulders and she leaned her head on his. "Friends write sometimes, you know," she almost whispered into his sleeve. "They call once in a while."

"I know," Asher surrendered. Her hair was clean and sweet and familiar. "I have no excuse. I did in college—thought I did, anyway. You know how it is in college."

"I *do* know how it is in college. Don't try to blame me for not calling, Asher Daniel. I told you once why I didn't call first."

"I could say I had the same reason."

"Are you going to?"

"No, I suppose not."

A squirrel scolded from high up a hickory tree. The branch on which he sat bobbed and swayed in the wind, but he didn't seem to notice anything but them far below.

Kimberly put her arm around Asher's waist. Her hip rolled against his as they walked and he thought of the last time they'd been on this path, her hair wet and legs tanned and smooth in the hot moon's shine. He tried to count the times they'd been here, but he couldn't. This was the first time in the winter. This was the first time they'd had to worry about the cold.

"How's everything going in Boston?" Kimberly hesitated.

"Fine," replied Asher in kind.

"You're working for some sort of publishing company?"

"Sort of. Online publishing, databases, that kind of thing. For investment banks, mostly."

"Do you like it?"

Asher shrugged. "I just got promoted."

The path cut between two boulders. Had they broken apart suddenly when they fell from the bluffs, or did they split slowly as they stood there, too rooted to move away as each year's rain and snow and ice and wind found even the tiniest fissures and cracked them, one by one?

"That's not what I asked, you know." Kimberly's voice sounded louder in the boulders' lee.

Asher let her go ahead of him through the narrow gap. Out of habit he checked for snakes, in spite of the season. The roar of the water rose up again on the other side, where the current piled up against the foot of one boulder before being sucked past the glassy stone. You could see from the polish that the water got much higher, sometimes surging up through the gap they'd just cleared, washing away anything blocking its path. Except for the boulders. The gap might widen a little bit every time, but the boulders were there to stay. Like it or not, they had nowhere else to go.

Kimberly had stopped and turned on the other side of the gap. She looked up at Asher as he came around the rock and they took hold of each other without saying a word. They stood there for a long time, wrapped in the familiar.

"I'm not sure it's important, whether I like it or not," Asher finally said. He watched the stream careen into the boulder, one wave after the other, just as it probably always had and probably always would. He pressed his face into Kimberly's hair and kissed her ear. "I'm just not sure."

Julie had sat on the porch, staring out through the sprawling rose bush at the cars in the parking lot. The Indian summer sun was warm but fading, and she'd tucked her knees up under her chin and wrapped herself in an old blanket till only her head showed.

"I'm just not comfortable."

Asher had watched from the chair next to her, unmoving, silent.

"I'm not comfortable going home with you for Christmas. It just doesn't feel right to me."

"That's okay," Asher had lied. "You don't have to."

Julie had opened her mouth but no words came. She'd squinted as the sun dipped just enough to shine a spotlight directly on her face. One hand had emerged from the blanket and shaded her own eyes as she'd turned to search Asher's.

"I'm not comfortable being your girlfriend."

Asher had just stared. Julie had started to turn back to the parking lot, but, trapped by the spotlight, she'd just looked down into the blanket, at her legs tucked up against her chest.

"Why?"

"I don't know why. It's a feeling, not something I can, you know, prove. I'm just not."

Asher had reached out and rubbed the back of her neck. She'd closed her eyes and bowed her head. Asher could feel her muscles relax, and he'd stood up and moved behind her chair so he could use both hands.

Julie had taken a deep breath, exhaling long and slow.

"I think you're too good for me."

"Don't you think that's for me to decide?"

Julie had shifted in her seat so he could reach farther down her back.

"No. You're too good. You'll decide wrong."

Asher opened his eyes and stared into the pool. He pulled Kimberly closer, standing behind her on the rock they'd shared that summer.

Kimberly leaned back and kissed him on the cheek. He turned and kissed her back. But when he closed his eyes again, Julie was still there.

"Where are you?" Kimberly whispered.

"I'm right here."

"But you're not here to stay, are you?" She offered another kiss, without much hope.

"That's where you're wrong, Miss Kimberly."

Asher kissed her again, eyes wide open.

The jeweler was open late that night, it being so close to Christmas. He smiled as he watched his determined young customer pondering carats and clarity and cut.

Charging and fleeing tend to look the same from a distance.

• • •

Twelve hours earlier, Eva Engelhart had planned to spend the evening blending into a crowd. At the Museum of American History, maybe, or the National Gallery. Or the mall, even, though she'd never been much of a shopper. Anyplace would do, provided nobody there knew her. Which shouldn't have been particularly difficult, given it was her first time in Washington, DC.

Her assignment had been simple: The clients of her company wanted to lure Phaeton to Germany. Her boss, Andreas, would organize a fictitious business meeting with a lucrative offer for Phaeton to attend. Eva was to pose as an employee who had been sent to accompany Phaeton to the meeting. Once she had delivered him to the appointed place at the correct time, her assignment ended. But now there was a sudden change of plans. Phaeton was making a surprise trip to Dubai and she was to follow. The text had been very clear: "The target is on the move, and we have a quick change of plans. Follow him. More to come."

Now she was on a plane to Dubai and was very consciously ignoring the glances of her neighbor, who wasn't supposed to know she was there.

Excellent work, Eva. Everyone is just going to be so pleased back home. Not that anyone has to know. As long as you complete the mission. That's what you're good at. Giving them what they need. As least, that's what they always think at the beginning.

Eva stared at the words on the page, but they fought back. The *New York Times* Best Sellers list really should be some indication of quality, she thought. Maybe she just hadn't gotten to the good parts yet.

Or maybe the best part was already past. Maybe she should never have opened the folder.

Nonsense. Al Green had been quite insistent that she open it as soon as she was on the plane and had some privacy. The doors had closed with the seat next to her empty, so privacy hadn't been a problem. The folder contained a series of photographs of her target—code named "Phaethon"—all apparently taken without his knowledge. It also contained a redacted personal profile, giving the particulars of his family, his work, his habits, his likes and dislikes—all without revealing any actual names, places, dates, or other hard facts. It wasn't her job to know who Phaethon was. It was just her job to get him to the planned destination, on time and unsuspecting. She felt a little pang when she saw that he had children. How could people put their families in danger like that? He must be a very worthy target, she mused, if he was so callous as to ignore his familial obligations. She would never put her father in danger, for example. Or her mother, if her mother had been around.

Ridiculous that you switched seats and are now sitting next to him. Are you going to pretend to read a book for the next four hours? Maybe Andreas was wrong about your abilities.

The flight attendant refilled their water glasses. She reached for hers at the same time he reached for his. His smile was friendly, but his eyes curious. She gave him a little turned-up smile in return and sipped her water.

He hadn't been difficult to locate. The photos were good, and one walk down the aisle to the lavatories had been enough to find him, a couple of rows back, on the opposite side of the plane. He'd been lying back, eyeshades pushed up on his forehead, reading a magazine by the light of the little reading lamp on the side of his seat. An older woman, large enough to make even the business-class seats appear uncomfortable, sat next to him. Twin movies flickered and glared in the thick lenses of her glasses.

Eva had gone into the lavatory. Bright neon drained the blood from her cheeks when she locked the door. She thought of Kai. Kai lying in her—their—bed in Berlin, waiting for her. Lying naked in the stifling summer dark, duvet folded all the way down under his feet, reading a book by the light of one tiny fluorescent bulb. Avoids making the room any hotter, he'd said. That weather had lasted what, a week? Two weeks at most. But it was the way she always remembered him first: His face lit flushed and damp, his blue eyes expecting her, his body shades of freshly washed tan curling toward her as she sat down on the bed.

An impish neon version of herself had grinned at her from the lavatory mirror and told her he was nothing like Kai. He's older, his eyes are gray, he wears his hair short, he's—well, he *probably* is, since he *is* American—but she wasn't listening. She'd washed her face and unlocked the door and tried to go back to her seat without looking at him again, but she'd had to turn to let another passenger pass her in the aisle and she'd seen him, lying with his face lit up behind his magazine.

She'd sat back down, alone in her seat. She'd looked through the pictures in the folder again and reread the bio. Studied humanities at a good university. Graduated with honors. Good job, nice house, wife, two kids, no known "extracurricular activities." Debts like everybody else in America, but nothing out of the ordinary. Had played in a band as a kid, was known to have "experimented," but again, nothing out of the ordinary—and those days seemed to be long gone. Doesn't really seem like the type, does he? She'd looked at the pictures again. In one, he was walking through a lobby of some sort, dressed in a business suit with a computer bag over his shoulder. He was looking down and away to the right of the camera. His eyebrows were raised but his eyes were tired and his mouth closed tight as if trying to keep quiet. Frustration? Despair? Eva had looked closely. Kai's face again, that Saturday a couple of months ago. She hadn't thought of it as despair until now. Maybe she'd been wrong.

Maybe she'd been wrong most of her life. Her mother had certainly thought so. But there was nothing to be done about that now.

Eva closed her eyes, but thoughts of Kai wouldn't let her rest. She sat up straight and peered back over at her target. His light was out and his eyeshades down over his eyes. The big woman still glared at her video screen. Trading places with her wouldn't be difficult. Would they approve of that move, to get closer?

Eva gave up on her book. She pulled the card out of the back pages and marked her place with it. On the front of the card, two cartoon mice with huge feet sat on a bench, holding hands and blushing. Eva laid the book in her lap and closed her eyes and leaned back in her seat. She knew the inside of the card by heart. It was written in cursive like they'd taught back in the '60s. "Just trust in yourself, the way I trust in you. I'll be waiting for you. I love you." The signature was simple and strong and completely illegible, like her father's. Everything Kai's was not.

. . .

Kimberly Daniel hung up on another voice mail system. Doesn't *anybody* answer their phones anymore? Sure, it's suppertime and all, but honestly, when you're out it seems like nobody does anything *but* talk on the phone. Where *is* everybody? And where *are* those kids?

The clock on the wall above the oven ticked off the seconds, unconcerned. The window over the sink, dark for the past hour, shadowboxed her frustration. An unfamiliar dog barked and the neighborhood chorus responded in kind. Plenty of sound and fury tonight. Plenty, at least, for those on the ground.

How could he just be gone, now of all times? How can it be, in this day and age, that there can still be someplace where somebody just can't be reached? I mean honestly, they talked with the astronauts on the moon, clear back in the sixties. Sure, there were a lot of beeps and hisses and people saying "over" and "roger" and all that, but they still managed to get their point across. You can be damned sure that if Neil Armstrong's wife had needed to talk with him, she would have been able to. If something had happened to—what was his name?—the guy Tom Hanks played in *Apollo 13*? Whatever. If something had happened to his kids while he was flying around up there in outer space, his wife would have been able to talk with him. So why can't I get ahold of Asher when I need him?

It's because men are still running things, that's why. Can't have cell phones work on the plane—God forbid! Might interrupt you while you're drinking your champagne and telling your little jokes and winking and smiling at the stewardesses and the cute little twentysomething "management trainees" running errands for their bosses while their bosses run off to St. Barts with their secretaries. Might force you to actually *deal* with a problem instead of saying you don't have time for it now and hightailing it to the airport as fast as your little legs will carry you. "Kim, can we talk about this later? I'm really sorry, but I'll miss my flight." Lord almighty, if I hear that line *one more time* I might just have to *scream*! I swear I can't remember the last time we had a real conversation about any not-so-pleasant subject that didn't, at some point, come around to some version of that refrain. Got a flight to catch. Got a meeting to get to. Late for a conference call. Got a dinner—won't be home till late. Do you think he ever says to somebody at the office, "I'm sorry, but I can't deal with this right now—I need to get home to talk with my wife?" You think he's up there right now saying, "No thanks, no more Chateau St. Somebody for me—gotta work on this problem I'm helping my wife with." "Sorry, sweetheart, but you'll have to settle for your teddy bear tonight—I'm married." Think that ever happens? Likely as a snowball in Hell. Likely as happy hour at the Betty Ford clinic.

The dog chorus stopped abruptly. The clock ticked on and Kimberly's eyes—her mama's eyes—glared at her from the black glass.

Okay, girl, now you're starting to sound like Grandma. Get a grip. Fact is, Asher's out of the picture, at least for the next ten hours or so. (And probably longer.) You're gonna have to deal with this all by yourself (as usual). You've left messages on both of their cell phones. You've texted them. You've left messages at the Flynns, the Cerniceks, and the Blakes. It's not that late, really. They should've called, they're *definitely* grounded, but they're probably fine. Take a deep breath. Think where you'd be right now, if you were them.

Knowing what I know? Anywhere but here.

The doorbell rang. Kimberly knocked her iced tea glass, barely catching it before it fell to the floor. Instinctively she fixed her hair in the window, and wiped the damp from the corners of her eyes. The entry hall was dark—she hadn't been in here since the sun went down. She switched on the chandelier over the stairway and the front porch lights and looked out through the glass next to the door. Nobody there. She unlocked the door and opened it carefully. Kimberly squinted at the gray of the lawn, the silver of the driveway, the black of the woods. Invisible leaves sifted a damp breeze, and she felt a chill she hadn't noticed earlier. Autumn was too close for comfort. Nothing else moved.

Kimberly opened the door further, spilling yellow light out onto the stoop. A plain white envelope lay tucked half under the doormat. She backed away cautiously, as if a snake were coiling there. "Hello?" No one answered, or perhaps no one heard—her voice came from a place she didn't recognize. "Hello?" The breeze taunted the envelope in its yellow spotlight. Kimberly couldn't look away.

• • •

The terminal looked like the inside of a big old 1950s flying saucer—six, seven stories high, cut in half crosswise, accented with dark wood and sea-foam tinted glass, decorated with palms and keyhole arches. Asher looked around for anyone he might recognize, more out of habit than actual expectation. But tonight, he recognized everyone. They were all him—wrinkled clothes, skin, hair, eyes—zombies with briefcases and roller bags shuffling one after the other through an endless night. They had left Washington educated, ambitious captains of politics and industry. But thirteen hours in a dark metal time machine had devolved them by three million years. Stow your carry-on bags and good breeding in the overhead bins. Have a drink or two, stare at the tiny screen in the seat back in front of you, and relax while we reduce you to thoughts of food, drink, shit, and sleep. Maybe the occasional bath, as long as the big cats have already eaten. Safer to skip the bath, sit in your tree and pick the lice out of your neighbor's hair. Behold the pinnacle to which the industrial revolution has brought us: *Australopithecus americansis*. Space-age primates. Children with grown-up shackles.

Thoughts of shackles reminded Asher about his BlackBerry. He switched it on and put it back in his pocket to find a network and download messages. He wondered if he should get started right away—head out immediately to try to locate Ahmed. That had been his plan, of course—his rationale for leaving right away. But what makes sense at home and what makes sense on the road are two entirely different things. He looked around for a clock: 8:30 P.M. Early, particularly here. Asher opened his eyes wide, stretching his face and, by extension, the left half of his brain. Of course you're going out, Asher. The sooner you find him, the sooner you find out what's going on. The sooner you get everything back on track. The sooner you find him, the sooner you get to go home.

The adrenalin and hunger that had originally driven Asher on this project was somewhat muted in the weariness of the air travel. What made sense was to keep moving forward, no matter what. And what if "forward" became a different direction, his mind wondered. But now wasn't the time to wonder about that.

The customs officer didn't even glance at him. Walk off a flight from half way around the world in Boston carrying nothing but a briefcase, they'd have you in the back room in no time. But not in Dubai. Asher had always been convinced he could stash a couple of AK-47s in a suitcase underneath a kilo or two of coke and nobody here would notice, or really care. Same thing in Hong Kong. Or Frankfurt, for that matter—minus the "or really care" part. Sure, they'd string you up if they caught you, but that would be more for embarrassing them than for actually bringing the goods through. Here, it was personal. At home, it was business. At least that's the way it seemed to him.

Outside was humid and the sky glowed orange. Asher gave the driver the name of the hotel and he pulled onto Airport Road. The drive would only take a couple of minutes. Check in, clean up, head out again. Ahmed and his cell phone would be out there somewhere.

People swarmed around the white glow of a mall entrance. A man in a dark suit leaned against a nearby wall, staring at his phone. Surrounded by many, but intent on the one not there. A veiled woman turned and stared straight at Asher as he drove by. One chance in seven billion of their having just made eye contact. Amazing coincidences happen all the time. Without expectations, though, you can't recognize amazing.

Significance is limited only by the imagination.

Australopithecus asherensis reached for his BlackBerry and looked away.

• • •

Jess Kelly stood in the elevator with eight other people, all of them gazing dutifully at the numbers above the door. All of them except Jess Kelly. She stared at herself in the polished metal door, and at the rapt congregation behind her. They look like the apostles in that painting at church, she thought, watching Jesus ascending into heaven. She smiled at her reflection, that held back a laugh. That would make the sixth floor heaven, I guess. The laugh emerged as a snort, and the apostles looked down on her. Her reflection turned red and stared, still smiling, at her walking shoes. The sixth floor's heaven, and we're all dead.

"Trampoline Jesus," they'd called that painting as kids, because of the way Jesus held out his arms and looked down at his apostles like someone at the top of his bounce, preparing to come back down to a springy Earth and do it all over again.

By the time she arrived at her desk, the nervous bees in her stomach had resumed their hums and buzzing. The red light was still there, glowing smugly on top of her phone. "You can't wait me out," it explained patiently. "You know what you have to do. But no hurry. I'm happy to sit here and torture you for as long as you like."

She'd thought last night about talking it over with her husband, but it wasn't meant to be. He came home late with something on his mind, and they'd eaten dinner on the living room sofa, watching *The Office*. She hadn't really warmed up to that show yet—reminded her a little too much of the real thing—but it made Jimmy laugh, and he'd seemed to need that last night, so she'd sat through it. But she'd been thinking about the phone calls, her boss's trip to Dubai, and her dilemma. Shutting down wasn't working so well this time.

She tumbled, alone, into the abyss of regret. If nobody had told her brother about her message, back then, wouldn't it have been better? She was silly to have left it in the first place, of course, but she'd needed to talk with somebody and her big brother was everything to her. He'd walked her home from school on her first day. He'd been there the first time she'd gone up the high dive, smiling up and telling her everything was going to be okay, kicking up water to show that the fall wouldn't be as far as she thought. Convincing her that everything her own mind was telling her was wrong. It had been him—not her father; her father had been out of town—who'd waited up in the living room for her to come home from her first date. He'd just sat there and smiled until almost two, probably, listening to her go on and on about all the wonderful things they'd done—the movie and the fried clams and the barefoot walk along the beach. She'd left out the kiss, but she knew he knew. He was her big brother. He just knew.

So how was she to know that day that he *didn't* know she had told the truth to the papers? How was she to know that the newspaper people call *everybody* when those kinds of rumors fly? How was she to know her message meant he either had to ruin their father's life or lie? She was only a freshman in college when it all happened—how was she to know any-thing?

She couldn't talk to Jimmy about this. She didn't trust herself. What if she messed things up for the two of them in some way that she couldn't even fathom? She'd felt the panic rise and excused herself to go lie down. Jimmy had brought her a glass of water and then went to sleep.

So she went to work the next day fairly well-defended. She sat down, changed into her office shoes, and threw her bag under her desk. It wasn't important *how* she should have known. She should have. She'd made a mistake. But that was six years ago. She'd learned her lesson. She returned the little red light's smug glare. She wouldn't make the same mistake twice. She was not going to give those people what they wanted. Let them get it from someone else.

Jess picked up the receiver and pressed the buttons for voice mail. Four new messages. In the first, the recorded voice was sterner than the live version—or maybe it was just that she'd never gotten back to him. It was definitely the same person from before– sounded like the bad guy in *Die Hard*. Please can we meet. Defiantly she jotted down the address and phone number to give her something to tear up later. Then she deleted the message.

The second message was from a guy with an English accent who called every week, selling ad space. She'd deleted every message from him for the past year, but he never stopped calling. She deleted this message as well.

The third message took her by surprise. The first word was little more than a long exhalation, off speed and far away.

"Hey, it's me."

Mrs. Daniel never called this number.

"Please call me as soon as you get this. It's—I need—please just call. I left a message on your cell, too." The voice of someone with no alternative.

Jess checked the time on the message—10:49 P.M. She switched on her computer to get to her address book. Before it had even booted up, though, the other line rang. Jess recognized the country code. But this time she didn't recognize the number.

five

The lights in Roy Daniel's office clicked off, leaving his face pasted in CRT moonglow while the rest of the room huddled in darkness.

"Smart building, my ass." He flapped his arms at the darkness and the lights sulked back to life.

Roy Daniel flipped through the pages of the latest report from the Ariadne project team. Pete Vasilescu's algorithm development appeared to be progressing—just slower than anyone had hoped. The client had approved a revised budget, funding their efforts for at least another year. Good news for the business—Morton would be happy, at least. But anybody more interested in results than in money had to be frustrated.

"I thought I heard you down here." Jabe Evans shuffled through the doorway on his way to the sofa. He didn't make eye contact, and for one of the first times Daniel could remember, he wasn't carrying his notebook. Daniel thought he looked more hunched over than usual, but maybe not. End of the day, yes, but end of the road? A little too early for that kind of talk.

"I was just having a little chat with our friends about the lights. Seems they can't tell the difference between motion and activity."

Evans put a steadying hand on one arm of the sofa and lowered himself slowly. "They sound like clients."

"That they do." Evans settled into the soft cushions of the sofa. "Can I get you anything, Jabe?"

"No, no, Roy, thanks, I'm fine. I just got off the phone with General Hayward." Evans leaned back and took a deep breath. He looked at Daniel as if just noticing he was there. "I swear, Roy, that man is one stubborn son of a bitch. If you'll pardon my French."

"No need for apologies, Jabe. You know my opinion."

"Sometimes I really wish we'd never met him."

"Well, I can't say the same thought hasn't crossed my mind a time or two. Not sure Mr. Morton would agree, though."

Evans smiled. "No, Bill most certainly would not agree."

"What's on the General's mind?"

"Oh, just the usual. He wants more of our people in theater. 'Boots on the ground, Jabe—that's what wins wars!' You know the pitch."

"Did you tell him scientists don't usually look great in combat boots?"

Evans finally smiled. He leaned forward on the sofa and started flipping the pages of a book on the coffee table. *CASTOR: The First 25 Years.*

"He likes what our guys over there are doing, Roy. I don't know if that's the good news or the bad news. He says they're dedicated, hard working, good at what they do. No General Order #1 problems. And they're smart, by all accounts. The perfect soldiers."

"The perfect soldiers—including not being soldiers. Easy to blame if things go wrong, easy to get rid of for any reason at all. And easy to bring on board, too."

Evans nodded. "And easy to bring on board. Every job that can be done by a contractor means one more soldier in the field, without any questions about troop surges, extended deployments, escalation—pick your term. Hiring us is his way of increasing the size of his fighting force without getting anybody excited about it."

"And the fact that we're scientists, not mechanics? Not shipping clerks?"

"We have a contract vehicle in place, Roy—that's our big advantage. He doesn't have to go back to the well for approvals. He can just order up a few more guys and there they are, no questions asked."

"Pretty soon, Jabe, we're going to be changing the tires on their Humvees. Or just minding the warehouse where they keep all the tires."

"I know, Roy, I know—it's not exactly what we had in mind when we started out. But we do have some guys doing IT work, you know. And there's more intel stuff going on than you might think."

"It's a win-win, then." Daniel sat up and drummed a quick, frustrated riff on his desktop. "Easy for him, easy for us. Everybody's easy, everybody's good. After all, what should we have against more work? Work we don't even have to compete for? Work we frankly get paid way too much for—what labor category do we use for oil changes, anyway?"

Evans turned the page.

"Did he even mention Ariadne, Jabe?"

"Of course he did. He said he understood these things happen, that he hoped we could get some results soon. But in the same breath he said our 'boys on the ground' were making a difference *today,* and that the best way for us to support our troops *today* was to get him more people *today.*"

"Guess you don't get to be a general by being subtle."

"I suppose not." Evans smiled and turned another page in the book.

"So? What did you tell him?"

Evans held up the book to show Daniel a picture of their old building in Georgetown. Skinny guys waved from the top-floor windows, wind blowing ties and what had once passed for conservative haircuts. Two of them stretched a CASTOR banner between windows. Another braced an American flag that fluttered out of the frame.

"Remember that day?"

"I sure do."

"How much was that contract for?"

"One point two million."

"We'd never seen that much money."

"Sure made it easier to sleep that night."

"It certainly did."

The lights in the hall went off with a click. Daniel stared into the dark. Evans turned the page.

"Where's the 'Application of Science and Technology' in all this, Jabe?"

"Maybe we need to focus on the 'Operational Realities' part, Roy."

"There are plenty of those."

"More every day."

Daniel stretched his arms out wide and looked around his corner office. "And without our dear General Hayward, none of this would be possible."

"Lights and all."

"They *were* his design, weren't they?"

"Maybe we should give him an award for *that*." Evans exhaled a laugh as he pushed himself upright. "You *are* going to be there tomorrow night, aren't you?"

"You know I will, Jabe. Wouldn't miss it."

Evans resigned himself to another laugh and mumbled as he walked into the dark hallway. "Theoretically, you know, if we moved fast enough, there'd be no light at all."

Bill Morton saw the old man walk past his doorway, muttering to himself. He carried no notebook. Morton wondered if he'd finally started to lose it.

"Jabe? Everything okay?" Never wake a sleepwalker. Never know what they might do.

Jabe Evans looked around absently. For just a fraction of a second, it seemed as if he either didn't see or didn't recognize Morton. Then he stopped and walked toward the doorway.

"Hello, Bill. It's getting pretty late. Don't neglect your beauty sleep."

Morton swiveled in his chair to face the doorway. "You're implying that I have any beauty left to preserve. I'm not sure I had any to begin with!"

Just a smile and a shaking of his stooped shoulders hinted that Evans was laughing. Morton stood up and shook the wrinkles out of his slacks.

"Jabe, at some point we need to talk about the latest numbers. Do you have some time tomorrow?"

"I don't know. Roger's gone home. Is it a long conversation?"

"No, shouldn't take too long."

"Let's just do it now, then." Evans motioned down the hall with his head and shuffled away. Morton looked around his desk for the report, picked it up, and followed Evans into his office.

Jabe Evans's office was notorious for two reasons. The first was that you never wanted to be invited there. Evans didn't do praise in private. If he wanted to see you, either you'd done something he didn't like or you were about to do something he wanted. Either way, you were in trouble.

The second was that it was a complete disaster. Every available horizontal surface was covered with paper—physics books, government reports, printed e-mails, faxes with notes scrawled in the margins. Even the pictures on the walls—signed photographs of sailboats, mostly, cutting across the Chesapeake, some with CASTOR spinnakers—had yellow Post-it notes stuck to them, or business cards tucked in between the frames and the glass. Only Evans's own chair was free. He sat down in it and started flipping through his notebook, which lay in front of him on the desk on top of a spiral-bound report stamped "Secret" in red ink.

"The numbers were good, weren't they?" he said to the first blank page he found.

Given no other choice, Morton remained standing. "They were, Jabe. Up over last quarter, up year over year, no write-downs to speak of. Time sold's as good as it's ever been. Absolutely nothing to complain about." Bill Morton crossed his arms and stroked his chin with one hand, studying his polished loafers as he rocked back on his heels.

"Except . . ." Evans was writing.

"Except that . . . well, they could be better, Jabe."

Evans still didn't look up. "Couldn't they always, Bill?"

"Well, sure, I suppose, the numbers could always be better—in theory, anyway. But I'm not talking theory, Jabe, I'm talking reality. We could do better. We *should* do better."

The room was silent except for the scraping of Evans's pen.

"These are historic times, Jabe." Morton stepped to the darkened window and addressed the reflections of CASTOR's two top managers. "These things don't happen every day. We have a chance to make a real difference here—to help our country, to help our world. The government can't do this alone, Jabe. They just can't move fast enough. They need companies like ours to help them ramp up quickly to the levels they need to be at."

"What exactly do you mean by 'companies like ours,' Bill?"

Morton contemplated his boss's reflection for a moment, then turned to face reality. "I mean strong, entrepreneurial companies full of smart, capable people who are ready, willing, and able to serve the needs of their country."

Evans put down his pen and looked his CFO in the eye. "The *scientific* needs of their country. Isn't that what you mean, Bill?"

"Yes, the *scientific* needs, of course, that's what we do. But don't you think we could go beyond that, Jabe? In this day and age, when the country needs so much more, don't you think we *should* go beyond that? Don't you think it's our *duty* to go above and beyond? Don't you think that's *every* American's duty?"

Evans was writing again, hunched over the scribblings only Roger Taylor could decipher with any degree of certainty. Morton held himself back.

"Pretty lofty ideals, Bill. You sure that's really what you wanted to talk to me about?"

Morton smiled, but his face reddened. "You understand exactly what I'm talking about, Jabe."

"I do, yes. I do." Evans didn't look up from his notebook.

"We're running a business here, Jabe." Morton turned back to lecture the window, arms crossed, chin up. "We have an obligation to our shareholders—to our employees, to their families. I *do* believe we have an obligation to our country, too—that's not just pandering, that's patriotism. But I just don't see the conflict here, Jabe. Our country wants us to step up. If we do, our shareholders will make more money. We live in the . . . the bastion of capitalism, Jabe. Where's the conflict? Why is this even a discussion we need to have?"

Jabe Evans was no longer sitting. "It's a discussion we need to have, Bill, because it affects who we are as a corporation. And since *we* started this corporation, it affects who we are as men." Evans wandered toward the door as he talked. "There are all kinds of problems the government needs help with, Bill. You know that, I know that—everybody knows that. But we're scientists here. Science is what we do, science is where we can make a real difference." He looked down the empty hall then turned and leaned against the doorframe. "Science can solve a lot of problems, Bill, but not all of them. Let's stick to what we're good at. Leave the rest to the others. Trust me—there are plenty of problems to go around."

"So we let 'the others' deliver fifteen, 20 percent growth to their shareholders while we plod along at five or six? And who says when a scientific mind can deliver the best value? Why should *we* make that decision? Why not throw our hats into the ring and see what the client thinks? Is it suddenly our place to decide what is and isn't the right thing for the U.S. government to do?"

Evans seemed to notice something on the windowsill and walked back across the office, past Morton, to rummage through the papers there. Not finding what he was looking for, apparently, he looked Bill Morton in the eye with a tired smile. Morton met his gaze but held his ground, arms still crossed, cheeks still flushed.

"Yes," Evans said quietly. "I think it *is* our place to help the government decide the best thing to do. That's exactly why we started this business, Bill. Because they, left to their own devices, will just do whatever's easiest. For them personally. Never mind the good of the nation. Somebody else needs to look out for that."

"You're saying the U.S. government is no more able to take care of itself than my father down in Florida is."

"Yes. That's what I'm saying."

"And that for some reason our shareholders—all these people who work so hard for you every day, not to mention you and me—need to suffer as a result."

Evans looked at the floor.

"Jabe, you're the boss. The buck stops with you. But it seems to me that you're letting a *belief* of yours—a belief no scientific method I ever studied can prove—get in the way of your fiduciary responsibility to this company. I'm just asking you to think about it. Sleep on it. We can talk about it again tomorrow."

Evans didn't move. Bill Morton faced his reflection and adjusted the flag pinned to his lapel. He hesitated as he walked through the door, turning to Evans one last time.

"By the way, when did you stop believing that science holds the answer to everything?"

Evans walked back to his desk and stared at his notebook. "Bastion of capitalism" was the last thing he'd written. He looked up and stared at the empty space in the window where Bill Morton's reflection had been.

• • •

Pete Vasilescu walked the fluorescent gray hall toward his office at NSA headquarters. The expression on his face—equal parts amusement and disgust—was the same he'd had leaving the Bucharest police station that bright, rainy day he'd received his first and last Romanian passport. The same physiological manifestation of the same feeling. Because in the end, government workers are government workers. It really doesn't matter which government. People are, on average, far more alike than all the ideologies of the world would have you believe. Ideologies are for big thinkers, and when it comes right down to it, there are very few truly big thinkers. Those there are tend to die young, ridiculed, vilified, institutionalized, alone.

There are many more people who try to *look* like big thinkers in order to get what they want. Their heroes are the big thinkers of yesterday—those no longer producing inconveniently new ideas, those whose teachings and views can be nipped and tucked onto ideological pedestals without risk of rebuttal. There are many such "big stinkers" in the world. Many of them find their way into politics.

But even in government, these aren't the majority.

For the majority—the great bureaucratic proletariat—even trying to *look* like a big thinker is impossible, or at least impractical. For the majority, the idea is simply to get to work as late as possible, to do as little as possible, and to leave work as early as possible while still having a job the next day. Make it to retirement without doing anything stupid—which generally means without really doing anything at all. Leave ideologies to other people—people okay with testifying before Congress. Ideologies get you fired, or killed, or make you work weekends. Just keep your head down, your to-do list short, and your cable remote close. That, my son, is the key to a good life. The meaning of life? Just have another beer. We'll talk about it after the game.

These were the people with whom Pete had just spent the last two and a half hours, locked in a windowless conference room that smelled of years of bad coffee and mixed messages. These were Pete's clients. These were the people who had hired CASTOR to create smarter, faster algorithms to sort through ever more data looking for increasingly complex patterns. Patterns that could help reveal even bigger patterns. Patterns that could reveal real risks. Patterns that could, ultimately, save real lives.

Algorithms that his clients couldn't write even if they'd wanted to and couldn't understand even if they'd tried. Algorithms written and tested by Pete and his team while his clients went home at four thirty and marveled at the contestants on *Jeopardy*. Algorithms that, if used properly, could reveal patterns that would make his clients look very smart indeed. Patterns that, if they proved misleading, could be blamed entirely on CASTOR— and that CASTOR, in turn, could blame entirely on Pete.

The reason that Pete Vasilescu had risked everything to get out of Romania that rainy week was that he'd believed communism had the exclusive rights to the "believe little, do less" worldview. He'd risked not just his own freedom, but also that of his family, his friends, and his colleagues, based on this belief. But now, more than forty years later, he realized that this worldview wasn't uniquely communist, any more than it was uniquely capitalist or fascist, atheist, or Christian. It was simply human. A lot of people just wanted to get by, and for those people, the government offered a pretty good deal. You won't get the view from the top—but you won't fall off a cliff, either. Fair trade. Sign here and you can be home in time for *Friends*.

Pete didn't regret his decision—not for a moment. In Romania, his future was decided before his twenty-second birthday. Top of his class in mathematics at the University of Bucharest, he would do his stint in the army, then become a professor—that was that. No room for debate, but also no room for failure. All he had to do was avoid pissing anybody off too badly and he was guaranteed a life free of misery. At least free of the non–self-inflicted variety.

In the United States, he was free to be as miserable as he liked. Which, he thought to himself as he walked into his office, was probably why he'd chosen to go to grad school. Which was where he'd met Roy Daniel. Which was why he was now living a life of luxury, with a whole government-furnished office to call his own, and a whole team of government-furnished project managers to spend whole government-furnished afternoons with.

He sat down and smiled again at the dark screen of his computer. Equal parts amusement and disgust. *That, I suppose, is my own personal worldview.*

Pete shook his computer's mouse and the screen came to life. Only the clock in the corner of the monitor told him what time it was. Only the "Images of Space" calendar on the wall told him what season it was. The day's e-mail was piled up in his inbox, and the red light on top of his phone was lit. *A couple more hours to go, at least—and that's before I get to do any real work. Another day spent busily getting nowhere.*

"But at least," he smirked, as Outlook announced the arrival of his sixty-eighth unread message, "I'm free."

• • •

Theoretically, if you moved fast enough, there'd be no light at all.

Roy Daniel sat transfixed by the ghost of Jabe Evans, staring through the blank space in his doorway, tapping his thumb to his lips, until the lights clicked off again.

He turned to his computer screen and flipped back to the beginning of the Ariadne project report. The executive summary gave him the month's highlights: a new time delay neural network approach to phoneme recognition yielding promising results. Target voice matching improvements of nearly 5 percent versus last month. Hardware upgrades significantly improving capacity and processing speed. All the usual stuff. Roy loved Pete, but he'd never shake the academic's love of the detail. Forget about the forest. Forests, Pete would say, are for poets, painters, lovers on their days off. For Pete, the mathematician, only the tree would do—or, better yet, the leaf, or a good, sturdy root, invisible without some hard digging through rocky soil. True understanding, in Pete's view of the world, came only through the study of the most fundamental elements, through a thorough understanding of root causes, through the relentless pursuit of yet another man behind the latest curtain. For Pete, God—not the devil—was in the detail. Take good care of the details and the big picture would take care of itself.

All of which was probably why Ariadne—Pete's project—had been behind schedule from day one.

Of course, Roy owed a lot to Pete's love of detail. The two men's paths first crossed during Roy's senior year in college. Pete was a first-year grad student, recently escaped from communist Romania, who, like Roy, worked as a substitute math teacher at the local high school to make some extra money. Without a way to go home, Pete was stuck at the university over the holidays, and since he hadn't yet made many friends, Roy invited him to join in for a little "Christmas cheer" that he and some of his housemates had planned. They all broke into one of the University of Washington's cheerleader's rooms a few nights before the Rose Bowl and stole one of the 3 × 5 cards that told each person in the Huskies' student section which color card to hold up when during the halftime show. They spent the next couple of days making up new cards, actually chemically treating them to look as much as possible like the originals. On New Year's Eve, they visited the cheerleader's room again and borrowed the master plan for the card show. The rest of their day was spent frantically changing—by hand—the instructions on more than two thousand individual cards to "improve" the show, in time to replace the old cards with the new before the cheerleader returned for the night.

So fast you couldn't even see it.

It was Pete who single-handedly worked out what each card's instructions should be. He'd originally planned to have the cards scroll "Spay the Huskies," but when it came right down to it, there just hadn't been enough time to physically change all the instructions. A simple "CALTECH" appearing near the end of the show had worked just fine.

Roy was convinced to this day that his involvement in the now legendary prank had kept him out of Vietnam. He and his cohorts had become quite the campus celebrities after their success, even among the faculty. One particularly admiring professor helped him arrange the grant money he needed to stay on for his master's and doctorate—delaying the inevitable service his ROTC scholarship demanded—and ultimately wrote a letter to the commanding officer at the Air Force Weapons Lab to secure him a place there in the New Mexico desert instead of the Southeast Asian jungles. So Roy Daniel could say with some conviction that Pete Vasilescu's attention to detail might well have saved his life.

Tonight he wondered, though, whether he'd done Pete any favors by luring him away from academics and into the "real world." He'd certainly made him richer. But happier? Who knew? Pete was never really happy. More successful? Who could say? What kind of a question was that, anyway? Certainly not one any mathematician could answer.

No one could fault Pete's dedication to Ariadne, or the brilliance of his approach. Roy had no doubt that, ultimately, Ariadne would be a success.

What that would mean for Pete, however, wasn't at all clear. Officially, the project didn't even exist. Hard to win a lot of fame and fortune from a nonexistent success.

What it could mean for the country, though, had held Roy's attention ever since he'd thought of it, ever since he'd talked with Pete about it, ever since Pete had called him back in the middle of the night to tell him what he thought was truly possible. "You have any idea, Roy, what we could do? All the phone calls, all the e-mails, all the text messages, all the bank transactions—everything they got, we can read. We can recognize their voices, establish call patterns, trace wire transfers. We can build a database of what any one of these guys does every day. As long as it involves electronic communications—and today, what doesn't?—we can track it. And we can do it *fast*. Given enough hardware, we can do it with so little latency—we're talking minutes here, Roy—not hours, *minutes*—seriously, Roy, this is good enough to let them work just about in real time. So fast, there's no way the bad guys will ever see them coming. How about that, Roy? This is big! I can't sleep. I've got an idea for detecting when events are probably not just coincidence. Bayes' rule, that kind of stuff. Gotta go. You sell this, Roy—you sell this tomorrow, okay? This is *big*!"

Nothing in government, of course, happens *tomorrow*, but this one had moved pretty quickly. Pete had worked up a little demo of what he thought he could pull off, using a week's worth of communications running through the CASTOR servers. The results were pretty impressive. Decent voice recognition, considering that for the demo they were basically just using commercial software. Pattern recognition identified with very high accuracy project teams, functional departments, and other groups of people working together. It even flagged certain male-female relationships with a high enough probability to give everybody a laugh—and to make Roy secretly glad that he and Sarah had the executive-assistant alibi to hide behind.

What really impressed, at least Roy, though, was the speed. Pete had been right: his algorithms were *fast*. Even in that first demo, they could recognize a voice on a new call and match the call to likely patterns within a few minutes. That with mostly COTS tools, and a PC or two, and only a couple of weeks' work. In that first meeting with Roy's Technical Support Working Group contacts, Pete rattled on about partial cues, self-organizing nets, fuzzy logic, subsymbolic processing—enough stuff no one understood that everyone concluded he must know what he's talking about. TSWG was sufficiently impressed that it set up a meeting a week later with representatives of the CIA, DIA, and NSA. All agreed it was worth funding a trial. And so Ariadne had its funding, less than three months after the idea was born.

So fast almost nobody even noticed.

The project team was based on-site at NSA headquarters up in Maryland, where they could have relatively unfettered access to the agency's huge databases, as well as to the real-time feeds streaming in 24/7 from all over the globe. Over the past year, they'd made steady progress, continuing to expand and refine Pete's algorithms and increasing their computing horsepower by many orders of magnitude. But they had yet to show any real results. Roy longed for the day when Ariadne would produce a name, a phone number—anything the client could use to take down a living, breathing bad guy. It would justify the project's continued funding, sure—people like Bill Morton never failed to remind him about that. But it would also prove that he'd been right back in that conference room. It would prove that it took more than just soldiers to win this kind of war. It would prove that science could—that science actually *had to*—make a difference. CASTOR—*his* CASTOR—could make a difference.

But instead, the team continued to build out their infrastructure, talking about how much more they'd be able to process, how much faster, how much more accurately, if they just made *this* revision. *This* code change.

This library mod. Academics striving for nirvana. The sound of one hand clapping: interesting, but probably not a great way to get anybody's attention. It was like watching a construction crew assigned to build the world's greatest skyscraper, but that never stopped digging deeper and deeper into the ground in order to lay the perfect foundation.

Roy Daniel continued through the report, page by page, looking for something he could use. Some nugget of real information. Real intel. Something I can run with—even if I have to do the running myself—before the race is all over, and this beautiful foundation gets plowed back into the Earth.

If we move fast, they'll never see us coming. It's the laws of physics. You can't argue with the laws of physics.

* * *

Sarah Anderson looked at her mother's alarm clock. She could hear it humming quietly now that the day noises had packed up and wandered home. Its square white plastic casing had been yellowing around the edges for as long as Sarah could remember. She used to think, as a little girl not napping on top of the bedspread in the sticky still afternoon, that the greenish nighttime number glow had stained it. She smiled, lips pursed a shade redder than fashion today required. Do you really know that that green glow *doesn't* stain plastic? She'd stopped believing it years ago, but she didn't really know why. Seemed childish, she guessed—that was all. She'd like to believe it, but she couldn't.

Sarah looked over her to-do list one more time. The arrangements for tomorrow night's dinner were all set. Tomorrow that's all she'd do, but there was nothing more to do tonight. She could work on Roy's presentation to the board next month, but her heart wasn't in it. She had a long time to get ready for that, anyway. Not tonight. She scanned on down the list for the most mindless task she could find. Expense reports. She could approve expense reports. Technically that was Roy's job, but he had better things to do and, frankly, she knew better than he did what did and didn't look right. She clicked on the link on the CASTOR intranet homepage, typed in Roy's password, and opened the first report.

The alarm clock did the little double hum it did every time the minute hand passed the two. You could only hear it when it was really quiet. Sometimes her mother would lay with her on the bed, running her fingers through her hair or singing a song Sarah couldn't really understand. Once she told Sarah the story of an old man who got magical things—a rag, a goat, an old hat—from devils in a shack by the side of the road. Every time he got something new he went to the same inn and showed it to the innkeeper, who then stole it. Even then she couldn't understand why he kept going to that same inn. Why not go to a different inn? But it did make her laugh when money came out of the goat's ears.

Sarah heard voices at the end of the hallway and a door closing. It was going to be a late night, apparently. Roy was still reading in his office, and Bill and Jabe Evans were still around. Strange that they weren't in the hallway, talking as they usually were by this time. She supposed Jabe, at least, was getting ready for his speech tomorrow night. Jabe Evans hated speeches. He had every right to—he was terrible at them. Roy was much better. Roy knew how to throw in enough useless details to keep the audience entertained. Jabe Evans didn't do useless details. Just the facts, and all the facts—hours' worth of facts, at times read off sheets of paper that he sometimes got in the wrong order. Last year Roger had had to come up on stage and sort them out for him. It was a good thing Jabe Evans was nothing short of a god to most of the people in the audience. It made his ineptitude endearing. People would have walked out on any lesser being.

The slides Roy owed Jabe for the speech had been done a week ago. He'd made sure he had everything to her before he left for his trip to

Ottawa. That gave her an excuse to "work from home" on Friday so she could have the slides ready for his final review with Jabe when he came back on Monday.

It was their first time away together.

Sarah's mother had told her another story about two sisters—one good, one bad. The mother—as bad as her oldest daughter—had forced the good sister out into the world when she was still very young. When the little girl found an oven in need of repair, she fixed it. When she found a spring plugged up with mud, she fixed it. She came to work for an old woman, cooking and cleaning and caring for the woman's dog. The woman told the little girl to put all the dust she swept up every day into an old chest, which became her reward when she left. The spring gave her wine and the oven gave her bread and meat on her journey home. When the little girl got home, she found the dust in the old chest turned to silver and gold, and the dog she'd cared for turned into a handsome prince. And they lived happily ever after.

The older daughter, of course, went out into the world the same way, but did none of the good things her sister had done. And in the end, she got nothing but an old chest full of dust.

Sarah had always wondered what it would be like to have a sister. Sometimes she'd pretended her mother's pillow was her sister. There was a crocheted afghan her grandmother had made that lay at the foot of the bed, and she'd drape it over the pillow so the fringe hung down and she'd lie on her mother's bed and braid her sister's hair and tell her sister her mother's stories.

The alarm clock double hummed and Sarah looked at the green-gold number, arranged around the golden circle in the middle of the face, and at the clear plastic second hand winding away another minute. She still had the afghan, folded over a chair in her bedroom. It and the alarm clock were the only things she'd kept when she'd cleaned out her mother's house before the sale. Sometimes she slept beside it hoping to smell the past, to hear the stories. But it would never stroke her hair, not even after she fell asleep.

• • •

"I need your help on this. I need this to work."

Jabe Evans hunched over his desk and tapped a pen on his notebook. After a long pause, he sat up as straight as he could as if addressing someone sitting across from him. There was a time when they would have been sitting next to each other, thick as thieves. Although that time had past, Jabe retained complete faith and trust in the man on the other end of the phone.

"Of course he is. But we need a little insurance. This is too important to trust to just one person."

Even from this angle, absolutely nothing was visible through the dark windows. Not a sound came from the hallway. Evans stood up and maneuvered the phone cord over the wreckage on his desk, over his computer monitor, and stretched to kick his office door shut with his toe.

"It's bigger than this one project."

He walked the cord back over his desk so he could stand by the windows, and looked down at the lights of the strip mall parking lot across the highway. It was almost empty now, except for a huddle of cars outside the sports bar. He'd never been in there.

"I can't tell you. But I can say that this one project has implications for the future of the whole company. You've always come through in the past and helped us make things right. I need someone I trust to keep an eye on this and keep me updated. Can you do this?"

The light at the intersection changed from red to green. A car in one lane didn't immediately move. Somebody honked. After a minute the road was empty. The traffic light swayed gently in the breeze, directing no one.

"Good. Thank you. Keep me posted, will you? Do you think you'll have anything to report by Friday?"

Seeing the breeze made Evans's mind drift, and he looked at the pictures on the wall. Nothing but physics involved in sailing. Patriotism, politics, fiduciary duties—none of them could make a sailboat move. He wondered what the weather was supposed to be like on the weekend.

Maybe Friday should be a sailing day.

• • •

Al Green fumbled in his shirt pocket for his reading glasses, wrestled them onto his face, and frowned down his nose at his ringing phone. Still frowning, he pushed a button and put the phone to his ear.

"Well, good evenin', sir."

The bar at the Hyatt Regency was a wood-paneled trade-show booth wedged into an otherwise uninhabitable corner of the main lobby. Men in dark suits loosened their ties and drank tall beers or short whiskeys. A few hunched at the bar and watched the ball game, practicing with the bartenders for their new careers as sports commentators. Others slumped into chairs designed for hippier hips and explained—more to themselves than to their half-listening colleagues—how the day hadn't really been their fault, and how their mission was really much more significant than it appeared.

"Sure, I think we can do that."

Al Green put his free hand to his chest to unsuccessfully hold back a burp, then reached for his beer. He filled an awkwardly low-backed seat turned away from the bar, watching glass elevators carry glassy-eyed guests into the glass-framed, Chrystal City sky.

"I know just what to do. Don't you worry 'bout a thing. It'll all be sewed up by this time tomorrow."

A tall man, hair bottle silvered and skin booth tanned, traded business cards in the middle of the lobby with a woman bleached and tucked for yet another assault on her glass ceiling.

"No, shouldn't be any risk o' that. We're s'posed to meet here in just a little bit, anyway." Al Green looked at his Rolex. "It'll all be face-to-face."

The tall man walked away toward the elevators. The bleached woman rummaged through her purse for a moment then hesitated in the direction of the bar.

"Well, hell, we'll get a room if you want." Al Green grinned. "That's right. Trust me. After that it'll just be a matter of the contracts boys wrappin' up the paperwork."

Al Green squirmed in his seat, aspiring to an upright position. He caught the bleached woman's eye and flashed her a pig's best smile. She countered with a downward glance practiced to mean anything or nothing to anyone or no one and kept on moving toward the bar.

"Look, buddy, I've got another call comin' in. I'll see you tomorrow night, though, okay? Okay. Don't worry. By next week we'll be in high cotton. Okay. You bet. B'bye."

Al Green stood up, put his phone in his jacket pocket, adjusted his Sansabelt, and followed his nose to the bar.

• • •

Tamara Maybin stood in a corner of the ballroom, watching the action. At this point, she really had very little to do. Very little except worry. Everything was in somebody else's court now. Nothing made Tamara more nervous.

White tablecloths covered round tables for eight that nearly filled the room. In a couple of years, Tamara thought, we're going to need a bigger space. Imagine that. The room seats four hundred and fifty and it's getting too small. Who would have thought, back what—ten years ago? Who would have thought Pollux would grow up so big?

Certainly not Evans. He still couldn't understand why a simple PAC wasn't good enough. The point, after all—how many times had he said this to her?—was to get money to politicians legally. There were rules governing these things. Just follow the rules and get it done. The less fuss the better. Words Evans had built a life around.

Roy Daniel understood—she was sure of that. He'd done his best to stay out of it all at first, but eventually he'd come around. After the first golf tournament. That's when he'd started calling her "Leda." It'd taken her an embarrassing amount of time to work out that he was actually referring to her when he said it. She was still trying to work out how she felt about his saying it.

The hotel staff was setting out the silver and the blue-rimmed dinner plates. The florists were wheeling in carts loaded with red and white roses in cobalt blue glass vases. The screen behind the stage was framed on each side by huge flags hanging down from the ceiling. The AV guys were adjusting the alignment of the picture between the flags and checking the microphones. She hoped she could at least get everyone besides Evans away from the podium. With him, she knew better than to waste her time.

Scientists. And she'd thought getting away from the military would make her life easier.

Actually, that wasn't completely true. If she was honest with herself, she'd thought getting away from the military would make her richer. And in the purely material sense, she'd been right. Financially, she was far better off than she ever would have been working in the military. Better off than she would have been even if she'd ascended to the highest ranks—which, of course, she never would have. An African American woman specializing in public relations was never going to get much further in the marines than she already had. Forget the African American woman part—*nobody* specializing in public relations was going to get much further in the marines than she already had.

Forget the marines. Nobody specializing in public relations was going to get much further than she had at CASTOR, either. But at least CASTOR paid better. And it could give her a path into *real* PR one day—maybe, eventually, her own agency—if she played her cards right. She'd gotten to the point where it really was up to her. Sink or swim—her own actions would decide.

In that respect, she couldn't thank the General enough. All those hours really had paid off, working on his press team during the Gulf War, running 24/7 interference for him while he did the only job he had any time for, any patience for, and (she could say this now) any real aptitude for: winning battles. Real battles—the kind with tanks and guns and air strikes and casualties. Real casualties. Other kinds of battles, other kinds of casualties, he just couldn't understand, even when he was right in the middle of them. He couldn't understand the enemy—had no idea what their motivations were. Without her support, he would have walked right into God knows how many ambushes.

With her support, he'd become a hero. Because being a hero isn't so much about who you *are* as about who others *believe* you are. It's about perception, not necessarily reality. She still wasn't sure he understood this. But at least he had, eventually, appreciated her help—that and other things, places she refused to go now. That's just the way the military works. Perception versus reality—one or the other—he'd appreciated it enough to make some personal calls on her behalf when she decided to leave. One of those calls had gotten her in the door at CASTOR.

Aside from the pay, CASTOR wasn't really all that different from the marines. Evans, Morton, Daniel, the General—they all appreciated the fact that, because she was there, they didn't have to deal with the press except on limited, highly scripted occasions. And they appreciated this because, Tamara was convinced, deep down they were afraid of the press—afraid of them because, in their minds, the press was completely, incomprehensibly irrational. The General would have stepped onto any military battlefield in the world without hesitation because—in his mind, at least—he understood the game. He understood that the enemy wanted to kill him, while at the same time not getting killed. Simple. But the press? He didn't really know what they wanted. To the General, talking to the press was like talking to a bunch of birds—seagulls, maybe, or crows. You could talk, and they might listen—appear to, at least—might turn their heads and hop a little closer and squawk at the right times to seem interested in what you had to say. And then afterward, they might do nothing, might just fly away, or might make a lot of noise and shit all over everything. No way to know. No way at all. Only thing you *could* be sure of is that, given half a chance, they'd steal your food.

Same with CASTOR. Tamara had been hired because Evans (or actually, she suspected, Bill Morton) had realized that CASTOR was now big enough to need to play the PR game, and to play it like the rest of the big boys. But he had basically the same impression of the press as the General had. There were no laws of physics governing the press, and in the absence of rules, he had no idea what to do. By default, he'd do nothing. Ignore it all and move on to the next solvable problem. But he was smart enough to know that doing nothing while your competitors do something is not generally a winning strategy.

And so she had a job.

She suspected she also had a job because someone had realized CASTOR needed to show a little diversity, but she tried to ignore that. One of Tamara's own personal rules—worked out during her first weeks in the marines—was that you couldn't pay any attention at all—none—to the possible implications of being a black woman. Ignoring it was the only possible option. Take the good, ignore the bad, and move on as if you were Bob Johnson from Fargo, North Dakota. Let yourself get distracted, veer off that great white road, dwell on those things—or those people—over which you had no control, and you'd never find your way back. Or forward. Or out.

The AV guys rolled the video so they could adjust the sound levels. Tamara watched as, one by one, the rest of the workers in the room stopped what they were doing and turned to watch. It *was* good, wasn't it? She knew her work. She supposed she owed her career to the fact that she—unlike the General, unlike Evans, unlike most of the rule-bound men she'd known in her life—had no problem understanding the press. They *were* just like birds—they *did* just want to eat. Nobody in the world was going to change that. So you really only had two choices: You could sit around all day trying to protect your food at the expense of whatever it was you were *really* trying to accomplish. Or you could make a meal just for them. Make one every day, and make it so good, they wouldn't see any reason to look for more. That was Tamara's strategy: to be the best damned chef those media birds had ever seen. To know just what to feed them, and when, to keep them not just from wondering what was going on behind the curtain, but from even thinking about the curtain at all.

The Pollux Society, explained the well-known voice narrating the video, was "dedicated to the health and welfare of our men and women in uniform, and to the families that support them." It was composed of the upper echelons of CASTOR management, plus like-minded individuals from the top ranks of government and industry. It donated large sums of money in very public ways to the Wounded Warrior Project, the National Military Family Association, and other organizations that sought to improve the lives of current and former service members. Images of men in wheelchairs rolling across finish lines and kids smiling precious and toothless as generals pinned medals on their superhero T-shirts wove in and out of footage of F-18s shooting off flight decks, and of dusty GIs giving the thumbs-up from the open hatches of Abrams tanks. The final scene—five perfect families representing the five military service branches beaming adoringly at one another in front of a flag-encircled Washington monument—played out to a crescendo of patriotic music. The audience would never know how much it had taken to select these five families—white, black, Asian, Hispanic, and Native American—and to get them all to Washington, all in a good mood, on a perfectly sunny day—all for less than thirty seconds' worth of footage.

The AV guys clapped and the others in the room smiled and murmured approvingly to one another and went back to finishing up the tables. Tamara smiled. Nobody here knew who she was. That made their approval all that much better.

"I asked for a PAC, not a charity!" had been Jabe Evans's reaction to her first presentation, two months after joining CASTOR. But she was convinced that wrapping the PAC inside something bigger than the company itself would ultimately work to the benefit of both—and more. Classic one plus one equals three—or maybe, in this case, four or five. So she didn't give in. She didn't promise a rethink and ask for another meeting a few weeks later. She looked Evans straight in the eye and said, "Sir, with all due respect, the last thing Washington needs is another PAC."

Evans had stared back at her, not used to a challenge. "Maybe not, but that is exactly what *CASTOR* needs. As, I believe, we've discussed, quite clearly, from the very first day we spoke."

Tamara took a deep breath. "You didn't start CASTOR looking to be just like any other company. You started it to be unique—and it is. So why should your PAC be just like any other PAC? Make it be more! Make it something memorable! Make it something so big that most people won't even think of it as a PAC at all!"

"There are rules." Evans searched for something in the pages of his notebook. "Rules we have to follow. I know I need to play this game, but I'm not about to stretch the rules doing it."

"Sir, perhaps I wasn't clear enough during my presentation. We're not stretching the rules at all. The PAC will be set up by the book, following every rule to the letter. We'll only take contributions from CASTOR management. No contribution greater than five thousand dollars. Pollux will, legally, be a completely separate entity. But contributing to the PAC will make you a Pollux member. Pollux will bring in other members, too, and other donations—separate bank accounts, of course, no mixing of funds. And Pollux will make the charitable contributions, while the PAC will make the contributions to political campaigns. The real point, though, is that publicly, we'll never talk about the PAC—only Pollux. Pollux will give us a way to keep the PAC out of the public eye while still making it one of the highest profile PACs in the country. It'll give us a way of doing all the work a typical PAC would do, but doing it while talking about far more popular causes: care for disabled veterans. Care for the families of those deployed overseas. You name it. There's not one cause in this arena that doesn't have off-the-charts public support. And all that support can flow back to CASTOR."

Tamara had looked around the room and seen all eyes on Evans. No one had spoken—not in her defense, but not against her, either. Given that she was far and away the newest employee in the room, she counted this as a win.

Evans stared down at his notebook. "I don't need the distraction. CASTOR doesn't need the distraction. We have real work to do."

Tamara smiled. "Which is exactly, sir, why you need the Pollux Society.

Focus on the real work: supporting the troops. The PAC—it'll be there, but almost as an afterthought. Out of sight, out of mind—of everyone, that is, except those benefiting from it."

Bill Morton had knocked on her open door later that afternoon and told her to go ahead. He didn't really say much more, but his smile told her everything she needed to know. He was on her side. But if it didn't work out, there'd be nobody taking the blame but her.

Tamara checked her BlackBerry. A couple of messages from reporters confirming that they'd be in attendance. One was the woman who'd gotten the first big Pollux Society fundraiser—"Operation Dessert Storm"—written up in the *Washington Post*. Hers was the only message Tamara responded to immediately—she owed much of what she had today to that woman's kind words. The rest she'd thank in person tonight.

One final glance around the room showed everything in order. The florists were wheeling away their empty carts and the AV guys were taping down cables and packing away unused gear. Just a check back in the kitchen, then I'll head upstairs to get changed. Tamara was heading for the doors at the back of the ballroom when Roy Daniel walked in. He smiled when he saw her, but his eyes were dark.

"Hello, Tamara."

No Leda. On this day, in this place, not a good sign. His mind was elsewhere.

"Roy, good to see you. Is everything okay?"

"Fine, Tamara, fine." Daniel glanced around the room, not seeing anything, not finding what he was looking for. "Look, I know you're very busy, but could I talk with you, just for a minute or two?"

Tamara felt an old familiar tug and looked around the room for what she knew wasn't there. She managed only a nod where she knew a few words would have been better.

The two of them stood there for a moment longer than either preferred, one thinking, one hoping the other would surely lead.

• • •

"Hey, buddy. How'd it go today? You get to talk to 'im?"

The hotel bar was empty except for a clutch of twentysomethings with espresso drinks in the corner. Their attention was on a laptop on the table. The bartender was cutting limes.

"That's good, that's good. So you think he's on board."

His Rolex read quarter of five. Time to get ready. Cocktails would be starting.

"I think that if civilian feeds are the only thing standing between us and success, then the General'll be havin' himself a big ol' civilian feed for supper tomorrow."

Al Green chuckled. A tall woman in a short skirt and high heels stopped at the entrance to the bar.

"You do good work, sir. We 'preciate ya. So when you comin' over?"

The tall woman was still standing there. Her loose, blonde hair obscured her face as she looked down to find something in her purse.

"Well, you get y'self over here early, and I got a special bottle with your name on it, you hear? The show's already started. Okay, buddy—we'll see ya soon. B'bye."

• • •

Bill Morton fingered his CASTOR cufflinks and smiled as the ballroom filled. Tamara Maybin had certainly been right about this one, all those years ago. He'd had a good feeling about Pollux from the beginning, but none of them had predicted—how could they?—the growth they'd seen since 9/11. You start things, you plan, you work hard, but at the end of the day, a big part of everything is just luck. He'd never say that aloud—CFOs can't officially believe in luck, after all. But before, they'd had to recruit, attracting mostly military brass and industry folks looking to curry favor with CASTOR, or with Jabe Evans personally. Filling the room for the annual gala had been mostly an exercise in finding a suitably small room. Now, they didn't have to lift a finger—prospective members contacted them every day. Last year they'd limited invitations to the gala to those contributing fifty thousand dollars or more, and Maybin had still had to scramble to find a bigger room at the last minute. This year was no different. Along the Beltway at least, not having a Pollux pin in your lapel was beginning to make people question your patriotism. Members were mentioning the Society in their Green Book listings. They'd even gotten an inquiry from their first Senator—first one, that is, not looking for handouts.

Bill Morton thought of his granddaughter, all cheekbones and sky blue eyes and cloud white smiles. You did everything you could. You sewed them pumpkin costumes for Halloween. You read to them every night before bed, tiny heads warm like fresh baked bread tucked up against your chest, sleepy fingers knowing when to turn the pages even before they could read the words. You made sure they got a shot at the best schools. You put away money for college. Maybe a little bit for later. But the rest was mostly luck—some good, some bad. The hardest thing for a parent to swallow—the good maybe even more than the bad. No parent would ever admit publicly that his child's success was just luck, any more than Morton himself would admit publicly that Pollux's success by and large had nothing to do with CASTOR's management.

Under their wise stewardship—that sounded better—the value of an honorary Pollux membership, like they were giving the General this evening, had risen with the Society's net worth. Being inducted into the Pollux Society came with a lot of press, nearly all of it positive. Maybin positioned these "nominations" as a "recognition of the best aspects of the American character," the nominees as "the embodiment of what it means to be a true American leader." And so far, it looked as though the press was with her. *The Washington Post* had moved their coverage out of the society columns. Fox News had apparently called, though as far as he knew they had yet to actually air anything. Even NPR had been talking with Maybin, although she'd been visibly disappointed when it became clear that their focus was on the fact that the Society was run by an African American woman.

"That new black girl," as Al Green still called her, although she'd been with the company for more than ten years now. But he never said it to her face, because what she was doing played right into his hands. The Pollux Society was made to order for Green's clientele, and Green knew it. Bill Morton could see it on his face right now, laughing and shaking hands and slapping backs as he waddled through the room, his blue cummerbund perched like a sow's bonnet over his most prominent feature. Colonel Jaworski followed, at a safe distance, stiff smiles and nods in Dress Blues. He kept a close eye across the room on the General, who was already seated at the table near the stage next to Jabe Evans, who hunched inside a tuxedo that had outgrown his shoulders.

The last time Bill Morton had seen his son, he'd looked a lot like that—dwarfed inside his huge, smeared jacket. Morton had tried to get him back from the hot, grimy pavement, back into the cool leathered safety of the idling family car. But his eyes were someone else's, fighting a world Morton couldn't see. "Liberty is wealth!" he'd declared, fist in the air, a dusty black garbage bag swinging over his other shoulder as he glazed past. Behind the wiry whiskers Morton could still make out the cheeks he'd once kissed every night before he turned out the lights. But not the eyes. Steel gray luck had stolen his son's green eyes.

Bill Morton found himself staring at Al Green. Green sat at the table just behind Evans's, just behind the General, just behind Morton's empty seat. Green laughed and shook his head as Morton finally acknowledged him, then closed his mouth and remained perfectly still for one sweaty heartbeat, eyes narrow and gaze determined. He winked at Morton and nodded just once, then turned to the Colonel seated next to him, slapping him on the back and offering him a flask from the inside pocket of his jacket.

Repeat after me, Bill: There's no good luck—just good planning. Al Green had said that to him once, sitting in a bar somewhere in a city he couldn't remember.

Bill Morton took one last look around the ballroom to assure himself everyone was in place. The accountant in him took a quick tally of clients: Well over 50 percent of CASTOR's revenues were represented in this single room. Morton chuckled to himself and adjusted his Pollux Society lapel pin. Way to go, Tamara. You certainly deserve some of the credit—don't let Lady Luck take it all.

Tamara Maybin was already on the stage, off to one side, chatting with one of the guys running the show—a lanky guy, long hair, scruffy beard, wild eyes. Bill Morton looked the other way. Out in the lobby, he saw the lights dim a couple of times, and the noise level in the room rose as the die-hard bar crowd returned, cocktails in hand, each hoping the others remembered where their seats were. He saw his own wife, Patty, walking arm in arm with Ellie Evans, tête-à-tête, patting her older friend's hand for emphasis. Ellie nodded in earnest. Morton smiled as he watched the two pass without noticing him. Ellie was everything Jabe Evans was not: charming, witty, fond of an evening out. Like Morton and Patty, Jabe and Ellie had known each other since high school. More luck. How many people in this room could you say that about?

Speaking of which: Where was Roy Daniel? Morton looked at the tables near Evans—no sign of him. He scanned back through the crowd toward the doors to the lobby—no Daniel. Morton glanced at his watch out of habit and walked into the foyer. Just a handful of people still stood at the bars, waiting for one last drink before the long dry spell ahead.

And Sarah Anderson, off to the far side of the room, stared at her deep red shoes.

Her wide, blue eyes caught Morton's before he could cross the room. Perhaps she shook her head. Morton stopped. Sarah held his gaze until the lights dimmed again and the last of the stragglers hurried into the ballroom. She held a cell phone in her hand. She looked at Morton as she answered. After a while she looked around the lobby, as if just realizing she hadn't left yet, and hurried off in the direction of the exit.

Bill Morton stood alone in the lobby for a moment, hands in his pockets. He considered the perfectly polished black-capped toes of his shoes as he rocked back onto his heels. Sure there's luck—you can say that here, Bill, nobody's listening—but we make our luck ourselves.

Behind this admission was his son's gunmetal stare. So Bill Morton willed it closed, just as he always did, and crossed the ballroom to the head table in this room filled with his life's good fortune.

six

Dad spent months looking for just the right shotgun. He was so proud when he found that old Ithaca 20 gauge in a pawnshop up in Dayton—that one at the corner, where the highway turns off and runs south down to the bridge. How he ever ended up in there in the first place I'll never know. Guess he must've walked into every place selling guns in fourteen counties, looking for a deal. Gotta say this for him, though—he did get a beauty. Not a scratch on it—hardly looked as though anybody'd ever had it outside. Dad couldn't stop smiling that Christmas morning, watching Asher unwrapping it, tracing the scrollwork with his fingers, aiming at imaginary ducks through the big picture windows and out over the lake. He was about twelve, I guess, eyes big as dinner plates. Gotta be a story behind that gun. Guess there's probably a story or two behind every gun.

Anyway, one time Asher and I were out quail hunting—I think it was the year after we got him the gun. Remember that place Jasper's uncle used to have on the river, over in Hardin county? Well, we were out there the week before Thanksgiving, walking an old dirt road. Field on the right had been planted in beans; on the left was thick brush along a creek that nobody'd cleared—at least not in a very long time. The day was overcast— low, flat clouds, smelled like snow but wasn't cold enough. Wind pretty strong, out of the northwest. Asher was walking down the right-hand side of the road, kicking at the clumps of grass with the previous year's leather boots and blinking into the wind from under his old gray stocking cap. Held his shotgun in both hands, ready for action, as always. Never did see Asher put that gun over his shoulder, or hold it one-handed down by his side. Always ready, from the minute he climbed down out of the truck.

He never got bored, not even when we didn't see a bird all day. Didn't seem to care. Dad used to call him our bird dog, back before we got him the gun. That was after old Burke died and Dad got that golden retriever that ran back to the truck every time we fired a gun. He started sending Asher out, just like a dog, to flush out the birds. Couldn't have been more than six or seven, first time. Dad'd laugh till his sides hurt, watching his grandson run off through the fields or into the brush, just his head bouncing, and his arms out wide like he was trying to take off, over and over again. We told him to fall down flat on the ground if any birds flew, and to wait there till we told him to get back up again. And he'd do just that, every time—fall flat on his face, just as if he'd stuck his toe in a gopher hole. At first he'd fall down for any birds at all—quail, doves, blackbirds, starlings, even sparrows—he didn't care. Get back up when we gave him the all-clear, all smiles, head tilted way back to see us, stocking cap pulled down almost over his eyes, dried-up grass and cockleburs stuck to it. But after a while he figured out the difference, and only fell down for the quail. Doves too, once in a while. Doves fool us all, the way they flush, flapping for what seems like forever before you finally see them, already flying too fast to hit.

Anyway, Asher and I were walking that dirt road, and hadn't seen a bird all day. I was starting to think they were probably all coveyed up, since for the past week it had finally started to feel like winter. I figured we'd either find a whole bunch of birds all at once, or nothing—one or the other. So I was trying to work out where they were most likely to bunch up, and the brush along the creek, right there next to the old bean field, seemed like a good bet.

But Asher, he didn't seem to care one way or the other. He was like that a lot back then—sort of off in his own little world, not really concerned with the things you and me think about. You and me—like most people, I guess—we think about where we're going, or what we're trying to get done. We think about goals. We set off down a road because we think it's the best way to get to the place we're trying to go. Asher, though, he never seemed to think that way. He didn't really seem to care where we were going. He'd head off down a road just because he liked the looks of it. He'd run off into a field and fall flat on his face just because we told him to—and I guess because he thought it was fun. Actually finding birds didn't seem to concern him much. Though he did always want to go find them after we shot them. Didn't work out too well, since he was always flat on his face when the shooting was going on. That made Dad laugh, too, watching the boy running off in the wrong direction. Funny how much I remember Dad laughing when Asher was around. Never thought much about that before now.

The dirt road took a turn to the left, away from the bean field, and into a little stand of oak trees. The trees blocked the wind, so it seemed pretty still in there, and open, too, with the ground not so choked with brush there under the trees. Almost like walking into a church. We stopped for a minute to look and listen. The wind rattled the bare branches up above us and the damp, brown leaves covering the road made the whole place smell like somebody's old cellar.

I heard them clucking before they flushed. Funny how good their camouflage is—I never did see them, even after I knew they were there. I whispered, "They're in here, Son," and he tucked the stock of his gun up under his arm, looking around. Don't think he really heard them. I took a step forward, looking off to the left where I thought I heard them. I hoped, because the wind wasn't so bad in there, that they'd fly instead of just running off into the brush along the creek, but I wasn't sure. I could actually hear them running, but you never can tell which direction.

The first ones to flush weren't actually the ones I'd heard. Ten, twenty yards up the road, just off to the right was the main part of the covey, and they all jumped at once just as Asher started to move again. The ones I'd been listening to jumped up right after that, and I got off two shots before they dodged off between the trees. Two shots, two birds—the first a nice crossing shot, the second flying straight away from me. I heard Asher shooting behind me, once early on, then again a little late, I thought. He had a tendency to wait a little long, aim a little too carefully, especially in a big covey like that where there were so many birds to choose from.

"Get any?" I asked, trying to work out where the main part of the covey was headed. I wanted to get a few more, if possible—enough to make a meal, at least—before we headed for home.

"Yeah, I got two," Asher said, sounding a little disappointed.

I was surprised, I have to admit, but I tried not to show it. "That's great, Son. That last shot sounded a little late to me—didn't figure you'd hit anything. One jump late?"

"No, that shot was kinda stupid. Bird was way outa range. Totally missed that one." I could see him looking off to the left of the road.

"Oh, well—that's the way it goes. Guess I missed your third shot. Only heard two." I started off through the leaves to pick up my first bird, which lay in plain sight just a few yards from where I was standing. Hit pretty hard. Should've waited a second or two before I shot, but—well, you know how it is, when the birds start flying.

"No, you didn't miss it." Asher picked up a bird that lay in the middle of the road. "I only shot twice. But I saw two birds fall on the first shot. Guess I hit two."

I stood up and smiled at Asher, watched him tuck the bird into his jacket pocket. Sometimes, out in a cold wind, that right ear of mine—the one I got a twig stuck up that time I slipped fishing—doesn't work too great. "You what?"

"I think I hit two. I saw two fall, at least." He headed off where he'd been looking at first—off the left side of the road.

"Did you aim at two? People do that sometimes, when a big covey like that jumps up—aim at the spot where two birds cross. Two birds always cross, they say."

"Naw, I just aimed at one. But I saw two fall."

Now, you know me—I've been hunting quail since the Truman administration. But in all that time, I have never hit two birds with one shot. Not once. Can't even say I've seriously tried. Old J.B., now, he was the one that told me there was a chance in every single big covey—claimed he looked for it every time. Claimed he'd hit a couple, too. But J.B. was one of the best shots I've ever known.

I started off toward where my second bird should've been—maybe thirty yards ahead, off to the left side of the road. Right about where Asher was kicking around in the leaves, looking for his second bird.

"How many did you get, Dad?" Asher looked to his right, kicked at a lump of leaves next to some sassafras, kept looking.

Now, I know what you're thinking. I did think about it for a minute. But I just couldn't work out what the right thing to do was. So I just pretended I hadn't heard him and walked toward the spot where I remembered seeing my second bird fall, right in front of a big holly bush. Asher was looking a little closer to the road, but was working his way toward the same bush.

I saw the bird first. A young hen, sitting all fluffed up just underneath the holly. One wing hanging a little funny. She looked up at me, then off to one side, then off to the other, trying to work out which way to run, even though she wasn't in any condition to run off anywhere.

I just stood there for a minute. Asher was still kicking through the leaves, working his way closer.

"Dad?"

"Yes?"

"How many did you get?"

Before I had time to answer, he saw it.

Asher bent down and picked up the bird at his feet. A rooster, not moving a bit. He smiled at me as he stuck the bird into his pocket.

"Lucky shot, huh?"

"*Good* shot, Son. Very good shot."

I bent over and picked the little hen from under the holly bush and knocked her head as hard as I could on the butt of my shotgun.

seven

Palm fronds rattled against the hot night breeze. Beneath the trees, the sounds of talk and laughter and clinking dishes cut through the smells of lamb and bread and shisha. Two women leaned close and whispered as Asher passed. The smell of Oud and Hermes hovered over their tea glasses. A table full of businessmen erupted as their whiskey glasses were drained. They slapped one another on the back and stared red-faced and sweating at the wreckage of their dinner. An Indian waiter hovered nearby in anticipation of the next round.

Ahmed was not among them. Asher's BlackBerry begged for attention, but he knew there was no message. Two voice mails and a text had gone unanswered since he landed. If he was going to find him, he'd have to do it the old-fashioned way.

Asher strolled as casually as he could around the edges of the restaurant, scanning the tables one by one. Two northern European men studiously dissected stuffed grape leaves with forks and knives. A group of young locals smoking tall shisha pipes laughed about something on an iPhone they were passing around. An old man's eyes reminisced while his children and their children passed plates and smiled and scolded. The littlest boy knelt on his chair with his elbows on the table. His eyes sparkled as he chewed, and Asher thought he could hear him humming.

No Ahmed.

Asher stepped through the door into the dining room inside. It was virtually deserted in the hot weather. A waiter pushed by him carrying a tray full of small plates and baskets of bread. In the back of the room was a bar where a man in a white shirt was arranging shots of whiskey on a tray. There were no customers at the bar.

Asher sat down. The bartender's eyes were tired, black bags under dull pools beneath thickets of near-gray eyebrows.

"Hello, Yassin. Jack Daniels on the rocks, please."

"Black?"

"Yes, please. Just the regular black."

The Indian waiter collected the tray of whiskey shots with a nod to the bartender and a nervous glance at Asher. He hurried back out through the door.

The glass was still warm and the ice cubes snapped.

The bartender took glasses out of a dishwasher, drying them with a white towel. "He hasn't been here in a week, maybe more," he said. He didn't look up.

The whiskey smelled like Asher's old backyard after a thunderstorm on a summer afternoon.

"Who was he with last time you saw him?"

The bartender shrugged. Asher drank and the whiskey smell filled his head.

"Was he okay?"

The bartender frowned and inspected a glass against the light. "Sure, he's always okay." He scrubbed, reinspected, then put the glass back in the dishwasher.

Asher almost missed his glance.

"Tell me, Yassin."

The bartender just shrugged again. He looked out the windows at the businessmen's table and set a clean row of shot glasses up on the bar.

"Have another?"

Asher shook his head and drained off the watery remains.

"I need to talk with him. He may actually need to talk with me. If you see him, please tell him so."

The bartender nodded, but not at Asher. He began filling the row of shot glasses with Johnny Walker black label.

Asher left too much money on the bar and walked away. Outside, the little boy listened and stared as the businessmen began singing in a language he didn't understand.

• • •

A bull in jeans muscled a tiny girl, giggling at her Manolo Blahniks, off the elevator. The distinguished gentleman who followed looked ready to follow them farther, but only paused before gliding off toward the restaurant.

Phaethon emerged last, wearing the same clothes he'd worn on the plane. His eyes scanned the room, and she eased away around the far end of the bar. He was coming her way, but hadn't seen her yet. Need to keep it that way. Eva turned and headed for the ladies' room.

So far, Al Green had gotten it right. He'd go straight to work, and at some point, he'd end up here.

There was a line. Blonde and brunette, fair skinned and dark, tall and short, laughing and quiet—all the women of the world united by a common need. Eva smiled to herself at the thought. Forget the UN. Just build big, clean ladies' restrooms in all the major cities of the world. Women from every corner of the globe would come together, queue up, laugh, cry, and share with one another, keep an eye on one another's children, help one another out. No need for skyscrapers or translators or bureaucracies for life. Just satisfy that one basic need and women would sort the rest out, all by themselves.

Eva stood in line for a few minutes, then walked carefully back to the far corner of the bar. She positioned a group of German businessmen between herself and Phaethon. He had his back to the bar, the man next to him making a point with his glass. The man next to him leaned in, unsteadily, said something, and waited. Phaethon looked at him, turned and hunched down, his elbows on the bar. He ordered another drink. Eva mentally scanned the pictures from the folder, trying to place the new man. Nothing. He was tall and broad shouldered, well dressed with a movie star's jaw. The two men huddled there, talking and drinking, for several minutes. They must know each other.

Eva ignored the Germans' slurred invitations and quietly moved away from the bar, away from the crowds, toward the windows. She took out her cell phone and pretended to look for a good place to photograph the lights of the city below. She casually looked back at the two men at the bar. They turned to clink glasses, and she took their picture.

The lighting wasn't great, but it would work. She saved it, and tiny versions of the rest of her pictures stared back at her. There was Kai with his backpack, two summers ago in the Alps. There was Freddie, their dog, his hiking handkerchief tied around his neck. Kai on his bicycle just before Easter, when he'd gotten it into his head to ride to Prerow or Zingst or wherever, all in one day. There he was again the next day, stiff from riding the train all the way back but still smiling to see her. He'd drunk a beer and eaten some noodles, taken a shower and gone straight to bed, hadn't even asked what she'd done while he was away.

And there, just before Phaethon and his friend, was Andreas.

Several groups burst out laughing. Eva looked up and the friend stared straight at her. Phaethon was signing his bill. He patted his friend on the back and headed for the elevator without looking back. Eva made her way quickly past a very drunk girl sitting on the floor, her tiny dress hiked up to reveal a very pink thong. A blonde gave her an icy blue Russian growl as she slipped into the space that Phaethon had just left. His friend turned and she smelled vodka. He was neither happy, nor upset, nor surprised to see her.

. . .

The lights by the palms and beach chairs fell away, leaving nothing behind the glass but dark water. The metal window frames tallied the floors as they rose. A tiny woman in plus-size heels giggled like some exotic bird as her body-builder companion's lips pressed her earlobe. Beside them, a man wearing a black *bisht* and carefully trimmed beard fingered his *kerkusha* and studied the bird's scant plumage.

Lights like eyes of jade and sapphire and ruby and gold descended from above and the elevator stopped. The bird glanced back at her dress in the elevator glass and giggled when she caught Asher's eye. The bodybuilder decided Asher posed no threat and half-carried her into the bar.

A Filipino band played something Asher didn't recognize. The bar curved around the room's middle, separated by a step and a railing from tables with panoramic views of the city lights and ocean darks. He walked through the expensive crowd—expensive smoke, expensive perfume, expensive talk, expensive girls. The first time he'd come here, the hostess had led them to a table by the window where the views slid off into the turquoise distance. Ahmed had watched the hostess walk away, scanned all horizons for people he knew, then—finding none—called someone instead.

"You slept well, my friend?" It had taken Asher a moment to realize he wasn't still talking to his cell phone.

"Yes, yes, very well, thank you."

"I spoke earlier with our Saudi friends. They were very pleased to meet you last night. You made a very good impression."

"I'm glad to hear it."

"They asked if we could meet again this evening. I think they're ready to discuss more details."

"That's why I'm here. Anytime they want to meet, I'm available."

Ahmed had smiled and stroked his cell phone. "Very good, my friend. Very good. I will tell them. In a couple of hours, perhaps, downstairs, for coffee?"

Asher had shrugged his consent.

"Very good. Very good. But now, perhaps, we should have a drink? Fill up now, before the Saudis come and end our fun?"

Asher had ordered rum. It seemed to fit with the heat and the blue and the mood.

Tonight he ordered whiskey. He squeezed in at the bar next to a tall man contemplating a clear drink. The denim across an African girl's skinny hip bumped his other side, and her jade eyes brightened when he noticed. The tall man looked up as the bartender turned away.

"They can't mess that up too bad." The tall man leaned close. His Cary Grant jaw had been neatly shaved yesterday. What had been reds in his combed-back hair were now mostly gray. His breath said the clear drink was vodka.

Asher smiled and shook his head. "Not much room for error."

"Steer clear of the mixers. If you're paying twenty bucks a drink, you at least need to know it's not just soda water."

The bartender traded Asher's drink for his credit card. Jade watched it leaving without her and pouted. The seat of her jeans pressed Asher's thigh as she turned and her bare shoulder lingered against his, black against white, as she assessed her prospects.

Cary Grant tried to focus on Asher while draining his glass and dangling it for the bartender to take.

"American?" Two syllables.

"Yes."

"Been here long?"

"Just flew in tonight."

"Well, welcome to town."

The bartender delivered Cary Grant's refill and the two men raised their glasses.

"You here on business?" Asher asked, looking past him for familiar faces.

"Two years." His thumb indicated his liberally loosened gold yellow tie. "Came over with Citibank. They actually put my wife and me up here the first time we came over, just to look." He forgot to say more and drained half his glass instead.

No Ahmed. Several stunt doubles, but no sign of the star.

"She was so excited to come. Had to wait till the school year ended, though. I stayed over there, at the marina." He waved his glass in no particular direction, noticed that it was in his hand, and finished it off.

Asher leaned his back against the bar and scanned the room. Jade glanced his way from just below the railing, next to a table of young Brits with tall pilsners ogling girls in tiny dresses and neon cocktails.

"Nice place. Eventually got an apartment over by the creek, though. Closer to St. Mary's—kids had to go to St. Mary's, no arguing." Cary Grant flirted with his empty glass. "Closer to the hospitals, too. Didn't think about that then."

Asher saw the dark grays of Cary Grant's suit jacket closing in around him. Asher glanced at the bartender, who was already holding a glass of water. The bartender placed the glass quietly in front of Cary Grant's pacing hands, which latched onto it and brought it to his waiting lips. As he drank he raised back up like a marionette being readied for a show by a puppeteer careful not to tangle his strings.

"You never think about these things, you know." He shook his head at his reflection behind the bar. "Never think about what might happen, what might be waiting for you right around the next corner." The puppeteer let his head flop in Asher's direction. "You gotta family?"

Asher turned away from a table of men in dark suits, none of whom was Ahmed, where Jade was circling. The puppeteer's voice suggested tears, but his puppet's eyes were polished gray blue stones.

"I do," replied Asher. "A wife and two kids. Boy and a girl."

The marionette's head bobbed on its slack string and smiled. "You love 'em?"

Asher noticed he'd finished his drink. "I do," he swallowed, turned, and nodded at the bartender.

"My wife has cancer," Cary Grant announced, his head still dangling sideways. "Doctors say six to nine months. What the hell do you do with that?" He shifted his weight slowly back to the bar and raised his empty glass to the bartender.

Asher heard the call of the exotic bird from the elevator over the sound of a saxophone and sipped his new glass. "That's rough," he said, shaking his head at his own reply. "I'm sorry to hear it."

"We had a date tonight. She has good days, she has bad days, but the last few days have been good days, so we decided to make the best of it. But I came home this afternoon and found her in bed, barely able to move. 'You go,' she told me. 'You go out and have fun. You need to have fun. I need you to have fun.' Whaddya do with that? So here I am. Having fun." He raised his glass to anyone listening. "Here's to fun."

The two men's glasses clinked and both finished their drinks in one pull. A pair of tall blondes circled. Jade glanced over, sitting on the edge of a dark suit's chair.

Cary Grant's eyes twisted to focus on Asher's face. His hand fell onto Asher's far shoulder. "I think you and I should go get a steak. There's a pretty good place just across the bridge. Not like home, but pretty good. Pretty good drinks, too. Whaddya say? Let's have fun."

"I can't." Asher shook his head and his voice was all wrong. "I'm sorry. I have to find a friend." Laughter erupted from the Brits at the table nearby and Asher saw one of their girls sitting on the floor, apparently (judging by her expression, and her very visible, very pink panties) by mistake. The men in dark suits laughed, too, though their eyes suggested otherwise. Jade and the blondes followed their lead.

Cary Grant sensed his new friend's eyes slip away. Behind the man, back by the dark windows alone, an angel with tropical blue eyes and sandy blonde hair stood and stared. Cary Grant felt fear and despair and maybe even relief, but all from a long way off, as if he were reading them in a book. After a while somebody patted him on the shoulder, and he turned to the bartender and ordered another drink. When it arrived, his new friend was gone, and the angel had taken his place.

• • •

Jess watched the phone until it stopped ringing. Then she hung up.

She found the Daniels' home number on her computer and dialed it. After five rings, it went to voice mail. Jess hung up.

Why are you returning the call anyway? The message wasn't for you. It's between the two of them. Stay out of it, mind your own business.

But the tone in Mrs. Daniel's voice . . .?

Here we go again. You'll call back, you'll leave a message, and that message will ruin somebody's life. It'll leave them with a choice they can't possibly make. Maybe not life and death, but still. Maybe something worse, because they'll actually have to live with the results. Career and family. Right and wrong. Choices that, in the movies, separate the heroes from the villains. Choices that priests and professors and politicians make their livings telling other people how to make, but—judging by the papers and the evening news—they don't do too well with themselves. But maybe you have to be bad at making those choices to get by in their worlds. Maybe, in their worlds, our good choices are the bad ones, and our bad choices are good. After all, your brother made the right choice, as far as you can tell, but your father would never forgive him for it.

Better not to try to understand it. You'll go round and round, lose a lot of sleep, come up with the right thing to do, and it'll ruin everything. Again. Just leave it, Jess—leave it alone.

The morning sun plated the windows in Asher's office gold and silvered the harbor beyond. The smell of fresh coffee stretched around the corner from the kitchen, and somebody laughed at an e-mail they'd received overnight. Jess stared and listened and hoped for an answer as the Hingham ferry scratched the silver on its way to the wharf. In a few minutes it would cut back the other way, and in an hour or so, it would be back. Different people, different light, but always the same boat.

Kimberly Daniel's purse rattled onto the edge of Jess's desk.

"I'm so sorry to just barge in on you like that, Jess. I know you must have just loads of work to get done." Kimberly Daniel shook her head slowly and spoke to her purse, which lay on the table in front of her.

"Please don't worry about it, Mrs. Daniel." Jess looked around the café for people from the office, but saw no one she knew. It was past the morning rush now. One of the waitresses was writing the lunch specials on the blackboard in pastel chalk.

"I just didn't know what else to do. After I left that message this morning, I started to worry about who might be listening in, who might be hearing all my voice mails, who might be *deleting* all my voice mails, and I guess I just panicked. I just drove. God, I must be a sight." She sat up, pushed her hair back, took a deep breath and looked Jess in the eye for the first time since they'd come downstairs. "I'm sorry, Jess." Her smile matched her apology. "I'm just a mess."

The waitress brought their coffees. "When was the last time you had something to eat?" Jess asked Kimberly.

Kimberly sniffed sarcastically and Jess asked the waitress to brink them two chocolate croissants.

"Thank you, Jess."

Jess shrugged. "You never need to thank me for having a little extra chocolate."

Kimberly's smile cleared but not her eyes. She and Jess sipped their coffee in silence until the waitress brought their croissants.

"Jess, somebody's got the kids."

Jess had almost taken a bite. Instead she just stared.

"They didn't come home after school yesterday. I missed one call from Tyler early on, before I'd really started to worry, but he didn't leave a real message. There was just some rustling, like he'd dialed my number by accident. I called their cell phones and called their friends and called the neighbors we know, but nobody answered. Then around 10:30 last night somebody left an envelope—a plain, white envelope—on the front porch. No writing on it. Inside was this."

Kimberly pulled a sheet of plain white printer paper, folded twice like a letter, out of her purse. She handed it across the table to Jess, who took it like someone might take a pink slip.

Four lines were printed at the top of the page in an unremarkable font. The page had been printed on a LaserJet printer, black ink. It didn't look as though anyone had spent much time on it.

Your husband will know what to do.

When he does, your kids will come home.

Talk only with him.

No police.

Jess looked up at Kimberly, who was picking at her food with her fingers. Way to go, Jess. Wrong again. So wrong she wanted to disappear.

"I called Asher, but of course he didn't pick up. He was already on the plane, I guess. Or maybe he just wasn't answering."

Kimberly peeled back the layers of her croissant, nibbling a piece of chocolate now and then. Jess had long since finished hers, though she couldn't remember how it tasted. She cradled her lukewarm coffee mug in both hands and sipped in silence as she listened.

"I didn't know what to do. I couldn't just wait fourteen hours till he landed. I couldn't call the police. I couldn't really talk with the neighbors, because one of *them* would just call the police. Of course maybe that wouldn't have been such a bad thing. I just didn't know, Jess—I just don't know. Anyway, I *did* know I couldn't just sit around, so I got in the car and just drove—drove down to the school, drove over to the library, drove out to that Ihop where they meet their friends sometimes—just looking for some sign of them. It isn't a big town, you know—by one o'clock I'd been pretty much everywhere there is to go, and I'd found nothing. The school was empty—couldn't even find a janitor to ask if he'd seen them. None of the waitresses at the Ihop had seen them. Neither had the cashier at the gas station. I drove by all their friends' houses, but our car wasn't there. Finally I just started driving down every street in town, hoping to find the car parked somewhere, but I didn't find it— didn't find them."

"By the time the sun came up, I'd stopped at every all-night restaurant and every gas station for ten miles up and down 495, but nobody'd seen them. A few times I thought I had—you have no idea, Jess, how many old Hondas there are driving around out there in the middle of the night—but none of them were theirs. Anyway, I started thinking about when Asher might be landing, and it occurred to me that it could be any time. I didn't really know—didn't know what flight he was on, what hotel he was staying at—didn't know anything, really, except that he was flying to Dubai. So then I started worrying that he might not check his messages, that his cell phone might not work there for some reason, or that—well, Jess, after our last little chat, he might just not call me back for a while, period. So I turned around and headed here, figuring you'd be able to track him down. So—here we are!"

Kimberly's mouth and eyes belonged to a much younger girl, grasping for brave on the first day of school. Jess, not thinking, reached across the table and took her hands. They were cold and her grasp uncertain.

"Things haven't been great between us lately, Jess. I don't suppose you want to hear that, but then maybe you already know. When he called last night on the way to the airport, I kind of let him have it. I'm not saying he didn't deserve it, but—well, regardless, it's not going to make him anxious to talk with me for a while. I may have to deal with this on my own."

Jess's lungs squeezed and fought for air. She faked it.

"It's going to be fine." Jess squeezed Kimberly's hands as she pulled them away to search her purse for a tissue. "I'm going to help you." Jess glanced down as she said it, but it was out now. Just like before. There was no going back. Why did these things happen to her? What was wrong with her that people trusted her with information she wasn't able to handle? It made her angry, in fact. How dare they entrust her with something that could cost someone his life? She felt the blood rush to her face. This was where it ended. No more blowing like a leaf in the wind of these complicated men. Somebody should have helped me when I was a child, Jess thought. And now these children were mixed up in something. This time she wasn't going to sit idly by and do nothing.

"Jess, I just wasted fourteen hours driving around while my kids are Lord knows where. What on Earth was I thinking?" Tears damped the corners of Kimberly's eyes.

Jess watched as Kimberly tried to dry them. It was no good. "What else could you do?"

"Oh, I don't know." Kimberly blew her nose and looked for another tissue. "It's just—what kind of a mother am I? My kids have been kidnapped, and I'm just driving around!"

"I'm going to help you. I am." Jess's eyes dared the room to disagree. "Asher's on a plane—still is, for another couple of hours. But once he lands, I can track him down. I can. That's mostly what they pay me to do, you know." Jess braved a smile and hoped her humor wasn't lost in last night's riddles.

Kimberly dabbed at the corners of her eyes and braved a smile in return. "I should go. I should be home. Maybe they're home already—or maybe there's another note. Anyway, I need to go. Please just call me if you do get in touch with Asher. Do you have my cell number?"

Kimberly scribbled it on a napkin without waiting for an answer, then searched her purse for her keys. She looked up at Jess and took a deep breath.

"I'm sorry, Jess—I'm sorry to bother you with all this. It must be the last thing you need."

Jess smiled and met Kimberly's gaze. "It's going to be okay. I'm going to help you, Mrs. Daniel."

"Kimberly, Jess. My name is Kimberly."

"Kimberly. I'm going to help you, Kimberly."

Kimberly nodded and the two women stood. Kimberly hugged Jess, squeezing her once more, tighter, just as it seemed she was ready to leave. When she was gone, Jess sat down and stared at the phone number on the napkin, its corners smudged with chocolate and mascara.

• • •

Asher leaned against the back of the empty elevator. More long hours of searching, hardly eating or sleeping, and that was the last of the obvious places. There were hundreds of other possibilities, but he'd tried all of Ahmed's favorites—all the ones he knew about, anyway. Finding him anywhere else would just be luck.

He should have seen this coming, really—from that very first day, he should have seen it coming. Ahmed's cell phone had nagged and sulked as they sipped their drinks until finally he'd finished his off in one gulp and left to go find the Saudis, promising to meet Asher later in the lobby. Asher had ordered another rum and watched the silver piping on the turquoise horizon cool to scarlets and ambers on deep indigo blues as the sun slipped in for her evening bath. Into the first sea civilization ever saw, more than likely. The first sunsets watched by people with time to look up and witness something new: beauty and wonder and meaning. To dream—dream of things beyond scraping and scratching for their next meal, and even beyond themselves—of gods and spirits and heaven. Dreams of better days. The very dreams from which civilization was born.

Asher's own phone had come to life as the same sun sinking into the sea before him rose over the sea back home. The usual morning mess of ads and newsletters and requests for meetings from people he didn't know. People he didn't want to know. People who had no idea how he spent his time, or what he needed to get done, or why what he was trying to accomplish now was more important than what they wanted him to accomplish for them. They wanted him to change—to work their agendas rather than to work his own. And sometimes that would be the easiest thing in the world to do. Just go with the flow, listen to everybody else, do what they wanted you to do, accept their praise. But do that and you'd end up where they wanted you to. And no matter what they might say, they weren't picking that place with your best interests in mind.

Asher had eventually made his way to the lobby and sat there watching the people come and go. Every person with an agenda of his own, or dreams of her own, busily running toward it or away. Dreams like those first people's dreams—those dreams from which civilization was born, first dreamed looking out over the very same waters Asher had just watched change from purple to black. They were the dreams that urged people on, even after the invention of a status quo. They were the dreams feared only by the priests and the kings—those for whom the status quo seemed too good to let go.

Asher had sat there for longer than he supposed he should have, staring down the effects of alcohol and jet lag, until finally Ahmed had appeared. He was alone. He sat down across from Asher and smiled and said he'd spoken to the Saudis. He said they wouldn't be able to meet with them that evening but that they were still anxious to work a deal. They were flying back to Riyadh that night, but their representative was staying to finalize the details. The feed they wanted needed to include information from a few specific firms—Ahmed had written them down. He handed Asher a slip of paper torn from one of the hotel's notepads. Asher recognized the names. They weren't particularly well-known. Ahmed explained that they were people with whom the Saudis had long worked—people whom they trusted. Trust was a big deal to people in this part of the world. Ahmed smiled when he said it, but his eyes glanced around the room and looked, just for a moment, like they had that evening in the sputtering New York candlelight.

Trust in the people they knew. The desire to maintain the status quo—to continue to do business the way they'd always done. And so came the dawn of that subtlest tool of the rich and the powerful, conceived to make people fear the very things that made them human. To make them fear their neighbors, and even themselves. To make them fear change, to fear progress, and to make them slaves to those with the most to gain by keeping things the way they were.

The loftiest dreams of the human mind harnessed by the rich and mighty to enslave the very people who needed to dream them most.

All of this had begun here, looking out over this same sea that loomed black through the clear, tall elevator windows Asher leaned against now. The sea he knew was there, though he didn't bother to look around. It had been there that day, and it was still there today. Some things never changed. As much as you might want them to, some things were simply never going to change.

Jade and a blonde slipped into the elevator just as the doors were closing. The blonde assessed her competition. Jade ignored it.

"You go home so soon?" Her lips pouted, but her voice was young and hopeful.

Asher could see her back reflected in the polished doors as they closed. Her blouse didn't quite reach the waistline of her very skinny jeans. Her blouse was the same color as her eyes.

The blonde inspected her own figure in the doors, standing up straight in her heels and turning slightly from side to side as she gauged Asher's eyes.

Jade brushed an invisible something off Asher's chest. The flat of her stomach pressed into his. Her short, carefully unkempt hair smelled like incense.

"I go with you?"

Asher felt the whiskey and the hour and the distance. The elevator fell. He closed his eyes and felt the back of Julie's fingers against his cheek. His arms wrapped themselves around her and she laid her head on his shoulder.

When he opened his eyes again, he saw Kimberly's glaring reflection. Well, *that's* convenient, she said again. Don't even have time to come home first? Don't know when you'll be back? You know what, Ash—fine. Just go. Maybe it's for the best. Just go, have a nice time, do what you need to do. Just give me a call when you find whatever it is you're looking for. No rush, though. Seriously, Ash. Until you're finished with whatever it is you're doing, there is absolutely no need for you to call.

Asher closed his eyes tight and buried his face in Julie's hair.

He thought about Ahmed and cursed the left side of his brain. The side that no amount of booze or weed or distance or women had ever seemed able to shut up completely. The side of his brain that had brought him here in the first place, six months ago, and that had brought him back now, to this very same elevator. The side hungry for the win, the modern-day version of the big kill—the kill that would feed the tribe for a month, maybe more, and make him a hero. The side that had convinced him it was a good idea to set up a trial feed for Ahmed's Saudi friends—those friends whom he'd only met once, with whom lack of a common language had precluded even the most basic of conversations—and to do so under his own account, off the corporate radar, away from all the questions and delays. The same side that, back in those days that we like to call primitive but that really aren't as ancient as we'd like to believe, would have left the women and children at home and gone out on the big hunt alone. Too dangerous for them, and besides, they might talk or sneeze or gasp or snap a twig at the wrong time and blow the whole deal. No food for anybody then. Better to just go it alone—better for everybody.

The ends, after all, truly do justify the means. History shows us that over and over again. Think about the Commodore, for Christ's sake—that founding father of his own dear alma mater. The guy was a pirate, for all practical purposes. Okay, a pirate with a license, but still—his fortune started out as someone else's, and was taken by force on the high seas. But he used part of that dubious fortune to start a first-rate university, and now he's regarded as a minor saint and portrayed as nothing more dangerous than some juiced-up Keebler elf, running around the field at halftime and pumping his stuffed white biceps when the home team scores.

Just get the deal done, get the tribe dozing full and happy by the campfire, and nobody'll ask too many hard questions about how you pulled it off. Assuming, that is, you *do* get it done. Which requires, generally speaking, that the dealmaker hasn't stopped calling entirely.

The elevator stopped. Asher let go of Jade and tried to shake it all off. The blonde didn't move as their reflections disappeared with the opening doors. Asher said, "Excuse me," and sidestepped her into the lobby. Jade grasped his arm and followed into the ebb and flow of the crowds at the lobby.

They were stopped midstream by a bellman. "Mr. Daniel, sir?"

Jade half hid behind Asher, holding his arm close.

"Yes?"

The bellman smiled to have gotten the right man. "I have a message for you, sir. Will you please follow me?"

Asher eyed the man suspiciously. "Can't you give me the message here?"

The bellman looked around at the crowds and indicated a quieter corner with a slight bow. "If you please, sir."

Asher broke Jade's grip with a gentle pat on her hand and followed the bellman. She stood and watched them go, suddenly fragile among the echoes and laughter.

"I have a message from Mr. Yassin. You know Mr. Yassin?"

Asher nodded. The bellman smiled.

"Mr. Yassin is a good friend. Mr. Yassin called me about one hour ago and asked that I watch for you, sir. He asked me to tell you, Mr. Daniel, that someone is following you, sir."

Asher looked across the room. Jade looked down at the floor.

"It is not this—young lady, sir." The bellman smiled, his eyes conspiring. "Mr. Yassin said a European woman, blonde hair, was in the bar earlier last night, not long after you left. She had a small picture of you, and she showed it to Mr. Yassin. She told Mr. Yassin that she was to meet you. Mr. Yassin told her that he hadn't seen you."

Asher looked around for the blonde from the elevator, but he didn't see her. He didn't remember her even getting off the elevator.

"Did she believe him?"

"Mr. Yassin did not say, sir. He only said that I should watch for you and tell you."

A blonde woman in linen was walking toward the concierge desk, searching for something in her purse. A couple of blonde girls were laughing and teasing and weaving toward the elevator he'd just left. A blonde woman stood staring at her own thoughts beside a man talking with the receptionist. None of them seemed to notice him.

Asher fumbled in his pockets and gave the bellman fifty dirham. "Thank you very much," he said. "Please let Mr. Yassin know that you delivered the message."

"Yes, sir. Thank you, Mr. Daniel. I will tell Mr. Yassin that we spoke."

The bellman bowed and smiled and walked away. Asher watched him blend into the crowd, watched the crowd churn and surge, listened to its crescendos and sforzandos and trills. Jade was a thin, dark reed in the stream. She swayed and beckoned him back into the cool flood, away from the rocks and scavengers on the shore. Asher watched, transfixed by the cool green, by leaving terra firma behind and floating away downstream and out to sea. But he couldn't move. His feet, it seemed, were rooted firmly on the bank, right where the left side of his brain had ordered them planted years and years ago. Only his head—well, half of it, anyway—was free to watch and listen and breathe and dream that anything more was possible.

. . .

The Mass Pike was empty. Kimberly Daniel fled the brass glare of morning, chasing the shadow of her SUV through the belly of the city, under the Citgo sign, curving away from BU and then back, away from Cambridge and the Charles, through the toll gates and away, the buildings becoming houses and the houses disappearing in leafy green shadows.

She drove under the familiar hotel. When the kids were little, they'd always wanted to stay there. She hated the way it looked, glazed and unwashed, squatting over the Pike without even a piece of good solid ground to call its own. But the kids couldn't get enough of it. Maybe they'd dreamed of lying safe and warm in its beds while the cars and trucks and buses rushed right under them, feeling like they could reach their little hands down out of the covers and catch the oily spray, see the headlights scurrying under their beds. "Not tonight," had been her stock response when they were little. When they got older, she'd resorted to reason, trying to explain that it made no sense to stay in a hotel so close to home. But they'd never stopped asking. It became almost a family ritual, like the old responsive readings at church when she was a little girl. Words you had to say at the prescribed moments, words you didn't really understand or even try to understand, words that made you feel good—even as you squirmed in your seat thinking of T-shirts and shorts and Grandma's for dinner and swimming in the afternoon—just by the sound of them uttered at the same, familiar times by the same, familiar people. Words that kept the sun coming up every morning, held the moon and the stars to their well-worn paths every night.

Words, words, words.

Kimberly glanced up as the hotel restaurant's windows flashed overhead. She imagined them staring out, still little, hands framing faces pressed flat and laughing to see her go by. But she couldn't see them, couldn't see anybody. Just the morning sun reflecting orange in the dirty-brown glass.

Asher probably would've let them stay there, if he'd ever heard them ask. She couldn't remember a single time they'd asked when they'd all driven under it together. Funny how kids divide up their lives. She remembered a boy she'd known in grade school. His dad was from Spain, and his mother was Swedish. He'd speak English like all the other kids on the playground, but when he got mad,then he'd start yelling in Spanish. One time she'd gone to his house to play after school, but when they went into the kitchen to ask his mother for something to eat, he'd started speaking Swedish,even to Kimberly. Each part of his life had its own language—one for play, one for anger, one for everyday necessities. She didn't remember thinking it was strange back then—only later, when she got older. He'd moved away by then. Kimberly wondered if he'd ever outgrown it.

What language do you suppose he'd dream in?

No, he didn't outgrow it—none of us outgrow it. We all have different languages for the different parts of our lives. You talk with your friends from home differently than you talk with your friends up here. Asher—remember that time you and Asher went to visit his best friend from back home, the guy he'd grown up with ever since the two of them were in the first grade? They hadn't even talked in complete sentences—just little phrases, meaningless phrases, but those phrases had made the two of them laugh hysterically. You and his wife had tried to keep up and laugh along, but it was hopeless—the two of them had learned this language as children and nobody from any other place or time could possibly understand it. You probably couldn't even learn it, even if you'd tried, because a single word stood for a whole chapter in a story even Asher couldn't remember completely.

The conversation at the company Christmas party was the same—a little more comprehensible, maybe, but only enough to lead you on. There were words that sounded familiar but, given the reactions they produced, clearly meant something else to native speakers. Which made it very difficult to be part of the conversation—almost more difficult than with the little boy in his kitchen speaking Swedish. At least there you didn't even *think* you could join in. At the Christmas party, you had a few drinks and laughed at a few jokes and started to think you knew what was going on. You let your guard down. And then you said something and noticed a curled lip or a darkening eye or a knowing glance or a misplaced smile. The walls started to rise. Suddenly there was "me" and "them," where a moment before there was only "us." And the strange thing was, the natives didn't seem to notice. They went on laughing and talking and giving you the occasional wink or friendly hug, treating you like nothing had happened. But you could tell. There were a lot of rooms in the house, and you weren't in theirs. The walls might be glass, but they were still walls. You could smile and wave and generally get by day-to-day, but when you reached out to touch a hand, or to kiss a cheek, there was always that cold, hard, invisible space that you just couldn't quite break through.

And when those glass walls start growing in your own house? You don't even see them coming—not at first, anyway. Not until that day when you need his arms around you, need him to whisper strong and low that everything will be okay, and you go running toward him only to be knocked flat by something between you that you never knew was there. Sometimes, maybe, if the walls are still new, you can break them down that way. But usually they form slowly but surely in the corners you never, ever visit, and by the time you feel them it's too late—they've taken root and that's it, you're stuck on your side and he's stuck on his. It's only then you realize that you knew it was happening all along.

Another tollbooth and she was free. Kimberly stepped on the gas and felt the big engine surge, pushing her back into the soft leather. She let her head fall back against the headrest and the gears whined in quiet succession as she sped away to the west. Leave the city behind, and the coming day, and Asher and his whole world. Or worlds—how many did he live in, anyway? How many were there she didn't even know about? Were her kids in one of them? Were they back there, back where she was running from? Kimberly felt her eyes swell and realized she had no idea. Absolutely no idea. But there was no way to turn around, not for several miles, anyway. And for that, at least, somewhere deep down, she was thankful.

• • •

Jess laid the napkin on the desk in front of her. The phone sulked in the corner, its red light dimmed by the brightening skies. She picked up the receiver and pressed the buttons. No hesitation this time. She stared at the napkin as she listened to the message.

It was a different voice this time. Still a man's voice, but softer this time. Gentler, but not necessarily friendly. "I regret that the matter has become so urgent. I'm sure you'll agree that it's critical we meet at your earliest possible convenience." Different address, different phone number, different attitude. Not a trace of anger this time, not a trace of the spurned lover. This voice had time to spare. Jess thought back to the note on the café table. *Your husband will know what to do.* This voice knew it had the upper hand. This voice lazed in the easy grace of conceit.

Jess wondered whether decisions were this easy for most people every day. Kimberly Daniel still stared at her from across the table, nose red, eyes damp and smudged, voice wrung out and wandering. She worried through all the dusty corners, leaving Jess only the bright spaces to work with. Without hesitation, Jess switched lines and dialed Asher's cell phone. How did the electrons or photons or whatever it was you could hear find exactly the right cell phone so quickly without even a hint about where it was? No hesitation in those clicks and buzzes, skipping through outer space and splashing along the bottom of the sea and skimming across waves in thin air. No looking back. Jessica toyed with the napkin as she waited. It was harder now to tell the chocolate from the mascara, but the navy blue ink of Kimberly's name and number had soaked deep into the middle of the white paper cloth and dried.

The phone on the other end of the line began that unfamiliar double ring that let Jess know she'd landed in another country. After five rings, Asher's recorded voice answered, telling her he wasn't available and that she should leave a message.

"Asher, it's Jess. Please call me as soon as you get this message. It's important."

Jess hung up the phone and sat for a moment staring at the napkin. She tried to think of what else she had to do, but her mind wouldn't have it. There was only one thing she had to do, one thing she really *had* to do. She picked up the receiver and dialed again.

Voice mail again. She hung up.

Redial. Voice mail. Hang up.

Again.

Again.

Again.

Jess wondered at some point why she didn't feel like she was wasting time, but she most definitely didn't. She couldn't remember ever being so certain she was doing the right thing. Not even on that day she'd talked with her brother.

"Hello?" Asher's voice, live this time. Jess could hear the rumble of voices and large spaces in the background. Someone laughed deep and hard and began to speak in a foreign language that drifted off into the spaces. Asher's breathing seemed heavier than usual. "Hello?"

"Asher—oh, good—I'm so glad you answered. It's Jess. Are you someplace you can talk?"

"Sure, I can talk. What's up, Jess? You don't sound quite yourself."

"Never mind about me, Asher. I need to talk with you about something important. And then you need to talk with your wife."

. . .

Eva stood in the descending elevator, willing it to fall faster. If Phaethon's drinking buddy was really anything more than that, he was a very good actor. If you lose him, Eva, you're going to have a lot of things to explain when you get back to Washington. Or Berlin. If you lose him, you probably won't be going back to Washington anytime soon.

And if you lose him, people really will start to talk about you and Andreas.

Put that out of your head, Eva. Don't waste time solving problems you don't have. Stay focused.

Andreas really did go out on a limb for you, though, giving you this assignment. Max and Rolf and Anja and Marion—any one of them has more experience with this sort of thing. I mean, not much more than a year ago you were basically just a proposal writer. Everybody thinks Andreas is just playing favorites. If you pull it off, he can say he saw promise in you and nobody can complain too loudly. But if you don't succeed—well, that's simply not an option. You *will* succeed. You *will* prove to everyone that you deserve everything you've gotten. You'll prove it to the office. You'll prove it to Andreas. You'll prove it to Dad. If Mom were still alive, maybe you'd even prove it to her.

And what will you do with yourself then, Eva, once you've become everything everyone's ever wanted you to be?

The sea outside swallowed the light from the city and the moon and glowed smugly beyond their reach. A cruise ship sparkled away into the Gulf and she thought of all the time she and Kai had sworn they'd never, ever want to spend their vacation stuck in a floating hotel with people whose idea of a good time couldn't push beyond food and drink and moving as little as possible. How could you say you'd seen a place if you hadn't even had to unpack? How could you say you'd experienced something new if the familiar was never more than a cab ride away? How could you really know something without leaving it behind?

Falling alone through the dark in a gilded glass cage, though, made those sparkling lights look like a secret, guilty pleasure, a floating *schuetzenfest* under a full summer moon where everyone's a neighbor and the unexpected is, by tradition, denied entrance.

Her crystal ball neared the earth and slowed to a gentle stop. Outside, palms swayed over the beach chairs and the pool bar. Inside, the doors slid open to the assembled masses. All eyes were on Eva.

Eva left the elevator and surveyed the lobby. Men and women from every corner of the globe were there to witness her performance. A group of older, well-dressed Europeans sat at a table and sipped coffee from tiny cups, more interested in themselves than in their setting. A skinny black girl wearing jade green contact lenses hurried toward the elevator with the air of someone late for work. Two men in radiant white robes confided hand in hand, nodding solemnly, walking aimlessly. A bellboy near the entrance seemed to smile straight at her. She felt her shoulders rise and her stomach tighten and her ears began to ring. *I've lost him. I've lost my chance. But it's not my fault. How could they trust me with such a task in . . .*

There he was.

Phaethon stood alone, away from the crowd, in a corner of the lobby. He looked up from his cell phone and stared directly at her. She started in his direction before she remembered she shouldn't. But by then it was no use. Both her wave and his were half-hearted afterthoughts, the gestures of children from behind the legs of their parents. His eyes were hollow, and the void drew her in.

"Hello," she said, intending to sound more cheerful.

"Hello," he muttered, and looked back down at his phone. "They have my kids. Somebody's taken my kids."

eight

Sarah Anderson lingered along the far side of the foyer, away from the big double doors, watching the crowd drain away into the ballroom. A few last-minute drinkers held tight to the bars against the ebbing tide—one last pull before the long dry spell ahead. Sarah considered her deep red shoes. She wasn't meant to have heard.

Bill Morton stood across from her, next to the ballroom doors, fingering his cufflinks. Still a good-looking man—tall, trim, plenty of silver waves combed back from a face tanned by years of Saturday morning tee times. He was looking for something, or someone. Only one person likely to be his target. Everyone who was anyone was already inside. So we have something in common, Bill—waiting for the one man who doesn't seem to know.

Al Green couldn't have been clearer. Standing there with the Colonel in the middle of the room, his head bowed in prayer over the amber holy water, muttering more loudly than discretion would advise but as quietly as the festivities would permit. The smile of a roast pig—only the apple was missing from his mouth. So intent on the bourbon and the intrigue that he hadn't even looked up on her first pass by. But she hadn't paused long enough to give him a fighting chance. Just slowed a bit and listened on her way to the nearest bar.

"Just you watch—by this time tomorrow you're gonna see just what Ariadne can do. And you and me both know just how fast ever'body's 'moral objections' disappear when something *this* sexy shows up."

She'd ordered a Chardonnay and tried to look like she hadn't heard, scanning the crowd in search of somebody else. Al Green and the Colonel were still there, still contemplating the drinks obscuring their navels, still oblivious to the crowd milling around them. Sarah had chosen her route carefully this time, first tacking left through the crowd in order to double back on them from behind, drink in hand, ready for a longer stakeout.

The Colonel had looked as serious as ever when she got back into position, but Al Green had been laughing hard and poking him in the ribs. The dew from his glass had darkened the blue wool beneath the Colonel's medals. ". . . design the world's perfect pussy, but wouldn't even wanna try it out. No, no, don't you worry 'bout him—he will *not* be an issue, I *personally* guarantee that. And as for old Daniel—well, let's just say I don't expect he's gonna wanna stay in the game after this next hand. Stakes'll get a little rich for his blood, I expect. So we'll have the table all to ourselves."

The Colonel had nodded, still serious, fretting a bit—Sarah could see the little glances he didn't want Al Green to notice—over the stains on his immaculate jacket. "Good, Al, that's good. You know how the General's been pressuring us on the civilian feeds. 'More intel at home, more boots on the ground'—that's what he's pushing for, every single day. And one thing you can say for the man—there is *nothing* that can stand in his way."

"Well, hell—you and me *both* know that! Seen that back in '91. And Colonel, we're gonna see that again. Hey now—what say we get ourselves a refill and have a little toast to that!"

Al Green had clapped the Colonel on the back and pushed him off toward the bar. As he followed he'd looked around and caught Sarah straight in the eye.

Did he know she'd heard? He couldn't be sure. But did he suspect it? Of course he did. Al Green suspected everyone. And besides, she'd been staring right at him.

Sarah watched Bill Morton methodically pan the room. How much did he know? No way to be sure. Bill Morton was a survivor. He didn't have the brains of Jabe Evans or Roy Daniel. He didn't have the connections of Al Green. What Bill Morton knew was how to play the game. Sarah was convinced that he knew far more than he'd ever admit. Far more than that kind-of-goofy, loveable, crotchety-old-man persona would ever let on. Bill Morton had perfected the art of playing the 'yes man.' He'd made a career of getting ahead by giving in. The opossum of the corporate world. Not the most glamorous way of winning the game, but still—glamor could be overrated. Real life didn't often read like a fairy tale. The rare and the beautiful lost with sad regularity. Opossums outnumbered unicorns by a wide margin. Princes, charming or not, were in short supply.

When had Bill Morton's gaze landed on her? Sarah stared, willing him away—him and all of the other characters on the stage. He seemed ready to cross, but unable. Sarah held his gaze until the lights dimmed again and the last of the stragglers hurried away into the ballroom. Her cell phone rang. Even as she answered, she kept her eyes locked with his. If she didn't, he might come closer. He might say something. He might tell her more secrets that she didn't want to know, hint at more trouble that she couldn't possibly avoid.

"Hello, Roy."

"Hello, Sarah. Are you still at the reception?"

"Right where you asked me to be, Roy. Where else would I be?"

"Oh, I can think of a few excellent alternatives."

"Can you, now?"

"Yes, ma'am. More than a few."

"Is this an invitation, Mr. Daniel?"

Roy laughed, the dark humor of a cautious man. "Sarah, you have no idea."

"Try me."

"Well, now that you mention it, I believe I will. But I'm warning you up front, Sarah, this isn't what you think it is."

"Oh? And how do you know what I think it is?"

"Well, I guess I don't, not for sure. But I think it's a pretty safe bet."

"Well—do you want to play twenty questions?"

"We need to meet, Sarah. There are a few things I think we should talk through, face-to-face. Anything happen at the reception I should know about?"

"Yes. I think so." Bill Morton was still there, watching her across the foyer.

"Okay. How quickly can you be at—"

Sarah thought they'd been cut off, the silence on the other end was suddenly so complete.

"Roy? Are you still there?"

"Sarah, remember that time I met . . . well, you remember, you made reservations, but that flight got canceled so you had to rebook someplace else? You remember that?"

Sarah frowned. "Are you talking about—"

Roy cut her off. "I'm sure you remember, Sarah. Took some doing, but ended up being better than the first place."

"Okay." Skepticism modulated Sarah's "kay" up an octave. "I *think* I remember. It was—"

"Just meet me there, Sarah. The second place, where you rebooked us."

Sarah looked around as if the place were hiding somewhere there in the foyer. "And if I've got it wrong? You mean—"

"You don't have it wrong, Sarah." Roy's voice like her mother's before a ballet recital, velvety low and reassuring. "You remember just fine. I'll meet you there in about forty-five minutes."

"Roy, I—"

Roy was gone.

Sarah looked around the foyer, half expecting to see Roy there, phone still to his ear, smiling at her reaction. Then she hurried off in the direction of the lobby, leaving Bill Morton standing there alone, suddenly unsteady without the force of her stare, nodding about something both funny and sad.

. . .

Brake lights turned the George Washington Memorial Parkway into a sluggish, red-scaled serpent burrowing into the capital's midsection. Lava from a ruptured Pentagon, cooling in a ruby-cobbled coil over the weary Potomac. Horns bleated, taxis butted and cut, giving up twelve feet left or right of where they'd idled before. Sirens up ahead, sapphires flashing at the head of the coil—must be an accident. Somebody's evening ruined at best, over at worst. But the indifferent serpent pushed blindly forward, the least common denominator of the plans, hopes, dreams and fears of a few hundred drivers.

Somebody turned up that three-note, back-and-forth hip-hop riff that had been on the radio since last summer. Fifth, minor sixth, minor sixth, fifth, repeat, ad nauseum, with a little out-of-tune penny-whistle thing that apparently served as a chorus. Roy Daniel listened, tapping his steering wheel in spite of himself. Was that Michael Jackson? Not unless he's had a shot or two of testosterone. Who knows. The background singers sound like a bunch of NFL linemen recorded mid-sack—not exactly Michael's sort of boys. Roy switched on the radio to his usual jazz station, but switched it off again as the two genres ducked and punched through his eardrums. Better one song you don't particularly like than two you can't even hear.

Soon enough, Roy Daniel stopped noticing the music altogether. The day's implications, hints, and possibilities kept any one thing from holding his attention for very long. He'd spent the whole day poring through the Ariadne report's backup files. There really was a pattern there—a pattern that could lead to a person, a person that could become a result. A real-life, tangible benefit—one less bad guy—brought to you courtesy of Ariadne.

The question was, did anyone else know about it? Pete had been with the clients all day. They were presumably just learning about it for the first time, and so wouldn't have had time to do anything yet. And nobody within CASTOR had seen the report—Pete always made sure it never went anywhere until Roy had reviewed it. Always had, anyway.

But what had Sarah seen at the reception? Was it evidence, or just coincidence? A pattern, or a fluke? Science, or science fiction?

Most of all, Roy Daniel wanted to sit somewhere quiet with a clean pad of paper and a good, sharp pencil and just think, sketch, and draw the connections, separating the things he knew from those he just suspected. At some point, he really needed to put in an appearance at the Pollux dinner—he checked in the rearview mirror to make sure he'd remembered to put on his tux—but something deep inside kept telling him there wasn't time.

Make time, Roy, said the voices of experience and reason that weighed down the other side of his head. Get the data. There's no way you can make good decisions with what you've got now. If you do, it'll just be luck—and you need a little firmer footing than luck at the moment. This is big—maybe even bigger than you realize. You owe it the most careful consideration and the very best planning that you can give it.

But you realize, of course, that it could all be over before you even get to "careful consideration. . . ."

One thing Roy did know: For Pete, the pattern *was* the goal. Pete's next step would be to make sure the next pattern showed up even clearer, even faster—not to follow this first pattern to its logical conclusion. Pete loved the hunt, not the meal at the end. He loved the elegant tool, not the beautiful object the tool could help him create. And so that was the focus of his report. But if you asked, he could help you use that tool better that anyone else around. He could help you get the meal on the table in minutes instead of hours. Hours instead of days. Days instead of months.

The sooner he could talk with Pete, the better. Roy Daniel dialed Pete's number for the third time in the past hour. Voice mail—again. Roy hung up and took a deep breath. Until he could talk with Pete, he really was stuck. The sooner the clients let Pete out of that windowless conference room Roy knew so well, the sooner he could start doing something useful.

The cars in front of Roy's inched forward. He glanced at the clock on the dash—he was going to be late. Maybe I should call Sarah back? She'll be late, too—stuck in the same traffic. Better to wait, leave as few traces as possible—just in case. Too many variables in the equation already—let's keep new ones to a minimum.

The back-and-forth riff was still going, but farther away now and lower as Roy's car moved slowly forward. Nowhere to get off here, anyway— just stay the course, as George, Sr. used to say. Roy smiled a little and looked out past the Washington Monument. A thousand points of light out there waiting to give you all the answers. But first you've got to get off this goddamned bridge.

Roy Daniel hit the DIAL button on his phone and listened as Pete Vasilescu's recorded voice said "hi" to him for a fourth time. He hung up. Then he did it again. Same result. Einstein's definition of insanity: doing the same thing and expecting a different result. Oh, well. Einstein was never stuck in traffic, and never had a cell phone. If he had, I'd bet good money he would have acted just as insane as the rest of us.

The sapphire flashers moved up ahead. Roy Daniel hit the DIAL button again. An ambulance's siren danced with the back-and-forth riff off in the distance. Penny-whistle chorus. That's all she wrote.

. . .

"Pete, it's Roy."

Pete Vasilescu tried to avoid the headlights from Route 3 coming in from his right and the taillights from I-97 approaching on his left as he adjusted the earpiece to hear his old friend better.

"Is this a good time to talk?"

"Sure, Roy, sure." The semi was going to merge in front of him whether he liked it or not, so Pete slowed. Someone behind him honked. "I was just going home. What can I do for you?"

"Everything go okay today?"

"You mean the meeting? Sure, sure—everything went fine, I think. As good as could be expected. Why? Did you hear something different?"

"No, no, just curious. Everybody's anxious to see some progress, that's all. Nothing new."

Pete signaled to change lanes, but the I-97 traffic was moving faster and had no intention of helping him out. "Sure, sure. You know nobody's more anxious than me, Roy. But if you had been at the meeting, you would have seen that that literally seems to be the case—*nobody* is more anxious to see progress than me. Nobody—except maybe you."

"Nobody said anything about the delays?"

"No—nobody. The NSA guys seemed totally fine. Honestly, I'm not sure they understand what we're doing, or how big it could be for them. Either that or they just don't believe we can do it. They just kind of sat and listened." Pete saw a break coming up in the traffic to his left and started to get ready to make a break for it. No blinkers, though—blinkers just give away your plans.

"Maybe they just don't want to look too eager in front of the TSWG guys. Don't want to get hit up for more funding."

"Maybe." The gap was there and Pete signaled and made his move. The guy behind him had the same idea and let loose with another blast of his horn. Pete sped up as fast as he could, but the guy stayed right on his tail, still honking.

"Listen, Pete. I saw something in your report that got my attention. It looks like you may have found somebody, Pete—somebody real. You didn't focus much attention on it—it was in the section about your self-organizing neural network modules—but Pete . . . Pete? You still there, Pete?"

"Sure, Roy—sorry. A lot of traffic. What—uh, I'm sorry, Roy. You mentioned the TSWG guys, right? Well, you know them. They don't ever care about finishing anything, as long as their funding keeps coming in. And they didn't seem to be feeling any pressure. The funding's in, the mod's done, everything's good—that seemed to be their opinion."

"Huh. Odd. But that's not really what I was calling about, Pete. I wanted to talk about the results you described in your latest report."

Pete was just past the semi when the car behind him started flashing its lights and serving back and forth. "Okay, okay," he muttered, signaling to pull over in front of the semi. "Where do you think you're going to go, anyway?"

"What was that, Pete?"

"Sorry, Roy—I was just talking to myself. There's some crazy guy behind me, I just need to get out of his way."

"Ah—okay, no problem. Do you want to talk a little later?"

"No, no—that's okay. Just a second. There's something I wanted to ask you about, too. Something that bothered me. I didn't think this was part of your idea. They mentioned something about opening up civilian feeds . . . Hang on, Roy." Pete changed lanes, and the car behind him downshifted and roared alongside. The driver was watching to make absolutely sure Pete saw his hyperextended middle finger.

Pete wasn't sure whether he really saw the car in front of the crazy man brake, but suddenly crazy man swerved into Pete's lane, tires screeching. Pete instinctively braked, too, and swerved to the right. The car in that lane, shadowed by the semi, didn't see Pete coming until it was too late, and the semi couldn't brake fast enough to avoid the broadside.

All of which, of course, Roy Daniel didn't learn until later. All he heard was a word he'd never known Pete Vasilescu say, followed by noises he wished he'd never heard.

• • •

The couple at the bar had no more to say. Glass empty, she checked her cell phone. He ignored the check. The bartender sliced a lime and pretended not to notice.

To the couple's right, at the farthest end of the bar, three women, still dressed for the office, agreed, loudly and simultaneously, with the incantations of the one swaying in the middle. Six eyes blurred over neon martinis as Roy Daniel, still in his tuxedo, took a seat at the other end. He ordered bourbon out of habit and nodded out of politeness. One of the women said, "Good evening, Mr. Bond"—quietly, she thought—and they all laughed and clinked. Roy took his cell phone out of his jacket pocket and checked for messages, hoping to avoid further engagement.

He had already tried the police station in Annapolis, but the woman manning the phones hadn't heard of an accident. Roy tried to trace in his mind the route between NSA headquarters and Pete's home, but realized he had no idea which way Pete would normally take, or which towns, exactly, lay between Fort Meade and Chesapeake Bay. He put the phone down on the bar. Where to begin? Outside on the sidewalk, a young couple tumbled by, girl tucked beneath boy's arm. Soft, happy notes drifted through the open windows, turning heads and silencing spirits at the other end of the bar. The bartender smiled and polished a glass. The couple at the bar gave up and left. Roy swirled the ice in his drink as the sweet music faded down the street.

Behind him, the door opened. The cadence of her heels on the hardwood floor and the glare of the martini chorus let him know she'd arrived.

"You did remember the place."

"Of course I remembered."

"What a girl."

Sarah Anderson ordered Chardonnay. Roy Daniel asked for a refill and pulled a pen out of his jacket pocket.

"Pete Vasilescu's been in an accident." He began to sketch on a dry corner of his cocktail napkin.

Sarah Anderson stopped rummaging through her purse and stared.

"I was on the phone with him when it happened. Just a few minutes ago. I'd been trying to reach him for a couple of hours, and finally got through just after I parked the car. Heard the whole thing standing on the curb out there. Don't even know where he was, exactly."

Sarah looked back in her purse and pulled out her cell phone. She dialed a few numbers and waited. The bartender brought their drinks.

"I already tried the Annapolis police. They didn't know anything. That's as far as I got before you arrived."

Roy Daniel kept sketching as Sarah talked to someone else. Her voice, sweet and efficient, lulled him off into an easy state of shock.

After a while, he noticed her hand soft on his neck and her whisper warm in his ear.

"Roy? Roy, can you hear me?"

The face of Pete Vasilescu stared up at him from the cocktail napkin. The chorus cackled at the other end of the bar. Sarah's lips brushed across his cheek.

"Roy." Her voice sang far away, there just below his ear. "You need to come back, Roy."

Roy Daniel didn't commit. "Did you learn anything?"

"Not really. Do you want to hear?"

He nodded, eyes still on the face he'd drawn from memory.

"Well, the Maryland highway patrol reported an accident at the intersection of I-97 and Route 3 less than 30 minutes ago. They weren't giving any details. I called a couple of hospitals in the area, but they couldn't confirm they'd received any of the victims. Honestly, the ambulances are probably still at the scene."

Roy Daniel nodded again and reached for a new napkin. "We should go up there."

"Yes. We should." Roy's first strokes were quick, punitive. Sarah took a tiny spiral notebook out of her purse and flipped through in search of her list. "There's a lot of things we should do."

Roy sat up suddenly, banishing his sketches to the back of the bar. He finished off his whiskey in a single pull and, with a quick glance and half nod at the bartender, ordered another. He sat up straight on his stool and looked around, agitation shifting in his eyes. "I need some paper. Could I have a sheet out of your notebook?"

Sarah tore out two and laid them on the bar in front of him.

"Too many loose ends. Nothing holds together. Time to get organized. Time to make a plan."

Sarah watched as Roy wrote a "1" at the top of the first sheet of paper. Next to it he wrote "Pete."

"Got to figure out what happened to Pete. Whether he's okay. That's priority number one."

The bartender set Roy's drink down in front of him. Sarah quietly put her own list back in her purse. Roy didn't notice.

"Priority number two: Ariadne. What's going on with Ariadne? From what I've learned today, I know the program's already producing actionable data. Do others know that? Are they already acting on it?" Roy ticked off these points below "Ariadne" on his list, then noticed the ice melting in his new drink and hurried to save it.

"Number three: Ariadne again. I guess two is what other people are doing, and number three is what *we're* doing. Did you get in touch with Andreas earlier?"

"Yes, I did. Got a reply back to my e-mail just before I left for the party. Good news. He said he's already on it. He has somebody in Dubai right now, making sure 'Phaethon' isn't late for his meeting."

"Who's 'Phaethon?'"

"He didn't say. The way he said it, I assumed you'd know."

Roy shook his head. "I have no idea."

He tapped his pen on the bar, took another long drink, forgave the cocktail napkins he'd abandoned on the bar and went back to his previous doodling. A hand emerged, delicate in black and white, holding a wine glass. The glass appeared to be empty. Maybe it just wasn't finished.

Sarah watched Roy's jaw work slow circles beneath his puzzling eyes. The lines in his forehead broadened and creased. She retrieved her notebook from her purse and turned back to the page with her list.

"Okay. So, leave number one to me. I'll keep trying the hospitals and police stations and I'll let you know as soon as I have anything certain. Try not to worry about that one. I'll take care of it."

The chorus at the end of the bar laughed for the first time in a long while and Sarah looked up. The bartender was leaning in close as if to tell them all a secret. They laughed again, one pounding on the bar. The eyes of the closest woman blurred and closed. Sarah thought she could see a tear on her cheek, even though she was smiling.

Roy didn't appear to notice. Shadows stretched across the hand on the napkin. Nails emerged from the fingertips.

"As for numbers two and three," Sarah went on, "it sounds like maybe you ought to talk with Andreas. The sooner the better, probably. I know his number's in your cell phone. You could call him from here, if you wanted to."

Roy nodded just enough for Sarah to know the idea had registered.

"Then there's one more point: Al Green. I overheard a little bit of the conversation he was having with the Colonel at the reception this evening. They were talking about Ariadne. And I think Al knows I heard them."

Roy looked up. "What did he say?"

"He said something about you, Roy. He said you weren't going to want to 'stay in the game after this next hand'—something like that. Something about the stakes getting too high. And with you out, they'd have the table all to themselves."

"Did the Colonel say anything?"

"He seemed pleased. He thought the General would be pleased. He said the General had been pressuring him a lot about the 'civilian feeds.'"

Roy glanced at the face on the other cocktail napkin still lying beside him on the bar. "He said that? 'Civilian feeds?'"

Sarah nodded and pushed back a strawberry-blonde lock that had escaped her French curl.

"And what did Al have to say about that?"

"Oh, you know Al. Just the usual stuff about perfect pussies and nobody but them knowing what to do with them. Nothing new." She took a sip of wine and glanced toward the other end of the bar. "Nothing we all haven't heard a thousand times before."

Roy Daniel added a "4" to his list. Next to it he wrote "Al Green—Civilian Feeds."

Sarah Anderson watched as he wrote. "If you want my opinion, I'd say just leave that one alone. You know how Al is—always trying to make it look like he knows everything and everybody. Always wanting you to think he's one step ahead. I'd say just talk with Andreas, make your plans, and go. Let me know if you need me to make any arrangements. But just leave Al alone. I'll talk with him, if it'll make you feel better. But he'll just be a distraction. That's what I think, anyway."

"Pete mentioned 'civilian feeds,' too. Said the customer brought them up this afternoon. He was about to say more, I think. It was just about the last thing he said."

The bartender appeared and asked Sarah if she'd like another glass of Chardonnay. She shook her head and they both watched Roy, his glass nearly empty, his drawing nearly done. Sarah looked up at the bartender with a shake of the head imperceptible to a less experienced man. One of the women from the other side wobbled by on her way to the ladies' room.

"Roy, let's go," Sarah whispered into his ear. "You need to at least make an appearance at the party. People will talk." The gray stubble on his cheek pressed against her lips.

Roy Daniel put down his pen and held up his sketch to critique. "The fingers are too short," he said almost under his breath. "The pinky's too fat."

"Don't be mean." Sarah kissed his temple, felt the muscles strain and release. "It's just the way I am."

Roy looked at Sarah for the first time in the past half hour. "You're perfect," he said, and she looked at the floor and smiled. "Have I told you that lately? Absolutely perfect."

Sarah took his hand in both of hers and held it in her lap. "Let's go," she said. They both stood up. Roy left too much cash on the bar.

Returning from the ladies' room, the woman from the other side noticed the abandoned napkins and the hand and the cash. She closed her eyes and began to cry all over again.

• • •

"Andreas. This is Roy Daniel."

Traffic was thinning on Constitution Avenue. Roy fumbled with his headpiece—this is supposed to be safer than just holding the damned thing?—and turned west off of 14th Street. He checked his rearview mirror to make sure Sarah Anderson was still behind him.

"Roy—hello! You are well, I hope?"

The flags surrounding the Washington Monument shrugged off the failing breeze. Daniel noticed that the SAMs were gone. Finally. He hadn't been against them, but still, one of these days, a picture of them with the monument and the flags in the background was going to show up on the Internet, with some smart caption. "Liberty and Justice for All." Better to have them tucked away on top of the office buildings nearby, where at least the tourists didn't have to look at them.

"Yes, yes, I'm fine, Andreas, just fine. Look, I'm really sorry to call so late. Do you have a few minutes to talk?"

"Sure, Roy, sure—no problem. Anyway, I wasn't asleep. What can I do for you?"

"Well listen, Andreas. I understand from Sarah that you're doing some work for us right now over in Dubai."

"Yes, that's right."

"Well good—that's great. And it's going well, I assume?"

"I believe so, yes. I know that last night my colleague arrived with the target in Dubai. I expect another report in the morning, but I'm certain everything is proceeding as planned. Otherwise, I would already have heard something."

Roy glanced in his rearview mirror again. Sarah was still there, following wherever he led.

"I'm sure you would have, Andreas—I'm sure you would have. So good—I'm glad everything's going well. But listen now, Andreas, I was doing a little research today, and I learned some things that make me think this whole thing might just be bigger than any of us had thought before. Bigger implications, anyway. So I need to get up to speed on what you've learned since . . . how long have you been working on this, Andreas?"

"A couple of weeks, Roy. When your people called and said they had someone under surveillance and asked us to send someone there for briefings—that was the first time we heard about it."

"Sure, okay. So since then—anything you've learned that we ought to know about?"

Off to the left, through the trees, Lincoln sat in his great white cabin, forever contemplating his legacy. What might have been. That "great task remaining."

Still nothing on the line.

"Andreas? Are you still there, Andreas?"

"I'm sorry, Roy. Yes, I'm still here. I'm just not sure . . . Roy, do you really want to talk about this now? In this way?"

Old Honest Abe had had a great view of the SAMs, too. Must've been curious about what that was all about. Still wondering whether government of the people, by the people, for the people, shall not perish from the earth. Still, after all this time, all those boys lost. Some things never change.

"I'm sorry, Roy—did you say something?"

"Sorry, Andreas—no, I was just thinking. So I guess you think it's pretty sensitive, then?"

"Yes. I think so."

"Okay. I can understand that. So let me ask you this: Given that I think this all might be more important than we thought a couple of weeks ago, do you think maybe we ought to catch up, trade notes, make sure we're all on the same page?"

"Yes." The low beginning, the drawn-out vowel, the upturned ending of the contemplative German. "Yes, I think so. But you know, Roy, we don't have so much time."

Roy checked instinctively to make sure that Sarah was still with him as he negotiated the S-curve onto the bridge. "I'm not sure I follow you, Andreas. Are you talking about the 'meeting' Sarah told me about?"

"Yes, that is what I'm talking about."

"Do you think I should fly out tomorrow?"

A pause. "I *think*. . . ." Andreas let the word hang like an off-hour church bell.

Roy glanced at the clock on his dashboard. Eight ten. Not much time for the party. No time to stop at home. But he just might make it.

"I understand, Andreas. I'll call you from the airport."

"Okay, Roy. But—Roy, you remember last time we met? A beautiful day, we sat outside?"

"Yes. I remember that. It was in—"

"Good. Fly there, Roy. I'll meet you there."

The line went dead. Roy wove through the exits on the far side of the bridge toward the 110. The Jefferson Davis Highway, maneuvering around Lincoln's back. Roy glanced briefly at the six bronze marines, locked in their eternal struggle to raise the flag just a little bit higher. Or were they just trying to keep it from falling?

If you moved fast enough, there'd be no light at all. But if you didn't move at all? Well, then you'd just be art. A monument. The backdrop for whatever stories everyone else had to tell.

Behind him, Sarah's car didn't flinch.

Sarah Anderson waited in her car, parked behind Roy's, away from the lights of the hotel doors. The valets leaned against their podium, knees and hips and elbows slack and laughing, waiting for the after-dinner rush. The tall one glanced over as he talked, dark eyes asking the only question they knew, flushed cheekbones used to a mother's attention. Ankles and wrists still growing out of pale beige cuffs, fighting the uniform. Sarah Anderson looked down at her lap, rubbing a ruby-polished thumbnail like a worry bead. "Wait for me, Sarah," Roy had said, hurrying toward the doors. He'd slipped a bill to the tall valet on his way inside. When Sarah looked up again, Tall Valet pretended he hadn't been watching.

He's younger than Roy's son, she thought—and not that much older than his grandson. How on earth does that happen without anybody noticing? A few months back Tyler had called, his voice creaking and humming like an old closet door, the lows and highs all jumbled up, agonizing through the introduction and body and conclusion of simply asking if his grandpa was there. How do any of us ever get through that phase? Sarah had listened in as he and his sister had sung "Happy Birthday" to Roy over the phone, Tyler clearly mortified, Sammy giggling all the way. Tyler hadn't said another word, letting Sammy carry the rest of the conversation, telling stories in her funny little pixie voice about their spring vacation, her vocabulary too big for the tiny thing—all limbs, helmet, and big white smile—next to the horse in the picture on Roy's desk. Enchanted by the music in her own words. Practicing bedtime stories for a whole new generation of Daniels.

Sarah couldn't remember her grandfather. She knew he and her grandmother had met on a ship sailing from Hamburg to New York—he from Sweden, she from a small town in Austria. One version of the story had them stowing away in pickle barrels, but the older she got, the less likely that seemed. Another of those things that you're told as a child and file away without question, then don't even think about again until one day when you tell them to someone else, and you see that look in their eyes as if you'd just suggested they go down to the park and play on the swings. Only you're twenty-seven now. Nothing dispels the myths of childhood as quickly as the mirror of another person's eyes. The myths of childhood, or the lies of parents.

It would have been hard to get pregnant hidden inside a pickle barrel.

A taxi pulled up to the doors, in front of her. An uncle had told her once that they put the word "yellow" on top of taxis so that colorblind people would know what color they were. She'd believed that one until college.

Sarah wondered how many more of those little stories were still hunkered down in the dustier corners of her head, clouding up her thinking, leading her daily down garden paths and blind alleys and dead ends. How could she know for sure? She couldn't even remember—could anybody?—the first four or five years of her life, and they say that your personality's basically set by then. How many of the things she'd been told as a baby had been stories? Half-truths? Lies? And those earliest things couldn't be undone. If she couldn't even remember them, there was no chance she'd roll one or two out after dinner some night, after one too many drinks, accidentally. No chance for her friends to laugh and embarrass her, holding them up to the light for her to study from a safe distance. No chance for her to see them for what they really were, and to take a dust rag to those corners of her mind to scrub away the false. The fiction. The fairy-tale ending.

Who knew what little time bombs her father had planted in there before he left, before she'd even had a chance to remember him. An image of himself, perhaps? A portrait of the artist as a young man? Was he a realist, or did he favor the abstract? A symbolist? What other "ists" could she remember from those art books lying around Roy's apartment? Dadaist? (Her father couldn't have been a Dadaist. He wasn't even a dad.)

Impressionist? (He made quite an impression on her mother.) Expressionist? (Not a chance.)

No way to know. No way to ever get to the bottom of it. Her whole way of thinking might be based on the wildest fantasies of people she didn't even know. But there was nothing she could do to find out.

Tall Valet ran by with a set of keys in his hand. A nice hand—long fingers, dark hair that matched his eyelashes. How did she know about his eyelashes? Had he looked at her as he ran by? Had she looked into his eyes, seen him blink, read his thoughts? She must have, she supposed, but maybe she'd just imagined it all. Not much to be sure of tonight. And at that thought, Sarah laughed. She laughed out loud sitting inside her car, watching the taxi pull away with new passengers in back. She laughed because she simply didn't know. Didn't know, really, who she'd seen, what she'd heard, what she believed, who she could trust. She didn't have a clue. And from where she sat tonight, waiting—because he'd told her to—for the one man she truly believed she believed in, she saw no way of ever improving the situation. She might, one day, decide she did know, but the foundation of that certainty might be nothing but fantasy. And wouldn't that make the certainty a fantasy itself?

Tall Valet returned in a red Lexus convertible. He saw the owner waiting under the lights. As he held the driver's door open, he looked back at the red Nissan that had been parked there for the past fifteen minutes. The woman inside was laughing, silent inside the walls of the car, framed in the windshield sort of like a painting he'd seen in an art history class. The person in that painting was supposed to be screaming. Is she? Is she crying? The hotel lights frosted the windshield glass, making it hard to make out what was happening inside. The woman looked up, seeming to wipe away a tear. Tall Valet looked back, thinking maybe she was looking at him, but it could have been she was just looking at herself, framed in miniature in the rearview mirror.

The owner of the Lexus pressed a bill into his hand. He didn't look to see what the valet was staring at. He just got into his car and drove away.

• • •

"Ladies and gentlemen, please welcome this year's Pollux Society nominee, General Grantham Hayward."

Whether the Society's enthusiasm was due more to appreciation for the General's good deeds or to relief that Jabe Evans's speech was over at last was hard to tell. Women in tight black, glittering red, and iridescent blue gowns; men in black tie and uniform—all stood and applauded as Jabe Evans tried to gather up his notes, clap, and move away from the podium all at the same time. Roger Taylor, whose only job this evening was to anticipate such issues, moved quickly from the wings to take the papers and gently turn Evans toward the stairs in time to shake hands with the General as he climbed onto the stage.

All eyes on the stage, Bill Morton glanced over at Al Green. Al Green winked at him, then turned and harrumphed something in Military at the stage.

"Thank you." The General waited a moment as one of the hotel's AV staff adjusted his wireless microphone. "Thank you all. Thank you, especially, to Jabe Evans." The General turned his eyes to the man at his right, who adjusted his glasses and nodded awkwardly at his feet as the audience renewed its applause. "I'm deeply humbled by your kind words, Jabe, and by the light in which they cast me and my career. It's a light I think I recognize"—the General paused and smiled past Evans at Tamara Maybin—"but in it, I'm not sure I recognize my own reflection."

The crowd in the room settled back into their seats. Maybin guided Evans down the stairs and back to his table, then took her own seat one table back. She glanced at the empty chair where Roy Daniel was supposed to be. Out of habit she checked her BlackBerry, but she already knew it didn't know, either.

The General paced stage right in his best pre-battle briefing style. "Part of what makes this honor so special to me is that it comes from an organization founded by such an exceptional individual. I first met Jabe Evans longer ago than I'd like to admit to having been alive. Jabe had just started a new company, struggling along like start-ups do, I guess—happy just to get through another day safe and sound, ready to catch a few winks, get up, and fight the good fight all over again. I was a young officer, recently returned from Southeast Asia, and that routine sounded familiar to me. I think maybe that's why we hit it off as well as we did. I'd just made it out of a war. Jabe had just started his. We understood each other. We understood that the only way to make it was to surround yourself with people you could trust. This room is a testament to Jabe's success in this regard, and to a large extent, to my own."

Al Green yelled something that could have been "hear, hear" or "oorah" or "hooah" or most any other two-syllable phrase, and broke into applause so enthusiastic that the rest of the room had no choice but to follow suit. The General scanned the room and nodded approvingly, a proud father at a family reunion.

"I met a soldier in Da Nang once whom I've never forgotten, even though our paths only crossed for a couple of minutes. He was just back from R&R—five days in Bangkok, which was bound to leave a guy feeling a little philosophical. We were both headed back to our units. He asked me for a cigarette, and I told him I needed an R&R story in return. I was just joking around, really, but he sat there smoking for a long time, just staring off past the choppers, off toward where the road disappeared around the side of the hill. He looked very serious. I'd just about given up on him, started getting my things together, making like I was going to leave. That's when he said, 'You know, sir, I don't think there's such a thing as fate. I think everything that happens, happens because of us. Bad things happen 'cause we make bad choices. Make good choices, good things happen. Simple as that. You get back what you give out.'

"I have no idea what happened to that soldier. A few minutes later, he boarded his chopper, I boarded mine, and we never saw each other again. I don't know his name. More than likely, he thought he was just talking about some Thai girl, but his words have stuck with me. Maybe the time and the place made them hit me harder than they would have otherwise. Doesn't matter. It seems to me that that soldier's words were some of the truest I've ever heard, maybe the best guidance anyone's ever given me on how to live a good life."

Bill Morton squirmed a little in his seat and looked at his watch. He looked again at Al Green, but he was gazing in rapt adoration at the stage.

Tamara Maybin saw Roy Daniel slip in, quietly closing the ballroom door behind him. It took him a few minutes to find her in the crowd. She smiled when he did and nodded. He smiled back, but stayed where he was, back against the ballroom wall.

"I don't know what Jabe Evans thinks about fate." The General paced back across the stage, studying each step, tapping his fingertips together beneath his chin. "It's one thing he and I have never discussed. But I do know that, of all the people I've met since that day in Da Nang, Jabe's one of the few who actually seems to live by that soldier's philosophy, day in and day out. To Jabe, nothing matters but what you do. Do the right thing, and the world will do right by you. Treat the people you work with—your clients, your employees, your subcontractors, your suppliers—treat them with respect, and they'll respect you. Fate has nothing to do with it. I've never heard Jabe talk about being lucky. He just focuses on the job at hand, confident in the belief that a job well done—and a job done well—is the only thing that really matters."

This time the crowd's applause required no catalyst. Even Jabe Evans joined in. Patty Morton applauded Ellie Evan's proud smile.

"Today, Jabe and CASTOR are doing many jobs in support of our great nation, and doing them well. I'm happy to report that my office has agreed to extend funding for the Ariadne project, which is just one example of the ways in which CASTOR is applying science to the effort to bring down the very real forces of evil operating—they think—under the safe cover of darkness. With CASTOR's help, we'll soon be able to shine a bright light into the darkest corners of their most secret lairs, and bring them to justice."

More applause. Tamara Maybin watched Roy Daniel applauding, smiling at her once again. The same unfamiliar tug she'd felt earlier pulled her eyes to her lap.

"But I'm proudest of all to let you know tonight that once again, Jabe Evans himself is putting action ahead of words. Earlier today, Jabe agreed to double down on CASTOR's commitment to this nation's military personnel. Jabe has promised that, by this time next year, CASTOR will have increased its number of employees in Southwest Asia by more than 500 percent, making it one of the largest private employers of American personnel in theater. This commitment means many things to many people, but one thing I can say for sure: it will mean better support for our men and women in uniform—better support for those soldiers who risk their lives day in and day out for the cause of freedom."

Al Green led the audience to its feet. Bill Morton smiled, and looked over at Jabe Evans. Evans stared at his untouched dessert plate, nodding vaguely. He raised his head and met Morton's smile with the same vague nod. His eyes were gray shot sunk deep in his skull.

"That, ladies and gentlemen, is the kind of support this country needs. That is what will make our nation successful in its war on those who would do us harm—those who would see us fail in our quest to make the world safe for all people dedicated to the twin causes of liberty and justice. That is what Jabe Evans is all about. That is what the Pollux Society is all about. And that, ladies and gentlemen, is what makes me proud to accept this year's nomination—a nomination from an organization that truly understands that, as that soldier told me all those years ago, we all get back exactly what we give out."

Tamara Maybin looked around just in time to see the ballroom door closing behind Roy Daniel.

"Thank you all. Thank you, Jabe. And thank you most of all to those brave men and women who, every day, willingly and selflessly put themselves in harm's way. God bless them. God bless you all. And God bless the United States of America."

• • •

Tamara Maybin sat in the dark, watching the Christmas lights twinkle on the planes gliding toward Reagan. They dipped their wings gently and waggled their tails in anticipation before disappearing behind the Crystal City skyline. Another perfect landing. Tamara smiled and looked around for her bottle of water. Just five more minutes—five more minutes of silence. She'd earned it. Five more minutes watching the planes and their passengers float down out of the faraway icy dark and back into civilization's sticky, warm embrace. Big, aluminum ornaments—make-believe turtle doves, French hens, and partridges—red and green and white lights twinkling, the faces of their passengers framed all in a row like one long family Christmas card.

Every year, Tamara hated the holidays more. When the decorations had gone up that first year on deployment she'd noticed the early signs— the little twinges through the back of her neck and the corners of her eyes and her gut. Then came the cards from her friends and the letter from her parents and the pictures of her little sister, a cheerleader at last, laughing before her first homecoming game. Tamara had locked herself in a bathroom stall and waited till the worst had passed. Waited till the naked tears had run their course, across her cheeks and down her neck, tracing for all to see everything she had been, everything she'd tried to undo, everything she needed to leave behind. Cordon off, command and control. She'd sat there locked away from the all-seeing desert glare and waited—waited until her sister's summer-cloud smile and jet-spark eyes no longer made her break; until her parents' old familiar voices in that handwriting from the little test-day notes in her grade school lunchboxes didn't melt her down. Then she'd torn up the picture and the letter and the cards, volunteered for every extra shift she could get, and held her breath till the new year came and brought her normal back.

Tonight was the best that normal had to offer. But that twinge was still there, and the holidays were still almost three months away. A quarter of the year. So it couldn't be the holidays, Christmas-card airplanes or not. She knew it wasn't. She just wasn't quite ready to admit it. Five more minutes. Five more minutes, then I'll figure out what to do.

Tamara drank down half the bottle of water in one long pull and watched the windows in the building across the highway. Not much action at this hour. A man in a bright blue T-shirt pushed a cart with a garbage can and mops and spray bottles between cubicles. His head bobbed in time to music Tamara couldn't hear. Two floors above him, a man in a sagging white shirt stared straight at her and talked on the phone. She stared back at him and wondered what he knew, why he needed to tell it to somebody else tonight, and whether it was making that somebody else's life better or worse. He pointed at her over and over again, emphasizing the point that Tamara, try as she might, couldn't hear.

She put the water bottle back down on the table and took a deep breath. Your five minutes are up, Tamara. White Shirt's not going to help you—doesn't even know you're here. Better make a move now, before you lose your nerve. While Evans still thinks you can come through. While you still have a choice.

There was a knock at the door. Tamara picked up her cell phone and dialed the number. Through the peephole glass she could see the man around whom her life had, for so long, revolved. Through the glass behind her White Shirt lectured, pleaded, swore. Tamara stood alone in the dark and listened. The phone on the other end began to ring. Another silent plane ducked behind the crystal towers.

All that glitters is gold.

• • •

The glow-stained alarm clock hummed past the two and hummed again, exactly as it had sixty seconds before. Still she hadn't moved. The cursor blinked at the end of an unfinished sentence. Sarah stared down at her candy-apple leather shoes. When she bought them last spring, she'd felt the way they'd move, saddle slick against the parquet floor. She'd seen the way she'd walk in them, hips tucked sidelong into the little red dress she'd still have to find. She'd dreamed of how they'd look, lying carelessly on the carpeting, and of how he'd look walking past them to get another bottle of wine from the kitchen.

She'd never thought of how they'd look sulking beneath the desk in her cubicle outside his office at ten past eleven at night, no polished floor, no coy walk, no bottle of wine in the naked flicker of a bedroom candle.

The office lights clicked off. Still she didn't move, staring down at the memory of her perfect shoes.

Her phone rang. Slowly Sarah Anderson opened her eyes and sat up straight in her chair. The lights sputtered back to life. The phone rang again.

Sarah glared at the familiar number on the screen. It's not his fault, she sighed, reaching for the receiver. Dammit. He doesn't even have a choice.

"Hello, Roy." Her voice had resigned itself to its fate faster than the rest of her had.

"Sarah. I'm glad you're still there. Thank you."

"You're welcome, Roy. Everything okay?"

"Yes, everything's fine. I'm on the plane. We're delayed a little, but nothing serious. Did you let . . . the folks at the other end know the details?"

"I did. They're good to go. He's arriving around the same time as you. Said you already knew where to meet him."

"Yes, that's right. Okay, then, I guess we're all set, then. What about Pete? Any more news?"

"No, nothing yet. I'll stay on it, though. As soon as I figure out where he is, I'll go up there myself."

Sarah could hear a flight attendant singsonging sweet nothings over the cabin speakers.

"Sarah?"

She realized she was staring at her shoes again. "Yes, Roy?"

"Sarah, are you sure you're okay?"

He'd seen her there in her car, trying to dab the mascara off her cheeks. He'd asked her the same thing then, but hadn't really wanted an answer. He'd needed his secretary, not his girlfriend. He was trying to check the box with the latter so he could move on with the former to set flight plans for him and late-night surveillance detail for her, all while still slipping off toward Dulles ahead of the Pollux crowd's grand exit. And he'd managed to escape Pollux, but not her. Success with the secretary, but not with the girlfriend. She hadn't convinced him. So he was asking her again. And again, he didn't really want an answer. He wanted forgiveness. He didn't really want his girlfriend right now—he wanted his secretary. But he did need to know his girlfriend was okay, tucked away carefree and warm until he had time to deal with her again, Barbie in her dream house smiling on the closet floor.

But dammit, he doesn't have any other choice.

"Roy, I'm fine." She knew she wasn't convincing. She wasn't even sure she really meant to be.

"Sarah—"

"Roy, stop. I'm fine. I know what I have to do. I'll talk with you when you get to Frankfurt and let you know what I find out. You just try to get some rest."

Sarah could hear the cabin noises, muffled voices, a woman asking if she could hang her coat. But nothing from Roy.

"Okay, Roy?"

Singsong flight attendant announced that the doors were now closed.

• • •

Tamara Maybin didn't hang up. She put her BlackBerry down on the table. She glanced in the mirror over the dresser, cocked her head just a little to the right, and faked her best smile. Nope—not selling it tonight. But don't worry about it. It's him you're selling, not yourself—and he won't even notice. The booze and the big screen and the after-dinner flattery painted too pretty a picture tonight for any mere mortal to resist. He'll be striding triumphant through a virtual reality of ego and alcohol and the privileges of rank. His own private Lara Croft, pigtail to jackboots, all shadowed eyes and shining guns—that's what he'll see. Not the flicker of doubt in the little PR girl's eyes. Not the hesitation on her lips, the tang of fear on her breath.

And the others—they can't even see you.

She smoothed out the wrinkles in her little black dress, took a deep breath, and opened the door. Places, everyone. General Grantham Hayward in the hallway, parade rest in blue and white, red and gold. A bottle poorly concealed by his barracks cover, behind his back.

Action.

"Have you forgotten already, Colonel? Never, never, *ever* keep a General waiting."

Maybin in the doorway, toying with her bracelets, shy smile avoiding his very direct gaze. "I'm sorry, General, but I wasn't expecting you. You knocked at a *very* inconvenient moment."

"Did I, now?" General smiling along, hunter's eyes prowling the room behind her. "Tonight of all nights? And after all I've done for you."

"And I thank you for everything, General. But it's not what you think. I was about to get in the shower. It takes a girl a little time to get back into one of these things. Without help, that is."

The General's eyes stand down. Tamara watches his Adam's apple bob along with his imagination. "Well, you didn't need to bother on my account," he rumbles, clearly hoping for a purr. "We can relax the dress code a little up here, can't we?"

"Sure we can," says Tamara, turning and walking back toward the window. "Feel free to unbutton your jacket if you want."

The General laughs. The door thunks shut. The General's big hands on Tamara's shoulders. His thumbs dig deep into the knots between her shoulder blades and she lets out a little sigh in spite of herself as her arms fall limp and her head slumps forward. He kisses the thin soft area right below her ear. I guess some things you don't forget.

Stay in character.

Tamara, eyes closed, the General's lips grazing down the back of her neck.

"I guess you needed that," he whispers, mouth returning to find her earring, hands still kneading her shoulders.

"Mmm hmm. I also need a drink. Was that a bottle I saw you carrying?"

"It was. A good one. But it'd be even better for dessert."

"I think"—Tamara turns, still avoiding his eyes, toying with the medals across his chest—"I think I might need a little appetizer first." Her fingertips drifting slowly down the stiffly pressed uniform. "I'm feeling a little"—further down still—"peckish."

"Are you now? Well, let's see what we can do about that."

Cut.

Tamara turned to the dresser, avoiding herself in the mirror. She retrieved two glasses from the minibar. She searched for a moment for a corkscrew, but the pop by the bed let her know the General had come prepared.

Get yourself together now. This is your big scene.

Action.

Tamara leaning against the dresser, wineglasses in hand. The General approaches, catching a glimpse of his own smile in the mirror behind her.

"It used to be your favorite, as I recall."

"Still is. The best things never change."

The General pouring, Tamara watching the glasses fill honey green.

"To you, General."

"To us, Colonel. Still the best damned team the marines ever fielded."

They drink. Tamara smiles into her glass.

"Thank you, General. Thank you for everything. You know that without you I wouldn't be here."

Tamara looks the General straight in the eyes suddenly, without hesitation, dead serious. The General off guard, starts to speak, thinks, takes a drink, shakes his head.

"And thanks for helping me out tonight. You don't know how much that little mention will mean to these guys."

The General still shaking his head, smiling.

"You're wrong, you know—you've got it all backward. Without you *I* wouldn't be *here*."

Tamara smiles and sips. "And I wouldn't be drinking this outstanding wine."

"No, no—I didn't mean it that way. Well, maybe—a little. But seriously—without your help all these years, I wouldn't be half the man I— The world wouldn't think I'm half the man I— Awe, shit. You're the PR goddess—you know what I mean, don't you?"

Tamara laughing, smile bright, eyes glinting, genuine.

"I do."

"And as for the mention—don't mention it. Least I could do, if it helps you out. Hell, everybody'll know all about it in a day or two, anyway. Surprised it means so much to them, but . . . anyway. . . . Least I could do."

The General raising his glass. Tamara's eyes darker, smile forced.

"What do you mean everybody'll know about it in a day or two?"

"Oh, there's some big sting going on tomorrow, maybe the next day—they're going to catch somebody that that program fingered. Should give them all the press they need and more—at least in the 'need to know' circles. Which is where these guys live, anyway. But hey—this is boring. Have some more wine. Here's to us." The General fills both glasses, touching his glass to hers.

"So the program's not in trouble?"

"Trouble? No! Hell, could be one of the biggest things CASTOR's done in years. From a PR point of view, anyway. Cute stunt. *And* it's gonna make opening up those civilian feeds for us look like somebody else's idea altogether, which gets me out of the spotlight, which is even better. But, like I said, this is boring. Come here. You look tired. You look like maybe you could use a little more . . . personal attention."

Cut.

The General put his glass on the dresser and turned Tamara gently toward the mirror. He took her shoulders in his strong hands and began to dig deep into those knots that never seemed to go away. In the mirror his head disappeared behind hers and she felt his hot breath, his rough familiar cheeks down the back of her neck, across her spine, into the low cut of her dress. But her own eyes remained fixed on themselves. Curiosity, wisdom, age beyond anything she'd understood before.

All right, Mr. DeMille, I'm ready for my close-up.

She closed them tight. They weren't doing anyone any good anyway, not seeing anything everybody didn't already expect, not learning anything everybody apparently didn't already know.

Fade to black.

● ● ●

Sarah Anderson tried to dismiss the sudden chill. She surveyed the empty hallway, searching for the staring eyes she felt down the back of her neck. Nothing. More out of habit than anticipation she checked her e-mail. Nothing. She shut down her computer. Her chair creaked and moaned about the hour as she rolled back to get her purse. She walked by Bill Morton's and Jabe Evans's empty offices on her way to the elevator. Nothing. No one. Just her red dress, red purse, and red shoes reflected in the polished steel of the elevator door, like a shop window on Valentine's Day.

Red button, pointing down. Blue eyes, looking up. Red numbers, counting up. Red lips, parting as the doors slide open.

Al Green.

"Well, well. Good evenin', darlin'. All dressed up, nowhere to go but work? Now ain't that a shame."

Sarah winked away her surprise and brushed just close enough to let Al Green feel the warmth in her perfume. Al Green swayed more than close enough to let Sarah smell his breath. Bloodshot eyes smiled up at her from beneath bushy gray eyebrows.

"In a hurry, sweetheart? Got someplace to be?"

"I do, as a matter of fact." She turned to face him and pressed the button for the ground floor. "Is there something I can help you with, Al?"

Al Green grunted a laugh and leaned hard against the open elevator doors as he considered the feet he knew were somewhere down below his cummerbund. "Honey, you have no idea."

"So I hear." Sarah rummaged through her purse for her car keys. "Don't stay too late, Al. I think you need a little sleep."

"Don't you worry your pretty little head 'bout me, Ms. Sarah. Everything's gonna be *just* fine."

Sarah Anderson held her keys in her hand and said nothing. Al Green laughed to himself, still contemplating his invisible feet. Then he half stepped, half rolled into the elevator car, executing a full two-seventy and landing against the back wall. He leaned there watching his reflection appear beside Sarah's, momentarily separated only by the CASTOR logo in the closing doors.

Sarah Anderson didn't move, staring up as the floor numbers began their slow descent.

"Ol' Mr. Daniel keepin' you up late again, Ms. Sarah?"

Sarah shifted her weight and glanced briefly at the reflections in the hard-polished doors. Her own face made her more uncomfortable than Al Green's.

"There's a lot to do. Hard to keep up." Her own voice annoyed her, the "do" and the "up" like midnight drips in a bathroom sink.

Al Green smiled at the reflection of her shoes, waiting for the next drop to fall.

"Well, there must be quite a bit goin' on. Not like ol' Roy to miss a Pollux party."

"He was there. Not for very long, but he caught the General's speech."
Drip, drip, drip.

"I saw that. Also saw he ran off pretty quick afterward. Where'd he run
off to, Ms. Sarah? Ever'thing okay at home?"

Sarah's full cobalt glare turned on the black-tied garden gnome beside
her. "Everything's *fine,* Al. Busy. But fine. Thank you for your concern." She
could feel her cheeks redden. She stared down at her shoes and closed her
eyes to hold back the inevitable. Just a few moments longer.

Al Green raised his bushy eyebrows, but didn't look up. His roast-pig
smile stayed smeared across his face, his eyes still fixed on the image of
Sarah's ruby-red shoes.

"Well, I'm glad to hear that. I was worried 'bout him. Thought somethin' might really be wrong. But I suppose he wouldn't go fly off and
leave ever'thing to other folks to mop up. That wouldn't be our Roy, now
would it?"

Sarah didn't move, didn't speak, didn't open her eyes.

"Course it wouldn't. Not *our* Roy."

The soft little bell, always in the background, rang and the elevator
doors slid open. Sarah Anderson stepped quickly out of the car and toward the front doors. She could see Al Green's reflection in the lobby
windows, watching her own reflection glide across the polished marble
floor in her candy-apple shoes, hips keeping time in her tight red dress.
His reflection moved only far enough to lean against the elevator doors,
blocking them open. Sarah thought she heard the hum of a cell phone
on vibrate, but it wasn't hers, and Al Green made no move. He just
leaned there, his usual grin a little wider, perhaps, than it would be in the
light of day.

"Good night, Ms. Sarah. Be careful out there, now. And oh, by the way,
. . ." Sarah paused as she opened the lobby doors, letting the humid orange

night into the stale air-conditioned fluorescent. ". . . please give Andreas my regards."

Sarah Anderson watched from across the lobby as the devil from her mother's story stumped back through the polished steel doors of his magical shack.

• • •

The elevator hummed and whirred and the red numbers clicked silently up toward thirteen. Bill Morton smiled, as he had as many times as he'd ridden this elevator, remembering the day he'd first seen the plans. The old man's finally losing it, he'd thought.

"You sure about this, Jabe?"

"Sure about what?" Jabe Evans scribbling in the rubble of his old office, the count of the ballet instructor downstairs pirouetting with the evening breeze through the open windows. The crew shells gliding along the Potomac to the fading count of the coach's megaphone, reality dwarfed by shadow in the setting summer sun.

"Well, I see you've got the executive offices on the thirteenth floor of the new building?"

"So?"

"Well, Jabe, I think most companies these days skip the thirteenth floor altogether."

"They don't skip it. They ignore it. It's there. Just count." Evans still refusing to look up. Tchaikovsky from below, the slippered thump and swish of tiny feet, four counts over and over again.

"Okay, fair enough, they ignore it. So don't you think we should, too?"

"Because everybody else does?"

"Yes. Because everybody else does—for a reason. Maybe it bothers certain clients. Maybe it bothers certain employees. Maybe it bothers me—who cares? Maybe there's some upside. There certainly isn't any downside."

"Sure there is. Makes us look silly. Superstitious. Unscientific. Like 'everybody else.' Which we're not."

"So it's actually on purpose—putting our offices on the thirteenth floor."

"Of course it is. What did you think it was—some kind of mystical confluence of the stars?"

Jabe Evans turning a page in his notebook, moving on from a conversation unworthy of acknowledging. Bill Morton laughing under his breath, just as he laughed now as the red thirteen lit up the screen and the shiny steel doors moved quietly aside, replacing his view of himself with a view of the CASTOR logo on the wall opposite.

To the left, down the hall, into his office. Al Green was already there, jacket missing, bow tie hanging, suspenders sagging, rocking back in a chair that looked alarmingly delicate by comparison.

"Come on in, Al. Make yourself at home."

"That you, sir—I believe I will."

"So—how do think the evening went?"

"How d'*you* think it went?"

"I think it went great. The turnout was great, the General came through—thank you very much, Al—what more could we ask for?"

Al Green rocked back a little further and smiled at his cummerbund like a carnivorous Buddha.

"Tell me, Al—what more could we ask for? Obviously there's something, or else you wouldn't have sent me that cryptic text. So come on, Al—I'm old, it's past my bedtime, and Patty's starting to think the two of us are more than friends. What's on your mind?"

Al Green chuckled and let his chair down on all fours, leaning his elbows on his knees and inspecting something on his right thumb he'd apparently never noticed before. "You look after that wife of yours, Bill. She's a fine lady. Somebody'll snatch her out from under you if you don't keep a good eye out."

Bill Morton smiled, sat down, and folded his hands across his stomach, but said nothing.

"Bill, I've got some good news, and I've got some bad news. Good news is, I talked to our German friends just a little while ago. Things are movin' right along. By this time tomorrow night, looks like we'll've caught ourselves a bad guy."

"Well that's *great* news, Al! *Really* great!" Morton stood up and examined his reflection, tall and proud, in the dark black windows. "And the General's guys know, just like we discussed? They'll be in there with us—ready to take all the credit we deserve?"

"Yes, indeed, Bill—told the Colonel to give the word, his boys are probably already on their way up from Stuttgart as we speak."

Bill Morton turned, hands behind his back, and stared down at Al Green, still hunched in his chair and biting at his thumbnail.

"So what's the bad news, Al? So far, seems like we're batting a thousand tonight."

Al Green examined his handiwork and then looked up, catching Bill Morton for the first time tonight squarely in the eyes. "Bill, I caught Sarah Anderson listenin' in tonight while I was talkin' to the Colonel at the party. Wasn't really sure why, or what she'd heard, so I came up here afterward to check things out. Found her here, and heard her on the phone, and I learned a few things. A few things I think you oughta know."

"Okay. I'm all ears, Al. Shoot."

"Well, first of all, seems Pete Vasilescu—you know him, that fella—Bulgarian or somethin'—college friend of Roy's—well, seems he got himself into a car accident tonight. Sarah tracked him down to a hospital up in

Maryland. I reckon she'll be on her way up there to see him any time now. Doesn't sound good."

Bill Morton shook his head. "Well, that's a shame. I hope he's okay. But between you and me, Al, that doesn't seem like something I needed to come in here in the middle of the night to hear. Is there something else, or am I missing something?"

"Well, way I hear, Pete's been pretty outspoken against using Ariadne on civilian feeds. And those civilian feeds are what we promised the General in exchange for his outstanding performance tonight."

Bill Morton tilted his head back and pondered the ceiling for a moment. "Well, Pete doesn't really have much say in the matter, does he?"

"TSWG guys think the world of him, Bill. Whatever he says goes with them. And technically speaking, it *is* their project. So I wouldn't be so sure."

Bill Morton sat back down in his chair, hands folded between his knees, and nodded his bobblehead nod.

"Plus," Al Green went on, "you know how close he is with Roy. And I think we both know what Roy would think about all this."

"Sure, but Roy *doesn't* know, does he?"

"Well, now that's the other thing, Bill. I heard Sarah talkin' with somebody about flight details. In Germany. Doesn't take a rocket scientist to figure out who she was talkin' to."

Bill Morton frowned down at his shoes, then looked curiously at Al Green.

"Roy's gonna be there, Bill—he's gonna be there for the kill. He caught the last flight out to Frankfurt, where I assume he's gonna meet Andreas. And you and I both know what Andreas knows."

Bill Morton stopped nodding and stole a glance at his watch. "What makes you think they're going to meet?"

"Come on, now Bill—is it really that late? I just called Andreas. Called him after my little chat with Sarah Anderson. And Andreas didn't say a word about either Roy or Sarah to me."

• • •

Jabe Evans slumped in the back of the town car as the Pentagon commandeered his view. It heaved uninvited alongside to port, tiny yellow eyes unblinking yet blind, drilled to overlook vessels of his slight beam and tonnage. Several classes above—Super Panamax to his twelve meters. Meet up with something like that in the middle of the night and it'll black the starlight out of your sky, churn the wave slap from your hull, smoke the sea mist out of your sails. Swamp you in her salt-rusted lee and leave you to founder in her bunker-smogged doldrums. Unable even to see you coming or hear your cries—innocent by reason of ignorance, unconscious of your fate. You unable to see or hear or smell anything else, guilty by reason of impotence; becalmed, bewitched, betrayed by her manifest destiny.

The driver stayed on the 110, which wouldn't have been Jabe Evans's choice. But for the first time in longer than he could remember he felt betrayed and defeated. Jabe couldn't speak. He simply didn't have the energy—something he would never admit to others, could scarcely admit to himself. Jabe Evans doesn't care. Those were words he was certain had seldom, if ever, been said. He'd built his company by caring—caring for his customers, caring for his employees. Caring—if he was completely honest—for himself; believing that his own abilities and his own judgment were simply better than most people's. He needed to care—he needed to gather the data, root out the fictions, consider the facts, make the decisions—because he was good at it, and the good of others depended on it. The good of the company. The good of the country. The good of the world.

Ego had never played a roll. As he stared into the passing shadows of Arlington Cemetery, he thought of how many times he'd admonished others not to think themselves too indispensible. He knew the world would get along without him. But he wasn't in any hurry to force it to do so. Because it would be hard. Jabe Evans didn't believe he made CASTOR successful, but he did believe he made it easier for the company to succeed. He didn't believe he made America successful, but he did believe his efforts helped the government make better decisions. And a United States of America that makes better decisions makes the world a better place—of this he was firmly convinced. The world did not know how to take care of itself. His earliest recollections of world events were of a world that would have been lost without the guiding hand of American might. It strained and bucked against this hand like a boat in a storm against the ropes holding it safely to the dock. But without those ropes, it would be lost, tossed up on the rocks and destroyed. The world needed a strong America like a child needed a strong parent.

And like children since the beginning of time, they would rebel against their parents.

Jabe Evans watched as the boys from Iwo Jima drifted by, forever fighting the inevitable forces of gravity. He could remember the war bond pitches, the scrap drives, the victory gardens, and the movies that showed him a world that needed his help. He'd begged his mother not to buy canned vegetables from the store for Thanksgiving, because if she did, the boys at the front wouldn't have enough to eat. He'd kicked himself every time he'd made a mistake on his homework, because he was saving his eraser for the next rubber drive. He could still remember the pride he'd felt on V-J Day, knowing he'd helped to win the war.

Of course he hadn't stayed home to run the family business, no matter how disappointed his father had looked the day he announced he was going to college. No matter how his mother had cried that they'd never see him again. But that was different. He knew they were wrong—he knew he knew better. And if he hadn't gone, he never would have been able to bail them out when the store went under and his mother got sick.

They needed him—that was the difference. They needed him to care. They needed him because he was just better at it than they were.

Oh sure, he used to joke with the guys at work about how Ellie was really the boss. On the boat, he'd always said Ellie was the captain. But wasn't it the very fact that it wasn't true that made it so endearing? "Yes," Ellie would say with a well-rehearsed smile for company, but an even more convincing one in private. "But you know you'll always be my first mate." The beauty of the whole scene being its fiction. Its pageantry. Like the Queen of England—would everyone love her half as much if she were *really* the one in charge? Of course not. What everyone loved was the fairy tale—the castles and balls and horse-drawn carriages—*and* the security of knowing it was all harmless. A game. A diversion from the brutal realities of the modern world.

If she were really in charge, they'd have had her head years ago.

Or, maybe they'd have just found a way around her and saved themselves the trouble. She was, after all, getting up there.

Jabe Evans took off his glasses and rubbed his eyes. The lighted spires of Georgetown University reflected in the water below as the town car made its way steadily across the Key Bridge. He tried to remember the passage from *Julius Caesar* he'd had to learn by heart so many years ago, but it wasn't there. Pushed aside by theorems and formulas and bylaws and balance sheets. Policies replace ideals. Ideals give way to laws. That's the way it's always been—the way it needs to be. The way the world needs to work in order to protect those dreamers in their ivory towers who . . . who what? Who encourage the young to go out and break all the rules. Dream their own dreams. Fight their own fights. Strain against their own ropes.

Just so long as the ropes don't break.

Jabe Evans put his glasses back on and looked at his watch. His phone rang in his jacket pocket, still set to the factory default. He took it out and tilted his head to read the screen through his bifocals. Tamara Maybin, maybe? Roger Taylor. Jabe Evans grunted and pressed the button and put the phone up to his ear.

"Roger, this is it for tonight. What have you got that can't wait for tomorrow?"

"Just wanted to let you know, Jabe, that the boat will be ready. I told them to be there by nine."

"And did they both accept?"

"Of course they did, Jabe. Who'd say no to an invitation from you?"

Jabe Evans just grunted and hung up the phone. The town car pulled up in front of his house. The only house he'd ever owned. Where he lived with the only wife he'd ever had. Where they'd raised the only family they'd ever raise.

The automatic porch light was on, but the rest of the house was dark.

nine

When I was five years old, I decided I could fly.

Now, it's important that you understand: I didn't decide to *learn* to fly. Lots of kids did that. Zach Ray wanted to learn so he could be a fighter pilot like his uncle Jimmy. Patton Fletcher and pretty much every other kid our age wanted to learn so they could be astronauts—including Penny Reynolds. She got so mad when we told her that girls couldn't be astronauts that Miss Marshall made her go and stand in the corner.

No, I wasn't interested in *learning* to fly. I just decided that I *could*.

My parents tell me that it all started when they took me to see *Peter Pan*. I don't remember that part. Honestly, I don't remember much—just a scene here and there, like looking through an old photo album. If the pictures in an album are taken close enough together—several in one afternoon, say, or a couple of pages worth in a single weekend—you can sort of follow the story. Or at least you can make a story up.

That's more or less the way I remember the time that I could fly. There are scenes in my head that I can remember perfectly—enough of them that I can pretty much fill in the blanks in between. Am I missing stuff? Of course I am. Does that mean I'm really making the story up? Well, let's just say my story is "inspired by true events," as they like to say in the movies.

Does that mean my story isn't true? Absolutely not. Not in my opinion, anyway. I guess you'll just have to decide for yourself.

One of those pictures stuck in my head is the view from our front-porch railing. The railing was a half wall covered in stucco that felt like sandpaper on my hands and my knees when I scrambled up from the porch to sit on top. It felt like the top of the world up there, looking out toward the street, though it couldn't have been more than six, maybe seven feet off the ground.

The picture is of my tanned, scuffed feet swinging over the bushes that grew right in front of the porch. The green bushes cropped flat on top, some of the cut leaves still stuck there, toasting in the sun between new sprouts the color of lime popsicles. Beyond the bushes, a thirsty, shadeless front yard. Our pond-colored station wagon farther out by the curb, the hot, stagnant afternoon wrinkling the air over its hood and its roof.

The sidewalk that defined the four corners of my universe buckled between the front yard and the car. On the other side of the sidewalk, terra incognita. People who sometimes waved but who I never talked to because they lived across that great divide—the street—that I wasn't allowed to cross. Did they speak the same language as we did? Eat the same kind of food? Watch the same shows on TV? Find the same butterflies on the flowers in their yards? I had no idea. Honestly, I didn't spend much time wondering, because there was more going on on my side of the street than I had time to keep up with, anyway.

To the right, my friend Zach's house with a big Sweetgum tree out front that, in the fall, dropped hundreds of spiny balls for us to throw at each other and drop down each other's shirts. To the left, old Mrs. Stone's house, always a source of butterscotch candies. Her house smelled like old wood and hand soap and was always dark, even in the daytime, set way back behind its wraparound porch and a huge magnolia whose branches reached all the way down to the ground. Those magnolia branches walled in a fort for Zach and me where we could suck on our candies and hide out from pirates and parents and other monsters and bad guys. It was from behind those branches with their big, waxy leaves that never dropped off that we watched Mrs. Stone one day, lying on a gurney carried by four tall men toward a bright red ambulance waiting at the curb behind our old green station wagon.

But that's a different picture.

On this side of the sidewalk, of course, our house, with its sky-high front porch and living room just inside and hallway that ran all the way through to the back door. The grate in the floor at this end of the hallway that I couldn't run across barefoot in winter because it would burn my feet. The screen porch out back where we kept the jars that Dad helped me put caterpillars in. "Always put in a stick, and lots of the leaves you find them on," he used to say, stuffing a jar half full of leaves and poking air holes in the top before screwing it shut. Eventually the caterpillars would turn into cocoons, and I'd check the jars every morning, hoping to find that one of the cocoons changed magically while I was asleep into a new kind of butterfly whose picture Dad would point to in his book and whose name he'd read me while I watched it drying its wings, hanging from the stick inside the jar. When its wings were dry we'd take it outside and twist off the lid and let the butterfly fly away. At first I'd leave the jar open, sitting on the screen porch steps, because I thought the butterfly would want to come home again. But none ever did, and eventually I stopped trying.

But again—different picture. Different page.

On the left-hand side of our front porch railing, there was a stucco pedestal that I could hold onto while I stood up on top. The stucco scratched my knees when I got up on them to start my ascent, and the top of the pedestal was hot where it stuck out from under the roof into the sun. Everything I touched was uncomfortable. But standing up there, I could see the whole world. When I stretched out my arms, I felt nothing but warm, nothing but soft. Only my feet still felt the rough grate of the stucco rail.

So I jumped off. If the butterflies could do it, so could I.

My flight was smooth but short. My landing wasn't great. I guess I hadn't thought about landing. The flat-topped bushes broke my fall. That's the next picture that I have in my head: sitting in the sun on the ground in front of those bushes, brushing the dry, cut leaves out of my hair and watching the thin white streaks across on my tanned arms and legs slowly turning red. And I remember thinking that I should have landed on my feet. Butterflies, birds—they all landed on their feet. Stupid of me not to remember. Next time, I'd have to make sure I landed on my feet.

I'm not sure how many more test flights I made that day. All I know for sure is that I made more than one. At some point Mom apparently noticed, because the next picture in my photo album is of her face right in mine, saying, "Asher, what on *Earth* do you think you're doing? You are *not* to jump off this porch—do you *hear* me? You're going to *hurt* yourself! Now come on indoors. Let's get you cleaned up."

I remember sitting on the kitchen counter next, Mom washing my cuts with the hydrogen peroxide out of that dreaded brown bottle, her blowing on it to stop the sting when it foamed up, and me explaining that I *could* fly, that I *had* flown. And her: "Asher, you can*not* fly. People can*not* fly. I don't want to catch you jumping off that porch again, do you hear me?"

She sent me to my room to lie down and rest. I could hear her turn on her TV show in the living room, the one where everybody talked low and serious just before the music got louder and the commercials came on louder still.

Of course I didn't believe her. I could fly. I had *flown*. And I lay there and looked for the animals in the spackle patterns on the wall by my bed and thought about how to practice my landings later on. After supper, maybe, when Dad was home. Then they'd be talking low in the kitchen like on Mom's TV show and not paying attention to me anymore.

ten
___

Asher suddenly needed to sit down. Adrenalin and parental instinct and that damned Protestant work ethic battled whiskey and jet lag and plain, old-fashioned fear inside his head, leaving little room for the basics—balance included. He found the nearest empty chair and sat down. His senses seemed to be shutting down one by one. His feet were cold stone. The voices in the lobby buzzed like distant insects. The light was suddenly unbearable, and his vision narrowed to block it out. He put his elbows on his knees and his head in his hands and caught a whiff of his shirt and realized it had been a long, long time since his last shower.

He felt a hand on his back, tentative at first, then slowly rubbing his shoulders, soft fingers pressing on the back of his neck. He breathed deep and slow. Jet lag was winning. He needed to sleep.

"Are you okay?" He realized it wasn't the first time she'd asked. He nodded, head still in his hands, and began to slowly try to swim back to the surface. No time for sleep now. Somebody's got your kids, Asher. Focus. Sleep will have to wait.

He heard dishes on the table next to him and low voices behind him. The back rub stopped with a gentle squeeze. He looked up, blinking in the bright light, and saw espresso and bottled water and cookies on a tray. She signed the check and handed it back to the waiter, who smiled and thanked her, then walked away. A slight holier-than-thou glance in his direction? Why not. He probably deserved it.

She sat down on the other side of the coffee table and poured a glass of water. "Here. You should drink this." He took the water and drank. "How do you like your coffee?" He drained the glass and put it down on the table.

"Sugar, please. Two sugars."

She stirred the sugar into the coffee as he refilled his water glass. He filled a glass for her, too, and she smiled. "Thank you." Just like on the plane. Just a little hint of a language other than English having been her first.

They drank their coffees in silence. The warm smell filled Asher's nose, and he could actually feel the sugar and the caffeine soak through to the back of his head. He drank another glass of water and ate a couple of cookies. He was starving. It must be time for a meal back home. Which meal? Too hard a question right now.

"I need something more," he said.

Here eyes fluttered up expectantly.

"Like a sandwich. I'm starving," he said, clasping his hands together to stop the tremor.

Asher finally dared a glance across the table. Her eyes were still the first things you noticed—blue like the water off the Keys, deep and clear and cool. Her left eye seemed to squint a little more than her right, giving her a mischievous look, like she was about to wink. But there were also shadows beneath her eyes, and the skin of her cheeks, perfect apple white on the plane, looked a little pale here in the light of the lobby. Her sand-blonde hair fell across the left side of her face when she looked down for a cookie, and when she glanced up and found him still watching she smiled like a little girl—like Sammy used to when she realized he'd been watching her coloring.

"Feeling better?"

"I am, thank you. I guess I was hungrier than I thought."

"No problem. You can't think when you're hungry."

Asher nodded and offered her the last cookie. She waved it away.

"It's quite a coincidence, you know, your being here just in time to rescue me." Asher looked her straight in the eyes, trying hard to focus only on her reaction.

She looked away, reaching for the water bottle. "It is, isn't it? More water?"

Asher shook his head, not letting her eyes go.

She refilled her own glass. "I guess here there are only so many places where people like you and I go." Her voice was certain, but he thought her eyes asked him how she was doing.

"What kind of people would that be? People who've just lost their kids? Did someone just take your kids, too?"

Her eyes had their answer.

"What will you do next?"

"I have no idea."

He put his head in his hands again and slumped over the table. Eva felt a stab of pity for Phaeton, although she knew that was a rookie mistake. Obviously, if they thought it was necessary to kidnap his kids to make the plan work, she should go along with the plan. She's got to use this, not feel it. A nagging thought wouldn't let go, however, as she imagined how her own father would feel upon learning she was stolen from him, held as collateral in some complicated, devious plot having nothing to do with her. The innocent should not have to pay for the sins of the father. But then again, this was her job. And she was going to prove to Andreas she was up to the test.

A new, young crowd entered the lobby and laughed toward the elevator. They paid no attention to the couple in the far corner, staring at each other across the dregs and crumbs and empty dishes between them.

"Let me help you."

Asher had no reason to trust this person, and warning lights pulsed behind his eyes, in the back of his brain. But she seemed to know something, maybe something valuable. How was it possible he hadn't thought that his family could be endangered by his attempts at heroism? He wasn't feeling heroic in the moment.

"Can you?" he asked without looking up.

"Yes," she said and took his hands.

"You know what I need to do?" He looked up and stared into the blue seas of her eyes.

She nodded. "Yes. I think so."

Asher watched her search the lobby carefully, expectantly, before she turned back to him. Her eyes looked very tired.

A kidnapper? she thought. Is that what I've become? Would Father be proud of that? She took a deep breath and nodded, her coral lips pursed at a regrettable, but inevitable, conclusion. "I think we should talk somewhere else. And get you some more food."

She waited for a moment, then stood up and offered him her hand. Asher watched her stand there, awkward, like a schoolgirl at her first dance. But she didn't lose her nerve, didn't back away, and finally he took her hand and let her help him out of his chair. She didn't let go once he was on his feet. He didn't let go as she led him off toward a new elevator.

• • •

Jess stood up, smiling around the office over the walls of her cubicle. The finance guys were all heads down over their spreadsheets. Their boss, Nick, was arguing with the whiteboard in his office, probably on speakerphone. Around the corner, one the other side of the elevators, she could hear the analysts chattering away on their phones.

She stood for a moment, smiling at the sun through the windows in Asher's office. She could feel the muscles in her neck letting go of her shoulders. Information was the heaviest burden she knew. Best to share it as quickly as possible, share the burden, breathe deep and get on with the rest of your day.

Jess stretched her arms up high and closed her eyes and rolled her head. Then she sat back down, picked up the receiver, and dialed the number on the chocolate-stained napkin. It rang only once before Kimberly Daniel answered.

"Kimberly, it's Jess. I just spoke with Asher."

"Oh, good." Expecting more.

"He—he does know what they're talking about. He knows where he needs to go. He knows what he needs to do." This last point was pushing it a little, but never mind—she needs some good news. "It's going to be okay."

Jess waited, but no response came. No breathing, no noise in the background—no hint that anyone at all was listening on the other end.

"Mrs.—Kimberly? It's going to be okay, Kimberly. Asher knows what to do."

Jess waited again. "Did *he* say that?" Skeptical, annoyed, exhausted? Hard to say.

"He did. He said that's why he's there. He said he's going to take care of everything."

"Hm."

"He said he would call you."

Okay, Jess, now you're just lying. Make her feel better, make her feel like help is on the way, but don't get her hopes up for things that aren't going to happen.

"Thank you, Jess." Different voice altogether, talking in public now, not behind closed doors. "You're a sweetheart to help. Let me know if you hear anything more, okay?"

Kimberly Daniel hung up. Jess felt the muscles in her neck begin to ratchet her shoulders slowly back up to where they'd started that morning.

• • •

The lock beeped twice, quickly, and flashed green. Eva turned the latch and walked in, holding the door open behind her. Establishing shot. Asher kept the door from closing as she continued away into the dark, but he didn't go any farther. After a while a light clicked on in the next room. A staircase curved up to his left. Behind a marble pillar, a living room in white carpeting wandered off to the right. She waited for his line. And . . .

"Nice room."

I'm on, she thought. She stood next to a blue sofa, fringed at the bottom in gold, and smiled. "I don't get to use it much. We get a very good deal."

"Who's 'we'?"

"My company." Look stage left and cross back to door.

"Who's your company?"

He didn't move.

Smile again. "Come in."

Asher smiled back. "Maybe we should just talk in the lobby."

Eva dug deep for authenticity and said with confidence, "That is not a good plan."

"The walk cleared my head. I'll admit I'm not at my best, but there's something about all this that just doesn't quite feel right."

Walk toward him, pause by the pillar. Lock eyes.

Asher realized this was the very first time she had looked at him like this. She came closer still and pushed him back into the hall, fingertips behind her back barely keeping the door from latching behind them.

"I agree with you," she whispered, standing on her toes so he could feel her breath in his ear. Her hair still smelled like mangoes, now smoked by cigarettes from the lobby. "That's why we need to talk. That's why we need to talk *here*."

"I'll get you some food. What do you like?" She walked over to the phone to call room service.

"I'll have a couple of scrambled eggs and toast. And Bourbon, please," said Asher, crossing stage right toward her, hands in his pockets, scouting the set.

"Jack Daniels, if you've got it."

A little orange box of dates sat on a low table in front of an ottoman. He took one and put it in his mouth, chewing its grainy sweet meat while he watched her empty two tiny bottles of Jack Daniels over ice. She put down the phone and twirled the ice in the glass noisily, then hand it to him. She popped the cork from a bottle of white wine and poured herself a glass. These were the classic props she had come to expect.

"Cheers," she said, holding her glass by the stem so it rang when she touched it to his.

"Cheers," replied Asher, studying her eyes. They both put their glasses to their lips, but neither of them drank.

"You said you could help." Asher watched as she crossed downstage and settled onto the sofa. He hadn't moved. How could she write him into her arms? She tucked her bare feet up under one of the gold-fringed pillows. Asher leaned against the bar and looked around vaguely for her shoes. This is your big scene, Eva. He's exhausted and desperate, the perfect moment to make your move. Just keep playing your part and find out what the kidnappers told him to do, and confirm his information coincides with what Andreas gave you.

"Yes. I think I can. But I need to know your plan. What did they tell you to do?"

Asher searched her eyes for his next line. She seemed to nod slightly, but maybe it was just his imagination. No stage manager whispered lines from off stage.

"Surely you already know?"

"No, I don't," she ad libbed. She'd need to run that line again later—the audience wouldn't buy it.

She waited for him to make the next move, idly tracing shapes on the sofa. He watched her soft, white finger stroke the blue fabric and, not thinking, took a sip from the glass he'd planned not to touch.

"They didn't tell me anything. They just said I'd know what to do. Which I don't." He thought back to his conversation with Jess, to the address she'd given him from the voice mail message, but stopped there and took another drink, never taking his eyes off his leading lady. He couldn't deliver the big reveal. Not yet. See what she suggests. You'll know if she's for real or not. His stomach lurched a little from the lack of food.

Keep up the pace, Eva. One beat. Two. She glanced up at him, smiled, and nodded again just barely, then looked back down at her invisible drawing.

"But surely you must have some plan?"

She looked at him again, this time nodding a bit more emphatically, pulling his eyes down with hers toward her finger. It did a little waltz there on the sofa, stroking down, down, across, down, down, across—careless, but still the same, over and over again.

"I wish I did." Asher tried to play a laugh, but it came out so badly it could just as easily have been a failed sob.

Her look called him a pathetic actor, but returned to her dancing finger. Still the same waltz, down, down, across, down, down, across.

It was an "H."

Asher's head jerked up in recognition. She was drawing an "H" over and over again. Carelessly enough not to make it obvious, not to make it look intentional, but an "H"—most definitely an "H."

Her eyes widened a bit and she tilted her head, urging caution and making sure he understood all in one motion. He looked down and tried to buy thinking time with another sip. Her finger was dancing a little more playfully now, but it was still an "H." She smiled vaguely as she did it, but didn't look at him anymore.

Somewhere the music had stopped.

One more sip of the drink. It's time to break the fourth wall. She obviously knows something that fits with what I know. It could be important, besides, what other choices do I have? "Hamburg," Asher said, trying for resignation, surrender. "Somebody left a message at my office, saying I should meet him in Hamburg."

"Yes," she said forcing herself to breath normally, like a Tony winner. It has to be right. The address Andreas gave her is in Hamburg. "I know people in Hamburg. Where are you supposed to meet?"

"I just have an address."

Let me see it, she wanted to scream. "Did they say when?" Eva said with measured speech.

"No." He showed her the piece of paper with an address she didn't recognize and her heart beat a little faster.

It wasn't the one Andreas gave her. It's in the right city but not the right street. There must have been another change of plans and he hasn't been able to reach her as yet.

Her white finger still danced across the blue fabric, but it didn't seem to spell anything out. Her smile was still there, but had turned inward. Asher reached inside his jacket pocket and pulled out his BlackBerry, searching elsewhere for communications.

"Well. Then we will go together." She rubbed the sofa as if to erase her doodling and stood up.

"Now?" Asher searched her eyes, but they were no longer hinting. They were telling. Everything was decided. The audience was on the edge of their seats.

Asher took another drink and stared.

"I can help you." She looked straight into his face, deep into his eyes. That was good. He wanted to look away, she could tell. In a movie, Eva would be ready for her close up. She moved her face within inches of his. "I will help you. That's why they sent me."

"Who sent you?" he asked like a drowning man reaching for rope.

"You know."

Asher wondered if he knew anything. He felt the need to sit down, and moved toward the sofa. She followed, not letting go of his hand, and sat down next to him. He felt her take his drink and rub the back of his neck as he closed his eyes and sank into the deep blue cushions. The soft kiss on his cheek was unexpected.

In the floor-to-ceiling windows, their reflections played it all the other way around.

• • •

In the hall outside the hotel room, Asher listened. Somewhere in Washington, D.C., a cell phone was ringing in his father's jacket pocket, or in his car's cup holder, or in his hand. Or maybe it was just glowing, silenced and tucked away, while the waitress at the Capitol Grill bar brought Martinis and Manhattans and orders of lobster mac and cheese. Men in dark suits and white shirts with agency cufflinks and ties in various combinations of red, white, and blue. Breath smelling of the day's stale thermos coffee and take-out sandwiches and a cigarette or two outside on the sidewalk. Suits smelling of wool and windowless conference rooms and bus exhaust. Eyes smelling a drink and hungry for a deal.

His father's eyes, concerned and distracted, calculating risks and rewards and the relative values of the various conversations.

The call went to voice mail. Asher considered hanging up, not worrying him further, but the beep came and he started talking, voice low and turned away from the door.

"Hi, Dad—it's Asher. Hope you're doing well. I was wondering if you could give me a call when you have a chance. Nothing—uh, well, it's a little complicated for a message, just give me a call on my cell. Need a little . . . advice. Thanks."

Asher hung up the phone and stared at his feet. This might not be a smart move. Kind of like dropping the bomb—you'll win, but at what cost? But then again. . . . He turned and pushed the door open just a few inches and heard a shower running somewhere upstairs. He was in the suite of a company whose name he didn't know with a woman whose name he didn't know probably being watched and listened to by people he would *never* know. The bomb doors are already open, Asher, and you're sitting on that bomb, just like Slim Pickens in *Dr. Strangelove*. So what the hell—are two bombs really any worse than one? Let 'er rip—the more, the merrier. This is gonna be one helluva ride, Asher. And like they say—misery loves company.

Asher pushed the door all the way open and stood watching the room's transformation. Soft night shadows faded as the blind, boney shadows of morning sniffed up the edges of the walls and around the corners of the ceiling. Their flight was still a few hours away. Behind him, the hall was empty, the promise of evening gone. He looked down at his cell phone, but it offered him nothing.

The door closed behind him with a discreet click as he followed the night's remains warily up the stairs.

• • •

Tropical blue eyes took in the lights on the gargantuan palm tree growing across the tropical blue sea. Ten years, they said—ten years before the giant leaves would be fully formed, visible from space, and the rich and mighty could dwell in their luxuriant shade. But ten years was a long time. A lot could happen in ten years.

Eva turned away from the bedroom window and walked into the bathroom. She looked at herself in the mirror. Who will look back at me when I look in the mirror in ten years? Will I recognize her? Probably. Will I recognize her as myself? Probably. But would this person I see now recognize that person in ten years as the same person? Would the me of ten years ago recognize this person staring at me now?

She turned on the shower and watched the woman in the mirror watching her undress. What was it she saw in that woman's eyes: Curiosity? Disbelief? Disgust? She confronted the woman, stripped naked now, as the steam began to fill the room. The same dimple here, the same mark there that she could remember as a little girl thinking looked like a puppy dog's ear. So there's proof—I am the same person I was. But would the little girl agree? The little girl answered from far, far away. Far enough away that Eva could nearly convince herself she didn't hear.

• • •

Kimberly Daniel set her empty glass down on the deck railing and watched the sun set orange and gold behind the Davises' red oaks, and couldn't get the idea to call him out of her mind. Jenny Davis would be able to see her out here, if she was looking. Which she probably was, because she'd been calling all afternoon. She'd be over eventually, and Kimberly would have to say *something*, and she couldn't see telling her the truth as it stood right now. Call the guy, now, she thought to herself. Do it now, before the neighbors start to pry and you're caught in some stupid lie.

She'd met the guy a few years ago at one of those big holiday parties Asher's dad liked to host. Whether Roy Daniel had scheduled it on purpose for one of the two evenings she and Asher were in town wasn't particularly clear. She wondered if Roy Daniel had indeed scheduled it on purpose, to ensure they were there. Roy had, of course, been very apologetic about the timing, and the fact that he was, at the time, short a wife/social coordinator ("cruise director," he liked to call them) certainly argued on his behalf. Still, Kimberly Daniel was suspicious. Had been then, still was today. She did, of course, tend to assume the worst about Roy. Asher was always quick to point that out. But most of the time, it seemed to her that the worst eventually proved true. The man, in her opinion, was basically an old letch. Brilliant, of course, and talented, obviously, but when it came to women, a letch, pure and simple. All of them were. And although she tried her best to keep her opinion to herself, she suspected she wasn't always entirely successful.

Anyway, they'd met just that once—she and that man whose name she could never remember. He'd introduced himself, slipping into the gap just after Asher had started talking with someone new and just before Kimberly realized she was no longer part of the conversation. He was taller than the rest of the men in the room—taller and tanned a shade darker—and had wavy silver hair that showed no intention of leaving. His voice reminded her of sugar just before it burns in the pan. His eyes were a cold pale blue that locked onto hers from the very first word and made her check her dress and blush as if she'd just noticed it was missing.

He'd introduced himself as something silly—Fred Furderburk, Hal Heffenreffer, something like that—and if he'd later told her the truth, she'd neither noticed nor cared. What she did remember was what he told her he did. "I fix things," he said, smiling at this obviously rehearsed answer to that most mundane of cocktail party questions.

Can you fix me? She almost asked. But hadn't, because that would have suggested some sort of conciliatory approval of the evening.

Roy would know his name, of course, as would Asher. And where were they right now in this minute? Had she *ever* called Roy? She didn't think so. She'd just never felt comfortable with him.

She probably just hadn't been very successful at keeping her opinion to herself. Roy was always a gentleman to her—but that was exactly what made her think he knew what she really thought. She watched him with the women he really liked—watched the way his smile and his eyes and his gestures seemed to widen, pushing tolerances to the limit. Maybe then some. But when Roy Daniel turned to Kimberly, everything was just as it should be. No lean in just a little closer than necessary, no laugh just a little bit too loud, no nearly invisible wink as he turned to check on his other guests. Not too hot, not too cold, but just right. Every word perfectly measured, every move mathematically precise. Calculated to shield every uncomfortable truth behind the comfortable, well-pressed etiquette of old movies and country clubs and breezy southern mountaintops.

"I see you met our resident fixer," Roy had said to her that same evening. "If you ever have a problem you just can't fix on your own, he's the one you want to call." A man with lost-boy eyes and shaped like a snowman with legs had overheard the remark and, his voice eager and yappy like a puppy just released from a cage, plunged into the tale of some South American country back in the day where those company men had gotten stuck, accused as spies and locked up by the junta and basically written off. And then one day Fixer had returned from a "long weekend" with those same men in tow, all of them looking tired and a little worse for wear but otherwise fine. And the water-cooler whispers about black-hooded men rappelling out of helicopters and secret air strips on narrow, foggy jungle ridgelines and private jets with no tail numbers, but none of the rescued company men saying a word. Roy Daniel's smile had gone from eager to indulgent to anxious and he'd finally excused them both, leading Frosty the Storyteller away still yapping away to anyone who'd listen whether they'd noticed that those men, standing on stage under that "Welcome Home" banner, had looked downright nervous, flinching just barely when Fixer put his arms over their shoulders to the crowd's standing ovation? Happy, sure, not to be forgotten in some rat-infested hole, but, having seen what they'd seen, wanting to keep as much distance as possible between Fixer and themselves for the rest of their days on God's green Earth?

Kimberly had looked around the room as Roy walked him to the door, but Fixer was nowhere to be seen.

Asher might remember his name. But if Jess had really talked with Asher—for some reason she had her doubts—and Asher still hadn't called, then she certainly wasn't going to call *him*. Call him and say what? I'm sorry? She wasn't sorry. I need your help? She did *not* need his help. Yes, you do, Kimberly. This is the one time you actually need his help more than any other time in your entire life. This could be the final time. But you do. You need him. Our kids are in trouble and we need to solve this together. Kimberly paused a moment and watched a couple of squirrels chase each other up one of the maples down by the creek. Its leaves were already starting to turn. Winter would be here before they knew it. But it was still plenty hot tonight.

I do *not* want to need him right now.

Her cell phone began to sing from inside on the counter, ditzy and cheerfully unaware. Kimberly Daniel narrowly missed knocking her glass into the lawn as she spun around and lunged into the dark of the kitchen. No number showed on the screen. No name to brace her for what lay ahead. Normally, without such reassurances, she wouldn't even pick the thing up.

"Hello?" Hours of silence had stolen her voice—it came out as nothing but an aspiring hiss, swallowed up at the end by the room's dark corners.

"Hello?"

"Mom?"

The first summer they'd sent Tyler to camp, he'd called them once—and just once—at about this same time of evening. The same time supper was usually just finished, the day air finally cooling off and drifting in slowly through the window screens toward that corner of the couch where he loved to curl up, stomach full, eyes heavy, to watch anything the television offered up and to listen to home's daily vespers—dishes clinking, water splashing, cabinets closing, sister laughing, mother—work done at last—sinking into the cushions beside him, offering with a sigh the shelter of her outstretched arm. Warmth and shelter and protection against the approaching dark of night.

"Mom?"

Tyler's voice had sounded the same that evening as it did right now

"Tyler? Tyler, honey—is that you?"

"Mom? Mom, it's Tyler. Sammy's here, too, Mom. We're both here. We're okay, Mom. We're both okay."

Kimberly Daniel sank to the floor, eyes closed in pure relief, knees hugged close against whatever might come next.

"Hi, Mommy!" Sammy's voice came from far away, amid scuffled whispers and a rustling much closer than either of her children.

"Hi, Sammy!" The crack in her voice surprised her. She wiped away a tear with the back of her hand.

"Sammy, Tyler, where are you?"

Papers rustled louder, the whispers sharp and insistent.

"Mom, we're okay. Dad's doing the right thing." Tyler's read-aloud voice, pitched a little too high, paced a little off balance, giant steps from word to word until finally dropping to the safety of the last syllable. "If he follows through, we'll be back home by this time tomorrow."

"Where are you, baby? I'll come and get you right now. Tyler? Sammy? Where are you, honey?"

There was no reply. The rustling was gone. She was talking into outer space.

The kids are okay. My kids are okay.

Kimberly Daniel lay her head down on the floor, pressing the throbbing in her temples against the cold, hard stone.

Do nothing, and they'll stay okay.

Outside, across the lawn, somewhere on the other side of the creek, a dog began to bark at something it couldn't see.

If I don't do something, I think I'll scream.

But if I *do* do something. . . .

Kimberly Daniel opened her eyes and sat up, leaning back against the cabinet doors. The room was dark now—just the vague, blue-green glow of the clocks and gauges and buttons of the best appliances money could buy serving only to illuminate the imperfections in the grout, the tiles that stood just a fraction too high, the gaps that spread just a little too wide. The door next to the dishwasher hung a little crooked, just like it had done since they'd moved in. It didn't really do any harm, honestly, but when you looked at it from down here, it looked much worse, made the kitchen look shoddy, unfinished, or just falling apart.

If he follows through, they'll be back home by this time tomorrow.

Asher had promised her he'd fix that cabinet door. Nothing to it, he'd said—just need to tighten up one of the screws on the top hinge, it'll take five minutes. That had been just after they'd moved in.

Trust Asher. He'll do the right thing.

Kimberly Daniel felt the blood beginning to rise. She crawled on her hands and knees over to the bottom drawer, next to the sink, where she kept spare change and rubber bands and the hotel pens Asher left lying around. In the drawer, over to the left, underneath an old butane lighter, was a screwdriver. She took it out, closed the drawer, and crawled over to the crooked cabinet door. Opening it, she searched in the shadows of the blue-green glow for the screw that would set it right. Without coming to any conclusions, she picked the one on the left, tightened it as far as it would go, closed the door, and examined her handiwork.

The cabinet door hung worse than it had before.

Kimberly Daniel drew a long, deep breath, paused for a moment, and then screamed—a long, gurgling wail, the kind you hear in horror movies, off in the distance, just after the camera cuts away from the approaching figure in the heroine's terrified eyes.

• • •

Jessica Kelly thought perhaps this evening she'd rather walk.

The number 7 bus was her normal route, out along Summer Street toward City Point. In the winter, leaning her head against a cold, damp window long after a lazy sun had called it a day, her breath would slow, fogging the pane, turning the red and white and green and gold lights along the way into magical abstractions, holiday bangles dancing across the frosting pane. It was comforting then, somehow, to be swaddled in this little capsule of light and warmth, alone and yet very much not, the people around her reading dog-eared paperbacks or searching bags for change or tissues or staring ahead or behind at the passing traffic or within at their own lives, sometimes smiling, mostly not. This time capsule—filled with living, breathing people, with the smell of wet wool and the sound of a cough and the occasional sympathetic smile—driving every day through her family's past, back and forth, along the streets where her father and grandfather and great-grandfather were borne and raised and married and buried—except her father, of course, who wasn't there yet but would be one day—and where she was borne and raised and married and would more than likely be buried one day, no real alternative plans in mind, but that was still a long ways off, plenty of time to worry about that later.

God willing.

On days like today, of course, the evening sun still hung high off over the buildings in Back Bay and the South End and the windows on the bus would all be open. The grinds and hoots and squeals of the road would overwhelm the feeble rustlings of the passengers inside and their sweat would disappear quickly amid the bus exhaust and the dinner-time meat smoke and vegetable steam and hot oil. Everything open, everything out in the streets, the people, the sounds, the smells—nothing private, nothing reflected, everyone looking out, not in.

On days like today, you could sit on the bus without staring at yourself, breathe without seeing the consequences, see what was going on across the street more clearly than what was happening behind your back. Days like this could be a gift, like the flutter of fairies' wings, the smiles of the children playing on the sidewalks all meant just for you. Or they could be hot and alien, just naked light and sound and smell, stripped to the bone of all rhyme and reason.

The only difference between one and the other, Jess Kelly knew full well, was her. She'd always known this. But apparently somebody wasn't convinced that she'd really learned her lesson yet, and so kept sending her reminders, just to make sure.

Mrs. Daniel didn't believe her. Jess kept playing that last conversation over and over again in her head. Her voice was different than it had been in person. More cheerful in a way, but a little higher, a little thinner, a little farther away. Back in that world she'd come from—that world that Jess knew nothing about. The bond was broken somehow. Too flimsy to stand the stresses of time and distance.

You should have known, Jess—I mean, really, were you born yesterday? You expect to build a bridge out of a little bread and chocolate and coffee and expect it to hold? You have one real conversation with a person and you expect the effect to last the rest of your life? You really haven't learned a thing, have you?

But a single conversation *can*, sometimes, have effects that never go away. And from her one conversation with Kimberly, Jess knew she had made a difference. The children were going to be all right, she felt sure of that one thing. It was a comforting thought.

Jess Kelly pulled on her walking shoes, picked up her bag, and headed for the elevator. The office was already nearly deserted, the warm sun and the knowledge that any such day might well be the last proving too strong a lure to resist—especially so close to the weekend. The elevator doors opened and closed, the car slumped slowly to the ground, and the doors opened and closed again, leaving Jess alone in the lobby. Her shoes squeaked on the clean tile floor. Outside, a seagull picked at something flattened into the cracks of the cobblestone alley. The bird looked around for something better, but, finding nothing, squawked some seagull obscenity and flew heavily away.

Jess pushed the front door open. Off to the left, the 7 was idling at the bus stop, windows open to the glare of the still, hot afternoon. The exhaust from the cars and the trucks and the harbor itself, stewed all summer long, had been left to simmer just a little too long. Up above, in one of the lofts across the alley—one of the few still haunted by the artists who'd colonized it years ago—someone played a flute, eighth notes tripping over halves, halves lolling between the open windows and along the baked brick walls, no breeze to hurry them away. Then, without warning, the world stood still. The traffic light turned green and the cars disappeared. The bus chugged away. The flute stopped singing. The gulls stopped complaining. For one, silent moment, Jessica Kelly was alone.

Jessica Kelly decided that, this evening, she'd rather walk.

• • •

At the top of the stairs, Julie was waiting. She leaned against the railing on the uppermost landing, soft skirts pressed against the cold, dark metal. Ivory smile and lacquer hair and polished pebble eyes framed against the gray buttressed ceiling over her head. Asher climbed up the stairs, circling the square, watching his view of her change, then disappear, then reappear, every four flights bringing him back to the place he could see her best. She reached out a hand to him, leaning down low over the rails, her hair falling past her cheek and over her shoulder and down through the stairwell toward him. But every time she came back into view she was farther away, higher above him, closer to the gothic vaults than to the step-worn stones beneath his feet. When finally she was scarcely more than an idea—a couple of finely etched strokes in a far-off woodcut—he heard their voices, soft at first, then tumbling louder down the infinite shaft to where he stood. Tyler, Sammy, laughing at first, chasing on the stairs, but then delight changing to surprise changing to fear changing to horror, louder now and echoing down the walls and the steps that had no base far below and no end up where they'd all disappeared.

• • •

Asher woke up reaching across a warm but empty other side of the bed. The sun was bright in the room; through a gap in the sheer curtains across the window, he could make out the shimmering of the gulf. Water was running in the bathroom behind him. He sat up, fear of the night replaced almost instantaneously by fear of the day to come. He looked around for his BlackBerry. It was nowhere to be seen.

His clothes were laid out over the chair in the corner where he'd left them the night before. He hurried into his shorts and headed down the stairs to where he remembered seeing another bathroom. The water was instantly hot and the fine shower jets stung his face and back. He'd hoped for a razor, but found none. Maybe there'd be one on the plane.

When he walked back into the bedroom, she was there, standing in front of the window, pulling on simple white panties and looking out over the water. The morning light played through the damp hair around her neck and made the down on her arms and in the small of her back glow like spun sugar. She turned to him, fastening a lacy white bra behind her back. Her eyes were a question mark, a little puffy, belying their tropical blue wink. Her smile was hoping for an answer.

"Good morning." No shyness in her voice, no regret, no fear. She walked toward him and, without stopping, gave him a kiss full on the lips before disappearing back into the bathroom. "You slept well." An observation, not a question.

"I did. Did you?"

"Not so well. Too much to think about."

Asher dressed quickly. His BlackBerry was in the back pocket of his pants. He sat down and opened his inbox. Just the usual garbage. The world, it seemed, had finally given up on him.

She returned from the bathroom, still in her underwear, a little color on her lips now and liner around her eyes. Another wink, frank and friendly, as she moved quickly toward the closet. Her bare feet left little pigeon-toed marks across the thick cream carpet.

If she'd been trying to get his attention, the effect would have been lost.

"Any news from anyone?" Asher talked to curves of her back as she slipped a little rose-pink dress off a hanger.

"No, nothing. They know when we arrive. I expect we'll hear from them then." She slipped the dress over her head, walked straight up to him, and turned her back. Her panties had a fine, lacy pattern that Asher hadn't noticed before. The zipper ran tight against them, easing up the hollow of her back and then pulling tight once more between the finely smoothed angles of her shoulder blades.

"You know . . . if we're really in this together . . ." Asher tried to pull her hair free at the collar but she was already off, back toward the bathroom, smoothing the fabric down her invisible tummy and not-so-invisible hips.

"It would really be handy to know what to call you."

When she returned from the bathroom, she turned out the lights.

"Just call me what you called me last night."

She'd pulled her hair back away from her face, and up off her neck, fastening it in place with a length of white ribbon. She was carrying a little cloth bag that she placed in her suitcase before zipping it shut.

"So." She stood and smiled, posing for the kind of pictures you see in history books. Pictures of people who never came back.

The smell of mangoes had followed her and was slowly filling up the room. Yesterday's Honeycrisp glow had returned to her cheeks.

Asher didn't move.

She looked down at her feet and, betraying her glow's true origins, fussed a little with the hem of her dress.

"You don't remember what you called me last night." Once again, not a hint of a question.

Asher looked around for his briefcase.

She picked up her suitcase and walked toward the stairs.

• • •

The big car barely made a sound as it glided onto the expressway, heading north. Acceleration and centrifugal force pushed Eva back into the soft leather seat and over against the heavy, padded door, away from the driver, away from Phaeton, away from everyone, back into herself. The forces of nature could have their way. The sun spun around them as they banked quietly through the curve, settling in just the right spot to glare onto her face. She bowed her head and closed her eyes. Friday prayers were coming. Traffic was light. They'd be to the airport with time to spare.

Somewhere deep in her purse, Eva's phone began to ring. The driver's eyes in the rearview mirror disapproved of the disturbance. Phaeton glanced her way, but only for a moment, returning to his contemplation of the waking city after a very brief, if reassuring, smile.

Asher wanted to ask her if she knew where Ahmed was, if he had sent her. If he had taken his kids (which he couldn't fathom). He had a million questions and no answers. His body moved forward and his brain tried to keep three paces ahead, just like his father had taught him when they went hunting, or fishing. You have to put your body on automatic pilot, rely on muscle memory, because you need to focus on the prey, the goal, and grasp it before it eludes you forever.

Eva glanced at the number on the screen and turned toward the window.

"Hallo."

Phaeton already knew where they were going, and her English, while good, wasn't *that* good. Switching to German would hide more than it would reveal.

"Good morning." Andreas's voice was solid, reassuring. "So?"

"Everything's fine. We're on our way to the airport now. We should be landing around three, I think."

"Very good. We'll be landing around the same time. You should go straight to the meeting, and let us know when you're close. We'll be right behind you."

Eva could tell that Phaeton was listening. Could it be that he understood? His file told her no. Even so, she should be careful.

"Understood? Eva?"

"Yes, yes—understood. We'll be there. I'll keep you posted along the way."

"Very good."

The car's air conditioner kicked up a notch, blowing cold against Eva's cheek. Outside, one long, low building after another, built as if only to give shape to the sand. Up ahead rose the giants, modern-day demigods in grays and glass, lording over the earth and the waters below and defying the winds above, tapping the fires of heaven itself.

"You're doing well, Eva. You're doing very well."

"Thank you." A small crack split her voice's smooth surface. She hoped it couldn't be heard from a distance.

Phaeton examined something on his thumbnail.

"Are you—is everything okay with *you*, Eva?"

Her father could always tell when she was about to cry, too. At those moments, he'd inevitably asked her that same question: "Is everything okay, Eva?" But why had he done it, if he'd already known the answer? What did he stand to gain from her tears? What did he stand to gain that he didn't already have—hadn't already had since before she could even remember?

"Eva? Don't forget what you're there to do, Eva. Don't forget what *he's* there to do."

Had he done it out of insecurity, out of fear that he'd finally lost the connection, one more mooring to this life's harbor loose? Were her tears a reassurance that all was still right with the world, that he'd still wake in the morning with the sun rising in the east and marking red in the west the day's hard-won end?

Is that what they were to her?

"Everything is fine …" She caught herself just before saying his name. "Everything is just fine."

Phaeton was looking at her now. She could see him reflected in the window, watching the bow of her head and the twist of her neck, and the way her wrist shook with her voice as she held the phone to her ear.

"I love you."

Eva hung up the phone. On their left appeared a wide swath of improbable green; on their right, the giants were upon them. Phaeton checked his thumbnail again, then reached his hand to the seat beside her. She considered it for a moment, then took it in her own, squeezing it gently as she looked away.

The driver pushed to pass a truck and she sank still further into her seat. The sun scorched the edges of the green and the sand returned, covered with earth movers and crane parts and early stacks of I-beams.

Phaeton squeezed her hand back. Just like Kai used to do. Kai and her father. And, yes, Andreas, too. And many, many others. But this was the first time that she hadn't known his real name. Something about Phaeton and his children got to her. Something very unprofessional.

eleven

Roy Daniel, as usual these days, had the feeling he'd forgotten something.

The big man next to him—free-ranging mustache and failed com-bover—watched a western, the wide blue horizons dulled into a fin-ger-smudged screen. He had quietly loosened his belt after dinner, glancing furtively at Roy as his fingers fumbled with the buckle. Roy smiled at the flight attendant as she cleared the remains of his dinner, and sat tapping his pen on his cocktail napkin—the only soldier left standing—and pretended not to notice.

If only there had been more time.

The list on the napkin charted the upcoming course of his wanderings. First was to confirm the location. Second, check the arrangements with local authorities. Andreas should have all that covered. Andreas had never once failed him when it came to facts and figures, places and dates and names and goals.

Then the wandering began.

His first wife had pointed this out to him early on in their relation-ship—before they were even married, actually. Should have tipped him off. She'd said that nothing seemed to escape him but the inescapable. He had to admit that it was a pretty good line, but he hadn't really understood what it meant. Still wasn't sure he understood what it meant to *her*. Still wasn't sure he understood anything about her at all—less and less, actually, as the years wore on.

That he and Ruth were married too soon, of that there could be no doubt. Hell, he'd even thought that on their wedding day. Sitting in the church office with his best man, listening to the ball game on the pastor's little transistor radio, realizing he'd far rather just stay there than walk out that door and into what appeared to be the inevitable rest of his life. The inescapable rest of his life. Which turned out not to be so inescapable after all. It had just taken him fifteen years to work out how to escape it. That's how he understood her line now, at least for himself. But how she understood it, then or now, he really couldn't say.

He couldn't really say.

Actually, had he ever really worked out how to escape it? Worked it out for himself, that is? Or had Helen simply worked it out for him? Helen an obsession from the moment he first saw her, there in the conference room in the Dirksen Senate Office Building. He'd sketched her in his notebook that day, and though he'd tried to be discreet about it, he supposed that doing so had required more attention than she could possibly miss. Inescapable. And so the meeting for drinks to discuss the upcoming committee hearings. And the dinner after that, because, after all, they both had to eat.

Maybe the rest hadn't been quite so inescapable, but at the time it hadn't felt that way. He'd showed her the sketch before the coffee arrived. She'd leaned closer to look and stayed closer than she needed to and asked him in her dark, dark accent if he wouldn't like to finish it and that was it. Entirely inescapable. Only way he could have gotten away was if he'd wanted to, which he most certainly had not. On that point there was no room for debate, then or now.

Certainly inviting her to the house that time she came to town on business wasn't inescapable. Only time she came to town on business, come to think of it. He should have known that Ruth would understand everything the minute she saw the two of them together. And she did. But at the time, inviting her over had seemed the natural thing to do. Colleague far from home, someone he'd mentioned to Ruth, mentioned what a breath of fresh air she was in Washington and how sure he was they'd get along. But in hindsight, he supposed that was what he'd wanted. He was tired of the arguments, tired of the charades, ready simply to get on with it. Ready to face the inevitable. Or, more accurately, ready to take the inescapable and make it truly so.

The plane hit some turbulence and shook from side to side. Mr. Mustache glanced up from his good guys and bad guys to seek reassurance in a flight attendant's eyes. If they weren't worried, he wouldn't worry—at least, not too much. But he couldn't find any. Roy looked behind him, back down the aisle, and saw two of them standing in the galley, laying out snacks and talking, smiling, laughing, nodding, apparently unaware that anything had happened. He turned back around and stared at his list. Still just the two items.

He knew there was more—knew he was forgetting something—but he simply couldn't remember what. Or maybe he'd never known. Maybe he'd just felt that there ought to be something more—something beyond the names and dates and times—but had never actually come up with what they were. Just knew they should be there, felt it so strongly that he ended up believing that once upon a time he'd actually known.

Which was probably what had happened with Helen.

The first couple of years were both the best and worst he'd ever known. The divorce, the move, the new job—behind everything old thrown off, ahead everything fresh and pure and new. Weightless, like the astronauts must feel after the crush of liftoff has passed. Like the mountaineer must feel upon reaching a summit and shedding his pack, gravity overcome, old foe turned best friend. But at the same time, unmoored, like the astronauts must feel when "up" and "down" lose their meaning, like the climber whose life goal, in one small step, ceases to be. Because all animals are creatures of habit, and the distance between man and those ancient steppes isn't as great as he'd like to believe. Because the difference between excitement and fear is nothing but a civilized conceit. From a safe distance, the brain can tell whether it's running toward something, or away. The body, on the other hand, knows only adrenalin. The animal, the astronaut, the mountaineer—they know that directions, like emotions, blur.

And so their emotions had blurred, and their directions diverged, and that was that. Easier than the first time, without all the baggage, but emptier, the wisdom of age making it harder to believe that he'd ever feel that old weightlessness again.

Which made it all the more satisfying when Sarah proved the old bastard wrong.

Oh, sure, the highs probably weren't as high as they had been back in his younger days. But the fact that he'd been so firmly convinced that no further highs were forthcoming worked like magnifying glass on whatever rays of sunlight he got, turning them into all the summer days of high school. Roy smiled and began doodling on the back of his napkin. Her face took shape between the advertisements for frequent flier miles and new and improved web sites. All my relationships seem to begin with a drawing, he thought. Maybe I actually draw the relationships myself.

Maybe I should learn to draw a little better.

Roy Daniel woke up convinced he'd missed it. His eyes opened instantly wide and searching, the muscles in the back of his neck tensed, the unwelcome familiar feeling in his belly telling him he had to hurry. All was not well. He had to catch up. He'd missed it.

The one thing he couldn't remember from the dream was what, exactly, he'd missed. That critical piece of information had somehow gotten lost in the shuffle of waking up. Its shadow still hung over him like a cold spot on a dawn lake—invisible, unmistakable, impossible to find again. But the thing itself was gone. Whatever it was that he'd missed, well—he'd missed it.

In the cabin around him, silverware jingled gently as the attendants' carts rolled through the aisles. Coffee and sausage mingled with perfume and hot towels to wash away the stale short breath of the lost night before. Mr. Mustache lay next to him in a static heap, blinders in place, mouth agape, unaware that the sun had outrun him again. Unaware that he'd missed it, too. Or maybe thankful that he had. One more thing removed from his control—one more thing for which he couldn't be held responsible.

Very few things made Roy believe that he wasn't in any way responsible. Over the years he'd built a life based almost solely upon compulsion. Which isn't to say that he didn't enjoy what he did—he did. At least most of the time. But the feeling he had down deep in his gut—the knowledge that constantly lurked in the darker corners and back alleys of his brain—was that it was *his* responsibility. It was *he* who had to get it done, or at least see to it that it was done and done properly. It was *he* who had to formulate the hypotheses and draw up the test plans and assemble the teams. It was *he* who had to work the late hours when everyone else had plans that just couldn't be changed. It was *he* who was responsible. At the end of the day, when all was said and done—insert your favorite corporate cliché of the day here—there was only he—only he who could make sure that *it* got done.

Whatever *it* was. At the moment, he just couldn't remember.

The flight attendant offered him coffee and he took it gratefully, even though it tasted like some sort of ashtray tea. Why it was they couldn't make a decent cup of coffee at 35,000 feet he'd never understood. Science certainly didn't preclude it. They couldn't say they didn't have the time, or the space. Anyway, the stuff still did the trick. Cut through the fog of the aborted night and made him feel, at least, as if he was ready to work. Ready to get it done. Made him feel—almost—as if he actually even knew what *it* was.

Roy Daniel knew that today would be one of those critical days. Most days, he'd learned, weren't much use in the greater scheme of things. Most days were just playing cards, stacked one next to the other, one on top of the next, building flimsy constructs that would never stand the tests of time. Somebody opens a door too fast, a little breeze comes in from a newly opened window, and the whole thing's gone in a second. In a few minutes, it's all been forgotten, and the same silly process starts over again from scratch.

But every once in a while, a different kind of day came along. A day born of sturdier stock, more solidly built, wood and stone and metal and bolts, more than just gravity holding it all together. Most of the time, these days didn't really announce themselves. Most of the time they started off just like any other days, and more often than not they ended that way, too, not revealing themselves for weeks or months or even years to come. Indeed, most of the time they *were* just like any other days, unremarkable when they dawned and nothing special by sundown. It was only the seemingly accidental links to other days—links that grew like crystals, imperceptibly slow but magically precise—that made them, one day, unlike any other days, days to remember, days to talk about, days to record in the history books and to mark in red ink on the calendars of the future. Because single days don't stand alone. Single points don't form a pattern. Single colors don't make a painting.

But every once in a while, you can see them coming. Every once in a while, when the crystal's nearly formed, you can see what the final piece will look like. Every once in a while, when the painting's nearly complete, an inevitable final brush stroke stares you right in the face. When you can see it coming, you can—sometimes—recognize its arrival. And today was such a day. Today, one way or another, this painting's final touches would be complete.

Of course, sometimes that's also how a new painting begins. But never mind. Analogies will only carry you so far.

Roy Daniel sat up, struggled free of his seat, and walked down the aisle to the lavatory. He latched the door and the fluorescent lights flickered on, mercilessly showing him what he'd become. My God, Roy, when'd you get so damned old? His reflection smiled back the only response at hand. He bowed his head and washed the sleep from his eyes and scraped a tiny plastic razor across his face. Brushed his teeth with a stubby toothbrush, then threw the whole lot in the trash. Do what you can with the tools at hand, then move on. Gather together all the available data, then make the best decision you can with whatever it is you've got. Then move on. Don't look back. Looking back is a waste of time. Leave it till retirement, when you have time to figure out where you came from. What the hell happened? Right now, don't waste your energy. Henry Ford was right—history is bunk. The only people doomed to repeat history are those incapable of an original thought.

The bad coffee had convinced his body it was morning and his brain was operating in high gear. Morning was always the best time for thinking. Some people had peaks and valleys in their days, but for Roy, it was mostly just one big slide from morning till night. Strike first thing, while the iron's hot—it's not getting any better than this. He went back to his seat, packed his things back into his old leather briefcase, and checked the screen. Forty-five minutes till landing. Forty-five minutes till the day really begins.

The "fasten seatbelts" sign lit up with a bell, and the flight attendants started gathering up the past hours' remains. One of them leaned across Roy and shook Mr. Mustache gently through his blankets. He gasped a final snore, peeled away his eyeshades, and blinked around at his fellow travelers, already washed and packed and ready for the day. He muttered something in German, then fumbled for the buttons that would set him upright.

If it were done, 'twere well it were done quickly.

• • •

Bill Morton's reflection on the mirrored wall panted back at him from behind the handlebars of the motionless bicycle. Around him swirled the hum and clank and rhythmic *thud thud thud* of seemingly boundless human energy. Wheels turned, rollers glided, bearings slipped in their greased sockets and rang low when pushed to their physical limits. But all of that was hidden. On the surface there was only metal, plastic, the latest in high-tech fabric, and sweat, quickly toweled away before anyone might notice.

All going nowhere.

A blonde woman leafed through a magazine while her long, tanned legs pumped the pedals of the bicycle to his left. Legs working furiously, fleeing some unseen foe, but eyes disengaged, more interested in the winter fashions than whatever it was that her body feared. To his right, a row of men raced on their treadmills, some quick, some nearly dead, but all focused on the screens ahead. CNN, ESPN, MSNBC, iPod. None speaking to the person beside them in line. Bodies in full-on pursuit or retreat, fight or flight, miraculous culmination of millions of years of human evolution. But minds—no one cared. Put a pretty picture in front of them and they're off and away, lost in the color and movement and sound of an artificial reality, carefully edited for maximum impact, the duller moments cut and replaced with advertisements for the latest ways to add to the distance from the inevitability behind.

Hurry—pedal harder, run faster, push harder—chase the rabbit you'll never catch because you—you very same people—spend your days inventing newer, shinier rabbits; and convincing newer, shinier people that they need to push just a little bit harder to catch them.

Bill Morton went back to reading his *Wall Street Journal*. Pretending to, anyway. He hadn't slept, and his mind wandered. He listened to the whine of the bike, felt the steady increase in his heartbeat, watched in the mirror as his breathing got faster and the beads of sweat got heavier at his temples, running down the sides of his face. The dark gray stain around his neck grew deeper and wide. He looked around, but no one noticed. His mouth grew dry and his breath smelled stale, but no one cared. The herd was in full stampede, but he was completely alone—each of them was alone—trying simply to keep up in a race even he didn't understand.

Jesus, Bill, you're one negative SOB this morning. The thought made his reflected self smile its crooked, 6:00 A.M. smile. It's just you and me, kid—we're the last of our breed. Better pump a little harder, or we'll get left in the dust, one of the stragglers picked off by the wolves when they smell that the fight won't be fair.

His phone rang some Caribbean jingle that his daughter had picked out on their last vacation. Gotta change that, he grumbled, and looked at the screen. He wasn't sure he was ready to talk. Hadn't sweated enough yet, hadn't kicked the dogs barking in his head enough to shut them up. Another twenty minutes on the bike, a few minutes of lifting, a couple of sit-ups to pull in the gut, then a shower, then some coffee, then okay— ready for the day. But not just yet. Hadn't had time to correct the chemical imbalances brewed up by the night before. Hadn't had time to transform those mongrels into happy puppies, or contented labs sleeping at his feet. Hadn't had time to replace the visions of his son and his upraised fist with that of his daughter, or of her daughter, glowing in her pumpkin costume.

Bill Morton stared at the screen for two more rings. The blonde pedaling to his left chastised his sweaty reflection over the scented pages of her magazine. As the steel drums geared up for a fourth chorus, he pressed the green button he'd had no intention of touching.

"Hello?" Although he knew perfectly well who it was.

The blonde went back to her magazine.

"So—what does that mean, exactly?"

"Okay. I understand. I'll make the arrangements." Bill Morton said to the figure only the mirror had allowed him to see. "Thank you for the information."

He hung up the phone and stopped pedaling, staring for a moment at the hair on his legs and the old scar beside his kneecap. When he looked up again, the figure was gone. Bill Morton turned to look directly at the place where she'd been, but no one was there. The blonde turned to stare at him, hand about to turn a new page. Her eyes were pale green, almost gray, like his son's. But when he stared back, she smiled, like the joke was all on him.

• • •

The bathroom door clicked quietly shut, letting Tamara Maybin know it was ending. She curled herself up tight under the thick duvet, hugging a pillow to her middle. The mounds of fabric were soft and warm against her bare skin. Her head burrowed deeper into the feather pillows below, and under the duvet above, blocking out the light seeping in around the curtains. We'll just stay here till he's gone, she thought. Pretend that we're sleeping and avoid all the drama. Start the day fresh when he leaves.

She could feel the regret start to work its way through her insides—the regret that always came after too much wine. Once she'd mistaken the feeling for emotion, but with age came wisdom—or at least a fading faith in the power of the heart. The heart was just another organ, in control far less often than most people wanted to admit. Far less often than screenwriters and novelists and greeting card poets wanted you to believe, anyway. Far less often than they were paid to convince you.

Cultural PR—that was all it was. The only difference between their jobs and hers was who paid them to do it. In PR, at least you were honest about it—people paid you, companies paid you, and you said what they wanted you to. No illusions about independence or responsibility or art. You were a mercenary, plain and simple, and not afraid to say so. Not afraid to admit the fact that they all really had in common: that corporations paid the bills. That if, at the end of the day, you didn't produce something that some corporation felt good about, you'd soon find yourself out of a job.

But come on, now, why do we have to start in on the serious stuff so early in the morning? So early on my spa day, planned now for months and months, massages and facials and pedicures only an elevator ride away, my gift to myself for a job well done? A whole day to work it all out of my system, leaving me free to hole up at home for the rest of the weekend, soft and pretty and clean and, best of all, alone?

The thought of "alone" made Tamara smile, and she rolled and stretched slowly under the covers. She felt the release in her muscles, felt the cool of the sheets as her toes pushed all the way to the bottom of the bed. Felt the tight stretch of clean cotton on her belly and her breasts, the fluff of feathers piling all the way down her bare back. For a moment, at least, the pure physical pleasure of it all shut down the workings of her brain. And that, after all, was the point of the day. She smiled again as the thought drifted listless through her mind's morning fogs. So much pleasure that there's simply no room left to think.

Wouldn't that be nice? Seriously, Tamara—but hey, be my guest. Doesn't hurt to give it a try.

She laughed a little, just warm puffs into the downy pillows.

In the bathroom, there was humming in the shower. Quietly, as always, trying hard not to interrupt her sleep. Considerate after all, just when you'd given up hope. She laughed a little again, to herself, not enough for anyone to hear. But the unwelcome feeling sensed the lapse in her defenses and moved cautiously forward, coiling and recoiling, blind as ever but ever alert.

It's only the wine. Nothing a little breakfast won't cure. A nice mango smoothie, maybe a little toast—everything light today, body and soul, nothing allowed that'll weigh us down. Today's the day for letting things go, for leaving behind instead of taking on. Because how long's it been since the last break in the "taking on," anyway? Way too long. Way, way too long.

The shower stopped. The humming continued. The water started running in the sink. Her BlackBerry started ringing. She buried her face deeper into the pillow.

Oh, please. Not today. Of all days, not today.

The ringing stopped. Tamara waited. It started again. The door to the bathroom opened just a little. Tamara rolled over and squinted through her hair at the wedge of steaming light.

"Sorry. I thought it might be mine." The General's voice ready to move on.

"That's okay." Her first words of the day, and as usual, a lie. She laughed into her pillow again. The General's face was half shaved.

"Do you, uh, want me to toss you that?" The phone had begun to ring yet again.

Tamara rolled over onto her back and shoved the hair out of her face. "I suppose you'd better. It doesn't seem to take a hint."

The BlackBerry landed on the pillow next to her, in the imprint of the General's head. The bathroom door closed quietly behind him.

Tamara grabbed the phone and stared at the screen. What were you saying about "taking on?" But seriously, Tamara, you should have seen this coming. I mean, you can't make a call like you did last night and not expect at least a little shit to hit the fan today.

Remind me again—exactly why *did* you make that call last night?

She laughed again as she pressed the button, just as the room's other BlackBerry jealously took up the cry.

• • •

"Good mornin', sir. I hope ever'thing's goin' okay?"

Al Green sat with his feet propped up on his desk, the ends of his undone bow tie smeared across his chest.

"Well that's good news. And it's still the same crew comin' along—same boys we talked about the other day?"

Except for the bow tie, Al Green was still dressed for the gala. His blue cummerbund had ridden up a little, exposing gaps between the lowest buttons where his shirt was stretched to maximum tolerances. The soles of his shoes had seen better days, but the uppers were polished with military precisions, reflecting the lights of the office like dark stars.

Al Green squinted at the starlight and nodded.

"Okay. Fair enough. Now listen. There's a little somethin' on our end that hasn't gone quite like we'd planned it. Nothin' to worry about—just somethin' I want y'all to be aware of. Seems that one of our top brass caught wind of the operation last night, and put himself on a plane to Frankfurt. We have reason to believe that he's settin' himself up to be at the party this evenin'."

Al Green's office was a windowless box, walls hung with photographs of himself. Al Green with Schwarzkopf, Al Green with North, Al Green with various men smiling in suits and robes and uniforms and flight jackets, in front of flags and helicopters and tanks and even a camel.

"No, sir, he wasn't briefed on the operation. But the Ariadne program fell under him, and that Bulgarian fella was an old college buddy of his, and—well, we figure he just put two and two together and decided he needed to find out what all the fuss was about."

In one corner of the room stood a bookcase filled mostly not with books, but with medals in cases and smaller pictures in frames. A purple heart in a small black case. On top of the bookcase, a United States flag folded into a triangular wooden box.

"No, sir, we have no reason to believe he knew anything about that."

On the wall above the bookcase, certificates, commendations, accolades in calligraphy, wax seals, illegible signatures.

"Negative, sir. Not a chance."

Al Green ignored them all, nodding at his shoes.

"I understand, sir. Now, sir, if I might just make a suggestion."

Al Green continued to nod, tried to speak, then finally got frustrated and kicked his feet back to the floor. He leaned over his desk like a portly gargoyle, holding the receiver to his head with one doughy hand and rubbing his mottled temples with the other.

"Yes, sir. Absolutely, sir. Now ..."

Outside, down the hall, he heard a door open and shut. Al Green glanced at his watch and wondered who'd be in so early. He picked the phone up off of his desk and walked over to the door, maneuvering the cord around the padded back of his big leather chair. The hall was empty in both directions, and for the most part dark. But down to the left the lights were on—there in the corner where Jabe Evans and Bill Morton had their offices.

Al Green grunted an occasional "uh huh" or "yessir" as he made his way back to his chair, trying not to trip over the cord by his feet that he, frankly, couldn't see. Finally he sat down, swallowed by the dark blue leather, and sighed deep and low like a ship's horn out to sea.

"Sir, with all due respect, sir, I want to make absolutely sure you understand what we're dealin' with here."

Al Green picked up a pen and began adding stars to the score or more already decorating his desk blotter. "Sir, I have no doubt that you and your men will handle the situation perfectly. But there's a small detail that you really oughtta know 'bout before y'all meet up—just one little bit of intel that might change who you put where."

To the final star, drawn in the middle of today, Al Green added rays, emanating outward to light the whole month.

"Sir, the gentleman we're talkin' 'bout—I think you need to understand just one more thing about him."

• • •

Sarah Anderson pulled over to the side of the road. It was an old road, narrow, winding past houses rambling back through the woods. One of those neighborhoods that always took Sarah by surprise. You never just happened upon these places by accident, on your way to somewhere else. They generally weren't far from the places you knew, places you lived, places like those that you saw on TV. But you knew when you reached them that you'd reached something rare. They were tucked into folds in the fabric of the everyday, hidden unless you knew just where to part the old, heavy curtains. They seemed revealed, not developed—a part of the landscape, just like the rocks and groves and streams. And the people who lived there—they were part of it, too, evolved like the animals to blend into the wood. You never saw them, but you could feel they were there. You could feel them watching. You could feel they belonged. And you could feel you did not.

She turned off her headlights, cracked open her window, and sat staring out through the blue hints of dawn. A sprinkler awoke hissing and spitting somewhere off to the left. Up above, leaves hung limp, listening for the day's first breaths. Birds chirped and chatted about the return of the sun, laughing and scolding at those with whom they'd awoken, at those with whom they'd lost touch, at those with whom they planned to spend the day, or the week, or the rest of their lives.

Sarah checked the address on the mailbox in front of her against the slip of paper in her hand. So Sandy's would be the next house up ahead—the driveway between the big rhododendrons. Glimpses of red-brick and slate were framed in oak and hickory and black gum leaves. One dogwood had already begun to turn, deep reds defying the morning's blues. The others would follow soon. Summer couldn't hold on forever.

Sarah Anderson waited.

The whole way here she'd tried to convince herself to turn around. At every exit she'd tried to find a reason to slow down, turn off, turn around, go home. But each passing sign offered her no such reason, and each passing hour found her that much more convinced that what she was doing was all for the best. The more she knew it, though, the more she wished it weren't true. Why couldn't there be an easier way? Like that time as a little girl when she'd finally let her mother talk her into jumping off the high dive. Watching the cracks in the concrete fall away as she climbed the wet steps; feeling the aluminum railings curve back and leave her as she dripped along the narrow blue plank; seeing her bare feet hesitate, toes clutching at the edge, the clear water below reflecting back the infinite depths of the summer sky above. Her mother sitting on the edge of the pool, feet dangling in the water, one hand shading her eyes as she beamed encouragement and pride. Tinier than her mother had ever looked, and farther away than she'd ever sounded. Sarah had wanted so badly not to jump, and the feeling had built and built until there, bobbing on the springboard's final inches, shivering a hundred feet above her tiny mother's distant cries, she realized at the same time that she wanted nothing less than to jump, and that she had absolutely no choice but to do so. The inevitability obliterated all traces of desire. Or did desire, when it vanished, steal away the last traces of hope? Even now she didn't know. Then, she didn't even know the question. Just the feeling. I have to jump. There's nothing I want to do less. So I have to jump.

A car approached around the bend in the road up ahead. Sarah Anderson sat up and rummaged through her purse, as if looking for her keys. She didn't look to see if the other driver looked at her. But of course he did. Or she. Why not look at the only other person on the road?

The car didn't slow down, didn't stop. Sarah watched it disappear in her rearview mirror.

The sky brightened by slow degrees, blue to gray to silver white. A wisp of cloud appeared, cotton-candy pink, then drifted in sugar-spun strands of tangerine and honeycomb. A breeze stirred, hinting of yesterday's mowing and the sticky heat to come. Fall would have to wait another day. Sarah closed her eyes and breathed in all those summer vacations past: sprinklers prickling crackerjack skin, soaking butterscotch hair; jellybean eyes licking up pure vanilla smiles.

And on the last day of summer you wanted nothing less than to return to school. And so you did.

Sarah Anderson felt the eyes, and opened hers. A tall man in baggy gray sweatpants and an old, thinning sweatshirt stood in front of the rhododendron bushes, stretching his arms into the air. He twisted his long frame from side to side, bony elbows sticking out right and left, hair chalky silver and wiry. When he bent to the right his eyes puzzled at the car, his thin lips narrow on his teeth. But then he bent back left, dropped his arms to his sides, shook it all off and jogged away down the road.

Sarah Anderson just watched him go.

He's not what he once was, she thought, and she smiled, the way one might smile at an ugly little puppy. Back in the day, when he was a

CASTOR regular, he towered above them all, hair trimmed and white, suits custom fit, eyes ever questioning what his assured smile knew best. But that was a long time ago. Back then, he'd had Jabe Evans's ear. He'd steered him through very rough seas. And as quickly as those storms had cleared, new ones had broken, requiring once again Sanborn McRae's expert guidance. Storm after storm safely weathered, but storm after storm nonetheless—until one day, Jabe Evans began to question cause and effect. Whether his suspicions were correct, well, Sarah Anderson was in no position to say. But after Sandy was banished from the inner circles, there was no doubt the seas had calmed. Oh, sure, the occasional squall still hit now and then, and Sarah knew Sandy was still quietly called on from time to time to help. But he wasn't the man he'd once been—literally, or figuratively. In the annals of CASTOR history, at least, Sandy McRae was now more myth than legend.

Sarah Anderson stared at the bend in the road around which their mythical hero had disappeared. There had been a time when he would not have run away. And there had been a time when, had he done so, she would have followed, without thinking, without question. He would lean against her cubicle, salt blue eyes distant but weathered voice whisper close, stories of courage under fire and valor and intrigue, all in the name of life and liberty and the pursuit of everything good and pure and just. He could have told her anything, asked of her anything, and she would have believed and obeyed. And he did tell her many things—stories she could only assume must be true, because if they weren't, how could he have ever dreamed them up? But he had never asked of her anything she wasn't perfectly willing to volunteer.

He'd been, in her mind, the perfect gentleman. Okay, the emphasis had been more on "perfect" than "gentleman," but still—those were different times, a different place. She hadn't been out of college that long, really, and he wasn't long out of the field. Always looking for a way back in.

That was the problem, they said—CASTOR was his way back in, whether CASTOR liked it or not. Still small enough to be influenced, still hungry enough to snap up the work that the big guys didn't want to touch. Which let Sandy McRae do the only work he'd ever truly loved. Work the nation needed done as much as it needed to deny. Work you can only do once—work you can't do and remain on the inside. That was the deal you made. Because you loved the work so much, you'd do it, but if you did it, you'd never be able to work again. The "patriotic paradox," he'd called it once, and now she finally understood. Then, she'd gone in with her eyes wide open—only those as young as she was could open them that wide. She'd looked, but hadn't seen; believed, but hadn't understood. And now she'd never be able to do it again, no matter how much she wanted to. Twice simply wasn't in the cards.

But you could keep at it forever, as long as you stayed on the outside. Vampires, cursed for eternity with that which you could no longer feel, lusting after that which you could no longer hold.

The rush of a passing car brought Sarah back to the street, the neighborhood, the dawn. Fairy dust danced in the sunbeams anchoring the trees to the ground. Somewhere a dog barked at the day's first squirrel. Another voiced his sincere, if distant, support.

"Good morning, Sarah."

Sarah nearly hit her head on the roof.

His face at her window had more wrinkles than it had last time they'd met. They glistened and dripped in the damp morning light. His hair was damp as well; he slicked it back out of habit, but it only stood straight up. The same glacier eyes, just a little farther back in his head. The same low-slung voice, just a little more gravel in the road.

"I thought that was you."

Sarah Anderson rolled the window clear down and did her best to smile at Sandy McRae. At the old man who'd unexpectedly turned up in his place. At the dark stains around the neck of his sweatshirt, the strong hands resting on the bony knees of his sweatpants, the uneven breath that hinted of a drink or two extra too few hours before.

"Good morning, Sandy. Haven't heard from you lately. How've you been?"

Sandy McRae stood up straight and held out his arms, acknowledging the cheers of his followers. "Old," he said. "I've been old."

"It happens to all of us, Sandy. To most worse than you."

"To you not at all."

Sarah smiled. "Just wait till you put on your glasses."

"Don't need glasses from over here. You don't look a day older than the last time I saw you. You're a wonder, Sarah. A vision. A charm."

"I'm just a miracle of modern medicine, Sandy. The best that money can buy."

Sandy McRae's eyes narrowed and he shook his head, smiling. "No, no you're not. You're the best, Sarah. Always were. Just the best."

The two looked at each other for more than a moment, and Sarah could feel herself start to blush. She looked around for her purse and searched it absently, then tucked it in her lap and squinted ahead at the sun.

"Would you like to come in, Sarah? Or are you just on an errand? Making sure I'm still alive? Hoping to find that I'm not?"

Sarah didn't turn to look at him. "Is Mims up already?"

Sandy followed her gaze toward the sunrise, an overture in gaudy whites just past the end of the road.

"No, she's out."

"Already? How early did she leave?"

"Nineteen ninety-eight."

"Ah."

Sandy McRae turned back to the car and chuckled at Sarah's red cheeks. "Come on in," he said, waving a long arm toward the driveway. "I'll make you some coffee. Or if you're still on last night, I'll make you a drink. Stick around for a while. I don't get a lot of company."

Sarah Anderson smiled up at him, still squinting, as if his face were the sun. Then she rolled up the window, opened the door, stood up, and faced him. He offered his arm and she took it, like a fond daughter on a morning visit. A dog started barking at the slam of the car door, and at the stranger trespassing the ancient rhododendrons.

• • •

Sarah Anderson stared into the bottom of her coffee cup. Where she'd swirled it a few minutes before, a long, brown eyebrow had dried, arced across the inside edge. On the outside, the last vestiges of her lipstick clung to the white porcelain rim.

Through the bay windows, the morning pink had warmed to an Indian summer haze. Gnats milled aimlessly where the breathless sunlight pooled through the trees. Inside, Sandy McRae leaned against the burnt-chocolate granite, eyes narrowed and dark in the shadows of the kitchen.

"And you haven't told anyone about this?"

Sarah Anderson shook her head, as if pitying the poor, sullied cup in her hands. "Just you, Sandy. I didn't know who else to tell. Roy was already on the plane."

"The police?"

"No." Still shaking her head, still pitying. "I know maybe that would have been the right thing to do, but . . ." She shrugged. "I don't know. It just didn't *seem* right. Seemed like. . . . I just wasn't ready to handle what would probably happen if I did."

Sandy McRae nodded at the floor and walked around the island to the coffee pot. He held it up in Sarah's direction but she just shook her head. He refilled his own mug.

"In other words, you want to control the outcome, not hand it off to somebody else."

"Just like you taught me."

"Just like I taught you."

Sarah Anderson put her coffee cup down on the table. Outside, a bird shrieked at someone or something that didn't answer. Sarah's eyes roamed the branches, unsatisfied.

"Except that I *do* want to hand it off to someone else. I just want to hand it off to someone I know. Someone we all know. Someone we know we can trust."

Sandy McRae nodded again, contemplating something on his right thumbnail. "You did the right thing, Sarah." He looked up and fixed his gaze on her for the first time this morning, so suddenly, so firmly that she felt herself holding her breath.

A clock chimed to no one in particular off in some empty room. The house smelled borrowed, sounded unused.

"Now tell me again, just to make sure I understand. All these calls came in while you were at the party, right?"

"That's right."

"And you don't have any reason to believe that anyone else knows about them?"

Sarah shook her head. "No, no reason. I didn't listen to them on speakerphone. And nobody else was in the office, except Al Green."

"Who heard you talking with Andreas."

"Yes. He heard that."

"So he could have been listening when you were listening to those messages."

"He could have been. But like I said, I didn't listen to them on speakerphone. So he couldn't have heard anything."

" 'Couldn't have' is a little strong."

"Oh, Sandy, come on. We're not in a James Bond movie."

"Speak for yourself."

Sarah smiled in spite of herself, remembering.

"I'm just saying. It's not impossible."

"Very few things are impossible, Sandy." Sarah stretched a little and yawned. "Almost as few as are likely."

Sandy McRae took a long drink of coffee and stared into the next room.

"Well," he said, "let me take it from here. I'll let you know what I come up with. But don't worry, Sarah—this doesn't sound serious. Amateurs—guys who've watched too much TV—that's my guess. I'd be willing to bet we have those kids back before this time tomorrow."

"Thank you, Sandy." Sarah Anderson carried her coffee cup over and set it down on the island beside him. She felt the color rise in her cheeks as she stood there, just a moment longer than she'd expected.

There was a loud thud against the bay window, like a tennis ball against a wood floor. Sarah spun around. Sandy McRae just looked up, but his arm was around her shoulders now. The outline of a bird, splayed wings etched in almost comic relief, smeared across the broad middle pane. Sarah looked in the bushes below. A downy puff fluttered in the nonexistent breeze.

"Don't worry about that," said Sandy McRae. "It happens all the time. Nine times out of ten, they just sit under those bushes for a while, then hop back up and fly away."

Sarah Anderson watched the tiny feather quivering beneath the pane. "You should keep your windows a little dirtier. If they could see them, they'd probably avoid them."

Sandy McRae shook his head and laughed, a little sadly. His embrace was suddenly awkward, the adrenalin ebbing faster than it once had.

"You'd think so, wouldn't you? But no, I'm afraid that wouldn't help. They don't crash into the windows because they don't see them."

"What is it, then? What do they see?"

"They see themselves."

Sandy McRae put the coffee cup in the sink and leaned back against the counter. He picked up the phone and dialed a single number.

"Good morning, sir. Are we still on?"

The window in the dining room admitted none of the light warming the dew outside. He watched the driveway until her windshield flashed and was gone.

"I understand, sir. That's already taken care of."

The bones of the big house creaked and popped. The refrigerator began to hum. Somebody outside was pulling a lawn mower's starter cord. The fax machine in his office began printing something he probably didn't want.

"Yes, sir." Spoken to the empty space between the rhododendrons. "I think we're in good shape. I'll call you back when I know more."

Sandy McRae hung up the phone.

He could still smell her in the warmth of the bay window, but she was fading, pushed to the corners by scorched coffee and old wood and furniture that no one used. Almost as if he'd dreamed the whole thing. He remembered thinking as a kid that the house smelled old, like his grandparents distilled into the doilies and fringes. Arm covers worn slick by generations of flannel and tweed. Dusty hooked rugs by the back door where the dogs lay and waited for someone to come or go.

But that was many years ago. Many years and, it seemed to him, two or three lifetimes ago. Grandparents gone, parents gone, wives gone, Sarah gone. Doilies, fringes, arm covers—all gone, replaced more than once by people who came and went. Sleek, cool, fashionable things—neutral tones, hypoallergenic, memory-free. The dogs no longer looked up and wagged their tails as he headed out the door. No room for care and feeding in this house. This assortment of bricks and wood frames and stone slabs that passed, from the outside, for something that fit, something with a past, something that belonged in that space for all time. This shell, this façade, this mask that hid an inner lack of any past or future or everlasting soul. Disposable living. Drip dry. Wrinkle-free.

Time to move.

Sandy McRae's tennis shoes squeaked on the wood floor of the empty hallway. He ignored the unmade Murphy bed in his study and sat down at his desk. He took an unmarked CD from on top of a neat stack of papers and put it into the drive of his desktop computer. He typed a few commands to start a backup. As the hard drive whirred to life, he turned his attention to the page on the fax machine. Another stock report from some anonymous broker who thought he cared. He added it to the stack of papers and fed the whole thing into the shredder under his desk. He checked his watch. Eight forty-two. The progress bar on his computer screen showed 30 percent complete.

Next to the shredder was a worn black gym bag, half filled with an assortment of crisply folded clothes. Sandy McRae emptied the shredder into the gym bag, and tossed the gym bag onto the Murphy bed. He unplugged the phone line from the back of the fax machine. He paused to stare again at the computer, tapping his fingers on the edge of the desk as the progress bar slowly crept across the screen. Then he stood up, walked over to the bookshelves that covered the entire back wall of the study, and pulled out an old hardback edition of *For Whom the Bell Tolls*. He tucked the big book into the gym bag. The shredded papers crackled under the weight of the book. Sandy McRae paused for a moment and looked back at the door. In the kitchen, the ice maker spat out its latest offering. Some crazed bird cackled and shrieked outside the bedroom window across the hall. The sound of the lawn mower modulated in the distance as it plowed into a stretch of deeper grass.

The CD drive in the computer whirred to a stop. Backup complete.

Sandy McRae removed the CD and tucked it inside the front cover of the book. Then he unplugged the computer from the wall, turned the CPU around so he could look in the back, and pulled out the hard drive. He dropped the drive onto the papers next to the book and zipped the gym bag shut. He glanced one last time around the room. Two old cell phones still lay on the desk. He pick up one, flipped it open, and scrolled through the call log for a number. When he found it, he pressed on CALL and waited. A joist popped somewhere up in the attic. A helicopter clicked by unusually low, but didn't linger.

"Final act. Take up your positions, then get ready to pull the plug. I'll be in touch with the go-ahead."

Sandy McRae hung up the phone, put it down on the desk, and picked up the second one. This time he didn't have to look. He just hit the green button and stared up at his books.

He'd been in this room when his third wife moved out. He'd had the door closed and she hadn't bothered him. He'd heard the dresser drawers opening and closing upstairs, the closet doors' familiar squeaks, suitcase zippers and rollers in the hall. Then the front door had opened, and he'd held his breath, not really knowing it, waiting for the pause. But the pause hadn't come. The door had just closed again, no hesitation, no final reflection on the threshold he'd once carried her over. Just the soft click of the latch and the clunk of suitcases pulled down the stairs outside. The car motor starting on the first try out in the driveway. Then nothing. Easy. Almost as if it had never happened. As if he'd simply fallen asleep at his desk and dreamed the whole thing.

He frowned down at the Murphy bed where he'd been sleeping ever since.

A voice was there on the other end of the line. Sandy McRae opened his eyes wide and stared up at the light on the ceiling.

"She's awake. Time for you to go to bed. I'm going to take a little vacation. I'll send you a postcard, let you know when I'm coming home."

How was it he'd never noticed, all those nights lying staring up at this very same ceiling, that the light fixture cover had, apparently, trapped generations of tiny bugs? Flying in from above toward the irresistible warmth, they ended up lying with all those who'd come before them in the dark, dusty silhouettes he could see clearly now clouding up the frosted glass that protected those bulbs that somehow never seemed to burn out.

"Good night."

Sandy McRae hung up the phone, powered it down, and pulled the battery and SIM card out of the back. He did the same to the other phone lying on the desk. Then he opened a side pocket of the gym bag and stuffed all the pieces in next to an assortment of other outdated cell phones. He zipped up the pocket, picked up the gym bag, and walked down the hall, through the kitchen, and out the back door to the garage. He pressed the button to open the door, then got into his old black Cherokee, tossed the bag onto the empty passenger's seat, and turned the key in the ignition. It started on the first try. He backed out of the garage, down the driveway, and into the street, then paused to shift out of reverse. The transmission rattled a little as the old SUV settled into first gear and made its way off down the narrow road.

The garage door was working its way slowly back down to the pavement when it disappeared from Sandy McRae's view, off beyond the old rhododendrons.

• • •

The man stood on the sidewalk, over toward the curb, wearing a brown department store blazer a few shades lighter than his slacks. His tie was striped in dusty greens, and in beiges that matched his shirt. His hat was the knock-off outback type men his age wear when they're feeling adventurous. Bill Morton himself had bought one a few years back when he and Patty visited the national parks out West.

In the man's hands was a stack of pocket-sized New Testaments. A white cardboard box of reinforcements heeled at his scuffed wingtips. Each little book was bound in black leatherette and bore a green-and-white card-stock sash proclaiming the "Good News!" contained inside. Bill Morton knew this because a few recipients had crossed to his side of the street. He could read the words from his car.

This man was no slouch. He worked the crowds of passersby, reaching out a hand to each personally, smiling as if at an old friend, looking each in the eye. Bill Morton couldn't hear his words, but he could see the looks on the passersby's faces. Some gave him a polite "no thanks," some waved him off, but almost no one ignored him. Almost everyone smiled back, at least a little. Most of those who took a book stopped for a few words before moving on.

Bill Morton counted out of habit. The man was averaging about one taker out of every ten to fifteen passersby. Morton had to think this was a pretty good rate, particularly because this was an entirely unqualified crowd. There were government guys and lawyers in dark suits; students in sweatpants and T-shirts—T-shirts Morton was pretty sure he'd worn thirty years ago; girls in skinny jeans and sweaters that looked, to Morton's eye, a little too homemade. Mostly younger, but a few his age. None older. Their numbers are dwindling, he thought—the people older than me. Seem to be fewer and fewer every year. Funny how that happens. Wonder where they all go?

Bill Morton grinned and tapped at nothing in particular in the middle of his leather steering wheel. The little jokes weren't working anymore. That old familiar feeling was on the rise.

No sign of his son today.

The man in brown offered a book to a middle-aged woman in black. Black hair streaming over dark, black-rimmed sunglasses down to black-sweatered shoulders; black leather bag syncopating one black-skirted hip. Black heels marching one two one toward some inevitable end. Marching without a sideways glance past the man in brown. His first complete whiff. The man stood up a little straighter, turned to his next target, smiled all the more brightly and offered up the same book she'd just rejected. A young man in a bright new Nationals ball cap met his smile, and reached out his hand to take it.

When his son had been a student here, Bill had sometimes parked on this same block. At first he'd made up excuses for himself—killing time before a downtown meeting, clearing his head after a particularly long one. But the truth had always been that feeling. It would creep up on him slowly, invisibly, like the daily changes in the bathroom mirror. By the time he noticed, it was too late. He had to go. Like the itching that makes you scratch the scab off an old cut. You know that pain and blood will follow. But the itch is simply too great. Instant gratification trumps the wisdom of years just about every time.

Mr. Brown offered his good news to a young couple. The boy's arm hung over her shoulders, her smile shy under his protective yolk. She took the little book and smiled up at the man in brown. The boy smiled, too, a little confused but eager to please. Anything to retain the privileges he'd worked so hard to secure. The man in brown laughed. The girl thanked the man, and the boy studied the girl's face. She leaned in closer but started reading the book as they walked away. Their familiar hips rubbed in matching jeans as they made their way down the sidewalk.

When it came to that feeling, Bill Morton had never been able to distinguish cause from effect. Was the feeling a result of the misgivings, or the misgivings simply his mind's misreading of a purely physical phenomenon?

He honestly didn't know—not to this day. But at least today he recognized the question. Back then, he hadn't even gotten that far.

At first he'd thought that the feeling was fear. Later, he'd decided it was more likely anger. But lately, it had come to resemble nothing so much as sadness, although Bill didn't believe the feeling had really ever changed. Maybe it was a distillation of all three. Or maybe—here's a thought—maybe all three are actually the same feeling. Deep down, maybe there's really no difference—no practical difference, anyway—nothing that science could discern. Like the same liquor cut with different mixers. The drinks might look very different. But raise the glasses to your lips and you'll breathe in that same aroma. Take a drink, break through the surface of sweets and sours and bitters, and you'll find the same bite, the same warmth, the same notes that float through the primal corridors behind your eyes and linger in the catgut synapses up the back of your neck. The only thing that lasts is the same. The rest is just window dressing. Seven veils. A thousand and one nights to charm the powers that be into sparing your life for just one more day.

The man in brown removed his jacket and folded it neatly into the white box of bibles. When he tried to stand again he showed his age, rising up slowly, a grimace creasing his face. He fixed his pained eyes on Bill Morton, sitting across the street in his big car, watching. Bill Morton looked away. The feeling jabbed at him low in the gut, creeping up his spinal cord, making his fingers go cold. He closed his eyes, willing it to go away.

When he opened them again, a familiar young man in a huge, dirty jacket stood on the sidewalk, unshaven for months, unwashed, unnoticed, unknown, unknowing. He stood and stared, but not at Morton—above him, through him, beyond him in space and in time. The man in brown reached out a hand, offering him the little black book that promised good news for the taking. But the familiar young man backed away, eyes wide, jaws working. He tightened his grip on the garbage bags that he held in each hand like withered balloons. He opened his mouth to speak, but if words came, they couldn't compete with the main stream of truck engines, bus brakes, and car radios Dopplering off down the street.

Bill Morton opened the door of his car and stood, ready to cross, waiting only for traffic to clear. But his son turned and walked the other way, one leg dragging a bit, shoulders shaking off some unseen weight. He punched to his right suddenly and the sidewalk crowd parted, unaware that they were not his target. They didn't realize they inhabited another dimension. He didn't see them, just like—except when he threatened, of course—they didn't see him, either.

The man in brown watched him go, hand still extended toward the place the young man had only just stood. A man in a dark suit took the book, thanked Mr. Brown, and continued on his way. Mr. Brown looked startled, and turned his head to Morton. But Bill Morton was already back in his car. It wasn't true what they said: Blood wasn't always thicker than water. Bill Morton knew what he'd done needed to be done. But that knowledge didn't stop the feeling from shooting up his spine like lightning and he closed his eyes tight, trying to hold it all in, hands digging tighter still into the safety of the leather-bound steering wheel.

• • •

Sandy McRae sat in his old Cherokee and waited. Seemed like he'd spent most of his life like this—sitting in a car and waiting. Or sitting in a hole in a jungle somewhere, waiting. Or in a desert. Hell, even when he'd had time off, more often than not he'd spent it waiting. Sitting at the bottom of some granite cliff, waiting for his partner to yell down to take him off belay. Sitting in some tiny tent, wind popping the nylon walls, watching the color darken as the snow piled up against the windward side. Waiting.

Waiting for things over which he had no control. Waiting for word from someone else. Waiting for people who knew next to nothing about what it was like where he was. What it was like to be him. What he was like. What he would like. And what he wouldn't.

One thing they'd always understood, though: that he needed to get paid. And at the end of the day, that was enough. That was all the understanding they really needed. Those people would never understand anything more, anyway, so why beat a dead horse? Take their money and run. Take a vacation. Disappear for a while out in the Red Rock Country. Find a little side canyon off the river, cool in the Kelly-green shade of the cottonwood trees. Set up camp in the warm, soft sand under rust-varnished cliffs and just listen. The rustle of the leaves and the swoop of the swifts as the heat of the day rises slowly into night. The slap of the catfish at the end of the line, hauled out of muddy water onto watery mud. The crack of juniper and the spit of hot grease and the chirp of the bats chasing moths from the fire. The chanting vigil of water on pebbles by the light of a million tiny suns. The excitement of grosbeaks and towhees and chats at the dawn that only they can hear. The far-off cry of the red-tail piercing the midday hush, lulling you off to sleep. And the rustle of leaves waking to long shadows and the ancient repeat that'll outlast us all.

The godforsaken places, as those people always called them. Those godforsaken places you spend all your time. Well, from what he'd seen of the world, it was a lot better off without gods. So forsake away, oh holy ones. Leave more room for me.

The suburban mid-morning was in full bloom where Sandy McRae had parked. Minivans piled high with white plastic grocery bags and with children still too young to go to school. Some women looked tired, beat down and dragging, like the load they were lifting might be their last. Others looked happy, at home in their element, ponytails perched high and gym clothes cinched tight. Most of the men just looked lost. So why the difference? Adaptation—the name of the game, no matter who, what, or where on Earth you were. None of us were really meant to be here. Evolution hadn't anticipated a life of asphalt and vinyl and AC and DC. It had all just happened too fast. Give us ten thousand more years or so, maybe we'll be prepared. The desirability of the fit human body erased from our common psyche, along with the longing for the great outdoors. Replaced by well-padded asses better suited for a life spent sitting on artificial surfaces. Wide, bulging eyes ready for all manner of visual stimuli—all except the sun, of course. Tiny, multifunctional fingers and thumbs ready to take on any manner of electronic device, but entirely incapable of pulling the rest of the body up a good 5.10 finger crack. *Homo suburbis.* The most sedentary species the world has ever known.

A man in dark-framed sunglasses and a new bomber jacket made to look old leaned against the wall by the supermarket doors. He appeared engrossed in his cell phone, maybe texting his girlfriend, but when he looked up, he looked straight at the old Cherokee. The third time he did so, Sandy McRae started his engine. He drove around to the front of the store and leaned over to roll down the window on the passenger's side.

"Sorry I'm late," he said.

The man looked around quickly and put his phone in his jacket pocket. "No worries, mate," he answered. "Just glad you turned up. I was beginning to think she'd talked you out of it."

Sandy McRae wasn't convinced that the accent was real, but the words matched up, so he unlocked the door. The man got in and sat down in the passenger's seat. He looked straight ahead as McRae waited for an old woman pushing a cart full of Kleenex and Campbell's soup to move out of the way.

"I heard—" the man started, staring at the shopping cart.

"Not yet," said McRae. He pulled forward, past the old woman, and drove off toward the other side of the strip mall. From there he pulled out onto a side street, turned away from the main road, and drove slowly into a residential neighborhood.

"Okay. You were saying?"

The man still stared straight ahead. "I heard from Danno. He said the monsoons have arrived early."

"Okay. Good."

"He also said he'd made it out okay, that the water was pretty clear, and that he was ready to break camp."

"Perfect. I think that about wraps it up, then. Just one last thing, I guess."

The man reached into his pocket and pulled out a folded handkerchief. "I have it right here."

Sandy McRae glanced over then turned left along a shady row of houses. He nodded. The man unfolded the handkerchief revealing a tarnished men's class ring.

"Okay." McRae turned left at the next street, making his way back toward the strip mall. "Leave it in the glove compartment."

The man in the leather jacket refolded the handkerchief, opened the glove compartment, and pulled out a brown envelope. He put the handkerchief into the glove compartment and closed it quietly. Then he slipped the brown envelope into his jacket and continued to stare straight ahead.

Sandy McRae made another left back into the strip mall, opposite where they'd left. He pulled into a parking space in the middle of several parked cars. The two men sat for a moment. No one was in the nearby cars. No one moved around them. The man in the leather jacket opened the door of the Cherokee, stepped out into the parking lot, and walked away. Sandy McRae waited for him to disappear. Then he started the engine again, backed out of the parking space, and drove off toward the strip mall's main exit.

At the stoplight, a little girl stared from a minivan next to him. Sandy McRae stared back. The light changed from red to green, and the minivan began to pull out. The little girl stuck out her tongue. She tossed back her head in a huge, silent laugh as Sandy McRae stuck out his own tongue in return.

• • •

Jabe Evans sat in the big, open cockpit of what he suspected would be his last sailboat and stared out across the channel at the golf course. The morning was warm—summer wasn't ready to concede just yet—and, aside from the planes tracing the river toward Reagan, as still as could be. He was trying to decide if what he was looking at near the far shore was a heron, or just a stick. Too far away to tell. More and more, things in the distance seemed to elude him. The only thing harder was seeing things right in front of his face.

A couple of young men Jabe Evans vaguely recognized from the club were making things ready up near the bow. Roger Taylor emerged from the cabin carrying a mug of coffee, a manila folder, and a black pen on an old wicker tray. The pudgy man set the tray down next to Evans, squinted distastefully at the low sun reflecting off the water, and beat a hasty retreat below. Jabe Evans thanked his back as it disappeared. He took a sip of coffee, opened the folder, and leafed through the papers inside. He first read the pages marked with Roger's neat yellow signature stickers, signing each with an impatient scrawl. Then he began reading the rest, one by one, leaving no word to chance. On almost every page he wrote a question or comment, like a high school teacher grading essays. A few he just let go with a nod or a frown. One he folded and tucked into his notebook.

He picked up his BlackBerry, searched through his contacts, and pressed a button. He listened to the ringing in his ear as he watched another boat motoring out into the channel. An old Lawley sloop; forty-five, maybe fifty feet; nicely kept. The captain gave Jabe Evans a wave, and Jabe Evans waved back. He was anxious to be off himself. Anxious to get back out into the main stream, unfurl the sails, trim in close to the wind and hear the hull slipping faster through the water. The powers of nature harnessed, the laws of physics proved. The shore, with its powers of people and laws of men, left far, far behind.

The ringing had stopped on the other end of the line. Someone was repeating hello, this time more as a question than a statement.

"Good morning. Are you getting close?" Jabe Evans turned back to watch the boys coiling the jib sheets. Good-looking boys, tanned, wrinkled shorts and old boat shoes frosted with salt. He knew he didn't pay them much for their help when he took the boat out. He wondered what they really did, or hoped to do, or who paid the rest of their way.

"Okay, good. I'm glad to hear that. I think I'm going to need you here afterward. Up till then, though, we'll be okay."

Who knows—they might not need to do anything at all. Might not even need the money he paid them. He didn't know a thing about them, or their families, or their situations in life. Didn't know a thing about what made them show up when he called—when Roger called, that is—or about what they did when it was all over, sails folded and battens fixed, ropes fore and aft made fast to the cleats on the dock. Did they splash a little water over their wind-burned faces, wash the rope grease off their hands and rush off to other jobs? Did they take the cash Roger gave them and head for the nearest bar? Did they wander back to their parents' houses and watch Andy Griffith reruns till their mothers came home to make them dinner while their fathers worked late again?

The voice on the other end of the line had stopped. "What?—no, no, nothing like that. I just think some of the guys will be surprised, or at least surprised that I know. Might need a little looking after."

One of the boys stood up and stretched, arms high over his head, faded polo shirt hiked up to his navel. Shorts defying gravity, held by friction alone to the clean tanned lines of youth.

"Okay, okay, whatever you think's best. I think it's overkill, but suit yourself."

The boy dropped his arms and shook his shirt back into place. His cohort stood up and smiled at something one of them had said. Or maybe it was a smile about something that, these days, went without saying. Some new universal truth. Some law of nature that Evans's generation hadn't ever learned.

"No, she won't be with us today. She's got a date with the ladies."

What were they saying? What did they think? What made them do this—what, or maybe who? Were they using the money to pay for college, or college girls? Or just girls? The two snuck a quick glance back at Jabe Evans as if they'd heard the thought. Empathy? Sympathy? Mockery? Disdain? Or maybe nothing—maybe they were looking right through him. Watching the old sloop passing in the channel beyond. Watching the heron rising with the heat of the day in search of quieter waters downstream.

At this distance, he simply couldn't tell anymore.

"Still in Colorado—yeah, that's right. Anyway, get here as fast as you can. Let Roger know when you're nearby."

Roger Taylor poked his head out from below and collected the manila folder and pen. He frowned in the direction of Evans's gaze then disappeared again without a word. The boys sat down at the bow, legs dangling over the rails. Down the river, another plane bore its passengers skyward. Jabe Evans stood listening to the roar of the jets, already fading, and watched the swinging of the boys' legs, shoes dangling precariously from the tips of their toes.

He wondered where the plane would land.

• • •

Al Green opened his top dresser drawer in search of a clean pair of socks. Wouldn't open more than six inches. Only thing in full view was a silver 1911 in a sweat-polished leather shoulder holster. He threw it on the bed. Spare set of keys, fraying nylon wallet full of cards he never used, aviator glasses with scratched yellow lenses, envelope full of fading color prints—he pushed all these off to one side. Damn drawer still wouldn't open. Al Green rattled it a few times then gave it a good yank. The left end checked up, caught on something back out of sight. He reached in and felt around—cardboard ammo box, just a fraction too tall. Wondered why he'd jammed the damn thing way back in there in the first place. Never mind— he ran his hand right across the back of the drawer, herding everything he touched over toward the front corner. A pair of navy blue socks hid in a tangle of wadded-up boxer shorts, handkerchiefs, and ancient gym socks. A silver tie tack. The button strip from some tuxedo shirt he no longer owned. A picture frame, face down. Her old-fashioned handwriting on the cardboard backing.

Gotta clean up all this crap one of these days. But not this morning. He grabbed the blue socks out of the tangle and threw them on the bed, next to the gun. Too damn much to do.

Al Green felt that all-too-familiar sting in the pit of his gut and hurried down the hall to the bathroom. In the medicine cabinet, the value-sized bottle of Tums was nearly empty. Al Green shook a few into his only-slightly-shaky palm and shoved them into his mouth. He stared for a moment at his reflection as he shut the cabinet door and chewed the pills. Eyes too damn small (and too damn red), nose too damn big (also too damn red), hair too damn gone (and not a trace of red left). Chins: too damn many. Too damn many gray chest hairs poking up out of the collar of last night's T-shirt. His wife used to tell him to do something about them—wear newer T-shirts with tighter collars, whatever, just so long as they stayed down out of sight where they belonged. And he had tried, once upon a time. Once upon a time, he'd tried damn near everything a man could think of to keep that woman happy. Once upon a time. But not anymore.

Al Green splashed some cold water on his face and tried to change his thoughts. Ran his electric razor quickly up his neck, over his chin, and across his cheeks. Combed what little hair he had left to comb, then stumped back down the hall. Six years already since he'd moved in here, and it still felt like somebody else's place. No pictures on the hallway walls, no curtains on the bedroom windows. He pulled up the plastic shades and squinted into the plastic morning sunlight. He cracked the window open a little to fight off last night's stink. He turned away and searched the closet for some pants and a shirt that didn't give away the general state of his wardrobe. Gotta keep up appearances. After all, appearances are more than half the battle. If you can just manage to look like you've got your shit together, most people will believe it and treat you accordingly. Give them just a hint to the contrary, though, and they'll be on you like roosters on a sick hen. Or—didn't it usually work the other way around?—like hens on an old, sick rooster.

The old roosters will be out in force today. So watch yourself. Don't let them see how you really feel. Just get through today clean, get the lay of the land by sundown, and go from there. Sometimes it pays to plan ahead. But not today. Sometimes—like today—you've just got to follow your nose. Trust your instincts. Keep an ear to the ground and a finger to the wind and don't think too much. Just feel. You'll know what to do. You always have before.

Well—almost always.

Hell, Al, come off it—you sound like one of them damn self-help books. Al Green sat on the edge of the bed, pulled on his socks, and pushed those old thoughts back into the dusty corners where they belonged. Maybe I need to write one of those books myself. *Seven Habits of Fuckin' Pathetic People,* or something along those lines. Make me a fuckin' killin'. Hell, just turn on the TV most anytime regular people have better things to do—late at night, or in the middle of the day. People will buy just about any damn thing, listen to just about any damn body, if they don't have any better damn thing to do. Any better damn thing to think.

Just plain lazy, most people—can't be bothered to get their fat asses off the La-Z- Boy or their flabby brains off the tube long enough to get themselves a life of their own. Gotta sit there with their remotes in one hand and their dicks in the other and watch somebody else's life instead. And then go online and write about how stupid all those TV people are, like those dumb-ass, *Survivor*-watching, Sleep-Number-dialing morons could do any better themselves. Hell, at least those TV people are out there doing something, stupid as it might be. They might be idiots, but what does that say about the folks sitting at home just *watching* the idiots?

Jesus Christ. Gets my heart rate going just thinking about it. "Self-help" my ass. You bought the book, didn't you, you dumb fuck? A little unclear on the concept? Why don't you buy yourself some old army surplus boots and a bowie knife and go get lost in the jungle for a few months. We'll get a few gooks together to come 'round now and then to use you for target practice, just so you don't get lonely. Drop a little napalm here and there—just a little "friendly fire"—to keep you on your toes. And oh yeah—watch out for the snakes. Have a few months of that, then we'll see how you feel about "self-help." Assuming you're still alive.

Assuming you're still alive, you won't need no damn "self-help" book. Hell, you'll be able to write the damn book, assuming you're still alive. Except by then, assuming you're still alive, you'll understand how fucking stupid the whole idea of a "self-help" book really is. Wanna know how to "self-help?" Get out and help yourself, dumb-ass! Just do it! And leave Nike out of it, while you're at it. A dying man's last words, selling tennis shoes. Jesus Christ. And back then, we thought it couldn't get any worse. Guess we were wrong. Both of us were wrong. All of us.

Al Green took a deep breath and looked around at the room's bare walls. Time to get moving. The old man wasn't the type to wait around, and if you missed *his* boat, then you'd really and truly missed *the* boat.

Al Green stood up and patted his pockets for wallet and keys. He picked up the holster from the unmade bed, stuck his arm and head through the wide leather strap, and tightened it down. He removed the pistol from the holster, checked the magazine, grunted and turned to his dresser drawer. He wriggled and jerked at the ammo box until it tore free from its corner, then filled the magazine, shoved it back into the grip with a Hollywood click, and slipped the pistol back into the holster. He eyed the ammo box, lid crumpled, still lying in the open dresser drawer. Next to it the same tangle of wadded-up boxer shorts, handkerchiefs, and ancient gym socks. The same silver tie tack. The same button strip from some tuxedo shirt he no longer owned. The same picture frame, facedown. Her same old-fashioned handwriting on the cardboard backing.

Al Green shoved the drawer shut, crushing what remained of the top of the ammo box, then turned around again and contemplated the bed. He rolled his eyes at no one. Oh, Jesus Christ. Will she never leave me in peace? Al Green made up the bed, creases to military specs, all traces of human occupation smoothed over and out. Then he pulled on his CAS-TOR windbreaker and left the room.

The plastic morning sunlight illuminated nothing that might disappoint that spirit that, seven years departed, had yet to move on.

• • •

The café was built into the belly of the stone wall that held up the south bank of the river. Stairways embraced it from either side, leading from its roof of tree-lined sidewalks down to its unassuming front door. The entrance looked out onto wooden picnic tables beneath white canvas canopies and, beyond them, across another bike path, the river. Across the river towered the glass and steel spires of Europe's latest financial crown.

Roy Daniel sat at a wooden table facing the water. The day was warm but overcast, not a breath of wind stirring the green-granite surface of the river. An empty coffee cup sat on its saucer on the table. A woman rode by with a basket full of cut flowers slung on her handlebars. She wore big, Jackie O sunglasses and had sandy blonde hair pulled back straight and tight over the high collar of her jacket.

Roy Daniel held his BlackBerry to his ear, listening, for the second time, to those ones and zeros on a Virginia server that somehow resolved themselves into a voice.

Does the change really come all at once, or do you only notice when what you need to know just isn't there? Like looking into your favorite pool on your favorite trout stream and realizing you've lost your favorite sunglasses. The superficial surge and ripple dazzle for a while with their endlessly changing patterns, their color and light changing with the hour from diamond to platinum to soft polished brass. Endlessly changing, and yet the same—the same as you've seen a hundred times before. The same pool, the same rocks, the same falls and ripples and eddies. But when you go to land a fly in just the perfect spot, right in front of the nose of that old speckled brown—it's then you realize they're gone. All the depth beneath the glitz. All the meat behind the sizzle. All the substance behind the form. All gone. And you only realize it now, when you really need them. When the sun's going down and your creel's still too light. When the first whiffs of pine smoke drift downstream from camp to remind you that you haven't eaten since breakfast. And neither has anyone else. And you're the only one fishing. And now you're fishing blind.

"Hi, Dad—it's Asher. Hope you're doing well. I was wondering if you could give me a call when you have a chance. Nothing—uh, well, it's a little complicated for a message, just give me a call on my cell. Need a little . . . advice. Thanks."

Asher's voice sounded quiet, slow, like it always had when he was tired. Was that all there was to it—exhaustion? Was he drunk? Hard to tell. Roy Daniel realized then that he'd lost that depth perception that every parent had. Sure, when Asher was little it'd been easier. His voice would crack a little and you could tell he was about to cry, tell you he was scared to get on the camp bus with the kids he didn't know or that he was homesick at his grandparents' and was ready to come home. There were more tells back then, and bigger, making the messages easier to read.

But maybe they were still there? Maybe the tells had changed while he wasn't looking, but they were still just as big and easy as ever. He just didn't know anymore what they were.

Roy Daniel pushed the button again and listened to the message for the fourth time, looking for clues.

Maybe Kimberly knew the tells, could hear them just as easily as he'd heard them all those years ago. But then again, maybe not. With his first wife, he'd only ever been able to hear anger. Whether that was his fault or hers, it was certainly part of the problem. With Helen, second time around, he'd done better. He'd probably tried harder—or simply realized for the first time that he had to try at all—but regardless, he'd been able to hear a lot. He could hear whether she was planning the vacation, or just dreaming. He could hear whether she was enjoying the party, or just being polite. He could hear whether the double entendre was a joke or an invitation. He could hear whether she was listening to the kids, or merely enduring them.

But he'd been busy and she'd been busy and time had passed and so had his ability to hear the differences. Which is probably why she'd waited till he came home to break the news.

So maybe Kimberly wasn't any better off.

An elderly couple walked slowly by on the bike path between Roy Daniel and the river. They walked hand in hand, but showed no sign of affection. No sign of animosity, either. No sign of anything—not even any real interest in getting wherever they were going. But their hands were gripped tightly together, a mutual offer of mutual support. To each according to his abilities, from each according to his needs. Whether out of willingness or resignation, no one could know—no one but them.

Roy Daniel looked through his BlackBerry contacts and found Asher's cell phone number. He pressed the CALL button and waited, elbows on the table, for the line to connect. He watched the couple inching slowly away along the river. Maybe even they didn't know. Maybe at this point, it simply didn't matter. Maybe they were back to where they'd started, like children with their parents, the differences between need and desire indistinguishable. Incomprehensible. Irrelevant.

But then again, maybe not. Roy could only see the surface. It was a two-dimensional painting, beautiful in its way, but flat—at least to him. Perhaps primitive, perhaps modern—telling the difference required knowledge. Knowledge that Roy Daniel didn't possess. Empathy that he'd seldom mastered. Maybe the only science that he'd never really understood.

Asher's cell phone went to voice mail.

• • •

The last time Roy Daniel was in Frankfurt, it was the middle of June. About as nice a day as they ever get in this part of the world, he recalled. Green grass covered with picnic blankets. Picnic blankets covered with young mothers watching naked toddlers. Teenaged girls like new butter-flies in the sun. Packs of teenaged boys, bear cubs in springtime, bodies and appetites grown awkward and unfamiliar. Young men drinking good beer, and arguing and laughing over subjects Roy didn't understand. Older couples sitting on benches, watching and listening, remarking on the weather, remembering the rest.

Roy Daniel couldn't exactly remember the reason for the meeting. Some dilemma. There was always a dilemma when you were talking with Andreas—that's why you talked with him. But Andreas, this time, brought up a dilemma of his own. Something about some surveillance work that the BKA was doing at that mosque up in Hamburg. Asking if CASTOR might help out. Asking whether they had anything new in the works—anything that might be useful. Roy had thought of Ariadne, suggested Andreas talk with Pete. Andreas wrote down the name and the number then tucked the little black book and expensive black pen back into his green tweed blazer. Looked at Roy over his tiny, rectangular glasses. Then asked him if he'd like a beer, and got down to the real dilemma.

The sun was hot and the beer tasted sweet. Roy Daniel had watched the long white legs strolling by and the red lips laughing on the lawn and listened as Andreas described the inevitable end of his marriage. When the conversation became a soliloquy, Roy had begun sketching on a pad of Marriott notepaper. Andreas, his back to the table, elbows on his knees, talking to the beer in his hands, gesturing toward the happy crowd as he described the saint who'd been his wife telling his kids that he'd lost his mind. Andreas, leaning back against the table, empty glass at his elbow, watching another girl pedal by who looked *exactly like her*. Andreas, casting a conspiratorial glance back at the man he knew had lived through all this before. Asking him what he was writing. Laughing without joy or interest when he saw the answer.

There were no happy crowds today, no giddy children, no teenaged blood simmering in the afternoon sun. An average weekday, lunch hour over, nothing special to trump a return to the office. Andreas was wearing dark slacks and a brown blazer. Sensible shoes. Expensive tie. He checked his cell phone one last time before coming into earshot. Frowned at it for a moment, then tucked it away in his jacket pocket, looked up at Roy through his tiny glasses, and smiled.

"Hello, Roy. So good to see you."

The handshake was firm and the smile sincere.

"Andreas. Always a pleasure, sir. Thanks for coming all this way to meet me."

Andreas shrugged, eyes closed, frown dismissive. "It's a small country, Roy. The sea is much bigger. Thank *you* for coming all this way to meet *me*."

Roy Daniel sat back down and Andreas joined him, facing away from the water toward the café door. Andreas raised a hand for the waiter and ordered coffee. With a glance at Roy, he asked the waiter to make it two.

"So, Roy, I suppose first, I owe you an apology."

Roy Daniel considered for a moment, Andreas's beard neatly trimmed, his dark eyes intent on holding Roy's attention. Roy considered the possibilities. "Why do you say that?"

"Well, last time we met, I wasn't quite myself. I drank a bit more than I should have. I talked *quite* a bit more than I should have. I shouldn't have troubled you with all that. I'm sorry. I hope we can just forget it."

Roy Daniel nodded, still considering the other options. He smiled a little and shifted in his seat. "Forget what?" When he saw Andreas was actually going to explain, he waved him off. "Of course we can forget about it, Andreas. But there's no need to feel bad. We all need to blow off steam every once in a while."

"Yes, of course," said Andreas. "Of course this is something that is normal. But still, I feel it was not right. It was a business meeting, after all. I believe even you Americans say one should not mix business with pleasure."

"Pleasure? Was that what you were talking about? I'm sorry—I think I must have misunderstood."

Andreas chuckled, watching the waiter approach with their coffees. "No, I suppose you're right. Anyway, thank you for understanding. Now, I believe you're here because you want to know what we know."

Roy smiled and dropped a lump of sugar into his cup. Love the way they get right to the point. "Yes, that is why I came. That, and why you think it's so important that we only talk about it in person."

Andreas sipped his coffee. "Yes, yes, of course, that's right. So perhaps I should simply start at the beginning."

Roy Daniel stirred the sugar into his coffee and waited as Andreas polished his glasses on the back of his tie.

"Of course, until we spoke last night, I naturally assumed that you were aware of this project." Andreas frowned down at his glasses, put them back on, and considered something away to his left, up the river.

Roy Daniel followed his gaze. A man with a briefcase walked quickly in the other direction.

Andreas turned back to Roy, stern at the corners of his mouth, but eyes sympathetic over his tiny, frameless lenses.

Roy Daniel shrugged.

Andreas took another sip of coffee. "So I must apologize again, Roy. You have always been good to me and to my company, and I should naturally have informed you. But"—he moved on with that shrug that involved his whole body from the arms up—"as things stand now, I should not be talking with you. You must understand that you and I did not meet here today."

Roy Daniel looked the other way, down the river, at the smattering of people walking, standing, biking along the water. He held his cup to his lips, inhaling the old smoke-rich smells that lingered like nothing America could engineer, before taking a long, slow drink. Turning back to Andreas, he shrugged again, his gesture smaller, disposable, gone almost as soon as it appeared. "But we did, Andreas. We did meet here. And no amount of silence from us will keep it a secret. So let's not play spy versus spy. Let's be grown-ups. We'll agree not to go talking about it—no harm in that, might even buy us a little something. And of course whatever we say to each other, that stays between us, at least insofar as it's not already out there now. But let's admit, if only to each other, that if anybody cares, they probably already know we're here, today, together, talking."

Andreas was nodding, contemplating his shoes. Another shrug accompanied the end of Roy's monologue. His shrug this time imitated Roy's, quick and resigned. But when he looked up he was smiling a little, and his voice was optimistic. "Okay. Maybe they assumed you knew, too. Maybe, when they said 'nobody,' they didn't mean you."

Roy Daniel smiled and nodded. But still Andreas hesitated. Looking from his shoes, up the river, and from his coffee cup, down the river. A river cruise ship appeared from under a bridge, pushing against the current toward them.

"Andreas. Who's 'they'?"

"They've caught someone, Roy," Andreas finally said, still looking at the cruise ship that barely moved in the stone gray water. "Using information provided by Ariadne. They've caught someone big. At least, that's what they've told me."

"That's good." Roy Daniel watched the ship, too, for a moment, then turned to study the side of Andreas's face. "Who's 'they'?"

"I'm not sure it matters, Roy. I'm not sure it will help you to know. The important thing is that Ariadne's a success, right? Isn't that what's important to you? To CASTOR?"

"Of course I care about that. Sure I do. But I don't just care that it works. I care about who's using it, and for what. And how. That all matters to me, Andreas. And it matters to CASTOR."

Andreas finally turned to look Roy squarely in the eye, his chin dropped, his eyes angling up over the lenses perched out over the tip of his nose. "Are you sure about that, Roy? Are you sure all that matters to CASTOR?"

Roy Daniel stared into the other's eyes as a man in bright blue overalls biked past behind him, smoking a cigarette. The smoke lingered in the warm, still air long after the man had pedaled away, out of site.

"Andreas. Who are 'they'?"

"Some of our people—BKA, mostly. Some of yours—military, marines, I think, though it's sometimes hard to tell. And some CASTOR people, too, of course, helping with the difficult work. Doing most of the difficult work, I suspect—isn't it always so, Roy?"

Andreas laughed without much hope of a response. Roy Daniel studied his eyes, glancing up and down the river, always coming to rest back on the ship, like a grateful sea bird far from shore.

"Andreas, you've convinced me that someone in CASTOR is up to something you don't approve of. If that wasn't what you were hoping I'd learn here, I suggest you tell me now."

Andreas's eyes remained comfortably perched on the prow of the approaching ship.

"Roy, if we can assume that anyone who cares already knows we are sitting here today, speaking with each other, can we not also assume they already believe I am telling you things I should not?"

Roy Daniel finished off his coffee, cold now, in one long pull, wishing it were something else. "I think that's a safe assumption, Andreas." For the first time, he was aware of the jet lag, a tone in his voice more suited to another time zone.

"So I'm not helping you by hiding things you would really be happier not knowing."

The ship was close enough now that they could see people standing on the front deck, scanning the shoreline.

"I didn't fly all this way to be lied to, Andreas. I can get all I need of that without ever leaving D.C."

Andreas smiled and laughed a little, just a quick burst that shook his chest and belly. He kept his eyes fixed on the approaching ship, as if looking for someone he knew.

"Andreas. Please tell me who 'they' are."

" 'They,' Roy, are not your friends. You may work with them every day, and I'm quite sure you think that you know them well, but you don't, I'm afraid. If you haven't learned all of this from them by now, then—well, you understand, I think. You're an intelligent person."

"So you're going to make me guess?"

Andreas finally turned to Roy and smiled. "As much fun as that would be, Roy, no, I couldn't do that. You've done too much for me. But that's exactly the reason I'd also prefer that you didn't know."

Andreas's eyes remained on Roy this time. A lot like an old hunting dog's, Roy thought—kind and sad, tired and excited, hopeful and resigned, all in the same moment.

"Come on," said Roy, standing up and stretching. "Let's take a walk. I've been sitting for way too long. You can tell me a story or two along the way."

Andreas stood, took his wallet out of his jacket, and handed some coins to the waiter. "That's a good idea. And you can tell me a story, too. You can tell me, for example, about Sarah Anderson. I spoke with her last night, but much to briefly. I'd like to hear more from her, but more *about* her would be okay, if that's all I can get."

Roy Daniel picked up his briefcase and put an arm across Andreas's shoulders. "I'd be happy to oblige, Andreas. Talking about Sarah is one of the few pleasures still left to me. And what about Eva? Do you have any more to tell me about her?"

"Eva," Andreas said, smiling, "is the best part of my story."

• • •

In the hospital parking lot, the morning rush was in full swing. Doctors just arriving at the office, frowning at their cell phones. Nurses in pastel scrubs with little teddy bear broaches, trying to remember where they'd left their cars the night before. Interns, pale and unshaven, guarding precious cups of coffee as they dodged from one building to the next, squinting up in passing at the sun as if it were some curious new phenomenon.

Sarah Anderson sat, engine running, blinkers blinking. An elderly man and his wife searched for their keys, unlocked the doors to their elderly car, sniped at something each thought the other should remember, resigned themselves to negotiating the heavy doors when neither of them did remember it, collapsed into their seats with some difficulty, searched again for their keys, struggled to pull the heavy doors closed, rested for a while after the effort, once again searched for their keys (this time finding them in the ignition), started the engine, put the car in gear, inched forward, hit the brakes hard, recovered, put the car in reverse, backed out as if into heavy crossfire, braked again, put the car into drive, started forward, thought they couldn't make the turn, braked hard again, shifted into reverse again, backed up again (clearly upset that Sarah, some twenty feet away, was too close), braked yet again, put the car into drive again, and just like that were off on their way.

Sarah Anderson smiled in spite of her rising blood pressure and silently wished them well. She pulled into their vacated parking space and shut off her engine, accomplishing in ten seconds what had taken them nearly five minutes. Soon enough, she thought, that'll be you. So be patient. Do unto others. Float like a leaf.

When her mother had been in the hospital the first time, the full set of possibilities hadn't really dawned on her. Just the superficial—another set of chores piling up on top of an already teetering to-do list. Rush in after work, try to sit still for a few minutes, try to smile, focus on the present rather than on all the things that still need doing in the immediate future. Fold the afghan at the foot of the bed; pick up the magazine from the cold, scuffed floor; try not to look at the clock more often than was absolutely necessary.

Funny how you could concentrate so hard on the superficial but still miss the signs literally right there on her face, telling you that everything had changed for good. Like the fact that she was talking about herself—trying to, anyway—and didn't seem to notice that everything around her wasn't neat and tidy. Didn't even seem to care.

Make sure the curtain hadn't slipped down the tenuous little wire, revealing the tubes and needles and inputs and outputs on the doctors' science fair project next door that had once actually been a human being. There, but by the grace of God.

Maybe you concentrated so hard on the superficial so that you *could* miss all those signs. There's only so much a person can deal with, after all. At some point, the defense mechanisms kick in, you go on autopilot, and the instrument panels in your brain simply stop displaying the perfectly obvious things that, if you saw them, would surely bring you to your knees.

Sarah Anderson walked across the parking lot and through the big sliding doors. Coming toward her, a man pushed a woman in a wheelchair, the woman holding a car seat in her lap. In the car seat was a neatly wrapped bundle of blankets. In the midst of the blankets, a tiny face. The face mottled crab apple red and pinched tight, as if having cried itself to sleep hoping the past couple of days had all been a bad dream. Dark circles under the woman's eyes, never leaving the baby, filled with the joy and the dread of a child's, strapped in for her first roller coaster ride. The man gripping the wheelchair as much to support himself as to propel the woman forward, out the doors, into the paparazzi morning, too adoring to be welcome. The man laughing at something the nurse by his side had just said—easy or exhausted, Sarah couldn't quite tell. His eyes reached out instinctively to Sarah as their paths crossed for the first time, and probably for the last. Casting out an anchor in the storm. Or maybe just looking out longingly from the life raft at that glittering ship that he'd always taken for granted, now sailing off into his sunset.

At the reception desk, Sarah Anderson asked for the ICU. Up the elevators, down the hall, through the double doors and to the right. The lobby was bright but overly warm; CNN and the local news competing for the attention of the people dozing in chairs. The elevator was huge and slow. Exiting it, the hallway smelled of institutional-grade cleaning supplies and, as she passed one open door, urine.

That was what had finally woken her up, the third time her mother had been admitted. Walking into her room and smelling that smell so foreign to everything she'd ever known about her mother. It was then that she'd finally noticed the glassy eyes, the confused questions, the hair that simply fell out when Sarah tried to brush it back from her face. And her mother not caring. Her mother not caring about anything, apparently—just lying in her bed, staring at the ceiling, or at the television, or at something only she could see midway between the night table and her childhood. It was then that Sarah knew how much she had to catch up—how big the real task was, and how critical, and how trivial the chores were that had so consumed her before. But by then, of course, it was too late. The mother who had cared for her was gone. The mother whom she cared for—well, she simply didn't know her. And so Sarah cared for this stranger whom she knew was her mother, for three more months, every day hoping for one more glimpse, but every day secretly knowing that she'd missed her chance. She'd never known where she really needed to be until that place was gone.

The nurse in the ICU asked Sarah Anderson if she was family. Sarah explained that she was a coworker, sent to see if there was anything they could do. The nurse considered her without a word, eyes steady but not hard. Not like some ICU nurses. Maybe she was new. Whatever the case, the long, sympathetic silence made Sarah worry. She had seen such silence before. It wasn't a sign of anything she wanted to hear.

The nurse stood up and quietly motioned to Sarah to follow her. Sarah stayed a little bit behind, studying the way the nurse moved. Not in any hurry, shoulders a little slumped, not looking back to smile or make casual conversation. Sarah unwittingly let herself fall back another step or two. Finally, the nurse paused outside an open door and turned to look back. Sarah noticed a little smudge across her cheek, just below the left eye, where you might wipe the back of your hand. The urge to wipe it off—to lick her thumb and rub it hard like her mother used to do—was almost more than she could handle. The nurse could see the look in her eyes Maybe she misunderstood it. In any case, she turned and looked through the open door and Sarah followed her gaze, standing in the middle of the hall beside her.

The nurse suddenly gasped. "Oh, my God," she cried under her breath, and ran back down the hall in the direction they'd just come from.

Inside the room, Pete Vasilescu lay on the bed, tubes leading into his arms and up his nose and down his throat. His left leg was suspended from a complicated array of wires and straps. His face was so stitched and bandaged and bruised and swollen that Sarah wouldn't have recognized him if she hadn't been looking for him in the first place.

But none of this was what took Sarah Anderson's breath away. None of this was what had sent the nurse running back down the hall. The silence—that was what did that. The complete and total silence. Of all the machines that stood around Pete Vasilescu's bed, not a single one made a sound. The screen at his head was dark. The respirator's familiar hiss and click were gone. Nothing moved, nothing flashed, nothing beeped.

It was the silence, and the eyes. And the hand.

Pete's eyes were wide open, glazed and staring up at the ceiling. His left hand was hanging down awkwardly off the near side of the bed.

Sarah Anderson stared at the long, thin hand, purple bruises on gray pale skin, hanging there just above the floor. And although she knew now from experience that there were certainly a hundred things she should think about that were far, far more important, Sarah's mind stuck on the simple fact that she simply couldn't remember whether Pete Vasilescu had ever worn a ring.

• • •

"So what are you going to do?" Tamara Maybin sat on the bed, wrapped in the soft white duvet, knees hugged up under her chin.

General Grantham Hayward sat in the same chair Tamara Maybin had occupied not ten hours before, watching out the same window as planes rode the same path down toward the ground. His BlackBerry dangled in his left hand. The nervous knuckles of his right hand tapped at his lips.

"That's more your department than mine, don't you think?"

"That's probably true. But you're forgetting, my dear General, that I don't work for you anymore."

"And last night doesn't entitle me to any free advice?"

"I didn't realize I was going to have to pay for your services, General."

"I didn't realize I was going to have to pay for yours. Colonel."

Outside the door someone walked by talking loudly about how hard it was going to be for him to get home in time for something. What exactly "something" was wasn't clear. That it was important to the person on the other end of the line was, as was the fact that the person in the hall really didn't want to be there.

"Well. You know my advice is almost never to ignore the situation. The best defense is a good offense. Right?" The General just watched as another plane floated downward.

"Right." Tamara Maybin glanced at the screen of her BlackBerry, which was showing her another incoming call. She'd silenced the ringer fifteen minutes earlier.

You won't be able to keep this up indefinitely.

"So. What's the side of this story that you'd *like* to tell?"

The General kept up his lip tapping, eyes still glued to the skyline. "I'd *like* to tell *no* story. No story at all."

Tamara Maybin quietly banged her forehead against her duvet-padded knees. Why am I not surprised?

"Okay, let's put it this way, then. If you were talking with a friend at lunch, telling him about this project, how would you describe what you're doing?"

"No friend of mine would ever ask me to talk about it. How'd they even know to ask the question? Stupid question."

"What if *I* asked you?"

The General's eyes narrowed and sulked out the window, commanding another plane to make its appearance.

Tamara Maybin picked up her BlackBerry and began dialing. "Okay. Have it your way. You're the one who asked for my advice."

"If *you* asked me, I'd tell you it was for the good of the country. To protect your friends, your neighbors. Their families, and yours. To make sure that no one ever catches us with our guard down again."

Tamara put down her phone. "That's good. How?"

"If I told you how, it wouldn't work anymore."

"No. If you told the bad guys how, maybe it wouldn't work anymore. But if you told *me* how, then maybe I could actually help you."

Beneath the tapping, Tamara Maybin saw a quick upturn at the corner of Grantham Hayward's mouth.

"You need to trust me here, Grant. I mean, think about it. This story doesn't help me, either. I've based a pretty good career on the success of the Pollux Society. And the success of the Pollux Society is based largely on its reputation. The reputation goes, the prestige goes. The prestige goes, the money goes. And when the money goes, everything goes. So if it comes out in tomorrow's *Post* that last night's Pollux Society honoree is behind the wiretapping of America, it's going to hurt me just about as much as it's going to hurt you. Who knows, maybe more. The military, after all, has a way of forgiving this sort of thing. The private sector—there's not much forgiveness in the private sector. Things like understanding, sympathy, loy-alty, and forgiveness tend to go out the window pretty fast when they come up against real dollars and cents."

Another plane. A siren in the streets below demanded attention. The General considered something on the back of his right hand.

"It won't help you to know more about it, Tamara." He turned to face her for the first time since the morning's first call. His eyes were their usual wolf gray, but this morning they matched the skin on his cheeks and the color of the hair cropped up over his temples. "In the long run, it won't help you at all. I understand that you're trying to help me—well, help us both, really—but you don't know everything, and the less you know, the better. You need to trust me on this, Tamara. You don't know the whole story."

"You're right—I don't know the whole story. But I'm going to have to tell the story, anyway, and if there are holes in it, I'm just going to have to fill them. I'm in PR—that's my job. I can't just ignore the press when it's convenient for me. Next time I need them, they might not be there. Tit for tat—that's the way the business works. You understand that, Grant. Anybody who's gotten as far in the military as you have understands that game."

The General stared at her, expressionless, eyes kind but worried, maybe—or maybe just sad. He said nothing.

"So either you can help me fill up those holes in the story with something you wouldn't mind seeing in the papers—who knows, maybe even something you'd *like* to see in the papers—or I fill them up with something I just make up. And I'll do my best to make up things that look good for both of us, but I'm only human, Grant. I do make mistakes. You might not like the look of the picture when I get done filling in the blanks."

The General's BlackBerry suddenly lit up again and began to ring. He looked at the screen, barely moving either his hand or his head, pressed the END button with his thumb, and turned back to the window. Tamara Maybin could see his reflection in the glass, pale and fading like a ghost floating over the city he'd known so well, as confused by the reason for his searching as by the goal of the search itself.

"In other words, if I don't tell them something, you will."

"That's what it boils down to, I guess. Yes."

"You understand that I'm only telling *you* this. Telling you so we can work out the best story to tell the press. The best story for *both* of us to tell the press. A story that may not bear much resemblance to the story I'm about to tell *you*."

"I understand, Grant. That was my point all along."

The General opened his mouth to say more, but just sat instead for what seemed like an eternity, staring into the disappearing morning.

"How would they know about all this, anyway?"

Tamara Maybin hoped she didn't hesitate too long. "I don't know, Grant. But they do. So tell me. What exactly is 'all this'?"

" 'All this,'" the General echoed, yet another airplane passing by, head down and tired, ready for the barn.

Tamara Maybin waited.

General Grantham Hayward took a long, deep breath, exhaling with a finality that Tamara Maybin hadn't anticipated.

The hotel door closed with the soft, heavy *thunk* of an expensive car. Tamara Maybin reached back behind her and picked up her BlackBerry from the night table. She let herself fall back onto her pillow and kicked away the covers, staring up past the number on the screen to the blank white ceiling. No public opinion there. No moral guidance.

The bright morning light burned hot against the window, making the room stuffy in spite of the tinting. The smell of his aftershave still hung over the chair by the window. Another airplane floated down in the distance, beyond the buildings, smudged and ordinary in the light of another day. Just another in a long series, no different than yesterday's, not likely different than tomorrow's.

The BlackBerry glowed quietly in the midst of it all. Its speaker was silent. Tamara Maybin held it up above her and tilted it left and right, up and down, looking at her naked body reflected in the tiny screen, perfectly dark except for the number glowing across the middle. The blank canvas against which her existence seemed to play out. The frame outside of which she felt she might simply cease to exist.

Tamara disconnected the line and threw the little piece of blue plastic unconvincingly across the room.

• • •

Andreas drove the car himself. On some such occasions he might have used a driver, but he hadn't wanted to risk having someone else know where he was.

The huge brownstone arch of Frankfurt's Hauptbahnhof glowered to his left. Atop the arch, a corroding Atlas—comically small by comparison—struggled to hold a weathered world steady between his aging shoulder blades. A world not much bigger than the clock below it, or the Deutsche Bahn sign, whose fire-engine red attracted any eye that happened to stray in that direction. How many of the people hurrying across the street in front of him even knew old Atlas was up there, looking down on them with sad, weary eyes, bearing a burden no one even remembered? None of them looked up. None of them looked left. Almost none of them even looked at one another as they hurried to catch a train that would take them somewhere else where they'd just have to rush to beat another ticking deadline. No time for Atlas. No time for stories. No time for myths about times before science shrunk the world.

It had started to drizzle. Andreas turned on the windshield wiper; the Mercedes's long, single blade scraped a wide, grimy smear across the glass. The traffic light turned yellow, then green, and Andreas pushed past the last of the pedestrians and onward through the grimy mist toward the *Messe*. Beside him, Roy was frowning at the screen of his BlackBerry. He pushed a couple of buttons, then held it up to his ear and looked away, out through the window at the bikers squinting against the car's filthy wake.

Andreas had found Roy Daniel something of a mystery for almost thirty years. The two had first met while working at the Max Planck Institute north of Munich. Andreas was there as a postdoc, Roy as a visiting scientist. In spite of their differences in age and status, the two had struck up a friendship based on common interests and close proximity. A mutual love of science, obviously, had brought them to the same place at the same time. One day, at lunchtime, Andreas had found Roy sitting outside sketching a flower in his notebook—and so they discovered a mutual interest in art. Roy's questions about the cold soups in the cafeteria and the unmentioned holidays on which he'd shown up at an empty lab had revealed a mutual interest in each other's cultures. This mutual interest had led to a series of "typical" dinners at each other's apartments—Andreas and his wife doing their best to replicate German "specialties" that neither had eaten since those dreaded holiday dinners at their grandparents' houses, and Roy's wife obviously frustrated by trying to serve up genuine Southern cooking without the benefit of genuine Southern ingredients. A mutual love of German beer and American whiskey had become increasingly evident at each subsequent meal. And at each subsequent meal, a mutual interest in each other's wives had grown into almost a fifth guest at the table.

Roy Daniel had returned to the States after six months, before—as far as Andreas could tell—having engaged this new guest in any serious conversation. Why this was so was one of the many mysteries surrounding Roy Daniel that Andreas now assumed he would simply never unravel. Another of those mysteries was why a man as smart as Roy Daniel had apparently never realized that he was alone in this lack of engagement.

"Asher? Asher—it's Dad. Can you hear me okay?"

Roy Daniel was staring up at the metallic gray towers of the Marriott, as if searching through the leaves and drizzle for his son's face in some high window. Asher, the skinny blonde boy Andreas remembered from so many years ago, following his dad around the lab now and then before joining him in the cafeteria for lunch. Lying on the living room floor after dinner, looking at the pictures in some book while the adults talked and drank. Working just as hard at taking everything in as at trying to look like he wasn't. Smiling in spite of himself at the Tom Lehrer song on the record player, then suddenly realizing the tell, flipping the smile to a studied frown, and glancing around to make sure no one had noticed.

"I got your message just a little while ago. Is now a good time to talk?"

Asher—perhaps the only one who knew it all.

"Sure, I've got a little time. Go ahead. What's on your mind?"

Andreas navigated the knot of streets converging on the Messe, and out into the lanes leading to the Autobahn. Until just a few months ago, this road would have brought him home, to the neighborhood of red and brown and white brick houses, the neighbors' kids riding their bikes along new cobbled streets, built perfectly narrow and precisely curved to keep everything moving at a safe, slow speed. The neighborhood in which, in spite of everything safe and slow, his own kids had grown up far too fast, off on their own before he'd even really gotten to know them. Following in their parents' footsteps. Their parents, whose own relationship had narrowed and curved and slowed until they could scarcely see it, much less recognize it as that fast, exciting, oh-so-modern expressway along which they'd sped all those years ago. At those speeds, it was easy to miss a few minor indiscretions. By the time they turned your head, they were already well out of sight. But not so at the safe and sane thirty kilometers per hour of middle age. You can't outrun anything at that speed. Your own children on their bicycles pass you by, leaving you alone with yourself and your memories that never seem to reach the rearview mirror. They just idle along beside you, staring in through the side windows, studying, assessing, judging, waiting. How can any relationship withstand the weight of its own past? Like an airplane, it needs a certain amount of speed to keep it safely aloft. The more baggage it accumulates, the more speed it requires. The alternative being a spectacular, horrible crash, with all the accompanying casualties and lawsuits and damages.

Andreas realized that Roy Daniel hadn't said anything in a while. He turned and saw his friend still holding his BlackBerry to his ear, listening, no longer looking out of the window. He appeared more jet-lagged than Andreas remembered. Maybe he just hadn't been paying attention.

"Asher, I think you need to go home. Do you realize how serious this sounds?"

Roy rubbed his free thumb against his forefinger like a worry stone. Andreas glanced at the road, then back at Roy, trying to catch his attention. But Roy Daniel had slipped away, out of the car, out of the country, listening to the voice of his son through the tinny little speaker in the blue plastic case at his ear.

"Yes, okay, I understand. I know somebody I can call, hopefully he can give us a hand. But Asher—just get back there as soon as you possibly can. There's nothing in the world as important. You. . . ."

Andreas instinctively pressed on the accelerator, flashing his lights at the Opel in front of him. The little car jerked right, obediently, a chastised dog retreating to his corner.

"Just be careful, Asher. I'll call you back as soon as I hear something. Okay. Bye. Okay. I'm sure. Bye."

Roy Daniel hung up the phone and immediately began dialing again. Andreas kept his eyes on the road, questions in check, as the Mercedes lurched forward through the Opel's dirty wake.

"Sandy? This is Roy Daniel. Okay. Yes, it has been a while. Listen, Sandy, I've got a little bit of a situation here. I was hoping you could help me out. No, it's a personal matter. Do you have a moment?"

Andreas pushed his car faster, past the gray offices and factories and overpasses and bridges. He understood the words, but not the conversation. There was no mistaking the urgency. Whatever was going on, a little extra speed was probably a good thing. A little extra wind under the wings couldn't hurt.

twelve

I have never run so fast, before or since. I'm telling you, there is nothing that a sixteen-year-old boy, given a good dose of plain, old-fashioned fear, can't do. Nothing. No wonder the military drafts the teenagers first. Science will never come up with a more remarkable fighting machine than a scared teenaged boy.

To be honest with you, I don't have the slightest idea now why we decided to steal Stuckey's watermelons in the first place. I do remember that it seemed like a great idea at the time. Boredom probably had more than a little bit to do with it. School was out, and sure, we all had our summer jobs, but those didn't burn much adrenalin. Sports did a good enough job during the school year, but during the summer, you had to fend for yourself. Like the time we mounted a shotgun on top of that old Jeep so we could shoot at doves from the frontage roads. Or when we tried to turn that leaky old rowboat we found into a sailboat, then dared each other to sail across the lake before it sank. This was probably just another one of those things. Something to do to keep the radiators from boiling over on all those long, hot, sticky summer days.

Part of the attraction, of course, had to have been that Stuckey was so damned mean. Everybody said so. Okay, me—I didn't really know him. I don't know that any of us kids did. But he was one of those people in town that everybody knew *of,* and what they knew *of* him they didn't much care for. Why was a bit of a mystery, at least to us kids, but as kids we didn't much care about why. We'd see him in town every now and then, at the filling station or coming out of the hardware store. Little, skinny old man with a stringy white beard and eyes that were always looking sideways, never straight on like normal people. Always seemed to be in a hurry to get someplace else. Never saw him talk with anybody. Never saw anybody talk with him, either, except to take his money. So you just knew he was mean. What more proof did you need?

Whenever the name "Stuckey" came up, I remember my parents just shaking their heads. Dad always changed the subject. Mom once said something about how we all get what's coming to us, but she didn't sound too certain. Which, thinking back on it, was strange, because Mom was about the most certain person I've ever known.

Anyway, the three of us met up just after supper on Friday night—me, Joe Exum, and Wade Peckinpah, whose dad, at the time, was the sheriff. We all met at Joe's house, because he lived closest to Stuckey's place. Stuckey lived alone out on the east side of town, just on the far side of the golf course. We decided the best way to go about stealing the watermelons would be to hop the low wooden fence between the golf course and Stuckey's pasture, then cut across the pasture to the garden beside his house where he grew the watermelons.

Well, okay—where we *hoped* he grew his watermelons. You could see the garden from the road—a row of sweet corn, some snap pea vines. Wade said he'd seen watermelons in the bed of his truck last time Stuckey stopped in at the drug store. Big, fat watermelons, a little wet black dirt still stuck to one side of some of them, but slick dark green everywhere else, with markings like you see on the backs of crappie. Wade's summer job was at the drug store, stocking the shelves, sometimes working behind the counter. His uncle owned the drug store. We gave him hell about spending the summer indoors with the women, but really we were jealous as hell. Joe's parents were farmers—their place was right at the edge of town, across the road from Stuckey's—so if he wasn't in school he was always outside, helping his dad with one thing or the other. I was helping them put up hay that summer. I'd thought it would get me in shape for football season, which it did. What it did most, though, was convince me I was *not* going to be a farmer.

We sat on Joe's front porch and watched the sun go down, melting down red over the big pine in the cemetery down the road to the left. Joe's dad was sitting in the living room, reading the paper and listening to the ball game on the radio. We listened, too, waiting till it was too dark to see Stuckey's house across the road. We could hear the clinking from the kitchen as Joe's mom did the dishes. Usually, when she was done, she'd come outside and sit down in her chair and ask us all about our parents and our brothers and sisters and our girlfriends. We'd need to be gone before that happened. So even though it was still light enough to see the white sides of Stuckey's house, we left, heading down the road toward what was left of the sunset as if we were all going back into town.

When we were out of sight of Joe's house, we turned right off the road, scrambling down through the thistles and the tiger lilies in the ditch and up onto the short mowed grass on the golf course. It was too dark for anybody to be playing golf now, but we could hear that there was a party going on in the clubhouse, so we kept an eye out, just in case. Whenever there was a party in the clubhouse, there was a good chance there might be people on the course. We knew this from personal experience. Usually, of course, the people sneaking out onto the golf course at night were with people they weren't supposed to be with, so they'd be as anxious to avoid *us* as we were to avoid them. But we didn't think about that. In such a small town, chances were good they'd all be people we knew, or at least who knew our parents. People we didn't want asking what we were doing out on the golf course at night. That's what we were thinking about. Not that they wouldn't be particularly anxious to have us asking them questions, either.

The world's still pretty flat when you're a teenager.

We stayed over to the right side of the course, up from the clubhouse and under the big elm trees that grew between most of the fairways back before the Dutch elm disease took them all out. We didn't see a soul. At the top of the hill, we cut over to the old broken-down wooden fence and leaned there, staring into the dark at Stuckey's house and at the garden right there in front of it. Nothing stirred. The fireflies had come out and were blinking over the pasture like low, phosphorescent stars. The frogs in the creek back behind us had stopped to listen as we passed by, but now they started up again, grinding and slow, like old tractor engines starting on a cold fall morning. All the normal summer sounds. A little breeze stirred up the smell of warm grass and horse. A dog barked somewhere back in town. Crickets chirped in all the usual dark corners. Nothing seemed to suspect the great robbery about to commence.

Wade was the first to hop the fence. Working inside all day, he still had his full daily allowance of teenage energy to burn. He ran off through the pasture, Joe and I close behind, watching the silhouettes of the corn stalks growing taller. When we got to there, we made sure the stalks were between us and the house, then waited a while to catch our breaths, hands on our knees and listening for the bark of a dog or the quick creak-slap of someone coming through the screen door.

We didn't hear a thing. There wasn't even a light in a window. Everything dark and quiet except the frogs in the creek, now far behind us and happier for it. The frogs and the crickets, who'd apparently shut up to watch us run across the pasture, but decided now that we weren't anything to worry about.

We dropped to our hands and knees and slowly crept out from behind the sweet corn. As long as we stayed down, the pea vines were still between us and the house, but they wouldn't be for long if we kept moving in this direction. No sign of watermelons yet. Wade led the way, with Joe behind him and me bringing up the rear. I could see the lights of Joe's house way off to the right across the pasture. Watching the lights instead of where I was going, I planted my cheek hard into Joe's dusty butt, who hissed "Watch it!" looking at me upside down from under his armpit. He'd stopped for Wade, who was rustling off in the garden to our left. "Found them!" he whispered, loud enough to spook the crickets. Joe and I, no brighter, said "Ssshhh!!" in unison, and listened as Wade's pocketknife separated a big, warm melon from its fuzzy vine.

Wade passed the melon back to Joe, who sat back on his feet and passed it along to me. It weighed as much as a regular-size bowling ball, and for the first time I wondered how I was going to run with it. The crickets started gossiping about what was going on. Wade passed another melon back to Joe.

I heard Wade's knife blade click back into place, then watched as he stood up with a melon bigger than either Joe's or mine. He was smiling so big we could see his white teeth. He had his back turned to another click, lower pitched than his knife's had been, and to the squeal of a floorboard that made the crickets go silent.

"You boys hungry, are ye'?"

Wade froze, standing there with his back to the house. Joe and I couldn't see a thing, crouched as we were there with Wade blocking our view. The floorboards told us Stuckey took two more steps—probably in our direction. Wade looked down at us, and we looked up at him, eyes wide and empty, any ideas we might have had replaced by just one primal urge.

Run.

Once again Wade bolted first, leaving Joe and me right there in the open, kneeling before the old man on the porch like two poor sinners on judgment day. And it was only then, with Wade out of the way, that we realized where the clicking we'd heard had come from. Stuckey was tracing the path of Wade's retreat with the long, black muzzle of a big old, double-barrel shotgun.

The flash and the bang slapped us both into action. Joe made a beeline for his house, a path 90 degrees off the one that Wade was retracing back toward the golf course. I was back behind the sweet corn before the next explosion from the porch. This time, Wade howled and skipped, dropping his watermelon but not slowing in his race for the fence.

I just froze, all senses on high alert, listening to the floorboards creak and moan. Empty shell casings hit the porch. The old gun's cross lock snapped back into place as Stuckey finished reloading. Gunpowder smoke drifted between the corn stalks and up through my nose, and from there straight on into my bloodstream. My muscles tensed up, ready to run. Wade was almost to the fence now. It was hard in the dark to tell if he was still in range.

But no more explosions came. Just a wheezy, half-hearted cry of "You boys stay off my prop'ty!" Then silence. Silence that lasted what seemed like forever. But really only long enough for the frogs and the crickets to forget that anything had happened, which, honestly, probably wasn't very long at all, frogs and crickets being fairly similar to people in such respects.

I heard the screen door open and shut and I was off, following in Wade's footsteps as fast as my feet would carry me, ready at any moment for the roar of a gun behind me and the searing pain I only knew from books and movies.

The gory mess on the ground pumped by heart clear up into my throat and for a stride or two practically pushed my feet off the ground until I realized it was only Wade's dropped watermelon, not some shot-away part of Wade himself. Even so, the adrenalin had reached levels in my bloodstream that I'd never experienced before, and when I reached the fence I practically jumped clear over it, using the rails like stair steps and vaulting over the top like a horse in a steeplechase. I was moving so fast, in fact, that

I almost missed Wade entirely, huddled there behind a big oak tree on the golf course side of the fence.

"Wade! Wade, are you okay?"

Wade looked at me as if I were a stranger. He looked around behind himself, put a hand on his backside, then held the hand out for me to look at, babbling in a voice I'd never heard from him before.

"He . . . he shot me! Look! He shot me, Roy! He shot me!"

And sure enough, Wade's hand was slick and red, the seat of his pants peppered with holes and wet with blood.

"He shot me, Roy! He shot me!"

"Come on, Wade. We'd better get you some help."

I slung one of Wade's arms over my shoulders and put my arm around his back and walked him as fast as he'd let me down the hill toward the road. Wade kept babbling that the old man had shot him, which was true, but not particularly helpful, and finally I told him to shut up. He was walking well enough that I figured he couldn't be hurt too bad, and besides, I didn't really want to attract attention. The party at the clubhouse was still going on, and it didn't seem that anybody had noticed the commotion next door. I figured it'd be best if we could try our best to keep it that way.

I managed to maneuver Wade back across the golf course, back through the lilies in the ditch beside the road, and back down the road to Joe's front porch. Joe was already there with his mom, and his dad was inside on the phone. When Wade saw the phone, he immediately started to blubber again. "Don't call the sheriff! Don't call my dad! Please, Mr. Exum—please don't call my dad!" But Joe's mom just told him to be still and led him into the house and down the hall to the bathroom. Joe and I sat on the porch, not saying anything.

Eventually Wade's dad—the sheriff—drove up in his squad car, and Joe's dad came out to meet him. The sheriff had another man with him, dressed in a jacket and tie and not walking particularly straight. The sheriff asked Joe's dad where the boy was, and when Joe's dad pointed to the bathroom, the unsteady man nodded and wove down the hall. The sheriff explained that the doctor had been at the party at the clubhouse—that he'd picked him up on the way over, right after he'd received Joe's dad's call.

Joe and I just sat there, trying to be as quiet as possible, hoping they'd all forget about us. But they didn't, of course. The sheriff asked us what had happened. We told him Stuckey shot Wade. The sheriff nodded, and asked if we had any idea why. We told him he'd caught us in his garden. The sheriff nodded again. Then he asked us what the hell we were doing in Stuckey's garden in the middle of the night.

"Picking watermelons," we told him.

"Stuckey's watermelons, or yours?"

We didn't answer that one. The sheriff nodded anyway, and looked out at the car pulling up in front of the porch. My parents' car. My mom and dad got out of the car, and the sheriff stepped down off the porch to meet them. They stood there talking low, nodding sometimes, shaking their heads other times, looking over at Stuckey's house, and every now and then, looking up at me. I looked away every time they did. My mom, as usual, looked certain. Not at all the way she usually did when the conversation turned toward Stuckey.

After a while the doctor came back out to the porch and said that Wade would be fine. He held out a surprisingly steady hand for the sheriff and Joe's dad and my mom and dad to look at. In his palm was something small and irregular, like a diamond, almost, but dull, and a little pink.

"Rock salt," he said.

The sheriff nodded, and almost looked like he thought it was funny.

"Hit him pretty good," the doctor continued. "He'll have a hard time sitting for a week or so, but he'll be okay."

The sheriff shook the doctor's hand. "He was gonna have a hard time sittin' one way or t'other," he said. "Kind of Stuckey to do the job for me."

My parents told me to go sit in the car. They talked for a while to the sheriff and Joe's father. Joe's mother came out and they talked some more. Then they all shook hands, and my parents came to the car with the doctor. We dropped him off back at the clubhouse. Then we drove home.

Once or twice on the drive home I was sure that my mom was going to say something. She'd take a deep breath, look for something in her lap, start to turn around to look at me there behind her in the back seat. But she never did. Neither she nor my dad ever said a word. The next day, I went back over to Joe's to help with the hay. Joe and I didn't talk, either. We just rode out to the field in the back of the truck, tossed up the bales till our backs ached and our shirts stank, and then rode back to the house again, sprawled out between the bales. On the way back I caught Joe's eye, and he smiled, and we almost laughed. But we could still see Stuckey's house across the road. A lot of questions. So instead we just lay there on the hay bales in the back of the truck, and we stared at the old house across the road, and we watched as the hot sun sank low back over the cemetery, and instead of laughing, we just wondered.

thirteen

Asher tried reading the street signs like a gypsy reads the tarot.

Harvestehude. The pumpkin-yellow sign pointed in the direction their car was turning, their driver grumbling words that Asher couldn't understand. Asher had no idea what either meant. His German was limited to restaurants and train stations, hotels, and the occasional convenience store. Numbers you could do with your fingers. The things you wanted to buy, you could point at. Prices were all written down. A nod or a shake of the head, a smile or a frown, conveyed half—maybe more—of what most people ever needed to say to each other. Not being able to go any further kept you away from the sore spots. The world might be a far better place if nobody had more than a fifty-word vocabulary.

Of course, there was no limiting the vocabulary of the imagination. So the trouble would still be there, whether you could say anything about it or not. But still, maybe talking just made it worse. If you couldn't tell anybody about it—couldn't turn it into a good story with a little drama to drum up an audience—maybe you'd just get bored with the whole thing and forget about it. Problem called for lack of interest.

Harvestehude. Was "harvest" the same in both German and English? The more important the words, the more they tended to transcend languages. The tires of the car hissed over the grimy wet pavement and the door window fogged as he stared through the cold glass. They banked around a park, soggy brown leaves dripping from the trees, and turned onto a street with an impossibly long name: *Rothenbaumchausee*. Something about red trees. Harvest time, indeed. Maybe in a better year, leaves the color of ripe apples against a crisp, blue sky. But today, only brown. Harvest already come and gone. The earth torn up, everything worth anything already dug up and carted away. Apparently he'd missed the whole thing. Better go inside and sleep until spring. Nothing to see out here, darkness coming on hard now, nothing to do but try to stay warm and wait it out.

Not even an hour ago they'd still been living in the Persian Gulf summer, sealed into the plane when they'd shut the doors in Dubai. Asher sleeping through all the reasons he shouldn't. Every now and then something had shaken him enough that he'd opened his eyes, sandy and sticky in the bottled desert air. She was always awake. A cool silhouette against the white-hot window, a static hair or two floating in the stratospheric glare. Tropical blue eyes staring at somebody else's words, or writing one or two of her own, but mostly just staring out at the silent white dunes of that fantastic cotton-ball no-man's land.

Jungfrauenthal. Something about young women. Or was it virgins? No sooner had he made out the letters than the pure blue sign was gone.

Asher pondered his father's words, still fresh in his ear from their conversation just minutes ago in the airport. "I think you need to go home. There's nothing in the world as important." Easy enough words to say from a distance, their apparent truth increasing with every passing mile. Up close, though—well, actions did speak louder. Where you spent your time tended to say a lot about where you felt you were useful, and what you thought you could do. And you didn't always have a whole lot of time to think it over, or, when it came right down to a decision, a whole lot of choice in the matter. Most of us just go where we're pushed. It's a rare man who can see his goal from a long ways off and then stay a straight course till he gets there. Perhaps not so much rare as legendary—as in, existing only in legends. Reality doesn't tend to do straight lines. The stories we invent later to justify what we've done—that's where straight lines generally make their debuts.

Innocentiastrasse. Asher just smiled. No need to turn in there. A wise man knows not to poke around in places he doesn't belong. Nobody in this story belongs in there.

That very familiar stranger—latest in a long and distinguished line to cross the stage of Asher's life—talked with their driver. Asher, as usual, couldn't follow a word, but the gist was clear enough. Her lips and eyes were pursed in that Northern European sign of things not going according to plan. She stared at her phone and typed a quick message with her thumbs. If she noticed his attention, she didn't show it. She was back in her element now. Backstage with her people. Whatever indiscretions she may have allowed herself last night, well, that was just part of the play. That was there and then, but this is here and now, and there's no time now to worry about then, nothing done there that can't be fixed here.

Words Kimberly would most definitely *not* agree with, of course. All the world a stage—theater in the round—the lack of an audience more or less the same as the lack of oxygen to breath, or water to drink, or dry land on which to make a stand.

Asher tried to put their last conversation out of his mind. It hadn't helped then, when he'd thought of her standing there—center stage, spotlights set—and turned to drive in the opposite direction, toward the airport. It hadn't helped then, and it wouldn't help now. The only thing that *might* help now—the only thing that stood a fighting chance of fixing what they'd said or done then—was to finish what he'd already started, to see the thing through to its logical (or otherwise) end. It wouldn't be long now. If this stranger could really help, he'd know it soon enough. If his father really did have someone he could call, he'd already have done it. See where it all leads. If it doesn't work, well, you can start all over again.

But give it a few more hours. There's definitely nothing else that's going to work any faster. What have you got to lose?

And until then, there was no point in calling Kimberly. Talking would just make it worse. More words, more drama, more problems. Time for some action. Give the words something to justify later. Give them something useful to do for a change.

"Okay, we're almost there."

Her voice was pitched a half step higher than it had been, but sounded satisfied that everything was back on track. The driver navigated a series of complicated intersections and suddenly they were driving along a wide lake. A big man on a bicycle, wrapped head to toe in dark blue rainwear, rode on the bike path between their car and the shore. The trees above the path did little to shelter him from the rain, which was blowing more sideways than down with the wind off the water. On the other side of the road, people stared from the windows of an old hotel, looking confused. Confused, maybe, about why anybody would venture outside, away from the coffee and cake that came with this time, this place, and this weather. Or maybe they were just curious about how they'd managed to end up on their side of the glass. How they'd managed to be so lucky. Or unlucky. Or just shocked that they'd had so little choice in the matter.

Alter Wall. The Old Wall? Again, Asher didn't know if German and English shared "wall." But that was the address they'd given him. The driver pulled over and stopped.

Tropical blue eyes turned to him for the first time since the earliest hours of this already impossibly long day.

"Okay. This is it. Are you ready to go?"

The man on the bike caught up to them and rode on past, careful to stay within the bicycle lane's cobblestone lines. Somehow a long cigar burned between his lips in spite of the rain. The smell of it crept in through their car's cracks and seals and lingered there long after he'd already disappeared.

"I don't really have a choice now, do I?"

"Of course you have a choice. You always have a choice. Only this time, perhaps you've already decided? Last night—hadn't you then already decided?"

Asher watched her eyes, carefully, searching the clear, blue deep for the slightest hint that something wasn't quite right—of anything important that the cards weren't saying.

He saw nothing. Alter Wall.

"Yes. Of course." Still searching.

Long, soft fingers reached over and quietly closed around his. Coral lips parted, almost imperceptibly. For a split second it seemed she was leaning toward him, that her eyelids would flutter and close. But just as quickly she sat up straight, eyes wide open, glancing around outside the car. She tucked a stray hair back behind her ear. She gave his hand a squeeze before letting go. Her little gold ring, simple as a child's, dug into his knuckle.

"Me, too," she said, reaching for the door handle. "So. Let's go."

The driver sat staring straight ahead, along the Alter Wall, where the man on the bicycle was coming back into view.

The building was something from the previous century, its thick stone walls and patina copper roof somehow spared the fiery fate of so many of its contemporaries. The man at the desk behind the heavy wooden doors wore a blue blazer and a bushy gray mustache and typed their names one letter at a time into a computer that clearly baffled him. "Third floor," he said to Eva after considering the screen for some time, his deep accent resonating up through the dark oak paneling from the wet stone roots of the city itself. She thanked him and he nodded as Phaeton followed her up the stairs. She could see him glance at the elevator as they passed but it would be old and slow, and besides, after the flight, she could use the exercise.

Andreas's instructions had been very clear: Bring Phaeton directly to the meeting. Andreas was scheduled to arrive at about the same time as they were. But Andreas wasn't answering her texts. He probably hadn't landed yet. And the fact that some anonymous caller had told Phaeton to come to this address seemed suspicious. It all had to be connected. Coincidences this big simply didn't exist.

The old stairs groaned as they passed the first-floor landing. The wind outside volleyed fat drops of rain against the windowpane ahead. Across the street stood the *Rathaus,* Hamburg's city hall, its blank, dark windows stoic against the storm. They'd seen better days, but they'd also seen worse. Just hold on, stay the course, and soon enough the storm will pass. Just like everything else, this, too, shall pass.

Her father had said that a lot, back after her mother had died. He'd said it with the resignation of Job, his voice always ending on a downbeat, low, the whole phrase bracketed in a sigh. She would have done anything for him then, anything to bring him back, anything to prove that she was enough. Prove it to him, prove it to herself. She could take care of him. She could do the laundry, she could clean the floors, she could make sure there was bread on the table when he came home from work. She could do all this, and keep up with her school work, too, making him smile the way he used to when she brought home the grades that they'd all come to expect. She could be everything he needed—she knew she could, even though she was only fourteen years old, she knew she had it in her to make things right. To make things whole. To make things just like they used to be so he wouldn't feel the need for anything more. Wouldn't feel the need to replace her.

The wood frame of the glass door off the second floor landing was polished to a deep gold. On the other side of the thick beveled pane, an empty reception area gave way to a long, blue-carpeted hallway. A stylized compass was etched into the glass, and on the wall next to the heavy brass door handle was a black keycard reader and a small, white call button.

Inside, nobody stirred. Eva looked up toward the next flight of stairs. A little white box housed a hollow Cyclops eye that watched them patiently from the ceiling corner.

Phaeton stood beside her, staring at the compass. His hair, still wet from the rain outside, was the color of weak tea. His eyes reminded her of the North Sea on a winter day, narrow and sunk deep back in his skull. They betrayed no sign of recognition. No sign of connection. Eva resisted the urge to put her arm around him, rest his head on her shoulder, kiss life back into his pale cheeks. He wasn't the one, after all, that she was out to please. Wasn't supposed to be, anyway. He was a target in a file, a few photographs and biographical notes in a neat manila folder. He was a package, plain and simple, addressed to someone else. And she was just the delivery girl.

One floor up, an electronic latch clicked and cracked open. Eva heard footsteps on the landing above them. Phaeton looked up at the ceiling, then looked her straight in the eyes. Eva smiled unconvincingly and began to climb the final flight of stairs. She could feel his eyes still watching her as she moved away.

The look in his eyes could have been many things. Exhaustion, desperation, surprise, even fear. Eva didn't dare look deeper. She knew what she'd see if she did—it was the same thing she saw every time, if she looked deep enough. They all had the same eyes, after all. If she looked deep enough, all men somehow shared the same eyes. They all begged her to save them, but she never could. However hard she tried, eventually they always needed something more. Sometimes she knew it before they did. Something different. Someone else.

Eva rounded the final bend in the stairs. Phaeton was close behind her. Ahead, on the third-floor landing stood a short, compact man with dark skin and a trim mustache. He smiled without showing his teeth. The jacket of his dark gray suit was buttoned over a gold silk tie. A few wisps of silver hair were carefully combed over his polished scalp. His hands were clasped in front of him, left over right, and an expensive-looking watch winked beneath his spotless white French cuffs.

"Welcome, my friends." He spoke in English, his voice soft but deeper than his size had lead Eva to expect.

Eva arrived at the landing and held out her hand. The small man took it gently, as if cradling a pet bird, closing his eyes with a gracious nod. But he did not introduce himself. He turned instead to extend his hand to Phaeton as he climbed the final stairs.

"Mr. Daniel. I'm so glad that you've come."

Phaeton—Mr. Daniel, apparently—shook his hand, looking down curiously at the small man before them. It didn't appear to Eva as though the two had ever met.

"You must be tired," he continued, apparently unphased by the fact that no one else had spoken. "Please, come in. My assistant will bring us some coffee. You can freshen up a bit, if you like. Then we can talk. I'm sure you have many questions."

The man held a keycard to a card reader next to a door identical to the one a floor below. The latch released and he pulled the door open, stepping aside to let his guests precede him. Eva walked into a small reception area and waited for the men to follow. The room smelled of linseed oil and strong, dark coffee. On the paneled walls hung heavy-framed paintings of sailing ships and storms at sea.

A young woman in a dark skirt and jacket appeared and, although she was clearly European, the man spoke to her in Arabic. She nodded without a smile and, turning to Eva, asked—in English—if she would care to follow her. Eva hesitated, looking from Phaeton to their host, then back again. The door lock engaged again with a soft snap. Phaeton seemed about to speak, but their host stepped in first. He smiled at Eva, the same crossing of the hands, the same gracious nod, this time toward the young woman. "Please," he said, "make yourself comfortable. Kerstin will show you the way. When you're ready, you can join us in the conference room. It's all the way down the hall. We'll be waiting for you there."

Phaeton looked at her again. "Actually," he said, "I wouldn't mind freshening up a little bit myself. Maybe I should go with Kerstin, too, and we can both meet you in the conference room?"

Eva wasn't sure whether the shadow she saw cross their host's face was real, or just something she'd imagined. Either way, it was quickly gone.

"But of course. Kerstin can show you both the way. I'll be waiting for you there."

Kerstin nodded again, first to their host, then to Phaeton and Eva in quick succession. "Follow me, please," she said in very efficient English, then turned and walked back down the hall, her high heels silent in the thick blue carpet.

The restrooms were halfway down the hall. Kerstin turned just beyond them and offered them up with a gesture and a nod and a perfunctory smile. Eva thanked her and opened the door, looking toward Phaeton as she did. His color was back, and his eyes, when they met hers, were steely bright and steady. Winter clouds parted over the cold North Sea, low noon sun burning through the fog, unwilling to give up the fight.

Eva locked the door behind her and looked in the mirror, searching for whatever it was that they all eventually saw—that subtle but unmistakable sign that made them all realize that whatever it was they needed wasn't something they were going to find here. She turned on the tap and splashed cold water on her face, then looked again. Nothing. Nothing ever changed. No matter how hard she tried, she could never see whatever it was that no one but her seemed to miss.

Eva turned off the water and took her phone out of her purse. Still nothing from Andreas. She wondered if he'd been delayed, or if something had happened to his phone. Or if he, too, had moved on. If he'd arrived at the address he'd given her and, not finding her there—not finding Phaeton there—had moved on to plan B. Whatever plan B was. They always had a plan B.

Next door, she heard the flush of a toilet, and water running in a sink. The release of a lock, and the solid thud of a closing door. She needed to hurry. Don't give up now, Eva. You're almost there. Their plane's probably delayed, everything's probably fine. This has to be the new address. Andreas would have seen, and answered, your texts before he even got there, before he could possibly realize that you've gone somewhere else. The children are innocent, Eva. You cannot abandon the innocents.

And what about Phaeton? He just didn't seem like—didn't feel like—the villain he must be if you've been hired to trap him like this. Andreas only went for the bad guys, she'd been told. Only the bad guys, okay, Father?

Eva ignored the sick feeling rising up in her stomach as she opened the door. But Phaeton was there, waiting, and in spite of herself, she smiled.

• • •

The dawn sky stared bloodshot through the open windows as Kimberly Daniel opened her eyes. She lay curled up on top of her bed, still in the clothes she'd worn the night before, her hands clutching a corner of the comforter up under her chin. There was a cold bite in the morning air, a reminder that warm days like yesterday were living on borrowed time. Kimberly pulled the comforter up over her head and dug her feet down into the folds. The clouds would roll in soon enough. Instinct told her to burrow in warm and snug and wait for summer to come back to the rescue. But she just stared into shadows under the covers, unable to close her eyes again.

Her stomach remembered what was going on before her head did, and twisted angrily at her forgetfulness. She kicked away the covers and stumbled to the bathroom. From the toilet, she could see herself in the mirror above the sink. Her hair was matted and tangled, her makeup smeared and smudged. Kimberly buried her face in her hands to escape the contempt in her own eyes. She felt sure she was going to be sick but the feeling soon passed, leaving her no excuse to stay. She left her socks and pants and underwear crumpled next to the toilet. Across the room, she stepped into the big double shower, turned on both faucets and fumbled with the buttons on her blouse, suddenly unable to get rid of its warm, clammy, yesterday smell fast enough. Steam began to rise from the tiles and to fog the cold glass. Kimberly Daniel let the hot water beat down on her face and run through her hair and wash down over the rest of her cold, numb body.

She'd designed this shower big enough for the both of them. She and Asher had spent a good deal of time in the standard showers of their past, Sammy being (Kimberly was pretty sure) tangible evidence of this fact. Over the years, Kimberly had spent more hours than she cared to admit looking through design magazines, leaving no detail of color or texture or dimension unconsidered. A bathroom big enough to accommodate their dreams had been one of her top, unspoken considerations when the time had finally come to buy a new house.

But of course this new house had come with his new job (well—the other way around, really), and his new job had come with its new demands, and as far as Kimberly could remember, they'd shared this shower of her dreams exactly one time, and used it in the manner to which they'd once been accustomed not at all.

Kimberly found herself going through her standard wash-rinse-repeat without even realizing she'd started. Just like her mother had taught her, all those years ago. Some things your parents teach you really do stick. Parents and teachers. Especially if there's a pattern to it—order from chaos, like the familiar chorus of a long, rambling song whose verses you could never remember. Kimberly could still remember the dentist who came to her classroom in grade school to teach them all the right way to brush their teeth. Well—that's not exactly right. She couldn't remember the dentist at all. But she could still remember what he'd taught them—brush up and down, count to ten in each spot, then move on. She still counted that way, same as she'd started doing that very night before she went to bed. She could remember feeling so happy that she finally knew what she was supposed to do—finally had a routine she could fall back on. Happy to have one less thing to worry about. One less question in the world. One less thing that she might get wrong, that might get her in trouble, or that might get her laughed at. It was like learning where a new "base" was in a big, long game of tag.

Adults all like to go on and on about the wonders of childhood—everything new, everything a mystery, everything full of that magic that as adults we find we've lost. But if we're really honest about it, try to think back to the way we felt as kids, wasn't it all sort of scary? Isn't that why we were all so eager to learn—so we wouldn't get caught with our pants down (what kid didn't have that dream?), laughed at for not knowing something everybody else somehow already knew, sent off to the principal's office for not knowing you weren't supposed to spin the globe in the library as fast as the teachers said the world was spinning right that minute?

We always say we'd like to see the world again through the eyes of a child. But it seemed to Kimberly that what children want most is the certainty that comes with adulthood. Understanding how it all works. That safety of being big enough to look down on it all, instead of up for protection from the things that might hurt you. The security of knowing the words to the chorus that will come, no matter what, just as sure as the dawn after a long, dark night.

Somewhere along the line, of course, we all lose that love of familiar things—lose it, or just start to think it's embarrassing. Most of us do, anyway—for a while. Some lose it earlier than others, and some lose it for longer, but losing it seems to be as much a part of growing up as finding it in the first place. One day we decide that we've learned it all, that nothing can hurt us now, and that all those routines are just there to keep us down. So we set about breaking them all. But all we really seem to do in the long run is figure out which routines still work and which ones don't. The whole process is just another routine, really—every generation test-driving what their parents have handed down to them, working out which hold up and which don't before trusting them out on the open road. Quality control on civilization. Learn it, break it, fix it, pass it on. Amazing how the universe works.

Her mother's old routine, which she'd never found reason to break, guided Kimberly from head to toe, soaping the long, smooth curves and the hard, bony joints and the warm, soft undersides. Rinse from head to toe. Mission accomplished. Time to turn off the water, reach for the towel, and dry off, everything in the same order, nothing left to chance. Do something different, something gets missed. Something gets missed, something goes wrong. No telling what, but it doesn't matter, does it, as long as you follow the rules? Just stick to the plan and nothing can go wrong.

Your husband will know what to do.

When he does, your kids will come home.

Now there was a routine that needed to be broken. May have been good enough for her mother, but most certainly was not good enough for her. Kimberly wrapped herself in her damp towel and stepped out of the shower. Amazing how a little sleep and a good shower can suddenly make things crystal clear.

Talk only with him.

No police.

With all due respect—fuck that.

Kimberly Daniel walked out of the bathroom and looked on the night table for her cell phone. Not there. She took the comforter on the bed in both hands and flipped it into the air—nothing there. Nothing under the covers, either, or under the pillow. She could've sworn she'd had it with her last night, climbing the stairs in the dark. She got down on her knees and peered under the bed. Nothing. Okay, maybe not. Must've left it downstairs, maybe by her purse.

Her bare feet fogged a trail of prints down the honey oak stairs. Through the living room windows she could see the orange sun climbing out of the morning haze. Not as nice as it was yesterday. In the kitchen, she found her purse where she'd left it when she came back from downtown. But her phone wasn't in it. It wasn't on the counter, either, or on the breakfast table next to the door that led out to the deck. Had she left it in the cabinet that she'd been so set on fixing last night? She bent to open the door and looked in.

"You wouldn't, by any chance, be looking for this?"

Kimberly Daniel bolted straight up at the low voice rattling in the shadows of the family room's drawn shades. She almost hit the back of her head on the underside of the dark granite counter, eyes wide and searching, what she expected to be a scream emerging as nothing but a hot rush of air from deep down in her lungs.

• • •

The bus had only been half full. None of the usual stoplights had been red. Jessica Kelly had arrived at the office a full twenty minutes earlier than usual—early enough that she could tell that the sunlight was different. She stood by her desk watching through Asher's empty office and out through the windows at the harbor beyond. The shadows of the ferries were longer that usual, stretching toward Rowes Wharf across waves more gold than silver. The sun splashed unfamiliar orange shapes on the red-brick walls and over the soft, silent cubicles behind her.

The light on top of her phone was dark.

Twenty-four hours ago, Jess would have found this a relief. Twenty-four hours ago, she had wished for nothing more than for the calls to simply stop. But now they had, and she didn't know why. And the not knowing why was almost worse than the not knowing what to do.

Maybe the kids were already home. Jess felt a hint of anger spark somewhere back behind her temples, wondering why Mrs. Daniel hadn't called to let her know. After all, she'd tried to help, hadn't she? She'd tracked Asher down, gotten the message through, let her know what was going on—she'd even lied a little to make her feel better. What more did she want from her? Was it too much to ask for a little gratitude?

Jess sat down in her chair and pulled off her sneakers, throwing them in her bottom desk drawer and pulling on her office heels. She sat there staring at them for a long time. Once upon a time she'd been able to see her reflection in the patent leather toes, but that new-girl shine was gone now. She closed her eyes and waited for the little flame kindled behind them to go away, too.

One step at a time, Jess. One step at a time.

Once upon a time, you assumed your brother would want to know everything. He'd always asked, hadn't he? Have a good evening, Jessie? Everything okay at school? What's the matter, Jessie? Want to talk about it? And so she'd always told him, like she told nobody else—not even her mother, who'd just tell her she should have done something different, and certainly not her father, who was never around, even when he was sitting right there. She'd always told her brother everything, and he'd always listened—just listened, his eyes following hers as they wandered around the room, seeking out just the right thought from the sometimes almost overwhelming crush of them fluttering around her head, like butterflies over a field full of flowers. His deep green eyes almost a reflection of her own, and his voice, too, soft and low when she was worked up, bubbling up when she was down, never sharp, never rough, and steady as the long, low notes from the organ at church that lingered even after the congregation stopped singing. Even after you'd stood up and made your way down the aisle and out the doors and into the street and the wind was blowing cold off the harbor between the rows of weathered gray houses and bare gray trees—even then you could still hear those long low notes rumbling from behind the thick stone walls, just like they did whether it was day or night, stormy or fair, winter or spring, summer or fall. Always steady, always the same.

Except on that day. On that day, there'd been a crack in his voice. "Did you tell them that, Jessie?" Yes, she'd told them that. "Okay." And then the silence. Had she done the right thing? The silence told her. "Okay, Jessie." After too much time. "It's okay. But I don't think you should talk with them anymore, okay? Just in case they call you again." And he'd hung up. The next day he'd told the truth. The day after that, the police had taken their father away.

Don't blame Mrs. Daniel, Jess. You don't know the kids are home yet. And even if they are, a little coffee and a chocolate croissant don't suddenly make you best friends forever. Just because you made a few phone calls doesn't mean you're now the first person she calls when the credits start to roll on her happy endings. Just because you did your job—and not very well, I have to say, Jess, while we're on the subject. How long did it take you to even tell anybody? How many messages did it take before you ever said a word? Isn't that what you're there for, Jessica—to help people who need to talk with Asher get in touch with him? So don't blame Mrs. Daniel, Jessica. If she's not entirely thrilled with your performance in this whole comedy or tragedy or whatever it turns out to be, don't be too surprised. Certainly don't be too surprised if you're not first on her call list.

Way to go, Jessica. Well done once again.

Jess walked into the kitchen and turned on the lights. She poured last night's coffee into the sink and put on a new pot. The water sputtered and steamed in the reservoir as the coils inside warmed up to a new day. The dark stream percolated down out of the grounds and hit the bottom of the pot with a hiss. The smell of coffee drifted through the empty office, marking a new day, ratcheting the low morning light up a little closer to vertical.

Jessica. Get a grip. You don't know what you don't know.

She poured herself a cup of coffee and walked back to her desk. Somewhere in the cubicles behind her, she could hear the thud of a bag on a desk and the grumbling of a voice by itself and the clatter of a phone receiver lifted. Another day off to the races. A moment later the elevator opened and two women burst into the room at street volume. It wouldn't be long now. She sat down and stared at her phone. The little red light was still dark. It could do nothing right this week.

Don't blame the light, Jessica. It doesn't do a thing. Sometimes doing nothing is the best policy. Remember?

For a long time after her brother hung up, Jess had sat on her bed, looking around at her dorm room walls. Pictures of family and friends, freckle-faced kids lying on Maine beaches and rowing boats around New Hampshire lakes. She'd sought out her brother's green eyes, and then her own, comparing, contrasting, trying to make the connection. In hindsight, she'd known even then it was gone. That was the moment the denial had begun. At the time, though, she hadn't seen it. That was the thing about her. She never seemed to realize what was going on fast enough to change it. If she'd been quicker then, she'd never have made the call. If she'd been quicker this week, she might have made it sooner.

Or maybe it should have been the other way around.

Jess picked up the receiver and dialed the number on the crumpled, stained napkin still lying there under her keyboard. After a couple of those clicks whose meaning she'd never understood, it began to ring. The elevator opened again, full this time, emptying a new load of noise and life into the building. Friday laughter danced with footsteps and silverware and running water in the kitchen. Someone put on a yet another fresh pot of coffee. But on the other end of the line, only ringing. Ringing, and finally the voice of Kimberly Daniel, recorded a long time ago, inviting some-body—anybody—to leave her a message.

The beep was long gone by the time Jessica Kelly even realized that she'd dialed the phone.

• • •

Phaeton smiled back. His flinty eyes sparked silver and he leaned in toward her, his unshaved cheek almost brushing against hers, the breath from his lips warming her ear. Eva's eyes began to close and her heart began to quicken, but she willed her lids open and her pulse rate steady and she glanced down the hall toward the conference room door.

"Everything you expected?"

His whisper was slow and precise. His rough cheek was quickly gone and she could feel his gray eyes back on hers, then following them down the hall. She didn't meet his gaze. He stood up straight and adjusted his shirt, tugging the cuffs out of the sleeves of his jacket. But he stood his ground. After a moment she felt his eyes again, studying the hard pulse right where her hair was pulled back from her temple.

Eva nodded, then swallowed. Phaeton didn't move. For a very long second they stood, he studying her, she studiously avoiding his gaze, in the hallway stretching from one paneled room to another.

"Do you think we should go?"

Maybe he'd whispered the question. Maybe she'd only been thinking it herself. Eva looked at her phone, more out of hope than of any real expectation. Then she tucked it away in her purse. Still, she didn't look at the man at her side.

He took a deep breath and started down the hall without her.

If you want them to follow, you have to lead. If you want to go off script, you have to improvise. Ever wonder why they always seem to have a plan B? Because you don't, Eva—you never have. It's not them—it's you, Eva. It's only because you fail them that they're forced to change their plans. Find something solid. Somewhere safer. Someone else.

Phaeton was almost to the conference room, head held high, long stride steady and assured. Eva thought of Kai, the last time she'd seen him, walking away toward the Tiergarten and the Spree. Away from their apartment. When she came home later, he wasn't there. She'd packed her things up quickly and left. The boxes that arrived at her father's house later contained things she hadn't wanted, anyway. On that point, apparently, they'd actually agreed.

On that point and many. As long as we're finally being honest.

Eva tucked the usual stray hair behind her ear and hurried to catch up to Phaeton. At the conference room door, he paused and looked back. The man from the landing was standing inside, his back turned to them, looking out the window at the rain. Down the hall behind them, porcelain and steel giggled quietly on a tray, their secrets safe for another moment, at least. Maybe two, but no more. Kerstin hadn't seemed like one to keep them waiting.

Phaeton stood aside and, with a little smile and a nod, let Eva lead him into the room.

• • •

"Please. Have a seat."

The small man from the landing turned from the window as they walked into the room. He spread his hands wide as he spoke, offering them the whole table. The table was long, filling almost the entire room, sleek black legs supporting a thick glass top. Four green bottles of sparkling water stood in a row lengthwise down the middle of the table, each flanked by two small, spotless glasses. Kerstin was suddenly there behind them at the door, pushing a metal-and-glass cart that matched the table. On the cart were stainless steel carafes and spoons, white coffee cups and saucers, and little butter cookies arranged over a white doily on a wide, white plate.

Asher Daniel waited for his blue-eyed companion to choose a seat, then sat down beside her. Their host sat down directly across from them, facing the door. Kerstin poured three cups of coffee and laid them, along with the carafes and the plates, on the table. She nodded when their host said something in Arabic, and she closed the door behind her as she left.

Asher noticed there was no phone in the room. No electronics of any kind, as far as he could tell.

"I'm so glad that you have come. You have been rather hard to reach, Mr. Daniel."

The small man smiled at each of them in turn, his hands folded neatly on the table in front of him. Next to Asher, one French-manicured thumb rubbed the back of a milky white hand. She gave no indication that she was paying any attention to anything else.

Asher poured a little milk into his coffee and stirred, watching the liquid go from hard burnt sugar to caramel brown. The strong coffee smell glazed over the centuries of tobacco smoke seeping out of the old wooden walls. Outside, low clouds snaked between shadowy church towers and scudded off toward the North Sea.

"Well, I apologize if I've kept you waiting. I wasn't aware till last night that you were trying to get in touch with me."

Small Man's smile appeared as quickly as it was gone. He dropped four lumps of sugar into his cup and stirred carefully, in no apparent hurry to respond. Finally, he lifted his cup and sipped at the coffee. As he did, he considered the tropical blue for a split second longer than Asher thought he should have. She was still intent on her thumb.

"Well, never mind. You are here now, and that is what is important." Small Man placed his cup back carefully on its saucer and folded his hands in front of him once again.

"Do you have any idea why we have invited you here?" The question directed at Asher, and Asher alone.

Asher tapped a finger slowly on the glass table and smiled. "No, sir. I'm afraid I really don't know."

"But surely you have some . . . how shall I say . . . suspicions?"

"Yes, of course I do. But let me be the first to say I'm sure I don't have the whole story. That, to be perfectly honest, is the real reason I'm here."

"Curiosity." Small Man smiled and began to nod, a little quicker now, lips pursed in increasing certainly, until he settled the matter with himself and stopped. "It can be a dangerous thing, you know. I believe you have such a saying—'curiosity kills the cat'— yes?" His dark eyes were fixed on Asher, and they showed no sign of letting him go.

Asher held his gaze. "We have lots of sayings, Mr. . . ."

Small Man let it go, frowning a humorous frown and looking for his coffee. "Of course you do, Mr. Daniel. Of course you do. So." He took a long swallow, put his cup back down, braced his hands on the edge of the table and stretched back in his chair with a deep breath. He watched the tropical blue the whole time. She glanced up for only a moment, but went back immediately to rubbing her soft, white hand.

"May I speak freely?" To Asher again, with a quick glance in the direction of the blue.

Asher shrugged. "I don't see why not."

"We invited you here because we need your help. Ahmed, in particular, needs your help."

Asher looked Small Man straight in the eyes. "You know Ahmed?"

Small Man smiled his humorous frown again and nodded down at his hands. "Yes, yes, I know him very well. You see, Ahmed is my cousin."

Asher sat up straighter, elbows on the table, hands in front of his lips. "Is Ahmed okay?"

Small Man continued his nodding. "Yes, Ahmed is okay. For the time being, at least. We've made certain that Ahmed is okay."

"Where is he?"

Small Man looked up at Asher, then into the tropical blue, then back at Asher. "He is safe."

Asher noticed that she still wasn't watching either of them.

"Okay. That's good. I'm glad he's safe. I've been trying to reach him for quite a while now."

"Yes, we know that you have. That is why we called you. We hope you can help."

"Help how? What's the matter with him?"

"Nothing is the matter with him. Not yet. But we are very certain that there are people who would prefer to have it otherwise."

Both men looked now at the woman at Asher's side. She looked up, though clearly reluctant to do so. She took in one man, then the other, then back again, and shook her head with a little shrug. "I'm sorry. I don't know Ahmed."

Asher considered her for a moment then turned back to the man across the table.

"What has Ahmed done?"

"The question, really, Mr. Daniel, is not what Ahmed has done. I believe you already know what Ahmed has done. The question, Mr. Daniel, is what have you done?"

A gust of wind blew fat drops of rain against the windows of the room, reminding Asher of where he was.

"I'm sorry, sir, but I really don't understand."

Small Man sighed and stood up, pacing to the far side of the room. "Ahmed was helping you with a certain business deal, yes?"

"Yes. Yes, he was."

"And you met together with certain clients, yes?"

"Yes—only once, though. The rest of the time, Ahmed met with them alone."

Small Man waved a hand in the air, dismissively. "This is not important. You provided these clients with what they wanted, correct?"

Asher noticed that the manicured thumb beside him had stopped moving. She was watching him now, watching both of them.

Asher said nothing.

Small Man leaned on the back of a chair and stared out the window at the clouds racing low over the city. He watched Asher for a moment then focused on the tropical blue. She avoided the attention, taking a sip of the coffee that she'd let go cold in her cup. She looked around the room, as if searching for something, but whatever it was, she didn't find it.

"Mr. Daniel, I don't like to speak poorly of my guests, but I'm afraid I must say that you have been rather rude. You neglected to introduce your lovely guest."

Small Man's eyebrows rose as he said it, and he tilted his head just a little and held Asher's gaze. Asher looked from him to the tropical blue. She fidgeted in her chair but said nothing, and looked at nothing.

"I'm sorry." Asher said still looking at her. "I assumed that you'd already met."

"No." Small Man's deep voice slower now, smoother, a calm current beneath the waves whipped up by the wind. "I'm afraid I have not had the pleasure."

Her eyes looked up at Asher, reflecting a clear, blue sky that was nowhere to be found.

"Sir, may I ask you a question?" Asher with his eyes still sunk in the tropical blue.

"Of course."

"Where are my children?"

Her eyes widened, and she shook her head very slowly, almost imperceptibly. Asher turned and looked at Small Man leaning against the thin windows that shielded them all from the storm. His dark eyes, for the first time all day, looked truly blank.

"Mr. Daniel, I assure you: We know nothing of your children."

Asher turned back to the woman sitting next to him, still shaking her head, eyes lovely and daunting as the deep blue sea.

There was a knock on the door an instant before it opened. Kerstin leaned in and said something to their host in Arabic. He stared at her blankly for a moment, then turned his attention to Eva.

"Are you expecting someone?"

"No."

"Well, someone is on his way up to see you. The guard just called from downstairs."

Eva stared for longer than was probably polite. The little man's hollow dark eyes stared right back. Beneath his trim mustache, Eva thought she could see the beginnings of a smile. She couldn't be sure. But even the possibility made her wonder. She reached for the bag she'd left on the chair next to her and fished around for her cell phone.

"Perhaps now would be a good time for you to tell us who you are."

Eva could hear the little smile in the dark rumblings of his voice. But maybe only because the image of it there—an almost imperceptible twist at the corners of his thin, shadowy lips—was still all she could see as she flipped open her phone, buried in the clutter in her bag.

Nothing.

"No?" Teeth emerging in her memory of his smile.

Eva realized she was still shaking her head. She looked up from the tiny, empty screen. The little man's smile was much less certain than the one she'd remembered. No teeth in sight. Behind him, waves of rain played crack the whip across the darkening gray sky.

To her left, Phaeton was watching her every move. Not even a hint of a smile there. His eyes matched the weather.

Your move, Eva.

She took a deep breath to inflate herself and her courage. She sat up straight, holding her cell phone in both hands on the table in front of her. She needed a smile, too. She looked from one man to the next. She wondered if her smile was convincing.

"No. I don't think this is a good time for that at all."

The more she smiled, the less they reciprocated. So she went on, encouraged by their silence, which she decided then and there she was going to take as a sign of success.

"I am here with Mr. Daniel. For now, you have no need to know more. But *we* need to know more. We need to be sure that Mr. Daniel's children are safe."

"Madam, I already told you, we know nothing—"

"Yes, yes, you already told us. But unfortunately, I don't believe you."

The little man leaned back in his chair, considering her. His hands were folded across his stomach, thumbs tapping each other to some silent metronome. He glanced over at Phaeton. Phaeton didn't budge.

Eva's heart raced. She felt like she'd taken the first steps across that wobbly old log that lay across the creek in the woods around the fishponds.

As a little girl, on walks that summer in those woods with her grandparents, she'd eyed the log every day as they passed by on the usual path. The log lay across a deep, green pool, and when the sun was right through the pine branches she could see fish swimming underneath, over on the other side where the big, flat rocks made little islands in the pool. Every day, she thought about crossing that log and sitting on the big, warm rocks and watching the fish watching her in the sunlight. Maybe dangling her bare feet into the water and feeling the tickle of the fish pecking curiously at her toes. Every day she wanted to try, but every day she felt her heart race and her stomach jump and her feet continued along the path instead, watching the log fade away behind her as her grandparents' hands—one on each side—pulled her safely away. Every day until the last day—the day before her parents were coming to pick her up. That day, she pulled away from her grandparents' hands and ran down the bank to the log and put her right foot up on it and paused. Her grandparents' voices were far away as she pushed down with her right foot and brought her left foot safely to rest in front of it on the log. The creek gurgled loud beneath her feet now and the breeze smelled strong of pine and her heart raced just like it did at this moment. All those steps still to come before she would make it to the big, warm rocks on the other side. All that anticipation still inside her, still in front of her, nothing yet behind but the things she already knew.

"Why, for example, would you make Mr. Daniel come here? Why would you not meet him in Dubai? You, or somebody already there?"

The little man smiled, more openly now, and looked to Phaeton for sympathy. Phaeton smiled but shrugged and looked away, studying the low, fast clouds and the gray rain whipping across the windowpanes.

"We did not know, when we first called to invite Mr. Daniel to meet with us, that he was planning to travel to Dubai. Had we known, perhaps we would have made other arrangements."

"It does seem odd, doesn't it, that your calls should come at the same time as the disappearance of Mr. Daniel's children?" Eva raced on across the wobbly log.

His hollow, dark eyes hardened into black pebbles at the bottom of the deep, cold pool. They turned to Phaeton.

"Mr. Daniel, we have invited *you* here to discuss the safety of my cousin, your friend. Perhaps we will find we are also discussing the safety of your own children. I do not know this woman, or what she has to do with these matters or, quite frankly, with you. I am not sure it matters. But I do believe that we may not have much time. So . . ." Eva felt his quick, hard glance before he looked away again. "May I suggest we meet in private? I do not believe this woman's presence is—how shall I say it?—productive."

Phaeton held the little man in his steel gray eyes. His left hand played across the edge of the glass table, fingering chords only he could hear. Eva held her breath, balancing midstream, the rush of the water beneath washing away everything not here and now.

"I think," said Phaeton, looking away toward the end of the room, "that I'd like to hear your answer first."

Eva leapt toward the warmth of the big, flat rocks.

Behind her, beyond the conference room's closed door, Eva suddenly heard voices. Loud voices—a man's voice, and woman's voice, low and stern, still fairly far away. But coming closer. Their host heard them, too, and rose to his feet, absentmindedly buttoning his perfectly tailored suit and adjusting the white French cuffs inside the dark gray sleeves of his jacket.

Phaeton stood, too. Eva turned in her chair to face the door.

Kerstin appeared, her face red, adjusting her glasses. Behind her was a large man wearing dark blue rainwear, dripping water onto the carpeted floor of the hallway. Kerstin started to say something in German, then switched abruptly to Arabic. When she did, the big man pushed past her, carefully taking in each person before saying a word.

"Excuse me," said their host, standing with his back against the window. "This is a private office. I must ask you to leave at once, or I will be forced to call the police."

But everyone was ignoring him. While their host was still speaking, the big man took Eva's arm in one damp, meaty hand and gestured to Phaeton with the other. Phaeton hesitated. Eva didn't try to break free. The big man waited for just a second or two before grabbing Phaeton's arm and unceremoniously push-pulling him and Eva out of the room. Kerstin complained loudly in German but stood aside to let them pass.

Eva had made it across the wobbly log that day, up onto the big, warm rocks with the sun shining down on the deep, green pool. But when she'd turned around, smiling up in triumph toward where she'd left her grandparents, she'd found only angry faces, heard only scolding words, asking her what she thought she was doing, demanding that she come back that instant before she slipped or fell or broke her leg or drowned. The racing in her heart and the flutter in her stomach had died. She'd never sat there on the rocks with her bare feet dangling in the water. The fish had never tickled and pecked at her toes. She'd simply walked back across the wobbly log and let her grandparents take her by both of her hands, hauling her back up the bank to the usual path, around the usual loop back to their car and then home to clean up for supper.

Eva caught Phaeton's eye as they stumbled out onto the landing. She nodded as encouragingly as she could manage, but inside she'd gone numb, and she was afraid that it showed.

Outside on the street, the doors to their car were open. The big man shoved Eva into the front seat next to the driver, then closed the door and bundled Phaeton into the back. The driver started moving even before the doors were shut.

The security guard stood outside the old wooden doors, the rain beating down on his worn blue blazer. His mouth hung open behind his bushy gray whiskers as the car hissed away down the wet street. The big man pulled a cigar case out of an inside pocket of his raincoat and turned his back against the wind to light it. He crossed his arms and stared past the bewildered old guard at the thick wooden doors. And then he waited, his back to the Alter Wall, standing next to the bicycle propped against the heavy stone stairs.

• • •

"I just thought I'd stop by, see how you were doing. The last couple of days must have been a little rough."

Kimberly Daniel leaned against the counter, clutching the damp folds of the towel to her chest.

"So you won't give me my phone back?"

"Not just yet. Sorry about that."

Kimberly's tall, lanky visitor was moving slowly around the other side of the kitchen, preparing a pot of coffee. He seemed to know her kitchen almost as well as she did. Either that or he just had a sixth sense for where things should be. Never once did he ask her where something was. Only once did he have to open more than one cabinet door to find what he was looking for.

He looked older than she remembered, but she probably did, too.

"It's strange, isn't it, what people will and won't do?" He flipped the switch on the coffee pot and turned, leaning the skinny seat of his faded blue jeans against the granite, across the kitchen, on the other side of the island, pale eyes roaming the room. "Things that make absolutely no sense to one person seem perfectly reasonable to another. Why is that?"

The pot began to grumble and smack behind him. His eyes had landed on something in the backyard. Kimberly, somehow more uncomfortable when he wasn't looking at her, glanced down at her bare feet and said nothing.

"I just don't understand it." His voice was low but rough, and he coughed once into his fist, hoping to clear things up. "Time makes a difference, too, of course. There are things I did thirty, forty years ago that I'd never do today. But then again, there are probably things I'd do today that would have shocked me back then. Probably. No way to be sure, I suppose."

Kimberly watched as the stream of dark coffee began to trickle down into the pot behind him. The smell drifted across to where she stood, mingling with the scent of shampoo from her hair and warm, clean skin from her towel to make the morning seem almost normal. Kimberly looked up to find him staring straight at her.

"Do you ever feel that way?"

His hair wasn't as thick as she remembered, waves more chalky than silver. But his eyes, deep set back in the tanned wrinkles of his face, still had that icy blue calm that made her blush for no reason. He smiled and she looked back down at her feet. She felt her blush turn to anger at the damp, helpless footprints on the bare wood floor.

"When are they coming home?" Kimberly's words sounded foreign to her as they hung in the middle of the room, like her voice on an old LP played just off the recommended speed.

She heard him pick up the coffee pot and pour two cups. Then footsteps, slow and steady, around the island. "Soon," he said. "Very soon. I'm just waiting for a call."

The coffee smell didn't quite cover up the smell of his deodorant, rising up from inside his jacket, which didn't quite cover up the fact that he hadn't showered in a while. But she didn't move away. "Here." He handed her a mug. She took it and sipped, hot and strong and bitter.

"I'm just curious," he said as he settled in next to her against the counter. "How did you manage *not* to call the police?"

Kimberly's silence seemed to hit him harder than his words hit her. "Don't get me wrong, now—you did the right thing. Everything could have ended a whole lot differently, and not in a good way, if you had called them. But still. That's a long time. How'd you keep it together?"

Kimberly looked up at the old man standing beside her. His eyes were on her, looking down, not wandering anymore, not distracted. He took a sip of coffee, but his eyes didn't budge.

"What makes you so sure I did?"

"Well, you didn't call anybody, did you?"

"You tell me."

"Nobody we cared about."

"We?"

He smiled and took another sip of coffee. Still, his eyes didn't wander from hers.

"You did good. You helped. You should be proud of yourself."

"I did nothing."

"Exactly. Nothing's really hard to do sometimes."

"You don't know me, then. Nothing's my specialty."

The tall man shrugged. "At least you have one. Not everybody can say that."

A phone rang, standard default tone. The tall man fished a cell phone out of his jacket pocket and held it far enough away to see the number. Then he flipped the phone open and listened.

"Okay." That was it. He hung up. Then he pressed another button and put the phone back up to his ear.

"We're good. Ship the package." He hung up again and put the phone back into his pocket.

Kimberly sipped her coffee, waiting. The man at her side looked around the room, checked his watch, then looked down at her once more.

"You did good."

Kimberly Daniel shifted her weight, moving her body just a fraction of an inch closer to his. He didn't move, but didn't look at her again, focusing instead on his coffee and the floor.

Kimberly's bare feet looked tiny and pink next to his ancient leather boots.

The living room clock ticked. A car drove into the driveway. Kimberly put down her coffee and ran to the front door. It opened just as she got there. Tyler and Sammy hugged her like they were still in kindergarten or coming home after their first week of camp.

Back in the kitchen, her cell phone lay on the counter next to two half-empty mugs of coffee.

• • •

Waves were bucking the boats on the harbor as the sun neared its high point of the day. Restless flags struggled for freedom from their halyards. Lunch-hour pedestrians, heads ducked against the dust gusting from the cobblestone alleyway cracks, fought for wind-whipped liberty from their brown-bagged, desk-bound calm.

Jessica Kelly watched from the still of Asher's empty office. Watched and waited for the ring.

Mrs. Daniel had never called back. Jess had left her a message first thing this morning, then tried to find things to make time pass quickly. Expense reports were easy—not much thinking involved, just a lot of paperwork. She'd offered to help Mindy, the GM's assistant, with arrangements for the sales meeting. Mindy had told her that her sister had just gotten engaged. Descriptions of the ring and the proposal at the top of the Pru lasted half an hour or more, and for a while they made Jessica forget. But only for a while. He was in his second year of residency at Brigham and Women's—Mindy's sister's fiancé. Tall and dark and handsome. And soon to be rich. Some joke about all that playing doctor finally paying off in the end. Jessica had smiled and tried to giggle to be polite, but she hadn't really heard. Back at her desk, the red light still refused to shine, and that brilliant next move people like Mindy's sister seemed to just stumble across stayed tucked away somewhere it couldn't possibly threaten Jess.

"Want to come to lunch?"

Mindy's voice had sparkled in the reflected light of her sister. Jess had known she couldn't handle the glare for much longer. She'd smiled, said she'd brought her lunch, had a lot to get done for Asher before the weekend, was so happy for her sister, couldn't wait to see the pictures, and made her way back through the cubicle doldrums to the dull peace of her neat and tidy desk.

The phone rang.

Jessica turned from watching the blustering world below and stared at her empty chair. The phone rang again—she wasn't imagining it. She was there before it could ring a third time. The number was unfamiliar. International. Any other time, she would have let it go. But she'd waited so long for that little red light, she grabbed at the receiver before the third ring was over.

"Investors' Information—Asher Daniel's office. This is Jessica. May I help you?"

Silence.

"Hello?"

Jessica said it just as the person on the other end began to speak.

"Hello. I'm sorry, but I have only a little time. I must give you the address where Phae . . . where Mr. Daniel is at the moment. Quickly, please. Can you write this down?"

The woman's voice reminded Jess of a mountain brook tripping over a strip mine. An acoustic guitar in a military band. Jess always thought voices had looks—some were good-looking, some fat, some bony, some small.

This voice was pretty—a voice matched with bright, clear eyes and a soft, kind mouth. A voice for bedtime stories, laughing at sand castles and at snowball fights. But not for this. It was in too much of a hurry now, forced to be abrupt out of necessity, not out of practice or any natural inclination.

"Go ahead," said Jessica, her own voice rising to the panic on the other end of the line.

"Okay—good." Something in the vowels wasn't quite right—she wasn't American, and probably not someone who'd grown up speaking English.

Just then, Jessica's phone began to ring again. The light on the other line began to flash. Jessica looked at the number—she recognized the number. . . .

"The address is in Germany."

Jessica's mind froze. She'd waited so long for Mrs. Daniel to return her call that for a split second she was about to put the scared, pretty voice on hold.

The phone rang again.

"The street number is—"

Jessica grabbed the red pen lying next to her keyboard and a yellow sticky from her pad and wrote "Germany" at the top. She held the pen ready, all the while staring at Kimberly Daniel's number lit up on her phone's display.

Then she heard rustling, a few muffled words, and a click.

The other line rang again.

"Hello?" Jessica looked around the office, as if she might find the lost voice somewhere among the empty lunchtime cubicles. No one was there.

"Hello?"

The line was dead.

The phone rang again. Jessica pressed on the button for the other line, but only just as that light stopped flashing.

This line was dead, too.

Jessica heard footsteps and the jingle of keys coming her way. She quietly hung up the receiver. Mindy appeared at her desk, still beaming, fussing with a thread that had attached itself to her purse.

"You sure you don't want to come?" Still to her purse. "Sheila's coming, too. She's got pictures of the baby."

Jessica said nothing. Mindy finally looked up and her smile drifted sideways, her next words already forgotten.

"Jess, honey, are you okay?"

Jessica Kelly shook her head and wished that Mindy would just leave. But the tears she felt starting to run down her cheeks guaranteed that she'd give her no peace for the rest of the afternoon.

• • •

Asher Daniel slumped in the back seat, listening: The revving of the big car's engine as they leapt away from the curb. The hisses and squeals of tires on wet pavement. The growls and chatters and rattles of the slower vehicles. The urgent third of a siren in the distance. Passing laughter at a crosswalk. Somewhere down a side street, the steel cadence of a lone hammer.

All this the background music for the argument in the front seat. Its speed and vocabulary left Asher in the dust, but its emotion was universal. It had started with a simple question before they'd even left the Alter Wall. When the question had received no response, the words had multiplied, first in a low register, then rising in pitch and in timbre. Finally, the driver chimed in, just a couple of syllables, dismissive and distant. Those syllables, however, had opened a window on a whole smoldering room, causing flames to suddenly leap and crackle and with the heat to force the wise to turn away.

Asher closed his eyes and tried to focus through the din. He could feel the second wind that always arrived with evening, and the strong coffee he'd just drunk still tingled the back of his skull. All systems go, ready for action. But what action? What was he trying to do? A little late for that question, isn't it? Ready, fire, aim—that's what you've gotten yourself into. Again. Ready to do the right thing, but no idea what the right thing is.

Sandy blonde hair whirled in the front seat as tropical blue seared the side of the driver's shaved head. The driver's words like the notes of a kettledrum: short, low, throbbing the car's dark interior. In response, the full force of a string section, soaring and diving, slashing and coiling, ready to strike back. At one point, the driver didn't see a red light until the car in front of them was already stopped. Brakes shrieked, violins wailed, timpani boomed as they all lurched in the direction of the grimy windshield.

A brief moment of silence as they flopped back hard against their seats, braced against the crash that never came. A couple of beats of the windshield wiper. The patter of raindrops on the roof. Then the next movement opened with the kettledrums pounding, the driver's finger conducting each beat to the side of his string section's sandy blonde head. She perfectly still, counting her rests, making sure that he'd thumped out his dull final note before unleashing new furies at the traffic ahead.

Asher stared out the tinted window at the cars and the people and the buildings and the rain. You should have seen this coming from the start. How could you expect to track down real live terrorists single-handed? What made you think that even *trying* was a good idea?

The traffic light turned green and the car began to move again. The kettledrum announced a new mood in the front seat symphony. Tropical blue eyes turned on Asher now, their tone low and somber. Cellos, violas, *molto sostenuto*. She paused with that same coral pout Asher had first seen on the plane barely a day before. The kettledrums kept time, a dirge for some unknown hero. But apparently there was more to it than that. The blue and the pout turned once again on the driver and the violins joined back in, swarming low, building, gaining strength for their next great burst skyward.

Asher took it all in from a distance. He knew perfectly well what it was that'd gotten him here. It was always the same old thing: the need to do something right. The need to do something well. The need to escape the day to day and do something that really matters. The need to care again. The need to care about something that matters.

And, of course, the need to do something himself. The need to do something nobody else was telling him to do. The need to escape parents' advice and schools' prerequisites and employers' policies and governments' laws and society's unwritten codes of conduct and just *do* something—do something *real*. Do something *original*. If you just follow the crowd, you'll never be outstanding. If you just follow orders, you'll never be a hero. Heroes—and villains—decide for themselves. Those who just follow rules? They're subjects—nothing more.

Milky-white fingers and French-manicured nails indicated Asher's face as the string section as crescendo built. The driver's hand had a point to make, but his voice couldn't find a gap and he ended up looking like a timid pupil with a question. Suddenly the music stopped, and both of them looked at Asher—she frank, direct, he sidelong in the rearview mirror. Another traffic light turned red, and the driver saw this one in plenty of time. The car whispered to a stop, virtually silent inside and out.

So maybe it was time to write off the original plan. But it wasn't too late to do something right. It was never too late to do something right. No matter how hopeless everything might look, there was always something good you could do. Sometimes it just took a lot of looking to find it. And at times like those, society's great rulebooks were *not* the place to be looking.

The next boom of the kettledrum was a word Asher recognized, and was echoed by the cellos' soft pout.

Kinder.

Children.

"They know about your children." Her voice was thin and tired. Waves of tropical blue broke and crashed before Asher's eyes.

So the little man in the office had been telling the truth, then. He didn't know anything about the kids. He probably really was Ahmed's cousin, after all. He probably was just looking for help, trying to make sure Ahmed was safe.

And the little man most certainly didn't know this woman staring at Asher now. This woman who had told Asher she could help him. This woman who seemed to know "them"—these people who knew about his children.

"And you?" His eyes icy gray, his voice a stranger in the car, a woodwind playing in a different key. "Do *you* know about my children? Did you know before I told you about them? Is that why you talked to me in Dubai?"

If Ahmed wasn't safe, whose fault was that?

"No." Her eyes were cold but clear, wide open, nothing to hide. "They never told me."

But if his own kids weren't safe? Whose fault was *that*?

The driver's eyes were narrow in the rearview mirror, suspicious of the shift to a song he couldn't follow. They turned away when the traffic light changed, and he steered the big car slowly around a corner, out onto a bridge.

"You said you could help me." On the other side, Asher saw warehouses, brick walls all the way down to the water flowing under the bridge.

She nodded. Another blue wave crashed. She looked at the driver, then ahead at the warehouses. Asher followed her gaze. They were driving across a canal now, its dark, still surface reflecting the headlights and streetlights of cars and bridges identical to their own.

The wind lulled. The rain was, for a moment, soft. The whine of the tires modulated downward as the pavement regained solid ground. The ghosts of the innocent children haunted her, as did her failures. She failed so many men: her father, Kai, Mr. Daniel, probably Andreas. She was sick of choking on their disappointment and knew the only way to exorcise it was to take action. Now. Now, Eva.

Her voice broke the quiet—shaky, rushed, an unwilling soloist on a darkening stage.

"Hello. I'm sorry, but I have only a little time. I must give you the address where Phae . . . where Mr. Daniel is at the moment. Quickly, please. Can you write this down?"

The driver looked startled by her cell phone. But the street narrowed and twisted, momentarily requiring his full attention.

"Okay—good."

The driver's kettledrum voice rolled through the car. She turned away, shifting the phone to cover the ear closest to him.

"The address is in Germany."

Louder now, insistent, the driver raised his hand and reached for phone.

"The street number is—"

The struggle was short, her fragile white fingers no match for his meaty fist. The driver glared at the phone only long enough to disconnect the call, then stuffed it in the left pocket of his jacket, away from her flailing hands.

The string section soared to new heights now, the timpani glowering silent, waiting. The driver eyed the warehouses carefully and slowed, as if looking for an address. But she wasn't going to give up that easily. She dove almost all the way onto his lap, reaching for his pockets, her voice staccato and bitter. The driver pulled the car over and stopped. She was clutching something in his near pocket, but he crushed her wrist, making her gasp, and tore the handgun away before she'd quite managed to remove it.

She leapt out of the car, shrieking into the wind. The driver was out almost as quickly, gun in hand, facing the tempest. Her tempest on his behalf, Asher had to believe. A gust sprayed rain on the empty front seat as the orchestra crashed across the roof over his head.

And so it came down to a choice. Simple in the end. Action has a way of drowning out consequences.

Then suddenly she dove back into the car, all the way across to the driver's seat, and put her foot down on the gas pedal. The big car leapt forward, the acceleration swinging the doors shut, and the tires clawing at the wet street for traction.

Asher recognized the sound of a shot behind them, and ducked down instinctively into his seat. Another shot, then the pop and slap of a blown tire as the car lurched drunkenly to the left. Another shot, another pop and the car ground into the curb, her still at the wheel, cursing at the useless accelerator.

She was out of the car again, screaming, again, into the wind. But this time Asher opened his door, too, planting his feet firmly on the soaked pavement and raising his hands out and up into the storm. For a moment he waited, but the shot didn't come. And so he stood up, the gale at his back, the rain soaking his hair and running cold down the back of his neck.

"You have to run!" she screamed, a sudden gust almost knocking her over, forcing her to grab at the car door that swung there between them.

Asher turned, opening his mouth to say something, but words didn't come. He just shook his head as her eyes, equal parts anger and fear, pleaded for more. Solid ground. But he knew there was only one thing to do. Asher turned, arms still held up in the air, and fought the wind back toward the driver, who was standing his ground back where they'd started, frenzied yellow raindrops racing past him in the streetlight's sodium glow.

When you write down the rules, you write out the choices, and all of the thinking behind them. Morality is lost in the attempt to preserve it. Real virtue, it turns out, requires real freedom. Try to force one, you just end up losing both.

Behind him in the storm, he heard the string section one last time. The tragic finale of some infernal symphony, the score unfinished but the players too hysterical to stop. Fingers blistered, bowstrings fraying, no one to signal the cutoff. The end clearly near, but not nearly near enough.

Asher turned just in time to see the shadow behind her. The symphony stopped. Tropical blue rolled skyward as she sank back into the shadow's waiting arms. For the second time since willing himself out of the car, Asher opened his mouth without any words to say. He wanted to call out, but he didn't know her name.

The blow from behind set off a firecracker right in the middle of his skull.

. . .

Summer moonlight from the open window touched the hair over her left eye and turned jet black to silver white. It sparked in her eye when she glanced up and smiled and as she leaned back so he could kiss her neck. He ran his fingers up the trace of her spine and over her shoulders and into her hair, holding her head as she lay back on the pillow. His other hand followed the soft curve of her side, crossed the moonshine flat of her stomach and down, fingertips searching, muscles tightening, breathing faster now and warm against his ear.

Dew and roses scented the warm dawn breeze and the spirits of all who'd come before wooed them quietly as they slept, drifting in each other and the streams that draw everything and everyone into the past.

At least, they did in his dreams.

fourteen

Roy Daniel awoke with a start as the plane began to drop.

He'd fallen asleep as the little jet took off from Wiesbaden. Acceleration and jet lag pushed him down into his seat as the air grew too warm and thin for strong coffee to fight. Not even unanswered questions could keep his eyes open as the airplane raced up into the clouds.

He couldn't remember the other passengers' names—other than Andreas, of course. There were a couple of U.S. military guys who'd already been on the plane when they boarded. Special ops types, politely monosyllabic, unsmiling and distant behind scraggly beards and weary eyes. Virtually indistinguishable in dark civilian pants and jackets and heavy leather work boots. Presumably up from Stuttgart. They hadn't said.

The BKA were more forthcoming, though only by comparison. Same brevity, same eyes that sleep too little and see too much. One dark-bearded, more neatly trimmed than the Americans'. The other round-faced and clean-shaven, blonde hair cropped close and little square glasses with electric blue frames. Blazers and ties sober by German standards. Shoes and rain jackets ready for more than your standard-issue sit-down meeting.

Andreas smiled and nodded when Roy Daniel opened his eyes. The little round window between them was streaked with rain and damped by thick, gray clouds. The two BKA officers were across the aisle, leaning forward and talking quietly to each other. In front of them, one of the special ops guys was still asleep. The other quietly thumbed at his front teeth and stared out into the gray.

Roy leaned forward. "How long have I been asleep?"

Andreas shrugged and looked at his watch. "Only about a half hour. It's a short flight." He clowned a sad face and spread his hands in resignation. "Small country, you know."

Roy nodded, still leaning forward, resting his chin on his hands. He stared at the water shivering backward across the window, the unimaginable winds reducing it to tiny, naked droplets clinging for dear life to the glass. Finally he turned back to Andreas. "So what happens now?"

"Well, first, hopefully, we land."

Roy countered the sheepish smile accompanying these words with enough genuine annoyance that Andreas continued with barely a pause for a decent breath.

"Okay, so, as I told you earlier, it should be quite simple. The meeting is set for seven o'clock at the office we established. Once the target is in place, we lock down and begin the preliminary questioning. You will have the opportunity, of course, to watch and listen to everything from a room nearby."

The little plane bucked and the clouds began to break. Not far below, soggy fields in shades of khaki and brown were dotted with steep, charcoal-tiled rooftops and crossed by roads glistening cobblestone buff in the rain.

"It shouldn't take too long, really," Andreas continued with a shrug, following Roy Daniel's gaze. "But, of course, one never knows. Afterward, depending on what we learn, we will arrange to move the target to a more appropriate facility. And that's probably it, for you and me. We can go and get a beer, something to eat, perhaps. Celebrate a little."

Andreas smiled hopefully as the wing outside their window dipped and recovered.

"Celebrate the fact that it's over, anyway," he added, remembering present company's sensitivities.

Roy Daniel nodded absently and kept his eyes focused on the ground.

Andreas's phone began to chirp. He retrieved it from his jacket pocket and frowned at its tiny screen. A small chorus of beeps and buzzes spread through the cabin as the plane dropped back into cell range.

"It's just starting, Andreas. This is just the first little shot. You wait and see. This is the beginning, not the end. We've got a long, hard fight ahead of us."

Andreas wasn't listening. Still frowning, he began to type. The others in the plane were doing the same, or stuffing laptops and notebooks back into bags in preparation for the next chapter of their story.

The fields below gave way to a wide, green swath of freshly mowed grass, pegged with approach lights counting down the distance still to go. The runway appeared, shiny wet tarmac rubber-stained black by the hundreds and thousands who'd come before. They overshot the usual landing spot by a good hundred feet, nose defying the stiff crosswind with a cocky swagger. And then they were down, easy as one, two, three, and taxiing toward the white vans waiting to whisk them away to the ball.

"Gentlemen. *Herzlich willkommen in Hamburg.* Welcome to Hamburg. I trust you had a pleasant flight?"

The square man in full storm gear and with a dark, bushy goatee introduced himself with vigorous handshaking as Hansen of the BKA as they stepped down off the plane. The American soldiers moved past him toward the van in front with barely a nod. The men from the BKA lingered to exchange a few words in German then quickly followed to get out of the rain.

Hansen herded Andreas and Roy Daniel into the second van. As soon as the last door shut, the van lurched forward, chasing the first out of the runway gate. Hansen ducked into the passenger's seat, pushed back the hood of his jacket, rubbed his face vigorously with his hands, then turned his bird dog's eyes to his guests in back.

"I am in charge of the operation on the ground here this evening. The arrangements are all in order—nothing too complicated, so no problems so far." Hansen's voice rolled from low growl to midrange and back again over the course of each sentence with a slightly slurred Southern bounce. "The technical systems passed their final testing this morning. Standard security, of course, is already in place, and will remain so until I give the word when the operation is complete."

Roy Daniel nodded as Hansen's eager, over-caffeinated eyes searched his and then Andreas's. Andreas was still engrossed in his cell phone. He seemed not to have noticed anything else since its resuscitation shortly before landing.

Hansen persevered. "There has, however, been one unexpected event, of which I believe you should be aware." He was addressing Andreas, who did not appear to be listening. "Perhaps you are already aware?"

Andreas looked up abruptly. "Do you know where they are?"

Hansen nodded, frowning, like a father weighing his child's punishment. "Yes, of course, we've been following them since they arrived. We have people watching the place now. They drove directly there from the airport, you know. Judging by the route they drove, it appears they were planning to go there. It wasn't a last-minute idea."

Andreas just stared. He glanced down at his cell phone for support, but finding none, looked back to Hansen, eyes wide and searching.

"Why. . . . Couldn't you have stopped them?"

Hansen's grave, fatherly nod again. "Sir, our orders were not to interfere. I believe—"

"All of our orders were to ensure that—"

Andreas suddenly switched to German. Roy Daniel could catch a word here and there, but without any context. He could get by with waiters and bellboys and the occasional taxi driver. It was clear that none of these was the subject of the conversation at hand.

Roy Daniel checked his BlackBerry, scrolling through page after page of unread and unwanted e-mail. Nothing from Sandy. Nothing from Asher. Nothing from Sarah Anderson, either. No voice mail. He stared out the windows of the van. What little light had fought through the clouds today was exhausted now by the effort. The vans turned onto a rain-drenched residential street. Trees in brown and yellow and the occasional red whipped in the North Sea's invisible atmospheric whitewater. An exhausted leaf beached itself on the van's breath-fogged windshield, its brief sanctuary cut short by the creaking wipers' next relentless sweep.

Andreas was saying something in English. Roy Daniel turned to his old friend's anxious gaze. "Roy, our target has apparently gone to an unexpected address."

Excitement, fear, desperation, and fatigue percolated in Andreas's eyes. Roy Daniel watched them swirl, insoluble fluids in a brown glass jar, their relative volumes and viscosities unclear. He studied his friend for longer than either man was comfortable. Hansen coughed and mumbled something to the driver, who nodded with a glance in the rearview mirror.

"Okay." Roy Daniel waited, but Andreas offered nothing more. "So—why don't we just go to that unexpected address? He—he or she—is in Hamburg, right? Somebody's seen him, seen her, confirmed it's the person we're here for?"

Andreas nodded, the gesture unnaturally small, a man forced to decide too quickly. "Yes, the target is here. Hansen's men have seen and confirmed this."

"Andreas, what's the problem, then? Are the plans really that hard to change? Is this new address particularly problematic?"

Andreas's tiny nod morphed into an equally tiny shake of the head. "No, it's nothing special. But it's not the *correct* address, you see."

Roy Daniel turned to Hansen for support, but Hansen said nothing, his lips pursed in concern, with the kind of big, heavy nod that suggested to Daniel he actually had no idea what was going on.

"Andreas, look. This isn't like you. I may not have been right here with you on the ground, before, but I've heard plenty of stories. You're flexible, resourceful, adaptable—you adjust when things change, do what needs to be done to get the job done. That's why we work with you. So what's going on? There's something you're not telling me. People don't just change all of a sudden. Not in the real world."

Andreas looked away, out the window of the van, at the somber gray houses twilit through the rain. Lights were on in a few, and in one a woman was fussing with the curtains, scowling at a stubborn crease that didn't quite meet her approval. Fighting off that which didn't belong. Keeping the order within equal and opposite to the chaos without.

"She went with him." Andreas's voice speaking to the woman, back in the distance now, as tall trees flailed at the last of the light of day.

"Who?" Roy Daniel looked from the back of Andreas's head to the back of Hansen's to the rearview mirror, where the driver's eyes quickly turned away.

"Eva." They'd left the woman in the window behind now, and the windows on this block were all dark. But Andreas's voice had yet to catch up. "Eva went with him to the wrong address."

• • •

A muggy catfish gray had already muddied the morning sky's Wedgewood blue as the boat slipped away from the docks and into the still water of the channel.

Jabe Evans stood at the helm, weathered fingers embracing the wheel like the hand of an old friend. The boys slouched up toward the bow, one keeping an eye out as they cleared the boats in the last couple of slips, the other already on his way back to raise the mainsail. Once upon a time, Evans would've already had it up, believing anyone who called himself a sailor should actually be able to do just that—sail—without the help of anything but the wind. But for the past couple of years he'd begun using the motor to get in and out of his slip. He couldn't remember exactly when, or why. No one had called him on it, which for the most part wasn't strange, but this silent group included his wife, and this *was* strange. Ellie generally wasn't one to let him get away with anything. Evans considered the implications, but only briefly. He didn't much like the possible explanations, and decided (conveniently, one particularly strident corner of his brain continually reminded him) that it didn't much matter, anyway.

Bill Morton sat on the port side of the cockpit, his back to Evans, staring out ahead over the boats and the water. He wore a CASTOR baseball cap and a CASTOR polo shirt, pressed khaki pants, and boat shoes with no socks. As close to casual as Bill Morton ever got. A blue blazer was most certainly hanging neatly in the back seat of his car, just in case the need arose. Bill Morton was prepared for everything, as long as everything had something to do with work. And with Bill Morton, everything had something to do with work. Something to do with money. Of that, at least, Jabe Evans had no doubt.

Al Green was permanently prepared for work, too, but not necessarily for money. He sat opposite Bill Morton, hunched almost down to the sole, trying to shade his BlackBerry from the persistent glare of the great outdoors. Might as well have been in the basement of the Pentagon, for all he cared—probably would have preferred it. Farther from the light of day. Closer to the powers that be—the kind of powers he respected, anyway. Closer to the people who think the way he does. Who know for a fact that might is right. Or at least that might *makes* right. And that right without might is a theoretical thing of no use to anyone at all—least of all to Al Green.

The channel was clear and Evans cut the motor. One boy hauled at the shroud while the other furled the jib, and soon the sails fluttered and filled with the thick, lazy air that drew the boat slowly south toward the currents of the Potomac. Bill Morton looked across to starboard, searching the gaps in the far shore's trees for a glimpse of the golf course beyond. Where he'd most certainly prefer to be right now. Not that he'd ever admit it, of course. But Jabe Evans knew him well. They'd worked together, after all, for more than thirty years. Hard to believe sometimes, that it had been that long. Hard to believe that, after all that time, surprises were still occasionally possible.

"I assume you both know why we're here." Jabe Evans spoke to the telltales fluttering quietly from the jib. Hearing their cue, the boys quickly finished coiling the sheets and retreated forward, following Evans's gaze aloft but attentively ignoring the cockpit.

Bill Morton glanced, startled, up at Evans, away from his meditations on fairways and greens, eyes wide as a child's waking from an unwanted nap. He recovered quickly, though, and his head fell to its habitual bobble and he looked down at his unblemished boat shoes, hands folded in his lap, frowning a prayer for the unrepentant.

Al Green finished typing something on his BlackBerry then tucked it away in the pocket of his windbreaker. He planted small, soft hands on fleshy knees and heaved a meaty head back like a walrus on a beach. In Al Green's old yellow-tinted aviator glasses, Jabe Evans saw the twin reflections of an old man at the helm against a graying sky. Cloudy with a chance of thunderstorms as the day wears on.

"I thought so," said Evans.

A silver jet roared skyward over the starboard bow. Roger Taylor poked his head briefly out of the cabin, sniffed and frowned at the prevailing winds, and retreated below.

"So, who wants to go first?"

Bill Morton continued his bobblehead prayer, agreeing with either his shoes or the Lord.

It simply wasn't in Al Green's nature to hold his tongue.

"Sir, I'd be more 'n happy to answer any questions you might have. But you know me—I'm just an old, slow country boy. I'm afraid I don't quite know what you're gettin' at."

Evans considered his course, making for the row of square brick officers' houses, parade rest along the shoreline to port, this side of the War College. The boys sat at the hull's widest point, legs dangling over the starboard rails, sniffing the wind.

"Al, I find that hard to believe."

Al Green chuckled and glanced briefly at Morton, who was still nodding at his shoes. "Well, sir, it surprises me too sometimes just how slow I can be. Lord knows it used to surprise my wife, too, pretty much on a daily basis."

Bill Morton raised his head, forgetting himself for a fraction of a second.

"Please don't change the subject, Al. Not today. It isn't going to help."

But Al Green, for once, didn't seem to hear. His glasses reflected only water, slipping away for good behind the shadow of Jabe Evans's sails.

Bill Morton's shoes recaptured his undivided attention.

Jabe Evans stared straight ahead toward the tree-lined order of the army base ahead. "Did you know that back in the war of 1812, the Americans abandoned the arsenal up there. They took all the gunpowder they could with them, and dumped the rest down the well to hide it from the

British. When the British showed up, somebody threw a match down that well. Probably a very conscientious, resourceful soldier. Probably looked around and thought that the safest place to get rid of a match would be down a well. But of course the match set off the gunpowder hidden down there and the whole place exploded and killed and mangled the better part of the men that that good, conscientious soldier had been trying to protect."

The three men stared out ahead at the big red-brick building down at the end of the point. The sails fussed momentarily about the low noontime breeze and the keel hissed through the brackish water beneath their feet. Another plane set sail for the clouds. The boys watched it rise and disappear.

Al Green had recovered his aversion to silence. "Sir, does all this have anything to do with what the General said last night?"

Jabe Evans smiled at the wreck turned prison turned college up ahead. "Apparently you think so, Al, and that's good enough for me."

Al Green didn't pause to consider the implications. "Now, I know you might have been a little surprised by some parts of that speech, sir, but if you think about it, it's really all nothin' but good. I mean, he basically came out and said—"

"He basically came out and said, Al, that I'd committed to something I'd never come *close* to committing to."

Al Green sat frozen behind his yellow lenses, hands still gripping his knees, challenging Evans with his own image in stereo. A seagull overhead chimed in, but as usual took no one's side but its own.

"Sir, are you saying you and the General never discussed that beforehand?"

"Yes, Al, that's exactly what I'm saying."

The reflections in Al Green's glasses panned between Evans and Bill Morton. Morton looked up, surprised to find himself at the center of attention, but only nodded at nothing and no one in particular while considering a foursome teeing off across the water.

The boys began to stir at the rail. "Coming about," cried Evans, his voice well above the conversation at hand. The sails luffed and flapped and filled again as he set a course for the far shore. The motor would have been faster, he thought. Steer a course straight down the channel. But sometimes, getting there faster isn't really the point.

Al Green was still staring at Bill Morton. But Bill Morton, his view of the golf course now blocked out by the sails, turned away to nod at the red-brick houses marching off toward the point. Jabe Evans followed his gaze.

"That's also where they imprisoned the conspirators behind Abraham Lincoln's assassination. I think they hanged some of them there, too. Of course, that was all too little, too late for Lincoln."

"Well," began Al Green, frowning only then as the implications of Evans's last words sunk in, "I think Mr. Morton would agree with me that, whatever the circumstances behind the General's announcement may've been, it'll be a very good thing for the company. Financially speaking, of course."

"I think Mr. Morton will agree with *me* that when it comes to the direction this company takes, the buck stops with me, and me alone."

Bill Morton considered the retreating shore.

"Wouldn't he?" Jabe Evans's voice rolled low beneath the fiberglass slap of muddy water against the hull.

Bill Morton turned, head tilted back to see the old man's face from under the brim of his CASTOR cap. "Of course I would, Jabe." He ignored the twin versions of himself, motionless in Al Green's glasses. "You're the boss."

Al Green shook his head slowly, then turned to Jabe Evans and held up his stubby arms in a gnome's surrender. "You *are* the boss, sir. I agree with Bill there 100 percent. And if you want me to talk to the General, tell him there's been a misunderstanding, tell him you've changed your mind, I can certainly do that for you, sir."

Al Green looked from Jabe Evans to Bill Morton and back again, giving each a chance to call him off. Neither did.

"Hell, I'll do it right now." Al Green shoved short, blunt fingers into his windbreaker pocket, retrieving his BlackBerry and holding it up for all to see.

Jabe Evans swatted at the phone like a bee at a picnic. It flew out of Al Green's doughy hand and up into the air above the starboard rails. Al Green started up and spun like a wide receiver half his age. He lunged for the little blue square of airborne plastic just as it reached the apex of its short flight and began to tumble toward the sailboat's wake. And he might have had it, had he really been half his age, or twice his height, or half his weight, or all of the above. But he wasn't—not one of them—and a sudden pitch of the boat sealed his fate. BlackBerry and Al Green fell with two splashes—one small, the other very much otherwise—into the murky brown churn of the Washington Channel.

Bill Morton turned to watch the spectacle, but didn't budge from his seat in the cockpit. Jabe Evans bent to grab a life jacket from under the seat Al Green had just vacated and tossed it out over the stern. Al Green bobbed and sputtered unintelligibly.

"You know, Jabe, I'm not sure that Al can swim."

Jabe Evans held his course, still making for the opposite shore.

"Al's a resourceful guy. I'm sure he'll figure it out."

• • •

Roger Taylor, holding a cell phone in one hand, hesitated in the companionway, squinting back into their wake.

"Roger," said Jabe Evans, "could you please get us two beers?" He tried to hold his voice low and steady, a lone cello in an empty hall. Just far enough up the dynamic scale to damp the blood pounding the inside his skull. A firm hand to keep the bow from slipping, betraying a hesitancy no audience would tolerate.

Roger Taylor turned his squinting eyes to Jabe Evans. "Beer, sir?"

"Yes, Roger. That's what I said. Two beers, please."

Roger Taylor nodded in disbelief at what he'd just seen and heard. He turned to go back below, then remembered the cell phone and ended up executing a full pirouette, right there in the companionway.

Frequency and tempo.

"I almost forgot." Roger Taylor reached up as far as he could, off balance, unwilling to trust himself to the cockpit. "It's Tamara Maybin for you."

Bill Morton took the phone and handed it on to Jabe Evans. Roger Taylor performed another half turn and gratefully disappeared below.

Space and time.

"Hello, Tamara. I guess you know what we need to do."

Tamara Maybin's voice was also restrained, the silences louder than the words that separated them. A full symphony, the split second after the musicians stop playing. Strings and reeds and lips stop their vibrations, and for one ethereal moment there's only sound. No cause, only effect. Metaphysics, pure and simple. The music of the spheres.

"Okay. Thank you, Tamara."

Bill Morton was staring at him. Jabe Evans looked away.

"I appreciate that. I know it's hard. But it needs to be done."

Jabe Evans hung up the phone and zipped it into his jacket pocket. Bill Morton was still sitting there looking at him. Roger Taylor returned with two cans of beer. Bill Morton took them both, passing one on to Evans. But Jabe Evans wanted nothing to do with it. He had other plans. The boys understood. Without a word, they moved to starboard. Jabe Evans came about, no call this time. The boys hauled the sails in as close as those ancient laws would allow and Jabe Evans steered for a spot just off the point.

When the sails were trimmed and the sheets locked back in their cleats, the boys hiked back up on the rails, swinging tanned legs over the source of the boat's dirty wake, Bill Morton still sat there, holding out a can of beer to Evans. Jabe Evans ignored him for as long as he could, but eventually their eyes had to meet. They both knew how the laws of physics worked. The questions went both ways. Einstein might have taught that everything was relative, but Newton had been on the scene far longer. Equal and opposite—that was the law of the land. Some people could handle it, some people couldn't. After all these years, Jabe Evans and Bill Morton knew where they stood.

Tamara Maybin hung up the phone and pressed her eyes hard into the heels of her hands. Of course she knew what she needed to do. There was nothing else to be done. Jabe Evans had, once again, removed all possibility of any other outcome. "What" was now a foregone conclusion. Now it was only a question of how and when.

The release was half-written on her laptop, which lay on the unmade bed behind her. The wreckage of her breakfast lay on a tray on the table by the window. She tried to forget about the wreckage of her day. *Her* day, this was supposed to have been. *Her* treat to *her*self for *her* job well done. She deserved it. She *still* deserved it. The anger began to spark again up and down her spinal cord. Another plan shot to hell. Another *good* plan ruined by circumstances beyond her control. By people beyond her control. By people who, when it comes right down to it, don't give a *damn* about her. Don't give a damn about *anybody* but themselves. Who only think of what *she* wants when it might help them get what *they* want.

Tamara Maybin sat up and looked around, drying the damp heels of her hands on her bathrobe. She breathed long and hard. Maybe it's time to hit the showers. Nothing useful's getting written till you cool down, get a little perspective back. Of course it's not fair, but that's the way it is. For today, anyway. We'll see about tomorrow. That's the great thing about tomorrow—it can turn into anything you want. Trouble is, sometimes everybody else beats you to it. By the time you get there, the whole script's already written, and all the good parts are already taken.

She grumbled into the bathroom. The mirror offered a full-length view, but she ignored it and turned on the water. You already know what you'll see, and she's not going to help, either. After all, she's just like all the rest of them. No, no, don't argue—when it comes right down to it, you know she is. Not interested in your problems—not in the least. Just out for herself. Just like everybody else.

Tamara Maybin stepped into the shower and the water burned her feet. She shoved the shower head to one side and twisted the silver knob marked "C." The edge came off. Adjusting the head back into place, she closed her eyes and faced it square on, letting the jets needle her square in the face. The water soaked through her hair and began to drip down her back. She reached for the shampoo and emptied the little plastic bottle into her hand. She scrubbed hard, fingernails digging in all the way down to her scalp. Out in the bedroom, she thought she heard a phone ring. She kept scrubbing, the suds falling down onto her shoulders, down into the tub, and off to wherever the plumbers had condemned them. Long, long ago. They never got a vote.

Slowly, the warm water worked its way through Tamara Maybin's hair and washed over her face and down the back of her neck and doused the flames arcing across her vertebrae. She stood there, trying just to feel. This was the way it was supposed to be. Today I was supposed to do nothing at all but feel. Touch and be touched. But, as was generally the case, the world had other plans. Needy men required her immediate attention. So, what else was new? Needy men had always required her immediate attention.

Apparently, that's the way the world worked. What was it her grandma used to say? "Men require, women perspire." Made a lot more sense to her now than it had back then, when she'd thought it was just about cooking.

Her grandma had been there the afternoon Tamara received her acceptance letter from the Naval Academy. She was there in the kitchen, a bowl of fresh green beans and a cup of strong, black coffee on the worn Formica table in front of her, when Tamara burst through the screen door waving the letter over her head, pure joy in the spark of her eyes and the flash of her smile and the tilt of her chin toward the sky. Body and soul already in flight. Grandma had smiled, too, and there'd been a spark in her eyes, as she rose slowly to her feet. She'd spread her arms out wide and with that little twitch of her fingertips silently called her granddaughter into the midsummer embrace of home.

Looking back, though, Tamara Maybin couldn't distinguish that embrace from the one after falling off her bicycle as a little girl, asphalt scraping up the side of her leg and knocking loose a baby tooth, filling her mouth with blood. Or from the one as she left for her first homecoming dance, dressed up in baby powder and lip gloss and bubble-gum princess costume lace. Or even from the one after Grandpa's funeral—the one she should have been giving Grandma but that somehow ended backward— standing in the cemetery, the big magnolia shouldering the weight of the gloriously indifferent spring blue sky. The same accepting embrace, the same patient smile, the same eyes glimmering on the verge of tears—of joy or of sorrow, it didn't matter, the two being opposite sides of a single, precious, well-worn coin.

Tamara Maybin turned off the water and stood for a final moment staring at the steam swirling around the lights on the ceiling. She reached for a towel on the rack above her head and began drying herself off. Her skin was no longer that of the little girl her grandmother had cleaned up in the kitchen sink, gently brushing away the road grit with a faded pink washcloth and a bar of Ivory soap. It was no longer that of the bigger girl shimmying out of her long dress after the dance, staring as if for the first time at that metamorphosis in the mirror that so fascinated the boys. But it wasn't yet the skin of her grandma, either, thin and loose-fitting like the soft dresses she wore in summer, fragrant with a lifetime of kitchens and bedrooms, vegetable gardens and children. It still clung close to the flesh and the bone that it covered, not yet ready to relax its grip. Still convinced of its power to defy time and space, history and gravity. Old enough to understand the causes, but still too young to concede the effects.

Wrapped back in her bathrobe, she returned to the bedroom and lifted her laptop out of last night's musky sheets. She set the computer on the desk in front of the mirror, and opened the curtains up wide. She sat down and began to type. Tamara Maybin paid no attention to her reflection, and her reflection paid no attention to what Tamara Maybin was doing. No time for reflections. Ideals, when it comes right down to it, are selfish, childish things. In the real world, there's too much at stake to let ideals—however beautiful they may be—get in the way. Too many people depend on the outcome.

By the warm light of evening, melancholy flows from every living thing. But if there's only one truth, it's this: Every morning, like it or not, the sun lights everything the other way around.

• • •

By the middle of the afternoon, it was clear they were in for a storm. The sky had gone from hot tin to sweaty wrought iron. The sweet, eager breath of warm summer rain was running with the boat up the channel. Bill Morton blinked at the wind, back at the trees sweeping the storm clouds on either shore, little whitecaps creasing the channel between. There was no sign of Al Green. Either he'd made it safely, or he'd already gone under.

Others might have worried, but Bill Morton had known Al Green for a long, long time. Bill Morton was betting on safely ashore.

Jabe Evans still stood at the helm, squinting ahead at the docks. His boys were milling around up front, fussing with the ropes, stealing a glance now and then at their captain and their remaining leeway. Bill Morton could tell they'd sailed with Jabe Evans before. They treated him exactly the same way here as most CASTOR employees treated him at work. Collaboration? Might look that way, but really it was simple obedience. Those puzzled lines that bunched on their foreheads and tugged at the corners of their eyes? Curiosity—never doubt. More like dogs than humans. Each party knew its place. Neither ever seriously considered a trade. Dream? Sure, probably. But ask? Never. Demand? Unheard of. Mutual acquiescence—that was the name of the game. Because at the end of the day, everybody knew what was in his or her own best interest.

Things did go wrong, of course, occasionally. Mother nature isn't perfect. All these scientists like to talk about their laws of physics—cosmic formulas that govern everything we do, like it or not, and that nothing in the universe can change. But those are just the rules of the game. They don't have a thing to do with the quality of play. The rules of, say, baseball are, after all, the rules of baseball, whether you're talking about Little League or college or AAA or the show. Basically the same game, if the scientists' view of the world holds true. Which it does, of course, as far as it goes. But don't tell me that even the most casual fan would say that what they see from that grassy hillside in Williamsport is the same thing they see in Fenway or the Friendly Confines. The rules are the rules, sure, but they leave the field pretty open to the vagaries of fate.

A muggy gust ran them up alongside the marina's first boats. Bill Morton saw Jabe Evans nod and the boys dropped the sails to the deck. Evans turned on the motor but let it idle for the time being, drifting toward the dock and his slip. Friction comes in handy every now and then. Strange that most physics classes start off assuming it doesn't exist.

Things go wrong all the time, actually—who am I kidding? People went off on their own, off the reservation, made stupid decisions or made no decisions at all. Didn't think about the consequences of their actions. Or did, but didn't take into account all the forces at work. Ignored the friction, which made all the difference in the world. And generally they paid for it. Equal and opposite reactions. Everything balanced out in the end. After all, for every mistake, there was generally an equal and opposite success.

Jabe Evans would say that that's the laws of physics at work. Things balance out. The universe doesn't fly off its axis. For every mistake, there's a success to balance it out. For every great breakthrough, there's a failure to keep people from getting too comfortable. Losing their edge. Believing the rules don't apply to them.

But Bill Morton knew there was more to it than that. The rules were all well and good, but somebody had to pay attention to all the space between the lines. There was a lot of gray out there, lurking between the blacks and the whites. Somebody had to keep an eye on it. Free will may not affect the movement of the planets and the stars, but it's alive and well down here where we live. The laws of physics may say that what goes up must come down, but there are a million ways to come down that don't break any laws.

That's really the difference between us, isn't it? Jabe and the scientifically inclined are fascinated by what's going to happen, leaving the rest of us to worry about how. And don't tell me people don't mostly see the "how." Hell, if physicists wrote all the stories, they'd all be, basically, "He was born. He grew up. He got older. Then he died." That's all the rules dictate. Everything else is in the "how." The parts that really matter are all "how."

The wind felt stronger now without the sails to bind them together. Jabe Evans backed the motor briefly to slow their progress, then turned the boat carefully between the docks. The boys stood by, one on either side, staring down at their progress through the water. A seagull hung motionless above them, letting the atmosphere move instead of his wings for a change. The swing of their mast barely cleared the white feathers padding his breast.

Alongside their waiting slip stood a man Bill Morton hadn't seen in some time. Tall and thin, a little lost in the fabric of his faded jeans and windbreaker. Less hair than last time, but still—didn't they all? The man stood still, his back to the wind, watching the boat glide closer. Jabe Evans was looking straight at him, but if the two men had acknowledged each other, Bill Morton hadn't seen the exchange.

The parts that really matter are all "how." Even Jabe Evans would have to agree, if he were truly honest with himself. Remember how he'd never use the motor? "How"—100 percent "how." Earlier today, Bill Morton had thought about calling him on it, but it had already been clear that this was not a day for jokes. The old man was not pleased today. But deep down, he knew what had had to happen. His silence on the way back had told Morton all he needed to know. He didn't have to like it—didn't have to like the "how"—but he did understand how the laws of physics worked. As long as the "what" balanced out, the "how" could take care of itself—that was the way Jabe Evans saw it. Or—put another way—somebody else could take care of the "how." Jabe Evans really didn't want to know.

The boy on the left jumped down onto the dock holding a rope tied up near the bow. Jabe Evans killed the motor as the other boy jumped, too, and the two of them gentled the boat into the slip. The tall man waited till the boys had the fenders in place and the ropes tied up to the cleats. Then he walked quietly to the stern, his eyes on his feet and the weathered wood of the dock pacing off the distance to the end.

Roger Taylor emerged from the cabin and stopped at the sight of the track shoes on the dock. The tall man drew up even with the cockpit and turned.

"Gentlemen. Good sail?"

The man's tone of voice bordered on distastefully bright, in Bill Morton's opinion, but he kept the thought to himself.

"Glad you came, Sandy. Everything okay ashore?" Bill Morton tried to match his saccharine tone, but the mix was off. Jabe Evans was checking his pockets, handing his cell phone back to Roger Taylor. He wasn't looking at anyone.

"Everything's fine. A little hot and damp in places—a little steamy, I guess you might say. But nothing serious. Nothing time and a little bourbon won't cure."

Bill Morton watched Jabe Evans inspecting the cockpit, nodding but still not looking anyone in the eye. Some things were necessary, after all, but you didn't need to be happy about them. Turning to the man on the dock, Morton saw that Sandy McRae's smile was still the same, pure pleasure on one side running to disbelief by the other.

Bill Morton nodded. Sandy McRae returned the gesture. Neither spoke a word for what seemed like far too long. McRae unzipped his jacket a bit and pulled a handkerchief out of an inside pocket. He handed it down to Bill Morton, watching all the while as Jabe Evans knelt to look for something under the seats on the other side of the cockpit.

"I found this this morning while I was packing," said Sandy McRae, a little quieter now. His eyes risked a quick turn, suddenly clutching Bill Morton's in their icy grasp. "Seems somebody left it behind last night. I thought it might have been you."

Bill Morton took the handkerchief, felt the hard, round object inside, and tucked it into his pocket. He tried to force casual into his voice, squinting up at the familiar face with its twisted smile studying him from the dock. But no words came, and just as quickly as they'd turned on him, Sandy McRae's eyes were gone again, back across the cockpit to Jabe Evans's hunched frame, then back across the water to whatever lay beyond.

Sometimes it was best to just let well enough alone.

"Well," said McRae, "looks like you gentlemen have everything under control. I guess I'll be heading off, then. I may not see you both for a while. Been wanting to get away, and did you know that I'm not getting any younger? Came as a surprise to me, too. Anyway, unless there's anything more you need, I think I'm gonna be on my way."

Jabe Evans was finally still, standing and watching the two men carefully. McRae caught Evans's eye now, his nod almost imperceptible. Then he turned without another word and walked away slowly down the dock.

Bill Morton watched him go. He turned to Jabe Evans, but once again, words failed him. Because there's a lot of gray there lurking between the blacks and the whites. Somebody had to pay attention to it. For every wayward son, there *was* generally a bright and beautiful grandchild hiding somewhere in the wings. But either one could quickly become the other.

How, you ask?

Exactly my point. Exactly why somebody needs to pay attention.

Al Green saw the tall, familiar figure walking across the parking lot long before the tall, familiar figure saw him.

Al Green's clothes were still damp, but he wasn't leaving footprints on the pavement anymore. He'd wrung most of the muddy water out of his socks. His old black shoes didn't suck up much water, anyway. His CASTOR windbreaker was already dry, and he zipped it up all the way to cover the white shirt and T-shirt that went all see-through when they were wet. And to cover up the damp leather holster that was stuck to them, down by the side of his ribcage.

Al Green hadn't actually laid eyes on Sandy McRae in years. Back in the day, they'd spent a lot of time together—back when McRae was running security for all the CASTOR guys working in places the company decided were "dangerous." Back when McRae was still the big swinging dick, with an office just down the hall from Evans and the standing noontime running date with the old man whenever both of them were in town. Sandy McRae, the man with a story for every occasion. And a lady, too, if you believed the rumors.

And who didn't believe the rumors? No reason not to believe them, after all—at least, no more reason than not to believe the stories. And come on, face it—*everybody* at CASTOR wanted to believe them. *Everybody* wanted to be able to say that they worked with a guy like Sandy McRae. Nobody tried too hard to figure out whether the stories were true or not because, when it came right down to it, *everybody* wanted them to be true. Just knowing a guy like that made you cooler. Just like high school, really—people don't really grow up all that much. From the day they're old enough to realize other people are looking at them to the day they're too old to realize it or care, everybody wants to be cooler. Everybody wants the perks, at least, that go along with being cool. Or at least with standing next to somebody who is.

Al Green squeezed sideways between a white Ford pickup and an ugly Japanese something that were parked across from Sandy McRae's old Cherokee. McRae was fishing his keys out of his jeans pocket. He smiled and straightened as he saw Al Green, squinting in the afternoon sun. Al Green thought he looked a little rough around the edges, but knew he wasn't in any position to talk.

"Al Green. I'd pretty much given up on seeing you today."

"Sorry to disappoint you, Sandy. Lord knows I tried."

The two men shook hands. Sandy McRae looked Al Green over, obviously ignoring the bulge under Al Green's jacket.

"What happened to you, Al? You go for a swim, or is the heat just too much for you these days?"

Let's not get smug now, Sandy. Those days are gone. I may not be the big man on campus today, but at least I didn't flunk out altogether.

"As a matter of fact, Sandy, I did go for a swim. Seems the old man thought I could use the exercise." Al Green gave his damp gut a good pat with both hands and grinned. "Hell, maybe he's right. Been spendin' a lot of time at work lately, you know. Maybe I should be takin' a little better care of myself. A little more 'me' time—isn't that what they say now? Maybe that's just what I need." Al Green patted his stomach like some men pat their favorite old dog. " 'Me' time."

Sandy McRae still had a smile on his face, but it was drifting a little, and his eyes were slipping from curious to suspicious. He said nothing. Al Green's smile wrinkled up his nose and narrowed his eyes and lowered his bushy gray eyebrows.

"So, Sandy, you see the old man and Morton? They back yet from their little three-hour tour?"

Sandy McRae rocked back a little in his old white sneakers and bowed his head, pursing his thin, dry lips at the car keys in his hand. When he looked up again, his smile was gone, and his eyes had retreated far back inside his wiry gray skull.

"Sure, Al, I saw them. They just got back. But they didn't have too much to say. Not sure they're really ready for company."

Al Green felt a drop of something slip down his side. Whether it was sweat or river water or something entirely different, he couldn't really tell.

"Well, maybe they just ain't ready to see *you*. I reckon I'll just head on down there and see how they're feelin' now that the old man's had a chance to think things over."

"I wouldn't do that, Al." McRae's voice dragged the bottom of a dried-up creek bed. The backs of his lips stuck to his teeth like wallpaper. "I think he needs a little more time."

Al Green squinted at the implications.

"Now, Sandy, I know you're just tryin' to help, and I 'preciate you doin' it. But Jabe and Bill and me, we've got a few things we still need to sort out. So—good to see you, Sandy. Hope you have a nice day."

"Al. Don't go down there."

Al Green felt the tug of the leather beneath his jacket. But he knew Sandy McRae better than that. He crossed his arms over his damp chest and faced the tall man full on. McRae just stood his ground, squinting against the wind, bouncing his car keys in one bony, weathered hand.

"Now Sandy, this doesn't have anything to do with you. Jabe and Bill asked me to do a job for them, and there's been a few misunderstandin's along the way. I just need to sort those misunderstandin's out before they go and do somethin' stupid. This is a pretty important day for CASTOR, Sandy. I know maybe you don't care anymore, but I do. So—again—nice seein' you. You have y'self a good evenin', okay?"

Al Green turned to leave, but immediately felt McRae's hand grip his shoulder. Once again the leather beneath Al Green's jacket tugged at his right hand, but before it could move, the grip softened to a friendly shake and the two men were walking together, McRae's arm draped over his good friend's shoulders.

Sandy McRae's voice was gravel in a clear, fast stream. "You know, Al, Jabe Evans is one of the best men I've ever known. Now, he and I haven't always seen eye to eye—you know that, everybody knows that—but that hasn't changed my opinion of him. I know he gave you a job to do. He gave me a job to do, too, Al. They both did. And I've done that job as best I know how, and I've gotten the results they asked for. What they do with those results—well, that's not my business, is it? And it's not your business, either, Al. So just walk away. I'm telling you this as a friend, Al—believe it or not, it's true. Just turn around now and walk away. There's nothing to be gained from going back down to that boat right now."

Al Green felt his heart beat slower as the tall man's cool voice rolled low through the muggy afternoon heat. He closed his eyes and for a moment heard the doctor's voice—strange that he'd never noticed the resemblance—delivering the very same message. Didn't seem that long ago. At some point, you've got to just let go. But it just wasn't in Al Green's nature to let things go without a fight. A good fight—that's what it was. Why couldn't they see that? He was fighting the good fight, and yet everybody kept telling him to just let it all go.

His heart started to race again. Al Green ducked out from under Sandy McRae's kind but unyielding arm.

"Sandy, I said it before, and I'll say it again, I do 'preciate you tryin' to help me out here. I really do—I mean that, Sandy. But the fact is that Jabe and Bill—they just don't know the whole story. They don't know all the things I've done for them. The old man, especially—hell, he thinks right now that I'm lined up right alongside the devil himself. And that just ain't true, Sandy. Everythin' I've done's been for the good of this company. Not just this time—*every* time. All these years I've been there, goin' to the places they don't wanna go, talkin' to the people they don't even wanna know...."

Al Green stopped himself, looked down at his feet, and felt that feeling for only the second time he could remember in his entire life. He looked back up and into the wind, hoping to dry away the evidence. He laughed a little, trying to cover up the shake in his voice.

"Shit, Sandy, I'm even startin' to rhyme now. Folks gonna think I've gone queer or somethin'."

Sandy McRae followed Al Green's gaze away into the coming storm clouds and tried to echo the big man's laugh. "No, Al, I don't think there's much danger of that. But we could take a little drive over to Dupont circle if you really want to make sure."

The two men stood side by side on the pavement and watched the sun slide farther and farther away.

"So what'd they ask *you* to do?" Al Green cleared his throat loudly and spat, relieved that the moment had passed. A couple of rows away, a diesel truck cranked and fired. Yet another jet roared off into the afternoon haze, pretending—for a few hours, anyway—that gravity no longer applied.

"Not to tell anybody."

"Hell, Sandy, ain't that always part of the deal?"

"Sure it is. The only part that never works out."

Al Green glanced at Sandy McRae, but the tall man's gaze was still fixed on the horizon.

"So what's the part that *did* work out?"

"You're still up here with me, aren't you?"

"You son of a bitch." Al Green shook his head and waddled off toward the docks.

"Can't let you do that, Al."

Al Green could tell by his voice that Sandy McRae hadn't moved an inch. Green turned around and patted the bulge beneath the left side of his jacket.

"Sandy, with all due respect, you've got nothin' to keep me here."

Sandy McRae nodded. "That's true, Al. I don't. But when have you ever known me to travel alone?"

Al Green looked around the parking lot. The diesel was still idling somewhere off to his right. A plain navy sedan was cruising slowly down the next row over to the left, looking for a place to park.

Al Green wrinkled up his pig's nose and spat again, then stumped slowly back to where McRae was standing.

"Seriously, Sandy. What'd they ask you to do?"

Sandy McRae squinted down into the pudgy man's eyes. "Clean up after you. As usual."

"And? Did you?"

"Sure, I did. Lord knows I've had enough practice."

Al Green cracked a crooked smile. "And everybody's okay?"

"Go home, Al."

Just like the doctor ordered.

Al Green stood his ground for a couple of seconds longer, then shrugged his shoulders and walked away—away from the docks, away from the sinking sun. After a while, he looked back, but McRae was gone.

"Home? Where the hell's that?" Al Green asked, anyway. Just as he'd asked then, in the hospital, all those years ago. And just as then, he received no answer. The only difference between then and now was that then, he'd actually thought he might get one.

• • •

A handful of grimy plastic chairs blocking the way from the door to the hallway were all that was left of the waiting room.

It hadn't always been that way, but its fate was predestined. The waiting room was the hospital's unwanted stepchild, a space reserved for "them"— the outsiders, the unwanted, the people who only made "our" lives more difficult. The emptier the waiting room, the better the day. So over the years, the hospital staff had quietly colonized the waiting room, annexing it piece by piece while management (approvingly) looked the other way. Billing built a fortress in the back corner, walled off with thick glass pierced with intercoms to minimize conversation and outfitted with card readers to expedite payment. Triage took the adjacent quarter, throwing up permanently temporary cubicles to fortify the ER door against uninsured incursions. And so today, only this small reservation remained, a space so uninviting that no one objected to leaving it to the great unwashed. Not even the great unwashed, apparently, who seldom stayed long enough to complain.

It was empty, as usual. Which made it perfect for Sarah Anderson.

She sat in the middle of the row farthest from the door and dialed the number he'd given her. The 406 area code puzzled her. It rang for a long time, but never went to voice mail. Finally, the ringing stopped. She heard voices muffled on the other end, then a short scuffle, a needle pulled abruptly off vinyl.

No one said a word.

"Hello?" The echo of her own voice made Sarah Anderson squint like the fluorescent lights overhead. She bowed her head to talk quietly to her lap. "Hello?"

Sarah Anderson closed her eyes as Sandy McRae's voice wrapped her in old flannel.

"Sandy. Do you remember Pete Vasilescu?" She thought she heard him hesitate, but maybe it was her.

"Yes. Yes, that's right. That's him. So—he was in an accident last night. Driving home from work. Roy was on the phone with him when it happened."

The big glass doors behind her opened and closed. A thirtysomething man with a thirty-six-hour beard nearly spilled a Venti-sized Starbucks drink down the front of his green scrubs, pretending to check the time on a watch that wasn't there.

"No. No—that's why I'm calling you. He's not okay. He's not okay at all."

A wave of warm morning air followed in the green man's wake. It smelled like hay and coffee and car exhaust, but it lasted only a second, lost in the antiseptic latex tide flooding out of the corridor beyond.

A voice was telling her not to stay.

"But—Sandy, I can't just leave. I need to find out what happened. I need to—I just need to. Something—it just doesn't seem right, Sandy."

Sarah Anderson saw the faces on the other side of billing's glass wall look up. The nurse in triage stood and disappeared through the ER door. The day she'd tried to explain that her mother didn't know who she was, the nurse had had the same expression. She'd heard it all before, and knew she'd hear it all again, even though she wanted almost anything but. Not because she didn't care, but because she did. She cared as much as she had on her first day out of nursing school—maybe even more. But all that caring and all those years still hadn't given her an answer worth giving.

"Why?"

A final sentence, then the line went dead.

Once upon a time, Sarah Anderson had believed that the world really was full of magical shacks and handsome princes and silver and gold and happily ever after. And devils and witches and wicked innkeepers, too, but only to prove a point. Good over evil. Beauty over all. Black and white may be mixed up for a while, but not for long enough to let the story get dull. Everything gray scrubbed clean by the end. Cotton-candy days and marshmallow nights and warm bubble baths to soften all the rocky road in-betweens.

He knew.

She'd once heard her mother on the phone. Not just once, of course. She was an avid eavesdropper back in the day. Always afraid she'd miss something. She couldn't really remember the words her mother had said. What she could remember was her mother's face. The way she hadn't quite smiled when Sarah caught her eye. She'd tried, maybe even thought she'd pulled it off, but Sarah could tell, even then. Especially then. The fewer words you have to work with, the more you have to rely on other senses to fill in the blanks.

Her eyes skittish, little birds in a gale looking for a leeward ledge. The corners of her mouth turned down, her lips pursed tight, her whole head drooping like a puppet momentarily forgotten.

She knew.

Mostly, though, it was the sound of her voice. A river, not a brook. Words short, sentences long, vowels rounded, sinking slowly out of sight. Colors running, slurring across the lines. Not the bright, clean notes of her stories. This song was different, the melody worn thin by too many verses, a chorus that no one remembered.

Sarah had known even then. Sarah knew now.

It would be many years before Sarah Anderson could hear the beauty in that song. It was a song her mother always tried to hide, but that Sarah heard nonetheless, listening all the more closely to unravel its secrets. And it stayed with Sarah longer, spilling deeper into her memories, filling up the still places further from her day to day. It provided the weight that kept her head above water. It anchored the dreams that kept her memory of her mother alive. Even after she wasn't.

Her mother had never mentioned her father again. Not after that call. But Sarah could tell that he was still with her. She could hear the song, even though her mother never sang it. It was something that stayed with her, whether she liked it or not, and a bar or two slipped out, every now and then, usually when she thought no one was listening.

But Sarah was listening. Just as she was listening now. The big glass doors opened and closed again. The triage nurse returned to her post. The old plastic chairs in the space nobody wanted were still there. As usual, nobody sat in them.

• • •

He'd let it slip away again.

Andreas stared at his reflection in the fogging window of the van. Beyond his sagging eyes, the wind blew traffic lights red to yellow to green, and long lines of cars swirled like Christmas lights through the rain. Friday rush hour crowds swarmed like insects to the train station's glowing porticos, or through the orange-yellow rings around a planet-sized electronics store called Saturn. Anything your heart desires. Your money can take you home. Your money can also take you far, far away.

At university, Andreas had once had a professor who was fond of saying that the first priority of any government should be to invest in its people. Money spent on things is inevitably money lost. Things break, things decay, get stolen, go obsolete. Money spent on people, though—that, he said, is money well spent. Only people, after all, have the ability to create. Only people have the ideas that lead to new products that lead to new companies that lead to new jobs. Only people can create something from nothing. An investment in people, he said, was an investment in civilization. An investment in a building or a monument or a fleet, on the other hand, was no investment at all. It was nothing but a contribution to the museums of tomorrow.

These words had made a great impression on the idealistic mind of the young scientist Andreas. They were some of the few that had remained with him long after classes were over, long after real life had begun, long after the cold steel wheels of pragmatics commenced their slow, steady roll over idealism's defenseless horizons. They were words that still made sense to Andreas, and around which he still liked to believe his personal cosmos spun. But he could hear those cold steel wheels grinding closer tonight. The university's towers seemed far, far away.

Roy Daniel's reflection was there beside his in the window. He was looking out over Hansen's shoulder, contemplating the long, slow curve of red lights ahead. Roy Daniel had been one of Andreas's biggest investments.

On a professional level, the investment had paid off. Roy Daniel and CASTOR had been very good for Andreas's career. On a personal level, though, things were more complicated. They'd become complicated almost immediately, thanks to that side investment Andreas had never expected to make.

The first one he'd let slip away.

She and Andreas had arranged to meet at the little beer garden down by the Isar. The foehn winds had been blowing for a couple of days already, evaporating the last mugginess of summer and leaving the cloudless skies the color of cornflowers. The shadowy woods between their table and the river smelled of pine straw and the sweet black Alpine dirt laid down year after year by the spring floods. Once upon a time, anyway. Before the dams. Who knew where that dirt came from now. Some things were best left unknown.

How his wife had managed to endure him so long, for example. Or how Eva had slipped away without even a hint. All things best left unknown.

Perhaps.

The van stopped at a light across from the brick and glass Kunstverein. Bright lights inside illuminated a reception of some kind, women in black dresses, men in suits or jeans or both. Waiters offering glasses of wine and little hors d'oeuvres on trays. The kind of thing Eva loved to drag him to. The kind of thing he'd only be dragged to by her.

That day by the Isar, it was only a Tuesday, midway between lunchtime and coffee, and the beer garden had been almost empty. Ruth Daniel was already there when Andreas arrived, and staring off into the forest. He'd sat down across from her and ordered a beer. He didn't ask if she wanted one. She'd reached across the table and squeezed his hand tight, but her eyes didn't budge from the trees.

Hand-painted signs had advertised the coming *Fischfest*. At that same festival just one year before, they'd met for the first time. Ruth Daniel was a tiny brunette whose dark complexion made a romantic Andreas fantasize that she had Native American blood. She could neither confirm nor deny. She'd drunk only half a Radler and eaten even less, visibly worried that the fish still had heads. But she'd listened without judging, and laughed without blushing. As the summer sun disappeared, her chestnut eyes reflected the tiny white bulbs strung in the branches overhead. Andreas's wife had offered to show the Daniels around, get them acquainted with what the city had to offer. But Andreas's wife worked, too, and anyway, Andreas's English was better. Before the evening was over, Andreas had learned Ruth preferred wine to beer. Over the next couple of weeks at work, he learned Roy Daniel preferred physics to Ruth.

Traffic began to move again. The van inched its way through the packed intersection and slowly toward the bridge and the Speicherstadt, with its old canals and brick warehouses suddenly all the rage with lawyers and consultants and anyone else with clients' money to burn.

Physics wasn't all Roy Daniel had preferred to Ruth. Thinking back on it, Andreas should have seen it that first evening. But he wasn't paying much attention to Roy at the time, nor was he paying much attention to his own wife. *That* was a situation that had been going on for some time, and that was destined to continue for some time to come.

The second one he'd let slip away.

Andreas had only half-finished his beer when Ruth Daniel stood up and pulled him away. She'd led him by the hand through the beer garden gate and down the path that curved through the pines to the river. The sun was still high, and the tall trees sheltered the river from the dry, nagging wind. The stones along the bank were hot and smooth. Ruth had slipped out of her dress and folded it neatly on top of the biggest stone. She'd waited for him to catch up. Then she'd taken him by the hand again and they'd eased into the water together, up to her knees, up to her waist, finally up nearly to her neck, barely chest high on Andreas. Only then had she turned and put her arms around him, clutching her hands behind his back, leaning her head on his chest. Still she hadn't said a word.

Andreas had reacted as he supposed any man would, and Ruth hadn't resisted, but also—if he was honest with himself—hadn't really been fully there. Afterward she'd held on to him as long as she could, then smiled up at his face—a slow smile, designed for children playing on summer lawns and daffodils that'll be gone far too soon. He'd started to say something, but she'd known better and stopped him with a finger to his lips. Then she'd turned without a word and walked toward the riverbank. He'd watched her for a moment—watching the wet black hair stick to her tanned shoulder blades as they emerged gradually from the water—then took a step to follow. But she'd stopped him again without saying a word—without even stopping, or even turning around—simply raising that same finger in the air and continuing on toward the shore, rising slowly out of the tea-colored water until she stood dripping on the rocks, letting her dress fall over her tanned body and slipping her tanned feet back into her shoes. Only then did she finally turn to him, and with a final touch of her lips to that same, all-powerful finger, blew him a kiss over the water as she disappeared into the shadows of the woods.

By the time Andreas got back to the beer garden, she'd been gone. The hot, dry wind rattled the little bulbs in the branches over the tables. Andreas had never spoken to Ruth Daniel again.

The first one he'd let slip away.

That evening when he'd gotten home, the kids were already in bed. His wife was in the study, working on some proposal that was due the next day. He'd kissed her on the top of her head, given her shoulder a half-hearted rub and wandered away to shower. He hadn't heard her come to bed. When he woke up the next morning, she was gone. But not for the last time. They'd repeated that evening for years and years, before finally realizing what they were doing. Or, more accurately, what they weren't.

The second one he'd let slip away.

The van pulled up in front of the warehouse they'd selected for the operation. It wasn't leased yet, actually wasn't even finished out, so they'd been able to strike a good deal. Andreas saw Roy check his BlackBerry without much enthusiasm. Andreas looked at his own phone, but saw nothing new.

Eva had stopped replying.

The third one?

Andreas sat up straight and tried to shake the past out of his head. Don't give this one up so easily. Remember what the professor said, after all: Only people can create something from nothing.

• • •

Far, far away, the foreign ring. Once, twice, then the voice, just a gurgle, a cough.

"Roy?"

Sarah Anderson sat in her car, forehead on the steering wheel, eyes closed tight against the midday glare off the dash.

"Roy, we have to talk. I found Pete. In a hospital in Maryland. He's dead."

Her breathing was quick, her heart pounding too fast. Her voice came in short bursts, unsure of how long they might last.

"Completely sure, Roy. I saw him. But here's the thing. It wasn't the crash that killed him, Roy. Somebody did it to him here. And Roy—I think CASTOR was involved."

The car was hot, smelling of vinyl and last night's perfume. Sarah Anderson felt a drop of sweat begin its descent down the small of her back.

"I know it sounds crazy. I didn't want to believe it myself. I still don't. But I spoke with Sandy McRae just a couple of minutes ago. I told him about Pete. I told him what happened. And Roy—he wasn't surprised. He knew, Roy. And why would he know, if CASTOR didn't have something to do with it?"

Sarah Anderson opened her eyes, looking out across the parking lot. A woman met her gaze, squinting against the sun, as she pushed a stroller toward the hospital. Her face was contorted, nose sensing sulfur, eyes almost closed lest something evil get inside.

Even Roy was wary of her, thousands of miles away.

"Roy, I know Sandy pretty well. You know that. I can just tell. I could hear it in his voice, the way he reacted when I told him. And—well, I saw him this morning, Roy, to ask for his help with something else—something that I think might be connected to all this, too. Something that I'm sure's connected, actually."

There were voices on the other end of the line, voices not Roy's, foreign voices, low and unknown. Sarah Anderson tried to picture where he was, but the sun off the other cars blinded even her mind's eye.

"That's really why I'm calling you, Roy. I think you should come home. I'm not sure you're safe there. Even if you are, I'm not sure you want to be involved."

The voices were louder now. Somebody shouted. But Roy was icy cold, turning away.

"I will, Roy, I will. But right now you need to leave. I'll explain everything later. But right now, please, just leave."

Sarah Anderson realized she was crying. Roy's voice had disappeared. The foreign shouting was louder now, pounding her ears, and the screaming to be heard through the unknown, unknowable distance.

Suddenly Sarah Anderson was remembering a conversation she'd once overheard in Roy Daniel's office. Some scientist had created a perfect model for predicting the weather forty-eight hours in advance. He'd been testing it for about six months, and it had been right every day, without fail. When it predicted sun, the sun came out. When it said rain, the skies darkened every time. Snow? Sure enough—the flakes began to fall within an hour or two, tops, of when the model said they would. He'd really had it down. Television networks and newspapers and websites around the world should have been knocking down his doors, trying to get the rights to this Holy Grail of the weatherman's world.

Why weren't they? Well, there was just one small problem. This guy was running his model on the fastest computers the civilian world had to offer. And while it did predict the weather perfectly forty-eight hours from when the computers started crunching through the numbers, it took about sixty to seventy hours to finish the crunching. In other words, it was worthless. The fruit of years of work, the crowning glory of an entire career, a minor miracle of meteorological science, but in the real world, completely and totally worthless.

A man in a lab coat was knocking on Sarah Anderson's window. Out of habit, Sarah Anderson stole a glance in the rearview mirror. Her eyes were red, her eyeliner smudged, and the salty trails of tears were drying on her cheeks.

The telephone line had gone dead.

The man outside knocked again. He looked friendly, concerned, but Sarah Anderson just waved him away. He didn't know the whole story. The story of her life. Every time it mattered. Everything had already happened.

• • •

It reminded Roy Daniel of an upscale museum. The end of the old brick warehouse had been blown out and glassed in, the thick panes tinted the color of new hundred dollar bills. The rooms inside sealed up and abandoned—dioramas of life in the turn-of-the-century multinational. Below street level, fronting the canal, a high-ceilinged cafeteria was furnished in the latest shades of blonde. Above—with views of the outdoor stairway—offices, conference rooms, all empty now, Monday's reckoning still a long way away. Automatic lights still on here and there, some movement keeping them nervous and awake. Movement real or imagined? Such distinctions blurred in places like this, for whose occupants bugs of the virtual sort were much more real than those that drowsed around empty break rooms on analog summer afternoons.

The driver sat staring straight ahead, the engine still running. He'd turned off the headlights, but left the windshield wipers alone. With every gust of wind, raindrops rattled the side of the van. Roy Daniel noticed a dark figure wandering slowly down the stairs, disappearing along the canal. Another tried—and, from Roy Daniel's point of view, failed—to look inconspicuous, smoking outside an empty office building on a rainy Friday evening. But it didn't seem to matter, because there was no one there to notice. A gentrified tree falling in a corporate forest, with nobody around to hear.

Andreas studied his phone, his breathing heavier—or at least sounding heavier—since the van had stopped. Hansen turned and studied him, warily. The big, square man droned through his goatee, his eyes focused on some point outside in the rain. He adjusted his earpiece and listened, then nodded, spoke again, listened, and nodded again.

If Andreas had noticed any of this, it certainly didn't show.

Lemming raindrops crashed over the side of the van. Headlights appeared up the street, but turned before reaching them. A woman hurried by on the opposite sidewalk, holding her umbrella sideways against the wind. The heels of her boots snapped with the soggy wipers' whine in a sort of subterranean bossa nova. The driver stared as she passed beneath a solitary streetlight, her shadow emerging long from the shadows, then shrinking, swinging around the light pole, stretching long again, then fading. Hansen mumbled. Andreas sighed. The snapping of the boot heels faded, leaving the wipers to play only one hand of a musical riff written for two.

A phone rang. Roy Daniel jumped and fumbled in his jacket pocket. Sarah Anderson's name glowed white on the tiny black screen. He cut the second ring short and put the phone to his ear.

"Hello. . . ." Roy Daniel's voice caught and fell into a cough. The driver's eyes narrowed in the rearview mirror. Hansen looked the other way.

"Hello, Sarah." Smoother now, soft. "Sorry about that."

Andreas slowly rose out of his trance and studied his old friend's face. "He's dead? Are you sure?"

Roy Daniel looked right through him, his eyes drifting away, widening the gap between them in the dark back seat of the van.

"Sarah. Slow down. Take a deep breath. Think about what you're saying. How can that be true?"

Hansen began to talk again, still low, but the pace quicker.

Roy Daniel's voice, when he finally spoke again, was far, far away. "What makes you think he knew?"

His hand, acting on its own now, took a pen from his jacket pocket and tapped it absently on his leg. His forehead creased, pulling his eyebrows up and his eyes open wide. His teeth chewed slowly on his lower lip.

Hansen turned to Andreas, one hand on his earpiece, and said something that wasn't a question. Andreas nodded, but his eyes were still on Roy. The screen of his cell phone lit up as a new message arrived. Andreas ignored that, too.

Another set of headlights appeared up ahead. They approached fast, waving icy halogen banners through the rain careening sideways over the pavement. Hansen repeated himself, more urgently now, and glanced back over a broad shoulder at the headlights. Still Andreas said nothing, transfixed by Roy's every move, hanging on his every word.

"Okay. So—this other thing he's helping you with. What is that, exactly?"

Roy Daniel's voice froze over. "Sarah. Please answer my question."

The third time, Hansen couldn't be ignored. Andreas turned to him coolly and nodded, regarding the headlights and the car pulling up alongside the van. Hansen barked. The dark figure on the sidewalk ahead tossed his cigarette into the gutter and took up a position in the middle of the street, hands shoved deep into the pockets of his raincoat.

Sarah Anderson was telling him to leave.

Roy Daniel watched over Andreas's shoulder as the two front doors of the black Mercedes opened together. The driver got out, reaching as he did inside his jacket, and swung a handgun across the roof toward the passenger door. He shouted something as he did so, his words swept away by another volley of rain against the van. The person on the other side emerged and turned just as quickly to face the driver. The wind whipped her sandy blond hair across her face as she silently screamed something into the barrel of the gun.

Andreas rounded on Hansen like an animal, cornered and bleeding. His eyes flashed out of the dark of the van. His voice snarled and hissed, spit flying from the corners of his mouth. Hansen struck back, but Andreas's snarl became a roar and he slapped at the side of the van in search of a door latch that wasn't there. Realizing this, Andreas hammered at the window as if the van were sinking, filling with water with no hope of escape. Hansen was yelling in all directions—Andreas, the van's driver, the people on the other end of the line. The man in the middle of the street touched a hand to his ear and moved over to the far side of the street.

"I'll explain everything later, Roy," came the faraway voice in Roy Daniel's ear. "But right now, please, just leave."

The driver of the car started at the sudden uproar in the van behind him. He was distracted for only a few of seconds, but a few seconds was all she needed. The car leapt forward, the blonde now in the driver's seat, tires cursing the slick pavement.

Andreas raged against the windows of the van, but the car's former driver only turned away. The crack of his gun silenced them all, echoing off the brick walls and the thick glass behind and above and around them. A second shot, then a third, then the metallic wail of rims grinding concrete. The big car slumped to the curb. The blonde was immediately in the street again, her words stolen by the gale before they even left her mouth. The driver stood his ground, turning the muzzle of his gun toward her. Andreas wheeled back to Hansen, tearing at the collar of the big man's jacket. The van driver tried to separate the two, but sheer force of will—for a while, at least—can overcome even the most unlikely of odds.

So Roy Daniel saw him first.

The rear door of the car swung open, almost hitting the blonde. A man's legs appeared from the car, then two hands, held up for the gunman to see. For a heartbeat or two, the man in the car didn't move. The blonde appeared to be yelling at him. He stood up, deliberately, said a word or two to her, then turned slowly to face the gunman. He talked to the gunman, hands still held high, and began a slow walk, closer to the gunman, closer to the van. The rain pasted his hair to his forehead and soaked through his blazer, his slacks, his shoes. Nothing remained to protect him from the elements.

Roy Daniel hung on his every step, the commotion in the van fading into the background. The man's stride was familiar, the way he landed each step on his heels, the outward point of his toes. The rain blew hard across his body, pasting his shirt to his frame, no fat there, little muscle, just sinewy fibers binding skin and bone. The way he held his hands up with the fingers apart, weary, almost, ready to fall. The skeptical tilt of his head, and the rise and fall of his chin as his monologue to the gunman progressed. The cold squint of his eyes against the storm. The gunman yelled something—short, imperative German syllables that the wind flattened hard against the side of the van. But the man kept walking. He wasn't coming fast, but he wasn't going to stop.

The man inched slowly into a streetlight's orange glow, and then he knew. The realization arced across Roy Daniel's spine, thundering in his temples, charging the primordial deep inside. He turned to the other men in the van, their hisses and snarls and growls rushing back into his conscious mind. He yelled the name, but they paid no attention. He tried again, feeling his vocal chords strain, but still they seemed not to hear. So he grabbed at Andreas, gripping his old friend's head in his hands, whiskery cheekbones hard against his palms, the man's face to his own, his eyes latching on to those eyes he now felt he'd never seen before.

Roy Daniel's voice was no more than a whisper, but like the last gasps of the dying, the rusty hiss of a valve opened too fast after too long, it carried the van like flash flood waters, drowning the vain rantings of protocol and policy and rank.

"Asher!"

Andreas held Roy Daniel's gaze without trying to escape, unflinching but not defiant, steadfast but without hope. The eyes of a crippled bird, wing splayed useless across the wet grass, found out after all and unable to run away.

A quick move outside the van jerked Roy Daniel's attention back to the middle of the street. Asher had spun around, yelling back at the blonde woman now, hands still raised toward the wind and the rain. Behind the blonde, the man from the middle of the street was approaching cautiously, having circled around behind her in the dark of the opposite sidewalk. The blonde turned her head, as she did sinking to the pavement, melting inside clothes suddenly much too big for her. At the same time, the driver of the car slammed his gun against the back of Asher's head. The force of the blow twisted Asher's face toward the van. His expression was one of simple surprise as his knees gave out and his hands, still held high above his nodding head, tried to lean against the wind and the blindly falling rain.

The driver prodded Asher with his shoe, then tucked his handgun back inside his jacket, pulled out a wad of zip ties, and bound the unconscious man's hands and feet. The man down the street did the same with the blonde. They maneuvered the two into sitting positions, squatted down behind them, and, wrapping big arms around limp bodies, lifted them easily and dragged them out of the street, across the sidewalk next to the van, and down the stairs toward the canal and the green-glass doors of the empty office building.

Roy Daniel realized he was still squeezing Andreas's head hard between his hands. But his friend didn't appear to notice. His eyes were closed now, and his breathing had slowed. Roy Daniel turned and looked from Hansen to the driver of the van. Hansen wasn't paying attention, mumbling questions and scanning the empty street ahead for answers. The eyes of the driver ducked quickly out of the rearview mirror as soon as Roy Daniel's met them. They fled to the anonymous thousands of raindrops hurtling around the orange streetlight's glow, like so many insects, blinded by a solitary flame.

fifteen

"And I didn't cry, and I didn't sing, and I did dance."

I wish I'd taken a movie of that moment. All the preschool kids on that little makeshift stage in the basement of the church, after giggling through their final bows. Showing off their costumes to their parents and grandparents and brothers and sisters and God knows who else. Anybody who'd look at them, really, smiling and saying the usual "Look at you!" or "Why, that's not an elf—that's Cindy!" The kid who played Santa huffing "Ho, ho, ho!" at one person after another through his big cotton-ball beard. The boy with his flat little conductor's hat tilted way back and his moustache half off, twirling his stopwatch on a yellow plastic chain. The one little elf girl you could just tell had to pee so bad it hurt to watch her, crossing her legs in her purple tights and spinning and squatting and jumping up and down. Afraid to go, though, because when she came back, it might all be gone. A Christmas home movie, run in reverse.

There was this one little boy—he played one of the schoolboys, I guess, with a big scarf wrapped around his neck—pointing up at some lady's Star of David necklace and exclaiming, "*I'm* a Jewish!"—wide-eyed, amazed at his good luck, finding another one here, of all places.

I guess I *do* wish I'd made a movie of all that, now.

Asher was an elf, too. Not much else he *could* be, honestly, since he'd missed most of the rehearsals. We were moving right after the holidays, see. We'd taken him along, leaving him with Ruth's parents for most of the time while we looked for someplace to live. So he'd only been back in school for a day or two before the night of the big show.

I think he would have been just as happy not to be in the show at all. Shy to begin with, of course, and tired from the trip, and not really knowing what was going on—who could blame him? But the teachers didn't really give him a choice, and that's probably for the best, because in the end he seemed pretty proud of himself.

The kids were doing some version of *Frosty the Snowman* that the teachers had made up. They gave Santa a bunch of elves because they needed more extra parts and didn't want to make everybody be schoolkids. The elves all had little pointy felt hats with bells sewn on top, and for most of the show they just kind of hung around in the background and sang the next verse of the song when that part of the story came around. At the end, they got to do a little dance with the schoolkids while they all sang "Jingle Bells," and the elves were supposed to shake their heads back and forth to make the bells ring. Didn't work out that great from an artistic point of view, since the bells didn't really ring at the same time and all the head shaking just made the kids giggle more than sing. But it sure was cute.

And that, of course, was the whole point—show all the parents and grandparents and aunts and uncles how cute the school was making their kids, so they'd all be back next year, along with all their little brothers and sisters and cousins. Keep the old gravy train rolling. No such thing as a free lunch. You know the story. Same story everywhere.

That sounded pretty cynical, didn't it? Sorry about that. I didn't mean to go there. Honestly, the show was really cute. Can't blame the motives on the kids. Probably can't blame the motives on the teachers, either—they all worked really hard and put on a good show. So scratch those last comments. I'm just tired, and—okay, you ready for this? Make sure that thing is on—I'm only gonna say this once—I'm gettin' to be more than a little bit old.

What *did* make me mad, though, was watching those parents behind their brand-new Super 8s, another one of life's precious moments passing before their one good eye through a tiny little piece of glass. Didn't they know what they were missing? Didn't they know you couldn't possibly catch this whole experience on a little strip of celluloid? Sure, you could catch *something*. But was it anything like the truth? Not a chance. Not the whole truth. A little piece of it, maybe, but not the whole deal. You can't catch the whole truth if you're only pointing in one direction.

Anyway, where was I? Oh, yeah—Asher. So, he hangs out there in the background for most of the show, not really doing anything. Doesn't sing a word. Sort of moves his head back and forth to the beat sometimes, but mostly just sits there and watches what all the other kids are up to. Then that final dance comes along, and he moves up front with the other elves, and I can tell that he's doing everything he can not to cry. Kid hated being in the spotlight. Hated it even when he knew what he was doing, which certainly wasn't true in this case.

But he was keeping it together. Still didn't sing a word. But when they started into the dance—just a little hokey-pokey deal, nothing too complicated—remember, we're talking about preschoolers here—lo and behold, little Asher joins right in! Not a smile on his face—he still had that puffy-eyed look he used to get before he cried—but his feet are going through the steps, and his hands take the hands of the little elves next to him, and sure, he's watching what those kids are going to do next, but he's keeping up pretty good! And when the time comes to shake the bell on his head, he does it, and that's when I knew that he knew where we were, because when it was all over he looked us straight in the eye and smiled—the first smile I'd seen on his face all night. And we all clapped and he smiled more and we clapped more and the Super 8s whirred while those parents yelled because they didn't have a spare hand to clap with.

Who knows—maybe they did know what those cameras could and couldn't get. Maybe they just had to try, anyway, that packrat mentality that all of us share too strong, the shiny thing too shiny not to try to grab hold of and keep. Never mind the consequences. And anyway, they don't know now what they didn't see then.

I saw it all. Heard it all, felt it all, smelled it all, even. Remember most of it now—better than I remember most things from back then. So I followed my own advice. But now? Well. We're being honest, right?

I *do* wish I had a movie of that moment. I really, really do.

Because after all the clapping was done and we'd pushed our way outside, he looked right up from under his pointy green felt hat with those puffy red eyes that were sparkling now under that clear, nighttime sky, not so puffy anymore—not so puffy at all—and he said, in that way he had of talking back then—just the facts, ma'am, no nonsense, no lies—those words that I don't think I'll ever forget:

"And I didn't cry, and I didn't sing, and I did dance."

That one moment, more than any other, I'd like to be able to watch again and again.

Notes on the Text

For those readers who have developed a longing to know what happened to the characters who populated *The Road of the Innocents*, we can share with you that Bryan's notes show he considered two different endings. Here are Bryan's notes as faithfully recreated as possible:

One was to be an epilogue that was a press release, or a series of press releases from Tamara Maybin, as mentioned in the book, explaining the aftermath of the fallout. His notes are brief and only say:

"story to press, covering CASTOR and General, Open ended whether it works, Just wants to be out of it. Whole thing needs to go quiet, Civilian feeds PR (Evans, Morton, Tamara, Gen.), Protect son (Roy)."

We have not found any text that he drafted for these press releases, and from the final version of the book that he shared with us, we conclude that he decided not to pursue this option for an ending.

However, from these notes and the contents of his book, we can draw our own conclusions as to what he might have revealed. First, from the perspective of CASTOR, the Military, and General Hayward, the priority is to make the Ariadne program and the badly conceived sting operation "go quiet." CASTOR officials do not want any publicity regarding the wiretapping of America or the serious legal questions that might follow.

According to Bryan's notes, CEO Jabe Evans desperately wants CASTOR, his company, "to be out of it [the wire tapping business]" and he kills the Ariadne program, or at least CASTOR's involvement in it. Jabe Evans and publicist Tamara Maybin ensure any press for CASTOR remains good.

From Roy Daniel's perspective, the priority is naturally to "protect his son." What the press release might say about these attempts are not known, but he would certainly use his technical knowledge to try to prove his son's involvement was innocent and accidental.

As for the POLLUX organization, recall from Greek and Roman mythology that Castor and Pollux were twins, but while Castor was immortal, Pollux was mortal. When Jabe Evans told Tamara "you know what you have to do," he was telling her to remove all CASTOR support from POLLUX, and in the process let the POLLUX organization die.

But, based on the way Bryan ended the book, we believe he felt there were too many things that needed to be resolved, and that a press release would not be sufficient. Instead, he chose another option—a sequel as indicated by one final entry in his notes:

"Morton quietly watches everything unfold—like he watches his son. Generally satisfied. Not found out = opening for future."

We infer the "opening for the future" was indicating a continuation. And in conversations with family members, Bryan said he was thinking of a sequel, a story that would tell us more about what happened to his characters. They each have more stories to tell and Bryan complained several times in the last six months of writing that his characters had "taken over the book and were going in directions I couldn't control." He needed more time to bring their adventures to a close.

The sequel may have been a story of an epic corporate battle between Evans and Morton for control of CASTOR. It would have been a battle of competing ideals: science and public service vs. money and shareholder value. The sequel would also explain whether or not Al Green was ever charged and convicted as an accessory to kidnapping and murder. Sandy McRae, who disappeared at the end of the book, would foreseeably return to reveal all he knows about the ill-planned sting operation, including Bill Morton's involvement in Pete's murder. And, given the relationship between Sandy McRae and Jabe Evans, it is likely that Sandy would have been Jabe's ally in his struggles with Bill Morton for control of CASTOR. But don't forget that Sandy has his vulnerabilities. In his past, he has been the true mercenary who would do whatever he was asked to do for anyone who asked, as long as he was paid well.

Roy Daniel would naturally try to rescue his son, perhaps with the help of Sandy and Andreas. And what about Asher, Kimberly, and Eva? Would Asher and Kimberly resolve their marital differences or, quoting Bryan's book, "have the walls grown too high"? Perhaps Asher and Eva would find love in the post-capture struggles they shared together. All of these would be interesting stories to hear, but we will never know the details. As one reviewer wrote, "The tragedy here is that there is no one to write the sequel."

So we, the readers, must now draw our own conclusions about what happened to these interesting characters. In some sadly ironic way, that is just what Bryan wanted us to do.

Acknowledgments from the Rockwood Family

Bryan was a kind and gentle person with great intellect, curiosity, and a love for life. He aspired to be a writer, and though the demands of life delayed achieving this goal, with this novel he shows us all what a beautiful skill he cultivated with words and imagery. Bryan enjoyed a challenge and lived his life with the philosophy that one must not be limited by their fears. Face your fears and you will find the strength to overcome them. A great deal of Bryan's personality and philosophy burst through the pages in this novel and we hope you enjoyed meeting him.

The family, on behalf of Bryan, would like to thank his many friends who read early chapters of the novel and encouraged him to continue writing. We also give our thanks to Ms. Alison Leslie Gold, Mr. Michael Chaplin, and Ms. Nancy Williford for reading portions of the finished manuscript following Bryan's accident and for their strong encouragement to proceed with publication in his absence.

We would like to thank Ms. Dotti Albertine for designing the book jacket as well as the book, and Ms. Shona McCarthy for her astute copyediting. Lastly, we wish to give our special thanks to Ms. Danielle A. Durkin for her excellent professional support and steady and thoughtful guidance in our quest to find the best option to bring Bryan's art to the public. During the past year of this effort, in addition to being an editor for Bryan's work, she has become a true and trusted friend of the family.

Were Bryan here to write a dedication and acknowledgments, it is certain he would have dedicated this book to his entire family for all of their loving patience and support during the years he spent completing his novel. He created a wonderful piece of literature for us all to enjoy.

The Rockwood Family

About the Author
May 24, 1965 – July 12, 2014

Bryan D. Rockwood received his BA in comparative literature from Princeton University in 1987. His aspiration was to be a writer, but after graduation, the responsibility of providing for his family guided him into a business career. He was successful, and about four years ago, around 2011, felt he had reached a financial position that would allow him to turn to writing. *The Road of the Innocents* is the result of his efforts.